5

Best Wis

Biep Neilgel
Feb 2016

"Stella Jasper emerges from this tensely told mystery as a woman recognizable to many Washingtonians. She is a shallow socialite who finds herself caught up in frightening reality when she is abandoned not only by her husband but her friends and finds herself in the dark world of terrorism-related money-laundering and even struggling with involvement in a presidential campaign with all its unexpected dramatic developments. Mr. Neikirk's Jasper is a vivid character, a portrayal of a woman who finds herself suddenly forced to face the world as it is and not as she wants to see it. His plot builds steadily and, especially given the state of politics today, is most timely."

—*Muriel Dobbin, a former White House correspondent for the Baltimore Sun, now book reviewer for the Washington Times*

THE COPPERHEAD CLUB

NONFICTION WORKS BY WILLIAM NEIKIRK

Volcker: A Portrait of the Money Man

The Work Revolution: How High-Tech Is Sweeping Away Old Jobs and Industries and Creating New Ones in New Places.

THE COPPERHEAD CLUB

—· A NOVEL ·—

WILLIAM NEIKIRK

WILLIAM NEIKIRK, PUBLISHER ALEXANDRIA, VIRGINIA

William Neikirk, Publisher
www.williamneikirk.com.com

Publisher's Note: This is a work of fiction. Names, characters, places, and incidents are a product of the author's imagination. Locales and public names are sometimes used for atmospheric purposes. Any resemblance to actual people, living or dead, or to businesses, companies, events, institutions, or locales is completely coincidental.

Cover design by Megan Bradley

The Copperhead Club/ William Neikirk. -- 1st ed.
ISBN 978-0-9969624-0-7

For Ruth,
Greg, John, and Christa

WITH APPRECIATION

I began this project in the 1990s, and it is only with the support and encouragement from my family and friends that I have completed it. Words cannot adequately express my gratitude to my friend Art Pine, who made suggestions and helped edit the manuscript.

Woe to him who shall trouble the Copperhead's rest!

—BRET HARTE, 1864

DECEMBER

CHAPTER 1

McLean, Virginia

Stella hit the chirping alarm clock and reached under the Egyptian sateen sheets to touch the man she loved. He wasn't there.

"What's going on?" she said, still bleary from the fast wakeup. Abruptly, she sat straight up in bed, sensing that something had happened to Bob. Then she remembered. He had texted her from New York saying that he would be home late or he might have to stay another day—to finish a trade agreement between the United States and two European countries. "It's a big deal," he said in a phrase he used so often. He signed off SCC, a love code which only they understood.

So Stella rubbed her eyes and relaxed—not to worry about Bob—and she smiled as she remembered she was going to meet her closest friend, Alicia Valiant, for their annual get-together on the Saturday before Christmas. She and Alicia had decided many years ago that on that particular Saturday they would revert back to their teenage years. They would dress up in fabulous clothes, have lunch at their favorite French restaurant, and would talk about everything under the sun—everything that is, except her talent as an artist, which was a painful topic for her.

Stella had stopped painting, contending that she couldn't find a standout style that she could call her own. "Essentially, I am a copycat painter," she had admitted one day to a magazine reporter who had written a story about her. The story was about how she, a Yale graduate and failed artist, was a philanthropist with a good eye for art. With Bob's money, she had donated $25,000 to buy a small sculpture by a new artist who she predicted was going places. She was right. The value of the piece had tripled in two years. In the same magazine story, Stella Jasper was described as the lovely red-haired beauty and popular director of various art shows in Washington—shows that brought in more contributions and attention for Stella and her magic than any painting that she might have created and sold herself.

So she laid her talent and her hobby aside and kept her paintbrushes under lock and key.

Stella delighted in the fact that, due to her husband's job and her art show expertise, she had developed friends in high places. The couple was often invited to White House parties and state dinners with the President and First Lady.

As a conservative lawyer and economist, and lobbyist who often worked behind the scenes to push the President's economic agenda, Bob spent more time in the oval office than he did at home, giving him little time to enjoy the new tennis courts, swimming pool, and helipad in his backyard. Although he had plenty of opponents, he successfully closed private deals in locations ranging from Chevron's Brussels headquarters to leather-chaired bars near the Capitol.

Stella was proud of him. They were richer now than before he became a lobbyist; money was never an issue. Bob took care of handling the big money for their household and set up a separate account for her purchases—no restrictions. But wealth did not bring her happiness.

With Bob's workload and time away from home, she was alone too often in their six-bedroom mansion, a home that could be boring and unsatisfying. As an only child, raised by her aunt after her mother and father died in a car crash when they were only 35, she had always felt alone. She had longed for a child at one point in their marriage, but she was unable to conceive even though sex was frequent and enjoyable.

Stella looked into the mirror, checked for any new wrinkles around her green eyes and saw a 32-year-old woman with Botox-reinforced cheeks and pale freckles, who felt lonely and empty. Alicia would brighten her day. She and Alicia fancied themselves as women who became big shots because of their charm and their connections. Their names often appeared in Washingtonian magazine or in the Washington Post's Style section, and that only enhanced their reputations and invitations to state dinners. Stella learned early on that if she told Alicia anything embarrassing about public officials they didn't like, she could count on Alicia to see that it got into the press.

Sorting through her closet, she picked out a favorite dress and coat, but then changed her mind. Her new Louis Vuitton boots would look better with the Jason Wu dress and trench coat. She took one last look at herself in the hall mirror, set the house security system, and walked out to the car. The right front tire of the silver Lexus looked a bit low. "I'll have Bob take a look when he gets home," she thought.

"Hmm, it's cold but bright and sunny in Virginia," Stella mused. "We're lucky heavy snow has missed us so far this winter." She smiled and waved to Chief Justice Peter Horizon, who was walking his Jack Russell terrier, Wendy, along the side of the road near his house. "He's like me," she thought of the famous jurist. "We need to get away from the house every day even for a few minutes."

Fifteen minutes later, as Stella parked the car and walked to the restaurant, she could easily recognize her tall, willowy friend with long blonde hair waiting at the door. She was wielding a shopping bag full of little brightly wrapped packages. "Stella!" she said loudly, as the women kissed cheek-to-cheek. "Good to see you. Happy holidays!"

Alicia was dressed as if she'd been ready to go to a White House event that very moment. Stella noticed she was wearing a black, tight-fitting Valentino outfit and a pair of Christian Louboutin high-heeled shoes, their red soles clearly evident. She carried an Italian-made, outsized tote capable of holding a bunch of gifts, itself easily a $1,200 item.

"You look phenomenal as usual," Stella said. "You're still glowing from that state dinner with the Mexican president last month. The President and First Lady adore you." Alicia smiled as a few nearby diners glanced her way. "I really haven't seen you since then," Stella added.

Stella recalled with pleasure how President Everett and First Lady Pamela had called her by her first name that evening and thanked her for her efforts in promoting art in the city. (Translation: Thanks for the campaign contributions). Alicia said she and her husband, George, had gotten the same welcome, and the President had asked whether they were planning to take another trip to the Greek islands that both couples loved so much. "To be sure," Alicia had told him. "How can I resist sherbet sunsets over the Mediterranean? We can truly get away from it all when we are there."

Alicia said she thought the President had looked a little tentative, and, frankly, worried. She said that George knew the President was worried about the troubling state of world affairs, the danger of another terrorist attack, and the fact that he would almost certainly lose the next election if it were held now. The actual voting was only 11 months away.

Indeed, the President was behind in the polls, and to many of his conservative friends it appeared that he had little chance to turn around the electorate. As befitted their different demeanors, Stella said she hoped the polls would turn as the economy improved, while Alicia said the President already looked like a loser and needed to do something dramatic—the sooner the better.

They both noted how impressed they were with Placido Ramos de la Torre, or Ramos as he was widely known. Ramos, a tall well-dressed man who resembled the actor Benecio del Toro, was born in the U.S. to Bolivian parents who became American citizens before he arrived. A conservative, he had started his own software businesses in the U.S., and eventually had become renowned as a political consultant. Ramos contributed millions of dollars to various philanthropic charities—all good causes.

"I was so glad that Ramos came over to shake hands," Alicia said. "He seemed to know all about us. Impeccable manners. I wish George had them. And his wife, from Sweden, is absolutely gorgeous. What a couple!" But Alicia pointed out that Ramos had yet to support the President in his quest for another term. "The President needs him in his corner if he is going to win," she said.

Stella and Alicia lowered their voices when their conversation got more critical about the White House party, such as the First Lady's undistinguished taste in gowns, how the Defense Secretary's wife looked like a floozy, and about how Vice President Hill looked sick and in need of medical help. "Not to worry," Alicia said confidently. "He has the best doctors in the world."

It was time to exchange gifts. Stella felt obliged to relate the details of how she had come to find the Venetian glass vase in a little shop just off the Grand Canal and how she usually never liked Hermes scarves all that much until she saw this one. Alicia gave Stella an amber necklace in which little insects had been trapped millennia ago. She had found it in Riga, she said, when she and George were passing through on a business trip, and she thought it would complement Stella's red hair.

After they exchanged other presents, earrings and bracelets and exotic little packages of soaps, Alicia handed Stella the final gift, which she opened hurriedly.

It was a paintbrush with a gold-plated handle.

"It's time for you to start again," Alicia said.

Stella was plainly touched. But the thought flashed by: Why this, when Alicia knew she had abandoned painting out of pain and frustration years ago? She promised to try, but she knew that in her current state, she probably wouldn't.

Sipping the last bit of wine, they spoke of vacations—Buenos Aires, Tuscany, the Swiss Alps—and of visiting friends in the Hamptons in the fall. Stella said she had wanted to go to Israel all her life, but had always too scared. "You can do it," Alicia assured her. "Never let fears hold you back. Say hi to Bob. We'll try to get our men together soon."

They hugged one another. Lunch was over.

As Stella drove her silver Lexus through the traffic jungle around Tyson's Corner en route to her secluded enclave in suburban Great Falls, she smiled at Alicia's extravagance. Alicia was her usual fun self. Their time together had met her expectations for the day. Life was good. Bob would be home and she would surprise him with her new red negligee on Christmas Eve. She began to hum as The Metropolitan Opera on National Public Radio surrounded her with one of her favorites, "La Boheme."

As she turned from Dolley Madison Drive, she mused about how her husband had become such a good dealmaker in the finest tradition of the nation's capital. A long time ago, they had laughed together at the silliness they had observed in D.C.—the hypocrisy and the posturing. At first, they didn't fully grasp that the way to get ahead was to play each side skillfully, and never make enemies.

Now he was deeply into deals—business deals and political deals that he rarely talked about. Stella didn't probe deeply, for she was into her world of art. They lived in two separate worlds. Hers was a world that bored him as much as his dealing bored her.

Their sex was not boring, though. On the contrary, it held them together. Foreplay had always been worth every minute—sensual and fun. There was nothing like their crème brûlée forays. Every time Bob would order brûlée to go from Chez Louis, her body would tingle in anticipation of what was sure to come. Licking brûlée from her breasts brought on an early orgasm, often followed by another.

As Stella was turning down Old Dominion Drive, the winter wind was blowing tall deciduous trees into a frenzy, just as "La Boheme" increased in tempo.

She crossed over the Capital Beltway, turning left and then right, and then into her driveway, where she abruptly came to a halt. A police car was blocking her way. Another cruiser appeared out of nowhere behind her, lights flashing and blocking her in. An officer got out of the first car and walked over.

"Are you Mrs. Robert Jasper?" he asked. "Stella Jasper?"

"Yes…but what's going on? Why are you here? What has happened? Oh, no. Is it Bob? Is he okay?"

She realized she was shouting.

JANUARY

CHAPTER 2

Hopefully, Kentucky

B.J. Matson had never been one to move very fast, but this steep old trail lined with rock, dead weeds, tree limbs, and old briars would give a snail the edge in a race with any animal, including human.

"God, this is beautiful," B.J. said as he stopped to pull up his jeans over his ample middle. He wiped his brow and looked back at the hollow below and at the layer upon layer of mountains that seemed like waves on the horizon. The Knobs, a range of hills that loops around Kentucky's bluegrass region like a horseshoe, provided the stage for many of Daniel Boone's exploits. To the east was the Kentucky River. To the west the countryside rolled toward the bluegrass in the state's heartland.

It was good to get out on this unseasonably warm afternoon in January. B.J. wanted to check out the family's property on the hill, take some photos, and talk to Melody. Before leaving he made sure his mom's cell phone was charged and she was comfortably sitting in her old blue La-Z-Boy recliner while she watched her favorite soap opera. She would be good for an hour. He grabbed his tripod and camera, locked the farmhouse door, got into his red truck, and headed for higher elevation.

He loved the vista, even though most of the trees, except for a few evergreens, were bare. When fog and mist came, the trees seemed to weep with a profound sadness. But on a sunny day like today, B.J. found their untamed ruggedness exhilarating. Besides, he had a purpose for coming. He knew there was an even better scene at the top of the hill.

From a distance Copperhead Knob resembled a pyramid. Photographers loved it. The locals, though, took it for granted and treated it as a routine part of the landscape, certainly duplicated somewhere in another county. But B.J. knew better. Each mountain had its personality, and Copperhead's stood out, even to casual hikers. He resumed his walk to the top, taking care as he stepped on loose rock. He didn't want to fall and get hurt, or smash his new camera.

Here he was again, he thought to himself, paying homage to a creature feared for its poisonous bite. No one had ever feared him, he mused. But those copperheads get respect. In the knobs—gentle hills that merely introduced the higher, longer Appalachian ridges to the east—there were copperhead lairs everywhere, and woe to the unfortunate person who happened to step in the wrong place. People had died from these bites, although B.J. knew that that was rare. No need to worry about that now. It was winter, and copperheads hibernated. In a way, B.J. felt as though he was in hibernation, too.

Now 33, with thinning brown hair and an untrimmed beard, B.J. might have been in Lexington, Cincinnati, Chicago, Los Angeles, New York, or God forbid, Washington, D.C. Instead, he was living at home in the hills where he grew up. He told himself each day that life was unfair like that, but he believed that he had no choice but to care for his mother, who was withering away from the effects of Parkinson's, and other old-age maladies.

With four siblings, his family was big enough to share in the duties of that chore, but when the real test came, there were excuses that excluded each of them. His brother Zeke, now living in Ohio and working in a car factory, said, "Sorry B.J. We have two kids to raise, you know, and Mary has to work. We can't do this right now." Jake, a high-school teacher in Purcells, and his wife, Magladine, told him that maybe he ought to consider a nursing home for their mother. His older sister Sharon was working as a nurse in a hospital in a town in Pennsylvania and, as a single mother, she had her hands full. Down in Atlanta, brother Larry was still trying to find himself, and to B.J. that meant keeping himself sober long enough to put his shoes on the correct feet. And so that left him—the baby of the family—the last one, born when his mother was 42.

B.J. could have played this "sorry, can't help" game, too, but he was the only sibling truly available and the only one who loved these hills enough to abide the culture that went along with them.

At times, that culture seemed absolutely unbearable to B.J. Nothing drove him closer to the edge than yet another hour-long argument about religion or one more conversation about Kentucky basketball. In such cases, he could not resist being outrageous. Once he drew frowns in the Copperhead Café, a popular hangout, when he shouted, "Do you think Jesus had a good hook shot?" And he even chuckled to himself when he said, "You know that old John the Baptist could sure dunk 'em; he would have made a good Wildcat center."

B.J. had won an academic prize during his sophomore year in high school, and was awarded a big gold trophy. But his older brothers and sisters, who came home to visit now and then, used it as an ashtray when B.J. wasn't around. But they insisted that their trophies and photos, especially those for athletic achievements, be reverently displayed.

Despite B.J.'s sardonic wit, Hopefully's citizens called him "Doofus," because in their minds, he was an idiot. He and his mom lived in an old gray wooden farmhouse that needed paint and constant attention, chores that B.J. managed but could never seem to outpace. It was a farm in name only. In fact, it had never been a true farm. It was 80 acres, most of which were on a hill leading to the top of Copperhead Knob. What little flat country there was had been used long ago to graze a few head of cattle, keep a couple of pigs, and raise chickens and vegetables. B.J.'s late father, Bruce Matson, had worked on the railroad as a laborer, and lucky he was at that.

B.J.'s mom, unlike the majority of mothers in these parts, had worked most of her life, leaving the care of the kids to a favored aunt who had never married. His mom, unlike the other members of her family, was someone born to law enforcement. After two years at the community college, and with two kids at home, she had persuaded Hopefully's mayor (one of her high-school boyfriends) to put her on the payroll as a patrolwoman. The police chief was reluctant, but said he would give her a tryout. He thought she would do mostly routine police work, such as giving out traffic tickets or keeping the office in good working order, and making sure all the files were properly in place. But he soon found that he had miscalculated the tenacity and ambition of Molly Jo O'Cleary, who quickly saw through the police chief's efforts to marginalize her and immediately set out to prove her mettle.

Molly Jo, though short of stature with big green eyes and dark brown hair tucked tightly in a bun, was blessed with a big-boned frame and visibly capable muscles. She exhibited a stern demeanor on the job, even when filing papers. She insisted on addressing people formally, "Mrs. Smith, how are you? Good to see you, Mr. Horner. Hello banker Jones." It was always "Mayor Billingsley" or "Chief Larson," not Gilbert or Jim. She had that natural suspicion of others characteristic of good law enforcement officers. She believed most people were corruptible, no matter what their reputation. In her mind, half of them had proven that by their actions and the other half just hadn't been found out yet.

With Hopefully's small population at 3,500, Molly Jo had an advantage: she knew almost everyone. But that also was a disadvantage. When she began handing out tickets without mercy—even a minute late on the parking meter or five miles over the speed limit—they complained mightily to the police chief and then to the mayor.

Having remembered an intimate night or two with Molly Jo when they were high school seniors, Mayor Gilbert Billingsley was reluctant to upset her in any way. He knew first hand that Molly had a temper and could, if provoked, expose their relationship to his wife, Harriet.

Harriet had suspected that the two had been more than a mere item and she had quizzed Gilbert at length before they were married. Since Gilbert had political ambitions and didn't want the gossip to spread, he denied it to his future wife. And although Harriet didn't believe him, she thought that he'd probably stick with his story for as long as they were married—and likely never stray again.

Chief Larson was a cop who knew not to buckle under citizen complaints, or he would look weak to the voters, but he listened patiently to the grumbling at the Copperhead Café. "When you gonna get rid of that bitch?" said Gladys Winstead, the drug store owner, who'd had her share of parking tickets and one for speeding five miles over the limit as she was hurrying to open the store on time. Molly's position was precarious, and she knew it, but she felt all these corruptible people she'd grown up with had questioned her integrity, and she was not about to give in.

Molly had a few defenders, not the least of whom was banker Baron Schnepp, a trim little man who always wore a fedora straw hat and a bow tie and called everyone in town "honey." They in turn called him The Baron. People loved him because he was generous to a fault and a good customer, to boot. B.J. knew that his mom often visited the Hopefully First Citizen Bank to commiserate with The Baron about her troubles.

It was on such a visit that her fortune turned. She was in the bathroom on the first floor just outside The Baron's office when she heard a stir outside. There was a lot of shouting. A bank robber was ordering the 10 customers (who, incidentally, happened to be among Molly's greatest critics) to get down on the floor and keep their mouths shut, warning that he would blow their brains out if they didn't, and he would think nothing of it. At that, Molly burst out of the bathroom with her gun drawn and as the robber turned toward her, she put a bullet in his forehead. After that, the memory that most people carried of Molly was that she didn't hesitate a moment, and didn't fret about it later. Nor had the pool of blood on the floor or the horror of the scene seemed to faze her. Also memorable was that she had been genuinely kind to her critics. "Are you okay, Mrs. Billingsley?" she had asked. "How about you, Mrs. Winstead?"

The shooting not only made her a town legend, but it also generated a surge of appreciation for her aggressiveness—although it didn't produce enough warmth to persuade any to invite her to tea. "I hate that woman," Harriet Billingsley was heard to say, "but I gotta admit she's just what this town needs, and that's balls. My husband never liked her neither; he resisted her when she came onto him in high school, I know for a fact. But Gilbert knows how to put the right people in the right place."

As a result, over time, Molly's office chores and ticket-writing duties were reduced, and she was assigned to more tough cases. After a few years, she was the principal investigator on all the difficult cases.

B.J. had long wished he possessed his mother's inner steel and iron discipline. But, he admitted to himself, he had a soft heart. He knew that he was soft when his eyes would well up at movies, against his better judgment, and when he sympathized with a hard-luck scam artist out to cajole a buck or two from him. In high school, he had allowed himself to be pushed around. He was not a jock and, although he would have wished it otherwise, high school girls mostly treated him as a quaint curiosity and ignored his clumsy efforts to befriend them.

B.J., feeling bereft, developed friendships with others who'd also been ignored, such as Jack Bergman, son of the pharmacist, and Arthur Oakwood, son of the owner of the town's only construction company. But Jack and Arthur were nowhere around now. They had finished college and gone on to bigger things. Both had left town. They had left the state. They had left B.J. to rot in the hills.

Another of his friends, Noah Williams, the only black person in his class and perhaps the most entrepreneurial as well, took business classes in college and launched his own regional trucking business, and now he lived in the county, doing very well. Occasionally, Noah and B.J.

enjoyed a beer, but Noah was too busy to do this regularly.

Before his mom required so much care, B.J. had hooked up with another of his former high school classmates, Melody Meredith. With their school days behind them, he had surprised her with his knowledge and his sense of humor, and she soon concluded that B.J. would be quite a catch—at least compared to all the other locals who had never left the area. The other stay-at-homes were the real doofuses, Melody said. B.J. thought she looked a lot like Scarlett Johannson, and he found her highly appealing. Soon they were sleeping together, with a plan for marriage ahead. Melody got a job at a call-center that served several middle-sized companies, which forced her to drive 15 miles each way to and from work. All went well until the time she barely negotiated a hairpin turn on the main road, only to run into a loaded coal truck that had drifted into her side of the road.

Melody's death devastated B.J., and he retreated into his own quiet world, rarely venturing out, except to help his mother. Even as he walked toward the top of Copperhead Knob, he thought of her, speaking to her as if she were there with him. "Don't you love this?" he would say to her in a quiet voice. A decade after her death, he still adored her.

Reaching the top, he quickly followed a precarious trail to the other side of the knob, where the canyon with the creek flowing through it opened before his eyes. One look at that scene stirred his emotions. It was as if Melody had joined him there to enjoy the view. He whispered to her, "I don't know if you are here, but it sure feels like it. This was worth the walk, wasn't it?" The creek wandered through the canyon toward a knob in the distance and then seemed to disappear. (Although B.J. knew it turned to the right, no one could tell that from there.) At the bottom of the knob in the distance, just above where the stream seemed to come to a dead-end, a round rock with two slits on each side formed a shape that seemed unmistakable to someone with even a little imagination. Combining the rock's eyes with the creek's long body, anyone could see why they called it Copperhead Canyon.

B.J. took out his camera and attached an expensive zoom lens. When the tripod was set, he waited for the sun's rays to fall over his right shoulder and cover the canyon, highlighting the copper colors of the strange rock with eyes. He could hear the stream below and the birds in the trees behind him. It was so peaceful, so perfect. The sun finally appeared illuminating the rock just as he'd wanted. "There!" he said, and began snapping photos with abandon.

And then he heard it—voices, a struggle, a woman's raised voice. "Stop it, stop it, you son of a bitch! Leave me alone!" It came from the bank next to the copperhead's head. Fumbling with his camera, he focused the telephoto lens on the struggle. A man in a faded wine-colored jacket was wrestling with a young brunette, grabbing her breasts, and then her crotch with one hand, twisting her arm with another. She yelled again as he ripped off her coat and tried to subdue her. He hit her in the face with his fist knocking her down. She tried to run, but he tackled her.

B.J. knew what was next as the brutal scene below unfolded. He had no weapons but his camera and his voice. He hesitated, assessing his choices, whether he should or should not get involved. Although he had been passive all his life, all he could think of was the image of Molly Jo Matson drilling a hole in the head of a bank robber without remorse.

"Stop, you asshole!" He shouted into the canyon. "The police are coming. Leave her alone!" His words echoed loudly. The man stopped his attack and looked around in search of the voice. As he turned his face toward the camera, B.J. snapped the shutter. Through the lens, he could see the surprise on the attacker's face. The man said something to the woman and ran out of sight. B.J. heard his car starting and roaring away.

The woman composed herself and looked B.J.'s way, but by this time he had ducked behind a rock and remained quiet. She called out to him, "Hey! Come and help me!" But B.J. remained silent. He didn't want to be a hero. And he wasn't, despite her anguish. After calling out several times, she gave up. Instead, she got out a cellphone from her pocket and made a quick call. Thank goodness the newly installed radio tower was working. B.J. stayed hidden until another woman pulled up in a Volkswagen and whisked the victim away. She called out one last time before they left. "Thank you—I think," she shouted to the seemingly empty knob.

CHAPTER 3

Washington, D.C.

Dave Simon, Stella's lawyer, resplendent in a dark gray pin-striped suit, blue shirt, George Neale tie, and Ferragamo shoes, ushered Stella into his wood-paneled Watergate office overlooking the iconic Potomac River rushing past the Kennedy Center, where Stella had spent many happy nights there watching performances with hundreds of her "closest" friends—also known as donors—whom she was obliged to kiss on the cheek. Now the romance of the river was gone. As Simon was summing up his assessment of her financial situation, she remembered that first dinner with Bob long ago at that restaurant near the water's edge. He had tenderly touched her hand and she had fallen in love.

"He was a crook, Stella, pure and simple," said Simon, who got a kick from giving clients a truth so unvarnished that it might give them splinters.

"The bottom line here is that you are broke, and I am sorry because you really can't afford me. I'm doing this because you did me a big favor once, and well, because I like you." He managed a thin little smile. Stella recalled how she had suggested Dave to the head of the law firm as a promising talent back when Dave was a struggling nobody.

"As far as we can tell, he cleaned out the bank account and left you with all the debts, " Dave added, for good measure. "And the debts, you would need an International Monetary Fund bailout to pay them."

"How much?" Stella asked.

"Would you believe $25 million? Simon said. "He bought everything on margin and everything collapsed."

Simon didn't pause when she gasped. "Look, he was seriously into money laundering, and we don't know what else, maybe funneling money to buy weapons for the Middle East, too. He did have legitimate clients like the Export-Import Bank and also clients in Congress, and he dutifully did his work for them. He didn't get filthy rich, and I mean filthy in the worst sense of the word, from doing that kind of work; it was all this other shit he was into."

"How long has this been going on?" Stella asked.

"The FBI doesn't know exactly, but believes it could be as long as five years. Right now, they are skeptical of your story that you did not know about this, but they have no real evidence against you. Some of them, I am told, wondered how you could have been clueless about his real life, and the money rolling in."

"Dumb, you mean."

"No, stupid," he corrected. "That's why you have to be careful. I mean, it's difficult to believe that you never looked at his online banking or checkbook or that you never raised questions about any of his trips and what he was doing, and that you didn't notice any changes in his attitude that would have made you wonder if he was not what he was pretending to be. Did you two ever talk about terrorists? About problems in the Middle East?"

"No, not really," Stella conceded, "but yes, there were changes in attitudes, but I wrote it off to hard work and just the craziness of this city. You know what I mean? Here, they buy your soul. Sure, I was stupid. I let him handle all the finances because we were living well. I had my own bank account that let me live the life I wanted to live, and he was just so controlling about the rest. I signed the income tax return, but never looked at it, really. Look, I should have been smarter. I know it."

"The FBI agrees with you. But they also know that you're very smart

The Copperhead Club | 23

and that you could be faking a story. Look, it wouldn't take much for them to charge you with a crime, such as aiding and abetting a criminal act."

"But how do I clear my name, even though I haven't been charged?" Stella asked. "This is the situation that he put me in. Nobody is going to clear my name, except for him, and he has disappeared. How do I get my reputation back? Why would my husband treat me this way? And the police are going to be watching my every move, like I'm a criminal or something."

Stella remembered the agent who had questioned her, a tall, dark attractive man only a few years older than she. He had come to her home, and they had talked in the living room—a room she had filled with original paintings and expensive furniture.

"Did you and your husband have frequent sex?" he had asked her with a business-like look. He stared into her eyes to see if she turned away and at her face to see if she might blush. She looked down then raised her face to look directly into his eyes.

"Yes, I would say so," she responded honestly.

"Three or more times a week?" he had asked.

"God, I don't know! I don't keep a star chart of our sexual encounters. Let's just say he's good in bed, but for the last few weeks, his interest has waned a little—I thought because he was tired from long hours at work."

"Do you have a lover?"

"No," she said vehemently. "Absolutely not. And that should be fairly easy to check."

"Ma'am, I have to ask these questions, please don't get curt with me. But, yes, we have checked on that possibility." She knew they hadn't found anything because there was nothing to find.

"Did he have a lover?" he asked.

She looked at him for a bit. "I just don't know. I guess it wouldn't surprise me knowing what I know now. I'd like to think not." She paused and looked at him again, pondering the question he had just asked. "What do you know? Are you hiding something from me? Tell me the truth."

"I can't comment on our investigation," he said.

How do you read an obnoxious FBI agent, Stella asked herself. She couldn't stand these enigmatic responses to her questions. If the FBI had to undergo the same kind of treatment they dish out to others, she thought, the entire agency would sign a contract with the American Civil Liberties Union for help.

She took a lie detector test and passed it on the critical questions. She abided the questioning about putting millions of dollars into U.S. banks through front companies. The level of detail that the FBI had turned up and the extraordinary complexity of what Bob had been involved in without her knowledge bewildered her.

Simon didn't let up on her. "At the very least, they think of you as an idiot when it comes to money, someone who knows how to spend the stuff given to you, but having no idea how it's made or stolen or how to deal with banks or people who are trying to rip you off. But I know some of the hardened agents who don't believe your story. They're just waiting to see what your next moves are going to be. Just be careful of what you say or do. Tell me something, can you balance your own checkbook?"

"I've never had to," she said.

Simon's face flashed a look of disdain. By his facial expression, Stella knew what he was thinking: "You stupid rich little bitch."

In truth, the FBI could find no direct links to her in her husband's illegal dealings, and that seemed to be the basis for the agency's decision to stop putting the heat on her. The FBI was not a charitable institution, she had learned. Bob had run the whole scheme by himself, by investing the money he made into sundry enterprises and stocks. He kept her in the dark, or so it appeared. Worse, he was a terrible investor, converting his illegal payoffs into fancy financial securities just before the bubble burst again on Wall Street. He leveraged his cash to help start four companies that went belly-up in less than a year. He also borrowed heavily to make these investments, and his debts piled up even as the money rolled in.

The government seized all the cash and property it could, but Bob clearly had gotten away with more than enough to live on. He had been tipped off to the arrest at least 24 hours ahead of time, Simon surmised, and withdrew $3 million from seven banks in the area in a mere six hours.

"Do they have any idea where he is?" Stella asked.

"They think he might have skipped the country, but they can't be sure," Simon said. "He wasn't seen, and obviously he would be traveling under a fake name and passport."

"Do you think he's out of the country?"

"Could be, but I doubt it. He would be a liability to whomever he worked for, in or out of this country. Obviously, he knows too much for his own good. He knows way too much. In order to pull off what he did, he'd need a wide network of people to launder money. They'd form front companies, divide up the cash, put it into individual banks, and have the front companies write checks to each other, sort of layering it to make it look as if everything was on the up and up. Then the funds would be transferred to offshore banks and eventually converted. Meantime, Bob worked to get loans and favors for legitimate companies in Washington, but the FBI suspects that some high-level officials had something to do with his getting those jobs. They are also investigating "Security Now," the philanthropic group here in town that he was associated with. Apparently they have been funneling money to make arms purchases in the Middle East for the past year. My source tells me that there was some kind of a mix-up at a bank involving a large deposit in a foreign country. Someone there did not get paid on time and started talking. I'd say Bob's best chance of staying alive is for him to give himself up and go into the witness protection program. But my source doubts that he would do that now. He did not go straight to the airport here in D.C. or in Baltimore. He drove his car and left it at the train station in downtown Philadelphia. He could be hiding anywhere, but one operating theory is that he may have headed north to Canada. Anyway, the police have lost the trail."

The last time Stella had seen Bob was the day before her lunch with Alicia. He had told her he was going on a business trip to New York and would be back the next day. He even gave her the phone number at the hotel. She had desperately tried to call that number after the police showed up at her house. Then she called his cell phone over and over, but it never answered. They later found his cell phone, turned off and cleaned, on the seat of his abandoned car in Philadelphia.

"It's his calculation I can't abide," Stella said, gritting her teeth. "He was so cool—so believable."

"You were a naïve, Stella," Simon said. "It's like you pulled window shades over your eyes all the time you were married to this guy."

Knowing all this now, Stella regretted her first reaction to the police who had surrounded her when she'd returned from her lunch with Alicia. She'd called them "the Gestapo," and demanded to know why they were treating her so badly. She said Bob was in New York and insisted that he couldn't possibly be guilty of whatever they suspected him of. They should turn off those damn sirens and lights. What were her neighbors going to think? She was furious with herself for having gotten so huffy before taking time to see what was really going on. But that anger didn't come close to matching the gathering fury inside her now—all of it directed at Bob, who had left her penniless, homeless, and disgraced, and had duped her into believing all this time that he was a legitimate lawyer and lobbyist. *Time* magazine once had called them a "power couple," and her husband was frequently quoted by the national press on television about the great need for export credits to save the economy.

These days Dave Simon was one of the few acquaintances who would return her calls. Senator Oscar Taliman's wife, Penny, who had been in touch with her several times a week in recent years, had cut her off; she hadn't returned any calls since the story broke. Stella was beginning to get over her naiveté about Washington. She thought all the "close" friends she had made at Georgetown parties would rally behind her, but that was not to be. Columnist Frank Wright, once so chummy at parties, told her over the phone she was "radioactive" and she would have to recognize that. No one could be sure she wasn't involved, he told her. The real people who run Washington don't feel sorry for victims, he said, because victims lack the essential ingredient that Washington respects: power.

She ran into the White House social secretary, Penelope Campione, at Whole Foods Market. "Oh," Penelope said, "how are you doing? I'm so sorry. Look, I have to run today, but let's do lunch to talk this over."

"Sure," Stella said, she knew the Washington brush-off. But she put her pride aside and tried to call the next day. Penelope's schedule had suddenly turned so busy and she was "jammed" for the foreseeable future, she was told. Meantime, her friends in the art world in D.C., whom she never had considered pretentious and overly concerned about scandal, also treated her like a pariah.

Simon knew a few of the same people who were patrons of the Smithsonian, the Corcoran and the Phillips Collection. Now he reported to her: "They think you're a second-rate judge of art and a third-rate artist to boot, and never understood how you became so prominent, other than the fact that you had a lot of money to give. They, of course, think they are where they are on merit, naturally, and that their money is somehow more superior than yours, but that's another story." Simon said that it was only a matter of time before a local arts council would ask her to resign her position.

Such responses were the sounds of her world shattering. She amassed an impressive collection of fears to go with a palpable anger. Fear and anger were emotions largely unfamiliar to her until now, and want, real want, was something she had never known. "God, what do I do now?"

she asked Simon.

"Get a job," he said, not terribly sympathetic. He had known harder times than Stella. He could remember how uncertainty felt. He felt it had turned him into a real human being, self-sufficient and necessarily hard-edged. Stella needed that same edge, he told himself.

Alicia had been the only one to come through after Stella's life had changed for the worse. She had let Stella use one of the seven spare bedrooms for the past month and use one of her cars, a white 2014 Volvo that had only 2,000 miles on it. Alicia also lent her $10,000.

"You'll pay me back, I'm not worried," she said, as she kissed Stella on the cheek. She told Stella not to tell anyone where she was staying, because it might bring on the press hordes in front of her house. Stella knew there was another reason: Alicia was a social animal who did not want her reputation besmirched in the slightest by keeping the wife of a felon in her home, even if she was her best friend. That was just Washington, she said, nothing personal. Everyone understood it.

After the meeting, Stella left Simon's office and headed toward Alicia's house late in the day, fighting one traffic jam after another as she pondered her next step. She could not calm her emotions as she crossed over Key Bridge, caught the George Washington Parkway toward McLean, and rolled along the graceful tree-lined highway high above the Potomac to her right. She could see herself aiming a gun at Bob's head and blowing him away, and not feeling at all queasy about the bloody scene it would create. But first she wanted him on his hands and knees, begging her to take him back, begging her to protect him, begging her to save him. Yet she could see him now on some island, making love to a woman she did not know and stopping between sessions to sip a martini at the bedside. "That prick," she said to herself.

She pulled the Volvo into the circular driveway, parking next to Alicia's car and opened the door to a house that was purchased for $5.5 million in Great Falls, according to Washingtonian magazine. She went into the first floor den where Alicia usually spent most of her time, but she was not there. "Yoo-hoo, Alicia," she said on the house intercom. "I'm here." There was no answer. She saw nothing.

A search of the house yielded no Alicia. In the basement, though, there were signs of a struggle, as a table had been turned over, and an antique vase Stella knew to be worth at least a thousand dollars lay broken on the floor. Stella spotted a red spot on the carpet, and immediately thought it was blood. She felt cold air. The sliding glass door was open. She did not hesitate. She called the police, and then the office of George Valiant, Alicia's husband.

She sat on the floor and wept.

The next few hours turned into another exercise of wailing and staring at the wall, as the police searched the house and peppered Stella with questions. The police called Dave Simon to verify that Stella had left his office only 40 minutes before she arrived at the house, and had in fact been with her most of the afternoon. Before meeting Simon, she had had lunch at a small, darkly lit Chinese restaurant located in an Arlington strip mall. The proprietor, Mrs. Diem, a pleasant Vietnamese woman, knew her well and vouched for her story. Stella's alibi was seemingly ironclad; the police stopped questioning her for the moment.

Alicia was last seen at lunch at the M&S Grill in downtown Washington with Penelope Campione, her schedule no doubt cleared by the respectability of the company.

Stella wept over the disappearance of her friend as she remembered the happy moments they had together in social and in private circumstances. What happened? Where is she? With the blood on the floor and the sign of a struggle, it seemed that the person or persons who did this wanted her to be either dead or in captivity.

George was inconsolable over his wife's disappearance, and later became angry. He strode over to Stella. "I want you out of my house now," he said grimly. "You're poison. I can't believe this is not somehow connected with Bob, and that you know something. I wish I had never seen you and that you had never met Alicia."

"George, please believe me, I don't know anything," Stella said, looking dejectedly into his eyes. "I have no idea what happened. Don't you understand? I love Alicia. I wouldn't hurt her."

"Get your things," Valiant said coldly.

Stella went to her room and quickly gathered her clothing and other personal effects that hadn't been put into storage. In her haste a small brown leather-backed notebook spread open as it dropped on the floor. It was one of Bob's empty ones that she had kept to put in her purse. She noticed indentations on the pad as if Bob had used a strong hand in writing a note on the piece of paper that had been torn off. She found a pencil and lightly shadowed the areas where the indentations appeared. She couldn't make out any of the numbers, but two words showed up: "Copperhead Club."

CHAPTER 4

Hopefully, Kentucky

Loaded on his computer, B.J.'s digital photos looked sharp and clear. Views of the canyon and Snake Rock stuck out at B.J. almost like an agitated copperhead. He flipped through the photos rhythmically until he came to the attack.

In all the photos but one, the man who had fled through the woods had his back to the camera. B.J. zoomed in closer to make sure he was right about his initial suspicion. Using his photo-editing program, he clicked on the magnifying glass icon and then on the man's face, zooming in closer and closer. The enlargement sacrificed some detail, but it enabled B.J. to see enough to know that he had captured Jimmy Billingsley, son of the current mayor and grandson of a former mayor, committing a felony.

He was stunned.

Sure enough, it was indeed *the* Jimmy Billingsley, pride and joy of grandmother Harriet, who'd had great expectations for him, seeing him as a doctor or lawyer or engineer, and maybe one day mayor of the town like his grandfather and father.

Grandfather Gilbert Billingsley had also seen great promise in Jimmy, but never had harbored such grandiose expectations. Jimmy would create his own story, the former mayor mused, and it would differ from all the hopes that others had held for him, though the lad was certainly talented, smart, and very, very handsome. If Grandfather

Billingsley had known then what B.J. knew now, he'd have taken no delight in the fact that he turned out to be a better prophet than Harriet about how Jimmy's life would turn out—a previously benign prophecy that had just taken a major turn for the worse.

Jimmy had been all-everything in high school—an A-student, athlete, singer, guitar player, and saxophonist. In his senior year he had distressed his parents and grandparents with a rebellious streak, but they saw it as a passing thing. Yet, in his first year at Transylvania University—a small but prestigious college in Lexington—girls, alcohol, and dope occupied more of his time than his studies had.

This was not an unusual story for a college freshman these days, and Jimmy might have survived with the advance of maturity if he had not given in to that propensity for wildness that had manifested itself when he was 18. He had managed barely passing grades during this period. But one warm spring night toward the end of the school year, he and three buddies drunker than was prudent decided to pull an old-fashioned prank on Charles Mallory, the university's president. They wrapped some cow manure in a newspaper, dropped it in a plastic bag, and sneaked quietly across campus to the edge of the front porch of the president's residence. Jimmy took the loaded newspaper from the plastic bag, put it on the porch near the door, and lit it with a cigarette lighter. He and his friends ran as fast as they could to the nearest building and ducked behind it as the fire billowed up. There was a commotion inside the house, and Mallory opened the door to peek outside. He still had his suit on from all his official duties. "Holy shit," he said, not yet fully aware of how accurately he had identified the problem. He leaped over to the blaze and promptly stomped it out—only to discover that his entire trouser-leg had been splattered with warm cow dung.

"Dammit, you assholes, I'm going to get you if it's the last thing I do," President Mallory yelled into the night, knowing that his tormentors were watching and listening. He started to go inside to call the campus police, only to be stopped by Mrs. Mallory, who told him he wasn't coming back into her house until she cleaned the shit off his leg. Behind the building a hundred yards away, Jimmy and his friends were chuckling as softly as they could. It was painful to hold back the laughter, but as soon as they got back to the dorm, they exploded into a bevy of raucous whoops.

Certain that no one had seen them, they all went to bed that night thinking they had escaped. But the next morning, while Jimmy was sleeping off a hangover (and missing his English class), two campus policemen burst into the room.

"Get up, Billingsley, you're out of here—expelled," the older cop said. "The president wants you out of here by noon. Get packed. We'll stay and watch."

"What is this shit?" Jimmy had protested. "I didn't do a thing. Don't I even get a hearing, a chance to appeal?"

"Oh, you can appeal, all right," the policeman, said. "But that comes later, after you are out of here, and I mean *out* of here. Someone saw what you did last night, putting that little surprise package on the president's porch." Jimmy noticed a little grin on the officer's face. "Saw you put it there and light it and run off with your pals."

"That person was mistaken," Jimmy said. "It wasn't me—I swear it."

"That's not what the school chaplain says," the policeman countered. "You are no doubt familiar with him after all the trouble you gave us this year. He was having dinner at the president's house and just happened to be looking out the window when you did it. So let's move."

Jimmy was certain that he had taken all precautions and wondered if the chaplain or the president had guessed that it was he. Admittedly, he had been a troublemaker, prone to campus drunkenness and causing the university some embarrassment.

He left the campus that afternoon knowing that he would never be back but not knowing what was next for him. The reception at home was grim, and Jimmy stayed in his room for days before venturing out. He ended up using his music talent to get a job playing at the

Copperhead Club out on Route 7884, which certainly needed a talent like him.

From the club's point of view, he was a smash hit. The story of the university's president stomping on a package of burning cow shit became an immediate sensation—and a frequently told tale at the club. At the demand of the club-goers, Jimmy held forth almost every night, sparking boisterous laughter—especially around midnight, when the country music had ended and everyone was numb. In such a state, seasoned drunks are quite conservative in their taste for bar literature. They wanted to hear the tried-and-true standards, those that didn't require much mental focus and where everybody could anticipate the punch line.

Each time Jimmy told his story, he himself laughed and enjoyed it as much as his buddies did. It left the room rocking with laughter, and was always the pièce de résistance of any evening. Jimmy was the "clean-up hitter of laughter," but at the end of it all, when the crowd had thinned and he had received his handshakes and pats on the back, and heard lines like "that's a damn funny story, Jimmy, gets better every time I hear it," it always left him sad and surly. The attention was bittersweet because Jimmy knew the joke was on him.

As B.J. looked at the photos, he felt a sense of sadness about Jimmy, too. But he didn't know what to do with his pictures. He didn't recognize the young woman who'd been the victim. And he didn't know if Jimmy had recognized him when he yelled down into the canyon. It had been far away, but B.J. had such a recognizable profile with his bulging middle, big round head, beard, and stout legs and arms that Jimmy didn't necessarily have to see his face to identify B.J. If Jimmy had recognized him, B.J. knew he could be in trouble. He suspected that Jimmy must be hooked on drugs, perhaps methadone or oxycodone, the powerful painkiller omnipresent in the hills.

The oxycodone problem was especially tragic. Too many physicians had become lax about the drug, prescribing it for people who complained of back pain or other ailments. Dealers peddled it off particularly to young people, who crushed the pill so that the time-release mechanism no longer functioned. A young addict told the *New York Times* he had become hooked in seconds. Use of the drug played a big role in corrupting these once-stable small towns, where people liked to live to escape the evils of the big city.

B.J. scrupulously avoided befriending those who were getting hooked on oxycodone. Most of them saw him as a freak anyway, and laughed and called him Doofus to his face every time he passed them by. And Jimmy, he knew, was one of their leaders. B.J. had the good sense to know that the drug trap was an even bigger trap than the one he was in now, taking care of his mom, the land, and the few animals still left.

Deciding whether to turn Jimmy in was a real moral dilemma for B.J. He did not want Jimmy to go to prison and make his life even more miserable. He also knew that Jimmy's father, the mayor, his grandmother, and his grandfather, the former mayor, as well as all the rest of the family would be crushed.

B.J. was aware of stories that Jimmy's grandfather had once been sweet on his mom and had given her a job in the police department. On the other hand, Jimmy had shown himself to be an animal and might try to rape again unless he were stopped. B.J. did not want to be the one doing the stopping. Yelling at Jimmy was a courageous act by itself, and one courageous act was all he could manage for now. Not only did he not know the victim, but he was ignorant about the real circumstance of the encounter, or how the woman might testify if she were called into court. Perhaps it was consensual and just a rough kind of sex, and she would pass it off. B.J. briefly considered a clever form of blackmail in which he would send the copies of the photos to Jimmy with a note telling him he had better clean up his act or a Mr. Anonymous would send them to the police. But what if Jimmy figured out it was he? That would make him a target. Instead he decided to do as Scarlett O'Hara did, and think about that tomorrow. After all, heroes existed in books and movies and in the minds of inexperienced people who did not know what consequences flowed from excessive bravery.

The next morning, a car moved slowly up the road that passed by the house. Usually during the day, B.J. would leave the gate open so that delivery trucks, newspaper deliverers, or handymen could drive up to the house without being stopped. The car slowed and turned onto the dirt driveway leading to the house. B.J. rarely had visitors, and in his current state he feared them. He quickly saved his electronic files, shut down the computer, and ran into the yard to greet the visitor.

He did not want a stranger in the house disturbing his mother. He didn't recognize the old beat-up Chevrolet Chevette, but as soon as the car got close enough for him to see the driver, he recognized her. She was the woman in the photo. He was struck by how attractive she was in person. Her frizzy brunette hair rose in an airy fluff around her head. Her lips were bright red, and she had on heavy makeup in an attempt to hide a black eye and cuts and bruises on her cheek.

"May I help you?" B.J. asked when she rolled down the window. A light breeze hit her hair.

"Are you Doofus?" she asked.

B.J. swallowed hard. His worst fears were being realized.

CHAPTER 5

Arlington, Virginia

B ob Jasper's disappearance just before he was to have been arrested as a money launderer was sensational enough. But the news that Alicia, the best friend of Jasper's wife, had soon after been abducted or maybe even killed had gone viral in Washington and around the country. That was *her* blood on the carpet, The Washington Post revealed.

The Washington press corps gave the missing-socialite scandal full attention, surpassing even some of the presidential campaign coverage in an election year. There were blog posts and headlines about Alicia's high-school friends and Bob's sword collection. Such a juicy story didn't come around often, even though much of the coverage was devoted to the political impact that the scandal would have on the President and his party. The fact that Stella had been living in Alicia's house and that Alicia had dined with the White House social secretary just before disappearing gave the story all the juice it needed for 24-hour coverage.

"Dirty-moneygate," the media soon began calling it, and Congress began talking about a series of hearings.

The *New York Times* reported that the FBI was investigating why the Treasury Department had abruptly halted a probe into the overseas transfer of millions of dollars from one of Bob's companies, a pizza parlor in Chicago. President Everett and his supporters denied any knowledge of such illegality, but that did not stop the stampede of coverage.

"The sharks are in the water," Columnist Jackson Fisherman said on

41

the Sunday talk shows. "People are asking, 'What did the President know, and when did he know it?'" in the common reference to questions that the late Senator Howard Baker of Tennessee had asked during the Watergate hearings long ago. The White House deeply resented such references to the scandal that brought down President Nixon. The press secretary noted that the party's national committee had given back all the money Bob and Stella had contributed. Stella saw none of it. Her creditors got it first.

Now in demand by the networks and newspapers for interviews, Stella decided to go underground. She issued a statement through Simon that she knew nothing of her husband's money laundering and would speak about it in due time, but couldn't at the moment because of the on-going investigation, which would last through the winter months and into spring.

With a little money left from Alicia's loan, plus another $17,000 she had received from the sale of some of her belongings, Stella had rented a small room in the South Arlington apartment of Mrs. Rita Rodriguez, near Columbia Pike and George Mason Drive. Mrs. Rodriguez, a custodial employee whom she had gotten to know while working with an art show at the Freer Gallery of Art, was a hard worker, friendly, and very discreet. The neighborhood was a vast complex of 50-year-old apartment buildings that was home to some of the thousands of immigrants working in odd jobs all over the Washington area.

Stella felt comfortable with Rita as well as with Cynthia Aguillar, who lived in the same complex with her 85-year-old grandmother, Rosa. Despite Cynthia's efforts to dissuade her, Rosa insisted upon walking up and down the hall with her cane just to show that she didn't need that terrible wheelchair or walker all the time. But arthritis had gripped Rosa so that when she went outside, she didn't protest about riding in a wheelchair. Cynthia went to work every day, leaving Rosa behind in the apartment.

One day Stella met Rosa in the hall and helped her back to the apartment. Rosa, who could speak only a little English, said she had seen Stella's face on TV and that she knew she couldn't be involved in anything illegal. "Your face, too kind," Rosa said. She told Stella about coming to America from her native El Salvador, using her late husband's savings so that Cynthia could find a better life than in the village where they lived. Her husband owned a small restaurant, she said, but she could not keep it up after he died, and Cynthia, with a good mind and an interest in the wider world, had wanted to move to the United States. Now she was cleaning homes in the hopes of saving enough money to go to school, Rosa said, adding, "but is hard for her." Rosa offered Stella some lunch and tea and bade her goodbye with a big smile.

Alicia's disappearance had renewed the FBI's interest in Stella, and so once again she had to tell her story to agents who seemed to think little of her. Simon picked her up each morning when she had an interview, and ordered her to disguise herself as much as possible when she went outside. Sometimes the agents came to her apartment.

As another week went by, she still couldn't shake the fear she might be charged with a crime and end up in prison with violent murderers. Agents peppered her with questions about what her husband had told her and about the myriad calls from around the world, especially from the Middle East. Luckily, her own ignorance had bailed her out so far, but she was constantly petrified about what was next. Her anger for Bob grew with each such interrogation. Often, stories were leaked from FBI sources that she might be indicted if they found any suspicious connections, no matter how small. In fact, many of the questions surprised her, because they suggested a deep and intimate relationship between her husband and people with foreign names.

She had always been an upstanding person, soft and gentle with people, and so sophisticated that it would be difficult to see how she could harm anyone. But her ordeal was having a visible effect. She lapsed into a depression fed by the anger she felt toward Bob and the shame of being wrongfully victimized. Never a smoker, she took to lighting one cigarette after another. Each night she stared at his picture on her dresser while sipping a stiff martini. He had smashed not only her structured world, but also subjected her to an embarrassment so deep that it was nearly unbearable. How could she vindicate herself? With each day, she told herself that she wanted to confront him and insist that he clear her name and give her a life again. She feared that the FBI might find some document or some past comment suggesting that she knew more than she really did.

One unseasonably warm day, Dave Simon knocked at the door. He looked excited. With no elevator in the apartment building, he was huffing from the climb up the three flights of stairs. "Whew, that's a terrible climb," he said, wiping his brow. "Hey, why is your front door connected to a closet? Is this all the room you have?"

"Don't rub it in, Simon," she said. "It's all I can afford at the moment."

"Gee, you look terrible. You know missing sleep will quickly put new wrinkles on your forehead. You'll have to order up some more Botox," Simon said, smiling.

Stella smiled, too. She knew it was his idea of a joke and also knew that it was probably true. "What do you want, besides getting your sick kicks with your insults, Simon?" Stella asked.

"Look, you know Scott Herbert?"

"You mean the White House chief of staff?"

"He called me last night and said he believes that if you made a statement saying that to your knowledge the President never talked to your husband about any of this nasty business, it would help."

"What? How can I absolve the President of something I don't know about? That's crazy."

"I told him that, but he asked if you could break your silence and say that to your knowledge, your husband never had a discussion with the President on anything related to his work. In other words, they didn't confer on anything you know about, the President never called the house, and the two didn't talk about business when you went to the

White House on social occasions."

"Bob was a big contributor," said Stella. "I'd say that he was pretty deeply involved in the President's work, if not the other way around. Look, what's in this for me? I think such a statement would only get me in deeper trouble with the FBI."

"He's the President from your own party. Do you want the other joker in there because of this? He could ruin the country." Simon went on to describe the President's precarious political situation with the election only a little more than a few months away. "Many members of his own party think he's finished, considering the terrible economic climate and the President's own inability to deal with the long economic slide—plus the scandal involving your husband."

"I could say that the President didn't talk business to my husband because he was too busy looking at me all the time."

Simon just looked at her. "Stop it, Stella. Look, I'm hoping the FBI is mostly satisfied that you are not involved in this nasty business and Alicia's disappearance. I believe they would have charged you by now if they had any real evidence. It would just be a gesture to help the President. The FBI is not politically blind. They would know what you are doing, if you word it right."

"The fact that he's asking me to do this makes me suspicious about possible involvement, to be perfectly frank," said Stella.

"The President?" said Simon. "He may like women, but he's no crook. He's looking for political protection here. Although he can't promise anything now, when this is over, it might just work to your political advantage to do it."

"I just don't understand what's going on, Dave—what has happened to Bob and Alicia?"

"You know he was fucking her, don't you?"

"I'm sorry, what did you say?"

"Bob—he was screwing Alicia. I thought you had figured that out. The FBI knows."

"What?" she shouted. "Are you kidding me?" Her face reddened. "No way. She's my friend. How do you know this? I don't believe you."

"I have my sources. You've got to remember, Congress is investigating this, and there are some fine senators who leak from time to time."

"Dave, do you know where they are now? Dammit, I just want to know where they are! I want to stare in their fucking faces and give them a piece of my mind. Can you find out where they are? How could Alicia do this to me?"

She couldn't help herself. She was wailing, rocking back and forth in misery. Simon had seen Stella overwrought before, but not like this. She looked like a rhinoceros ready to charge. He wasn't sure he knew this woman at all.

As Simon left the building, the same black BMW with a man seated behind the wheel was parked across the street. He had a clear view of the front door. The FBI, he thought. They believe her, but they don't. Now they have to hedge against errors in their own judgment, no doubt the result of so many mistakes in the past, considering Hansen and Aimes, Ruby Ridge and Waco, and 9/11, he thought. "Poor Stella," he said.

As Stella predicted, her statement, issued through Dave Simon, didn't do much to calm the storm over the President's possible involvement in the scandal. The White House spokesman declined to comment on it, saying it spoke for itself. In the *Post* the next morning, an unidentified White House source was quoted as saying, self-servingly, that Mrs. Jasper had certainly dispelled the widespread perception that Jasper was a bosom buddy of the President's.

"It's clear it was only a social association, one of the thousands such associations he has," the source said. "He couldn't even remember Bob Jasper's face when the news came out." Stella knew this was a lie. Bob liked to remain in the background, but at one fundraising reception not known to the public, he made the President roar with laughter when he began to imitate the voice of his arch-enemy, Senator LaFont Vandergriffen, the chairman of the Senate Judiciary Committee.

A wealthy Southerner with White House ambitions of his own, Vandergriffen was about to give the White House additional trouble: He would be in charge of the hearings on the Jasper affair. They were scheduled to begin in February, with Stella as the first witness.

CHAPTER 6

Hopefully, Kentucky

66 I'm Julie," the woman told B.J. when she pulled her old Chevy up to his house. "Julie Whitwood. I live over in Purcells. Look, can I get out and come inside your house and talk to you? What I want to say is pretty difficult for me. In case anybody is watching, I don't want anyone else to see me."

"Sorry, I'll have to sit in the car with you," B.J. said. "My mom is old and sick, and I don't want to disturb her. She has a home-care person in with her." B.J. said this knowing that Molly was looking through the curtains watching the whole scene. He didn't want her to know about this and didn't want to be questioned by her about it.

B.J. got in the front seat and couldn't help but notice Julie's tight-fitting jeans and sweater revealing large breasts beneath. A fake fur jacket was draped over a cast on her left arm. Even though her face had bruises and lacerations, she was appealing.

"Look," she said, "I'm pretty sure you saw what happened to me over there in Copperhead Canyon. That S.O.B. Jimmy Billingsley tried to rape me, and if it hadn't been for you yelling at him, he would have done it. I need your help. I'm coming to beg you to help me. I was afraid he was going to kill me. If you hadn't yelled, he might have done it."

B.J. paused. "I'm sorry, lady, but, I don't know what you're talking about. I never saw any such thing."

"Well, Jimmy sure thinks it was you. He pushed me back when you yelled, and said, 'it's that goddamn Doofus.' He spit at me, and told me if I said anything about this I'd be dead, and so would that asshole up there on the mountain. Then he kicked me and ran off into the woods. Look, Doofus—B.J., is that right?—I can't go home because he knows where I live and work. I'm staying with a friend over in Lavender. I'm afraid to press charges without a witness. It would be just one of those he-said, she-said kind of things when I got to court, and the lawyers would question my past and my motives for going up in the canyon with him in the first place. Everyone around here knows that it's a place to make out."

B.J. put aside his natural shyness. "So you went up there to make out with him, and you say he tried to have sex with you, and now you want me to go to bat for you because he tried to do what you wanted him to do in the first place?"

"That's not what happened," she protested. "He promised me a ride home. I was visiting my friend here and we went to the Copperhead Club the night before, and had a good time. I met Jimmy at the bar and we talked. I told him I loved his music, which was true, and he tried to put the moves on me then and there. I said no; I believed in getting acquainted. So he said he had nothing to do the next day, and would pick me up. We would drive around, have lunch at the club, talk, and he would drive me home. He seemed very nice."

"Until the next day," B.J. interjected.

"We had a very nice date, a couple of drinks and a sandwich," Julie continued. Then he said, 'Before we go, I want you to see the canyon. It's beautiful up there, and there's this unusual rock formation.' As it turned out, we had to drive past your house down this dirt road to get there."

"That's where he wanted to get acquainted," said B.J., thinking he might want to do the same thing.

"He grabbed me as soon as I got out of the car, and when I resisted, he hit me. I think you saw the rest." She was sobbing. "He really hurt me.

Nobody should be able to get by with that.

"I agree, ma'am," he said. "I'd like to help. I believe your story. Jimmy's younger than I am, but I know he sure has a mean temper. The sheriff will believe you, and so will many people in town. But I can't be a witness if I wasn't there to see it. I'm sorry."

"B.J., Doofus, whatever your name is, I think you aren't telling me the truth, and I don't know why."

"I'm not lying to you, lady—can't you get the message?" He didn't look at her. He couldn't look at her. Instead, he looked at the window next to the front porch and knew his mom's eyes were watching every move he made. Julie didn't understand, he said to himself—she could never understand.

Julie leaned her head against the steering wheel and remained rigid—and quiet—for what seemed like a long time.

"I have to tend to my mom now," B.J. said, breaking the silence.

"There's a reason," Julie pleaded—"I know there's a reason. To tell you the truth, I wouldn't want to be you, Mr. Doofus. You seem like such a nice, truthful guy, and you even saved my life, for which I'm grateful. I guess I must be asking too much to help me now. However, I could tell the sheriff it's you. And then he'd be out here to question you, not me. I might just do that, Mr. Doofus."

"I'd tell him the same thing," B.J. said.

With that, Julie started the Chevette's engine.

"I'm sorry I can't help—I've gotta go," B.J. said again, and got out of the car. With tears dripping off her face, Julie said nothing and drove off.

"Julie, Julie, Julie." B.J. whispered her name over and over, either awake or in his dreams. Guilt-ridden, he climbed back up Copperhead Knob, where he could think. He remembered every word of their conversation, he'd gone over what he'd seen for days since he'd witnessed it, and he was still trying to tell himself he had done the right thing by not getting involved any more deeply.

For one thing, he thought, Julie wouldn't grasp the close connections and intertwinings between the Matsons and Billingsleys. B.J.'s brother Jake had married Magladine Billingsley after a secret high-school courtship that Betty Billingsley had tried to break up. His oldest brother, Zeke, and Larry Billingsley, Jr. had been high-school football stars and close friends who roomed together at Morehead University, and when both of them were in town, they made time for a drink at the Copperhead Club so they could share old times and catch up on what the other was doing.

B.J. and Joyce Billingsley were the youngest children in each family. Joyce was a natural flirt who had the goods to do it with. At 14, on a warm July afternoon, they'd had a fumbling, awkward sexual encounter on a secluded beach of the Kentucky River. It was perhaps the finest moment of B.J.'s teenage years, but Joyce soon told him that it had been a big mistake and she didn't want to see him again. She went on to be a cheerleader and married the captain of the football team before they graduated. He saw her now and then in town. She would acknowledge him, and then go on about her business, but neither had forgotten the moment.

Gilbert Billingsley's oldest son, Stewart, had replaced him as mayor, and for a time he appeared to be doing a good job considering the rough times that Hopefully had gone through. The Appalachian Regional Commission had developed grand plans for helping such small towns to attract new industry and jobs, but those dreams hadn't materialized. When the coal industry was down, as it often was, it had a ripple effect all over Eastern Kentucky, particularly on the railroad that carried the coal through Hopefully from the richer mine in the east to Bluegrass country. So, under Stewart Billingsley, Hopefully continued to wither. Most of its young people left to build their lives elsewhere; they called their hometown Hope*less*ly, even though they still had an affection for it. Even the railroad jobs gradually dried up. As the locomotives got bigger and better, the railroad discovered that it no longer needed to stop at Hopefully very often. Purcells, where Julie lived, was only two miles from an interstate highway, and the town had flourished.

Yet, the people who lived in Hopefully had a common bond that often unites those who live in depressed areas. They looked out for each other. The ones who'd gotten into trouble could be excused because they had endured more. And so in B.J.'s mind, Jimmy was both a member of the family and a victim all at once. As terrible as Jimmy was, B.J. could not bring himself to turn the man in.

Admittedly, B.J. knew that Molly Jo would think just the opposite if she had known about the situation. His mom had confronted him as he had returned from Julie's car. "Are you keeping something from me, B.J.? You get that girl in trouble? What does she want around here, anyway?" Her right hand quivered from Parkinson's disease as she pointed at him.

"No, Mom, just an old friend from my high school days who wanted to know where to find Jack Levi."

"She looked like she was crying to me," Molly said.

"They had been close at one time," B.J. replied.

His Mom backed off. "Where's the damned remote, B.J.? 'NYPD' is coming on soon, and I don't want to miss it. Where's my gun?"

"Mom, you know you can't have your gun anymore. It's dangerous to carry it around the house, and none of your friends want to come by when they know you still have a gun." He knew she would put it on the coffee table if her friends, like Mrs. Jackson or Mrs. Wainwright, came to see her. She did it to remind them she'd been a cop, and a damn good one, and because she still harbored suspicions about the corruptibility of any human being. B.J. would tell his mother's guests not to worry— that the gun wasn't loaded and that his mom was a little paranoid about their security living out in the country. Harriet Billingsley never came over, even though they shared grandchildren, but it was not because of the gun. The gun didn't bother Harriet. It was Molly Jo's tryst long ago with the man Harriet later married.

B.J. kept the bullets stashed away under lock and key in an old toy box that his dad had made 20 years ago. It was stored in the basement, and he never told Molly where they were because he knew she would get them. He kept a gun in his little office in the barn. At night he would bring it into the house as a security measure. He was a little paranoid, too. He had used the weapon once when he'd been sure a prowler was lurking on the property. He'd gotten up and walked out on the front porch, and listened. He'd shot into the air, just to let anyone out there know he was armed. He never saw or heard anyone, but the gun made him feel safer.

On a number of occasions, B.J. almost called Julie and told her the truth, to come over and plot a strategy for prosecuting Jimmy. He would have loved to tell her that he had the evidence—the photographs of Jimmy's brutal attack. But now he was afraid that she would hate him if he revealed the truth after so many days' delay. Yet, she might not if he could explain his reluctance. Once, he had punched the first six digits of her phone number, and then hung up, fearing the consequences.

Atop Copperhead Knob, B.J. sighed at the complexity of the situation. The old black-and-white cowboy movies that he'd seen as a child never covered these shades of gray, he told himself. Before the sun got too high in the sky, he took more pictures of the canyon as he sat on a fallen tree. He focused on the rock that looked like a snake's head, and it haunted him, as if he had been bitten with no antidote on hand.

FEBRUARY

CHAPTER 7

Washington, D.C.

Stella awoke at 5 a.m. after a fitful night of dreams. In the dream that finally woke her up, she was a one-eyed beggar on the streets of Washington, where uncaring passers-by either brushed her aside or stared straight ahead, refusing to look her in the eye.

She stayed in bed for an extra hour to let that image go away as she prepared for Senator Vandergriffen's hearing, now only hours away. Rita knocked on her bedroom door saying that she had made blueberry pancakes. "Come and join me for breakfast," Rita said.

Stella sagged into a chair at the breakfast table. "This is the day, Rita," she said. "This is really the biggest day in my life. I'll be asked about why my husband left me with the implication that I'm the guilty one. And if that weren't enough, they're going to bring up the affair between Alicia and Bob, and expect me to say I knew about it all the time. They'll try to turn me into a crook." Her eyes began tearing at the thought of it.

Rita got up and tried to calm her, rubbing Stella's back and urging her to forget about Bob, but Stella wouldn't hear of that. "I want to know where he is. I want to know where Alicia is," she said, seething. "I'm getting so desperate now that I want to see him and Alicia, face-to-face. Actually, right now I'm so mad I could kill him. I wish I could corner them against a wall and castrate him with a carving knife while she watched. Yep, Rita. I'd try to kill them both if I could."

Dave Simon picked her up and drove her to the Hart Senate Office

Building, where she would be given the third degree, subjected to hours of questioning under hot lights in an uncomfortable wooden chair. He told her to be responsive to the answers, but not combative—unless her questioners falsified the truth. "Then, let them have it," Simon said. "They might pull any trick, so be alert."

When they arrived at the Hart building, a large crowd gathered at the main entrance. Members of the Capitol police force, seeking to escort her into the building quickly, had to push people back. "Did you kill her?" one onlooker shouted." She didn't answer. "Were you taking out revenge because she was sleeping with your husband?" another yelled. Several carried placards reading: "MURDERER!"

Stella wasn't too distraught to take note of the most interesting signboard—one with the slogan, "IMPEACH THE PRESIDENT." Another said, "EVERETT EQUALS CORRUPTION." This could become a major issue for the President, Stella thought.

When she walked into the hearing room, the TV lights snapped on. Photographers from television networks and print media zoomed in on her. Behind her, she could hear someone say, "We're lucky we got in to see what the whole country is watching on TV. I can't wait to hear what she's going to say." Stella was nervous, but Simon calmed her down. "You are smarter than these clowns," he told her.

The chairman of the Senate Judiciary Committee, Senator LaFont Vandergriffen, a portly man with thick silver hair, rapped his gavel. Looking over his rectangular reading glasses perched low on his nose, he smiled, in courtly fashion, at Stella, who was ready to sink under the table.

"The committee welcomes you today, Mrs. Jasper," Senator Vandergriffen began. Then, reading the formal statement his staff had prepared, he said his interest and the committee's was merely to "get at the truth" in a case where there clearly had been a "concerted effort" to cover up the facts. "We all hope the President has nothing to do with this, as he claims," the senator continued, "and if he has nothing to hide,

I am sure he will fully cooperate with this committee and provide us with everything his administration has gathered about Mr. Jasper's alleged money laundering. We want to know why the Treasury Department did not move aggressively to prosecute him when it was clear that it should have, and whether this had any connection with his campaign contributions. As we say in the South, this case stinks to high heaven."

Stella was duly sworn in, and when Senator Vandergriffen asked her to present her testimony, she went over her entire story in an opening statement that Simon helped write. She also avowed no prior knowledge of either her husband's disappearance or Alicia's abduction. She said she already had been asked detailed questions about front companies, and layering of money, and foreign bank accounts, and why she hadn't questioned her husband's rapid rise to great wealth. She said she had to admit, frankly and humbly, that she had not paid attention to the details of her husband's business life, and instead had attended to their marriage. "I loved him once," she said as she approached the end of her statement. "But I had nothing to do with his criminality or with the disappearance of my friend, Alicia Valiant. You can cast suspicion on me all you want, but I swear to you that I am innocent."

Vandergriffen began the questioning, gently at first, then with increasing toughness.

"You helped advise people in the art world on what to buy and what to sell—is that right, Mrs. Jasper?"

"Yes, sir," Stella" said, "but much of the time I volunteered to help raise money for art in Washington, D.C."

"And did you enjoy your life here, you know, the large home you had out there in Virginia—the expensive cars, the parties and so forth, and your work in the art world? Did you find that all stimulating?" Vandergriffen asked in his thick Southern drawl.

"Yes, I enjoyed all that, I can't deny it, Senator, but that's not a crime." Stella said emphatically.

"Well, it seems to this senator that you enjoyed a great deal of privilege in this city, and that you were able to open a lot of doors that others couldn't."

Stella struggled to remain silent and expressionless.

"Don't you miss it?" Vandergriffen pressed.

"Now and then," Stella said.

"Didn't you ever feel guilty that you were buying influence with dirty money, Mrs. Jasper?"

Simon, sitting beside her at the witness table, waved his hand vigorously. "Senator, we have to object at this line of questioning," he said, obviously pained. "You know my client has denied any knowledge of her husband's illegalities."

The committee's ranking member, Senator Ferdinand Gugliermo, who clearly was sympathetic to Stella's position, underscored Simon's point. "That's uncalled for, Senator," he said.

"Well, let me ask it this way," Vandergriffen continued, not skipping a beat. "Do you now, at this time, right now, feel any sense of guilt or regret that you were able to enjoy a life of privilege and power here in the nation's capital by having to rely on your husband's ill-gained profits from laundering dirty money?"

"Some regret, yes," Stella admitted.

"No, I mean *shame,*" the senator said. "All those hardworking people out there watching this today earn their money through legitimate means. Yours was dirty money, whether you knew it or not, and frankly, with all that money coming in, you had to know something was amiss."

Stella lowered her eyes. Her face was beet-red. She didn't have to say anything. Her embarrassment was evident, but not for the reason the committee thought. The shame was not so much in mooching off illegal money. It was in Vandergriffen's crusade to humiliate her over it. She felt very hot. The tight-fitting black wool St. Laurent suit didn't help. She felt a trickle of perspiration going down her back.

Next Vandergriffen turned to the disappearance of Alicia, which Stella already had indicated would be painful for her to discuss.

"It seems strange to many of us that she disappeared not long after your husband. Just for the record, did you know in advance that something might happen to her?"

"No, I did not, Senator—and I've told that to everyone who's asked."

"Did you have any idea that she had any romantic relationship with your husband, as we see written in the newspaper all the time?"

"Sadly, I did not," Stella replied.

"Did you kill her, or have her killed, because she was having an affair with Mr. Jasper?"

"No, Senator," Stella said. "No, I did not, and even if I had known about the affair, I wouldn't have killed her or anyone else. I am sorry that you felt compelled even to ask that question."

"So her disappearance is a complete mystery to you?" Vandergriffen said skeptically.

"People can and do speculate about it, but it's a mystery to me," Stella said. "I have sworn to that."

"Many things seem to be a mystery to you, Mrs. Jasper. Now take this statement you made that appeared—and I use the word 'appeared' advisedly—to exonerate the President. Did you think that up on your own, or did someone else come up with the idea?"

Stella had anticipated this one. "I volunteered to issue this statement after all the intimations in the media that President Everett might somehow be involved with Bob and his business activities on a regular basis. I obviously don't know anything about Bob's dealings, but I am pretty confident that he never talked to the President about them. I can tell you for sure that the President of the United States did not call our house one time while I was there. We saw the President at a few state dinners and Christmas parties, but that was it."

"And fundraisers?" Vandergriffen asked.

"Yes, fundraisers," Stella said. "There were five or six of those in the last election."

"Let me get back to my question," the senator said. "Did you or did you not talk directly with someone at the White House about this statement?"

"No, I did not," she said.

"So you made this statement on your own initiative?"

"My attorney was in discussion about it with Mr. Herbert at the White House, but there was no pressure on me to say or do anything," Stella said. "I did it to clear the air and provide the facts as I knew them."

Vandergriffen looked at her with disbelief, masking the faint smile that was forming in his mind over how this once politically unsophisticated woman had so quickly learned how to spin the truth to suit her needs, just as he and everyone else in Washington's political class did all the time.

"Let me see if I get this," the senator said, a hint of impending mockery in his voice. "Your husband was deeply involved in this mess, yet you want us to believe you know nothing. Your best friend is gone, abducted or dead, even while you were staying at her house, yet you want us to believe you know nothing about that. Now you come forth with the incredible statement that the President had nothing to do with what you say you know nothing about. How can you expect me—or *anybody*—to believe that?"

The hearing-room erupted in laughter. Stella didn't answer until the clamor died down and the redness began to leave her face. She knew how Simon might want her to respond, which would be with a calm restatement of the facts she had presented. But she was angry—and she let it show.

"You can believe what you want, Senator—especially when you've apparently already made up your mind and you're running for something."

CHAPTER 8

Arlington, Virginia

S tella couldn't get herself to turn on the TV the day after her testimony, but she couldn't resist scanning the newspaper. She shuddered at some of the ridicule lobbed at her in the *Post*, including a front-page column by Severance Peig, illustrated with a photo of Stella crying as she left the hearing room.

Poor Stella. The wronged woman the world has been waiting to hear from showed up yesterday with a lame apology for President Everett and with a chip on her shoulder for Senator Vandergriffen.

Poor Stella. She was weepy and defensive, turning her eyes down at embarrassing questions and responding softly, as if she were a wounded bird, to gain sympathy. At least that is what many believe about poor Stella. She will be known as the woman who knew nothing. Never knew that Bob Jasper was a first-class launderer of dirty money and possibly guilty of other kinds of misbehavior. Never knew that he had been sleeping with her best friend, who disappeared later under mysterious circumstances.

Her insistence that she didn't know hasn't been proven or disproven, which puts poor Stella Jasper in limbo until this case develops with more clarity. Until it does, we may never know anything.

Stella had wanted to rip the column to shreds—until she realized that Severance Peig was essentially accurate.

Poor Stella indeed, she thought. Since that December day when her world fell apart, she had fought against an overpowering sense of helplessness. She longed to get away and find a peaceful spot on the planet where all the painful memories would be expunged and she could start anew. But she knew better. How could she start over?

Events had stamped her and become part of a memory bank that she couldn't suppress, hard as she tried. Furthermore, the hatred and anger she had developed for Bob had metastasized like a virulent cancer. Stella sensed that she had lost her center, and she was the star in a scriptless drama about herself over which she had no control. As the star, she was being tugged along by the drama instead of taking charge of it. She'd developed a habit of sitting on the kitchen floor drinking vodka from the bottle and scarfing down cheddar cheese goldfish and then curling into a fetal position on the cold tile.

As far as Stella was concerned, the only way to know how the drama would end and find peace was to find Bob, or at least try, as foolhardy and dangerous as that course might be. But she felt trapped, with so little money and such a daunting lack of information.

She doubted seriously if Bob would try to make contact with anyone in his hometown in Pennsylvania, for fear of setting off more gossip. He wasn't close to anyone back there anymore, even his own family. He thought he had grown beyond them, as he often put it, although it was clear now that "grown" wasn't the right verb. If Bob had fled the country, finding him would involve the kind of information and money she didn't have.

Bob could fit in almost anywhere. When he was in a crowd, he was an accomplished storyteller who could draw people to him. But he also knew how to stay in the background, listen well, and not interrupt, even if he thought the conversation was boring. He was a chameleon, but he was always calculating. She could tell that about him, as she watched him, time and again, work the room at Washington parties.

Despite Bob's current notoriety, it wouldn't be easy for people to spot him. He did not have any exaggerated features in his face or body.

His thick, brown hair was always well kept. His face was neither too round nor too long, his blue eyes not too big or deep-set, his nose neither too prominent nor too thin, his mouth not too wide or narrow. This provided him with a natural disguise. With a mustache or a beard, or perhaps sunglasses, he could escape notice almost everywhere.

If the FBI agents had any clue to Bob's whereabouts, they weren't saying anything. The press couldn't get a whiff of what they thought. Dave Simon told her that the phone calls Bob had made from the cellphone—the one he left on the car seat in Philadelphia—were all to legitimate sources. Bob was too smart to leave behind any incriminating evidence. Perhaps he had another cellphone, she thought—one that had been provided by his cronies.

Contemplating the cellphone, she could envision it sitting there, turned off, on the car seat. He had cut her off from communication as soon as he had left town. She remembered the notepad, with the words "Copperhead Club" written on them. She had dismissed the note because she thought it referred to a golf club that Bob had visited in his travels, or it might refer to his own favorite copper-headed golf club, which he used from time to time.

Then came something of an epiphany. He had given the golf club to a friend a year ago, and he hadn't mentioned playing golf for quite some time. So, was "Copperhead Club" something he had written recently or was this an old notebook with an old entry? She would find out.

Abandoning her toast and eggs, she grabbed her bathrobe and ran down the hall to Cynthia Aguillar's door. "Cynthia, could I borrow your phone for a few minutes?" she asked. "I want to take it downstairs to the apartment office and use the Wi-Fi to research something."

After 20 minutes of surfing, she came up with only three Copperhead Clubs in the United States. One was at a golf complex in Florida, the other at a country club in Arizona, and the third near an isolated Kentucky town named Hopefully. Thinking about Hopefully, Stella remembered that Bob had mentioned how beautiful the Kentucky landscape was as he flew over it on a recent trip.

Returning to her room, Stella began to plot how to escape Washington and find her way to the Kentucky hills. She decided if he were hiding in the continental United States, a little-known place would make more sense than some fancy golf club. Could Bob be there? It seemed far-fetched. She didn't know, but she wanted to find out for herself, and to see him face-to-face. Was Alicia there with him? Stella didn't have a gun, or have the slightest idea of how to use one, but she figured it couldn't be all that complicated, since some of the most unsophisticated people had figured it out pretty easily. Just load it and pull the trigger, she thought. No, she would be caught and put in prison, she mused. Better to find them and let the police deal with them.

Her first task was how to slip out without being seen by the omnipresent FBI agents who were watching the entrance around the clock. She went to Rita Rodriguez for help, asking if there was a way out of the building without being seen, such as some secret passageway. Rita said she knew of no such escape route. She looked at Stella with kind eyes that telegraphed that she understood her pain and her desire to flee from Washington.

"Rita, I will tell you the truth," Stella said. "I've got to try to find him, but I can't tell you where I want to go. I don't want to involve you in my troubles, because it could come back to hurt you."

"They proved nothing on you," Rita said. "You should be free to go. FBI should go away, leave us all alone. I'll ask Rosa."

"No, no, don't get Mrs. Aguillar involved," Stella said. "Let's just stop this right now. Forget I asked. I'll find a way out on my own."

Rita paid no attention to her. She was out the door. Soon she came back with Rosa and Cynthia, who suggested some escape possibilities. To make extra money, Cynthia had been a hairdresser. So, at Stella's request, Cynthia dyed Stella's red hair and eyebrows black and cut her long, flowing hair back so severely that it was only a little longer than a butch haircut with moussed spikes. Stella took off her elegant gold earrings, replacing them with large, red cheap ones. Also, she put on a pair of glasses with oversized frames. She was an unrecognizable hybrid of a 1980s-era punk rocker blended with a law student. With new clothes, such as a sequined T-shirt bearing a drawing of Mickey Mouse—which Stella never would have worn in her earlier life—it was, all in all, a clever disguise. Would this be enough to enable her to avoid anyone recognizing her? Would it be enough to help her escape from the people watching outside her apartment building? Maybe. But she wasn't sure.

She would need a front—a reason for traveling to a strange place like Hopefully. She got out her watercolor kit and checked to see if it had everything she needed to be credible. There were her sketchbooks, pens, pencils, erasers, paints, paper, and sable brushes, all packed neatly in a cosmetic bag. She took out a pen and a notebook and started to sketch herself. Looking in the mirror she said, "I'm Georgette, I'm Marlo, I'm Ingrid, no, I'm—I'm Ellie, a painter. This might work as a cover if I can make it to Kentucky."

The next morning, a light, cold rain fell in Washington. In a nondescript car outside the apartment building, FBI agent Jack Holtz yawned at first light. He jabbed his partner, Bill Simpson, who had dozed off, and offered him a cup of coffee from the thermos.

"What time is it?" Simpson asked.

"Five," Holtz replied. "Four more hours to relief."

"God, this is stupid duty," Holtz said. "Watching a woman just because the director is so paranoid. If he hadn't been responsible for so many dumb mistakes in the past, we'd be home now, sleeping with our wives. So much of our jobs these days is cover-your-ass."

"Oh, I don't know," Simpson replied. "You never know if she hasn't been holding back about her husband's disappearance. These lie detector tests aren't always accurate. I knew a guy once who killed three people in cold blood. He volunteered to take a lie detector test and passed it. This was before they found the gun with his fingerprints on it, and the blood of the three victims in his car. The jury convicted him. You got a doughnut in that bag?"

Holtz pulled a stale, greasy doughnut out of the bag. Scales of sugar came off on his hand. Leave it to Simpson to spout the bureau's line, he thought. He was younger and more ambitious. His mistakes were still ahead of him.

They passed the time playing games on their cellphones and listening to the radio. They were not basketball fans, so the daily sports news left them bored. Their ears perked up only when the announcers talked about the Nationals' upcoming spring training, the Capitals hockey team or the Washington Redskins' chances after last year's disastrous season. Football was a sport the FBI understood. "All they need is a quarterback, an offensive line, and a defensive line," Simpson said. "Otherwise, they've got a great team."

They watched as a stream of people emerged from the apartment building, most of them off to work in the menial jobs that immigrants were forced to take. More than half of them were women, Holtz noted, and wondered what that meant about the families that they left behind in Mexico, Colombia, Ecuador, and other countries represented in the complex.

At 8:30 a.m., a wheelchair emerged from the door. Cynthia Aguillar was pushing her aging mother toward her beat-up old Ford parked in the handicapped space in front. Cynthia often took her grandmother out at this time of day to go to the market and sometimes to see the doctor. Holtz had personally checked it out. This morning, Cynthia's mother carried an umbrella at such an angle that it blocked his view. Her profile also was a bit obscured as the wheelchair turned toward the car. A wool scarf over her head covered part of her face, and she wore an old olive-colored raincoat that covered most of her body. Holtz had seen this outfit before, and when she slowly eased her way into the front seat of the car with Cynthia's help, the agent noted the rotund shape compared to Rosa's.

Simpson was finishing off the last doughnut and sipping the last cup of coffee from the thermos. "Gee, when are those guys going to get here?" he wondered aloud. At 8:45 a.m., the relief agents arrived. Holtz and Simpson told them that Stella was still inside.

Upstairs from the window, Rita watched the scene. As the old Ford drove off, she turned around and faced the aging woman sitting on the couch. She smiled.

"They made it, Rosa," she said.

CHAPTER 9

Washington, D.C.

On a cold, snowy day in the nation's capital, President Everett summoned his chief political adviser, Jack Dudgeon, and his chief of staff, Scott Herbert, to talk about his chances for re-election.

The President knew what they both would say: "Not good." The latest poll showed that Americans did not trust Washington to solve their problems, and they gave the President bad marks for his part in the stalemate. Besides the continuing high unemployment rate, there was widespread concern about political unrest around the globe. Fears of terrorism abounded. At home, poverty was rampant, crime was on the rise, and mounting debt threatened the viability of the government's traditional safety-net programs—Medicare and Social Security.

"Sit down, fellows," the President said, motioning the two men toward two wing chairs in the conversation area on the other side of the room. "Okay—let's hear how bad it is out there."

"To be honest, Mr. President, I fear we are in the final days of your presidency, unless you do something—quickly," Dudgeon said. "You would lose if you ran today."

"Mr. President," he continued, grim-faced, "you know what I am going to say. First, you have got to go negative against Gonzalez." Dudgeon reiterated his opinion that Reyes Gonzalez, the hotshot governor of Ohio, was "far too young for this job, and simply isn't prepared for it. Negative, negative, negative. We can't hand this job to him on a platter." He reminded the President that Gonzalez had promised more dramatic government action to deal with the crises, much in the way that Franklin Delano Roosevelt had done during the Great Depression. In fact, Gonzalez frequently harked back to Roosevelt's programs, only this time, he said, the situation demanded even more government involvement. Everett, on the other hand, favored less.

"This guy is vulnerable to attacks—trust me," said Dudgeon. "We can say, for example, that he's soft on the drug trade coming in from Mexico, since Ohio has a lot of drug problems, and even though he was born in America, his parents were from Mexico. We can manufacture a lot of stuff that sounds legitimate. Once we begin attacking his record and casting doubts about his background, we'll start to see the benefits."

Everett hated distortion and simplistic solutions in a campaign, but at this point he was desperate. He nodded his head.

Along with re-election woes and the terrible economic climate, Dudgeon told the President that the Jasper incident had deeply damaged his administration. Herbert agreed.

"A lot of people think that where there's smoke, there's fire, and that you and Jasper or people in the administration were in cahoots," said Dudgeon, pointing his finger at the President. "And you can't clear yourself if he's still at large. The record is clear, Mr. President: You knew him as a friend who conducted business dealings with the administration, and the voters can relate to that. And, as we all guessed he would, Gonzalez is already making it part of his campaign.

"I know now that it was a mistake to take Jasper in as an adviser," the President conceded.

"We don't know how long he has been a money launderer," said Dudgeon. "From what I hear, it's been three, four years, maybe more. It's hard to tell because the evidence is so flimsy. Everyone will tell you that the money launderers are so clever in hiding funds, the law cries out for more reporting and regulation. And even more money is going undetected, since nowadays it's often little more than a digital impulse somewhere rather than cash or check. Smart people know how to move dirty money in order to clean it up."

Dudgeon continued, "There are rules and regulations, but these have to be updated and strengthened to deal with the times and these modern thieves getting rich on other peoples' money. It will take greater international effort to get that done."

The President said he was all for strengthening international enforcement tools against money launderers, but he knew many countries wouldn't cooperate, even in the face of evidence that the launderers were getting away with wholesale robbery. He had assigned his Treasury Secretary to step up the government's crackdown on money laundering, but whatever the result, it would come too late to help his presidency.

The President said he hoped they'd find Jasper soon, and get this controversy behind them. "The sad thing is, I always liked him," he said of Jasper. "Funny, isn't it? You never know who's a crook."

"Well," said Herbert, "we're searching the country. And now to complicate the matter more, we don't know where his wife is—or his girlfriend, for that matter."

"Damnation," Everett said.

"Justice is on it, I am told, and I hear that the FBI is actively engaged in the case. But I can't get details."

"Think he's left the country?" the President asked.

"It's possible, but I don't think so," Dudgeon replied. "I think he's afraid to come out of hiding because, frankly, I think he knows too much."

"If the press knows that Stella Jasper has run off, and the government can't find her, it'll be one hell of a story, and it won't reflect well on us," Herbert added.

"Let's try to keep this a secret if possible," the President said. "Do your best on that. Scott, I know you're working on this. The FBI is as well, but they don't always share their leads quickly. They're not sharing everything with us, simply because of suspicion that people on my staff or I could be involved. I understand their reluctance, since Jasper was a political friend, but I'm certain that my staff is squeaky-clean on this—especially you two." His chief of staff smiled.

The President told Dudgeon something that Herbert already knew: He was concerned about the Vice President's health. "He's undergoing a variety of tests, he said, and we should get word soon. He's having some weakness and double vision. Let's hope that it's nothing serious and that it's curable. But whatever you do, don't say anything about this to anyone yet. Of course, if it were something that would harm his functioning as Vice President, we'd have a real problem on our hands. As you both know, I'm very fond of him."

"And there's more bad news," Dudgeon interjected. "Placido Ramos de la Torre is refusing to openly support you, saying that for now he's staying neutral. If he abandoned you, sir, you'd most certainly be finished. You need to invite him here and stroke him."

The President viewed Ramos as one of the most respected people in the country. Everett knew the story of how Ramos's immigrant grandparents had moved to America from Bolivia. His parents pushed for their son to get a good education here. He knew all about Ramos's meteoric rise as a businessman, and, later, a prominent political consultant. The man's latest gambit was to set up a think-tank simply nicknamed: "*RAMOS.*"

"What credentials!" Dudgeon said in admiration, ticking them off. "At the top of his class at the University of Chicago and Stanford University. Small businessman, first in the Southwest, then a banker and finally a consultant frequently invited to speak on TV. I've heard that he's thinking of hosting his own television show—something like *The Daily Show*. He's also quite an active philanthropist, giving money to sick kids and education and all that. And he's never run for office." But most important for the President, Ramos's influence was strongest in places like Florida and Ohio, where the growing Latino populations could make the difference in whether the state—and thus the Electoral College—turns blue or red. He was a common figure in a series of television ads running on Telemundo showing an American flag blowing in the wind behind slow-motion shots of famous Americans. Recently, "Arribe Ramos!" was seen on a common T-shirt in Miami urging the businessman to run for the presidency himself.

Everett said the other party seemed far too liberal for Ramos, and that he didn't understand the man's reluctance to sign up with the administration instead.

"Mr. President," Dudgeon pressed on, "did it ever occur to you that you could destroy his reputation, if he remained so close to you at this time of your unpopularity? The man seems to act primarily in his own self-interest. Who can blame him? It's hardball politics he's playing. Nothing new. He's a real expert on hardball. He's written you off. You've got to give him a good reason to vote for you."

"He's not the same guy I've always counted on," Everett insisted. He baffles me. Is there some policy that I need to change to attract him? Could you check? Tell him that I'd love to meet with him and talk over the election. If it doesn't work, then maybe I'll try to go negative. Hell, maybe I'll go negative no matter what."

"That sounds better," Dudgeon said. "Maybe we can win this thing if we get on the attack. I'll call Ramos, the big self-important fart. Didn't used to be that way, but he needed us then. We have to make him need us again. We have to find out where his head is these days."

"Yes, we do," Everett said. "Another thing: I'd like for him to head a group of executives who would raise and spend money attacking my opponent. That would be ideal."

Since Ramos was withholding his endorsement, maybe he was getting an itch to run for public office after all, Dudgeon suggested. Ramos had once helped Everett win the presidency, but now he seemed reluctant to join up.

"Let's go all out to get this guy on board," Everett told his aides. "He could be the answer to our prayers."

"In Ramos We Trust," Dudgeon said with a smirk.

CHAPTER 10

Hopefully, Kentucky

The Baron, Heinrich Schnepp, looked at his watch. It was 9:44 a.m.—time for his second breakfast at the Hopefully Diner. Down the street, the diner's owner, Joe Baccardo, eyed the front door of the bank.

As soon as the door opened and The Baron took his first step outside, Baccardo yelled to his cooks and other staff: "Schnepp—biscuit!"

A flurry of activity ensued, with the chef slathering the top of an already warm biscuit with butter and tossing it into the oven to get it hotter and crispier, just as The Baron always demanded. If it were not made precisely to The Baron's specifications, Baccardo knew he would get a lecture on how quality had slipped, and the biscuit would be sent back to the kitchen.

"If I don't tell them to get it right, they will never learn," The Baron confided to the mayor one day. Baccardo had learned. From that day on, The Baron never even had to order. No sooner had he settled in his favorite booth than the coffee was put before him (one ounce of skim milk, please). Just as he reached for the napkin, the piping hot biscuit with a piece of sausage was laid before him. It was just like clockwork.

It was a ritual every morning.

"Why, thank you, honey, how did you know what I wanted?" he would say to Jennie, the waitress.

"Why don't you know, Mr. Schnepp, that I'm a seer on the side? I make money, reading minds. You're a snap, Mr. Schnepp."

This word play with his name amused The Baron. He moved the shakers of salt and pepper so that they fit his notion of symmetry, and put his glass of water just behind his cup of coffee, where it seemed precise and orderly to him. The knife, at an angle on the table, also was re-set, so it would be straight.

"You missed a crumb here, Jennie," The Baron said.

An impeccable dresser always in a vested suit and bow tie, The Baron was Hopefully's most sophisticated—and oddest—resident. Tipping his fedora to the ladies, he would often pick up their checks for lunch at the diner. Such behavior brought gratitude, but also suspicion: What had accounted for such generosity?

The local news reporter got an answer to that question: "Oh, I am parsimonious, really, if you want to know the truth," The Baron said modestly. "I only pick one person at a time, and pay their check, unless it's a family or friends together. Then I pay the whole check. But the main reason I do it? We all live in a small town, and I just like to make people happy."

When he looked into the mirror, The Baron saw a lean little man with a thin mouth and little eyes covered by small glasses. In contrast, he knew he carried a large personality that was based on three-quarters stagecraft and one-quarter glossed-over insecurity.

At the diner, people considered themselves lucky when they were at the cash register ready to pay and The Baron was either in front or just behind. "Hello, honey," he often said, "good to see you. Here, honey, let me take that check today." Protesting did no good with The Baron, but it was expected, so he could put his full act on display.

"No, I wouldn't have it any other way," he would say. "It's my pleasure." He would wink, reach over and give the cashier a crisp brand-new $50 bill. Of course, customers watched this spectacle with amusement. Each had been the beneficiary at one time or another. His generosity belied the image of a tight-fisted country banker, which he was in every measure when larger sums of money were at stake.

And though people appreciated The Baron's kindnesses, they figured that his charity with smaller sums was based less on altruism than on assuaging the hurt he had felt from having been slighted and ignored during his childhood. Schnepp had known deprivation and loneliness in his youth, but these had driven him to excel. His knowledge of money matters, gained from pinching pennies and saving obsessively, had helped him breeze through business and finance courses in college. At one time, he was consumed with becoming a big-city banker, but he realized upon graduation that he could achieve his goal faster in a rural area. So he settled in Hopefully, with visions of someday rising to the top at the local bank.

The Baron prided himself on being meticulous. Everything had to be in place at his home, at the table where he dined, and at the bank where he made his money. He knew details of all the bank's significant loans and on any given day could spout off the value of bank capital and assets and liabilities to the nearest $100. He expected tidiness from others and didn't hesitate to let them know if they did not live up to his standards—though he did so in a kind, country way. "Honey," he would say to one of the tellers, "you're $2 short for some reason or another. Tomorrow and every day after that, let's make sure you can have your mind on your business."

Over the past few months The Baron had been a bit puzzled that deposits were up more than usual for those months. Several companies in nearby Purcells had been using the bank of late—probably because of its reputation, he thought—and income was on the rise from a few local enterprises, most notably the Copperhead Club, which had become an extremely popular spot for country-music lovers and late-night carousers from the surrounding counties, many of which were dry.

The Baron had heard that Jimmy Billingsley, with his voice and music, was a terrific attraction, even if Schnepp himself had little liking for a young man who did not seem to have much respect for others. He had heard that things could get a little wild at the club late at night, and there were rumors that drugs were a problem, but The Baron was happy to have the extra money and told himself that bankers could not be overly judgmental about how people earned it. As a country banker, he was still suspicious of any surges in financial behavior, figuring what comes in can just as easily go out—and suddenly, at that. He determined that he would be as tight-fisted as ever in making loans even though his assets were suddenly looking better.

Right after the bank's closing time, The Baron would go out to see Molly Jo Matson. This had become a routine for him and the subject of some gossip in town, but The Baron didn't care anymore. Molly was an old friend who had had his respect even before she put a bullet in the head of that bank robber in his lobby long, long ago. Besides, The Baron's wife had passed away, and Molly was a widow, so what kind of convention was he violating to see an old woman with a load of health problems? None that he could think of. And, anyhow, damn the busybodies with all that prattle. He was going full speed ahead.

He had taken sympathy on Molly in the old days when the whole town was ready to strangle her over her excessive enforcement of petty law. She had come to him shortly after she had taken the police job to ask for advice for how to deal with townspeople who had grown to hate her. Though Molly was actually incapable of shedding a tear over potentially corruptible people, it enabled her to cry on his shoulder a bit about her situation. She'd said she needed someone with community respect to stand up for law and order.

The Baron was flattered. He was a clumsy man when it came to women, and no woman had ever come to him for advice before, especially one as fetching as Molly. He thought that in many ways she was the same as he was, outwardly strong, but inwardly vulnerable. He advised her not to back down so much, because it would make it difficult for her later. In the end, the town would respect her for being tough, he'd said.

"This little town needs some law and order, Molly, and you're just the one to provide it," The Baron told her. "One of these days, somebody's going to get hit by a car by these young people exceeding the speed limit. Just the other day, that Blevins boy was easily doing 40—15 miles over the limit—and he screeched around the corner so loudly, I could hear him in my office. You must have been somewhere else."

"Must have been my day off," she said. There was a pause.

"What about Harriet Billingsley?" Molly had asked. "She wants to run me out of town."

"Don't worry about Harriet," The Baron said. "I'll talk to her."

After he had patiently listened to her for an hour, Molly got up and prepared to leave. She kissed him on the cheek and thanked him.

The Baron, who was not an impulsive man, nevertheless did something at that moment that he would never forget. He grabbed her around the waist and kissed her strong and hard on the lips, and then put his left hand on her thigh and began to move it upward. But Molly pulled back with a strong push that nearly sent him back against the wall. She made a quick assessment that at the slightest vulnerability on her part, he would be on her again.

"Mr. Schnepp," she said sharply, "I'm married, I've got kids at home. You're married, too. Get yourself together." She knew she had the strength to deck this fragile little man without breaking much of a sweat, but she also realized that she'd made a mistake by sharing her vulnerability with a man whom she didn't know that well. She had breached one of her own rules: Every person was corruptible when the opportunity opened up. She had provided an opportunity.

The Baron realized immediately that he was taking great risks for a young bank officer who longed to take over the bank one day and become a pillar of the community, perhaps even known throughout the state. He loved his wife, he told himself, but Molly was just too beautiful and vulnerable for him to resist at that moment.

He'd always been a careful man, church-going and full of probity, usually the first person to step forward and volunteer anything for the community. What was it about this literal-minded patrolwoman—especially one wearing a pistol—that brought out a recklessness he never knew he had?

"Molly," he said. "I'm sorry. I…"

"I shouldn't have come over here like this, Mr. Schnepp. I thought I could trust you."

"I'm sorry. You are so…."

"You need your eyes examined," she said, stiffening her back. "You'd better understand right now you can't do anything like this again. If you so much as make the tiniest reference about this to anybody around here, I am going to file charges, and I will tell my husband. And believe me, you don't want that."

The Baron nodded his head, relieved that Molly would likely keep his secret. But inside, that relief became mixed with sadness. He had overplayed his hand, and now any chance he would have with Molly would be lost for the rest of his life.

"I won't say anything," he said. "I've never done anything like that. I just thought there was a way we could get together."

"You can forget that right now," she said. "I just needed some advice, not an attack."

The Baron put his hands on his forehead. Molly stared at him, turned, walked out of his office and headed for the restroom down the hall. Outside, in front of the door, the bank robber looked up and down the street, then walked into the bank lobby as Molly was freshening her face. She was on her way to becoming a town legend by killing him on the spot. After the day was over and Molly had proven her mettle as a patrolwoman, she wouldn't need The Baron for advice anymore.

This was a day that The Baron would long remember, when his desire for Molly had overcome him, when she had killed the bank robber without hesitation, when The Baron knew that she was not someone to be trifled with, when he realized he could not stem his feelings toward her. He could not talk himself out of loving her or into hating her. Molly made it difficult for him.

A month after the incident, The Baron drove absent-mindedly from home to work, not paying too much attention to his speed as he drove into town. He was thinking of Molly, fantasizing that she really did want him, but that convention had caused her to reject him. He had seen the same kind of scene in some movie starring Natalie Wood. The Baron told himself that Molly had that longing Natalie-Wood-look, even in rejecting him.

At first, he didn't notice the flashing lights of the police cruiser in his rearview mirror. But when the cruiser was virtually on the rear bumper of his black Lincoln Town Car, he awoke from his daydreaming. "Oh, damn," he said.

He pulled over next to the diner, where everyone inside could see what was happening. A patron was pointing her finger at him and guffawing. He heard the door of the cruiser open and close. Suddenly, Molly was looking into his window.

"Mr. Schnepp," she said loudly enough for the whole town to hear, "you were going 30 in a 25 mph zone. You know we can't let anyone, especially bankers, get off in this town. Try not to let this happen again. Now let me see your registration and license." She quietly wrote out a speeding ticket and handed it to him.

The Baron looked at her and then at the people in the café laughing. He smiled and turned to Molly, who had a stern, determined look, but a very wry little smile. "Of course, Officer Matson, you are right," he said. "I guess I was going a little fast."

Now, The Baron kept a copy of that pink ticket in his file drawer at the office. He didn't know why he kept it. Perhaps it was to remind him of his stupidity and ineptitude that day, or that it gave him a chance to reflect on a relationship that might have been.

He would pull the ticket out from time to time and see Molly's face at his car window. As The Baron finished his coffee at the diner, he found himself thinking of her again. "Are you all right today?" Jennie asked. "You seem to be a little preoccupied."

"Just thinking of work, Jennie," The Baron said somewhat wistfully. As he walked to the cash register to pay, Judy Blevins was just ahead of him. "Why, honey, how are you doing?" he asked her. "How's your babies?"

"My babies are 24 and 25, and just fine, Baron," Judy Blevins said.

"Well, honey, let me take that check, it's the least I can do. Here, Jennie, her money is no good here." Judy had no choice. She thanked him and smiled. "My babies thank you, too," she said.

"I wonder where God hid the mold when he made that one," Jennie said when The Baron left.

Promptly at 4 p.m., The Baron was out the bank door. "Hello, Mr. Banker," Mayor Billingsley called out to him. "You ain't broke, are you?" The lame humor had been mildly funny the first time, but the mayor had run it into the ground. He used it every time he saw The Baron.

"I ain't broke, but the bank is," said The Baron. "That means your next check will bounce to the top of the hill over there."

"You going out to see Molly again? Betcha you are."

"I might."

"Well, sure is a shame, her Parkinson's and old injuries and all that," said the mayor. "She was one hell of a police officer in her day. How old is she? Seventy-something? Damn shame. Looks a lot older. When did her husband die? Ten years ago? Yeah, I guess that's about right. Well, have a good trip, Baron, and keep that bank safe."

"Safe as a house on the sand," The Baron said dutifully. Hopefully had a tradition of having a mayor who answered his own questions and left no opportunity for the respondent to respond. He ran City Council meetings that way. The Baron remembered that his own father had the same odd traits.

He drove out of the parking lot next to the bank with a heavy foot on the pedal, turning left on Main with a screech of the tires, barely missing Mrs. Blevins's car coming the other way, and running swiftly through the next stoplight as caution turned to red. Molly would have ticketed him for that, he thought.

He went to see Molly because he liked her—yes, he still loved her—and in spite of all the years, she had spurned him. He had made a few passes here and there over the years, these more discreet than the first, but Molly would stop him instantly.

Also, The Baron liked B.J. and regarded him as the son he'd never had; he and his wife had had no children in 40 years of marriage. B.J. was a bright boy, The Baron had discovered, though still lacking in social skills. He liked to talk about Kentucky basketball, but he could engage in intelligent conversations about other things as well. For a mountain boy with only a few years of college, B.J. had educated himself thoroughly. He could easily discuss politics, science, theater, and economics. He had an affinity for Croatian history and would often recite Shakespearean soliloquies with no audience to hear them. Sometimes at night he would sit on the Knob, entertaining himself by using his self-taught skills in calculus to figure distances of stars in their galaxies and planets from earth. The Baron helped B.J. from time to time, lending him money for a new camera and for B.J. to build a special room for himself out in the barn. In return, B.J. ran errands for The Baron.

The Baron drove out Route 7884, through the valley, with the Copperhead Knob in sight. He passed the Copperhead Club, a two-story frame building with a gravel parking lot. It was 6 p.m., and the lot was already half-full. The Baron regarded it as honky-tonk hell, but if a little hell was needed to bring him business, that was all right with him. He took the dirt road to the right, kicking up a plume of dust as he headed to Molly Jo Matson's house.

The Baron's daily visits to Molly had been going on for a long time. They both needed the company after their spouses had died, and even after all these years, they had not shed their old traits of outer strength and hidden vulnerability. Only now, they didn't mind telling each other about their weaknesses.

As Molly once said, "Lord, if we are going to see each other so much, we need Topics (which she said with a capital T.") The Topics more often than not turned out to be themselves.

"God," Molly said on one of his first clearing-the-air visits, "you were the horniest asshole I ever encountered the day you groped me in your office. What was the matter with you, anyway? Weren't you getting any at home?"

"The God's honest truth—and don't you ever tell anyone this—is that I fantasized that you were Natalie Wood, as I saw her in the movies, and you were coming on to me with those earnest eyes," The Baron said, half chuckling.

She laughed. "Bullshit," she said. "You were one hair away from assault and rape and a prison term—and all because I had Natalie Wood eyes? When did a cop ever look like Natalie Wood?"

"I didn't say you looked like Natalie Wood. You remind me of her. There's a difference. Please, Molly can we drop this? Haven't I apologized enough? In my defense, all I can say is you were a beautiful, vulnerable young lady, and little old repressed me just came apart."

"What do you mean by 'were,' Baron?" Molly said. They both laughed.

"Let's not get too hung up on words," The Baron said. "I made a lot of passes over the years. I guess I thought I needed you."

"To me, you're still a goddamn felon," she said chuckling.

Molly was still a good-looking woman for her age, despite the toll of Parkinson's disease and a shoulder and back injury that she'd suffered when a drunken man, who had been beating his wife, threw her off his front porch. Her right arm shook visibly and she was in pain most of the time. The Baron could tell that the disease was also affecting her cognitive abilities. At times her mind was as sharp as ever, but at other times she could become disoriented. Her doctor said there were early signs of dementia, and maybe even Alzheimer's disease. Molly joked that she just had her senior moments. "A senior *decade*, in my case,"

The Baron replied.

The Baron hated being around pain and suffering, but with Molly he didn't mind. She had taken to feeling sorry for herself, very unlike her, and The Baron set out to lift her spirits and to help her in any way he could. That included helping B.J., too.

Molly was sitting in the rocking chair on the front porch when The Baron drove up and parked. "Shoot fire, I'll have to wash the car again tomorrow morning," he said. Molly was smiling. "Well, how's my felon today?" she asked. "Bring me anything?"

"Apple pie from the diner," he said. "Jennie's."

"Sweetie, can you get my medicine for me? This shoulder is about to kill me."

The Baron went inside the old house. The flowered wallpaper in the living room was beginning to come loose in places and was buckling in others. He would tell B.J. to get that fixed. He found the pills in the kitchen, in the cabinet above the stove where Molly had kept them hidden. "They've saved my life," she said.

CHAPTER 11

West Virginia

Stella felt as though she was on a wild carnival ride in the rocking bus. She fought off sleep-deprivation and fear for her life. Operating on three hours of sleep, she was at least grateful to get away from the frightening feeling that an unknown stranger might abduct her from the street. She would occasionally catch a tear building in her eye—such as when she caught a glimpse of a woman's perfectly sculpted azure toenails, which reminded her of one of Alicia's favorite ways of spending her time: $200 pedicures in Georgetown. She knew that outsiders would laugh at her calling herself *desperate*, but she didn't care—being alone was being alone. She still wanted her life back—not with Alicia or Bob, but with all her other friends, who had been frequent companions when she and Bob were riding high. Certainly the respect of your friends was worth fighting for, she told herself, no matter how painful it could be.

As the nearly empty bus rolled on the interstate highway toward Charleston, West Virginia, Stella decided she had to check out the Copperhead Club in Kentucky. She wanted to believe that Bob was innocent, but too many facts told her otherwise. She felt so strange being alone now. She knew now that Bob had pampered her, and that the trips to Bora Bora and the extra sets of diamond jewelry, were just devices to keep her in place as the other half of a fake normal life, under the pretense of love.

The bus driver, a man perhaps 10 years her senior, looked at her in the rearview mirror. Stella knew that kind of gaze. It meant that he liked what he saw, and was plotting how to get her to go to bed with him. She felt vulnerable, deeply angry. This was Bob's fault. Why did he like Alicia better? Why would he leave me in such a position? It was like being in high school again.

Soon she would be in Kentucky. The bus would arrive in Charleston well past midnight. She hoped the station would have a place for her to nap. She'd catch another bus at 5 a.m. that would take her to Kentucky, a place she associated with watching Kentucky Derbies during hat-fashion week and a coal miner reality show. Every Kentuckian she had met seemed kind and generous, but she only knew politicians or people in the art world. She remembered hearing someone say that Kentucky hillbillies can be scary, like the characters in the movie "Deliverance." She told herself that was ridiculous, remembering meeting Ashley Judd and seeing George Clooney at a White House dinner. "Hmm, who else was from Kentucky? Diane Sawyer, Jennifer Lawrence, Abraham Lincoln, Muhammad Ali, Colonel Sanders." Thinking about other Kentuckians provided some relief from her stress.

The books and news reports she had gathered indicated that Kentucky had a sizable drug problem, like most Appalachian states, and it had a high rate of poverty. She didn't know anyone who was as poor as those cited in news reports, those families of four earning under $25,000 a year.

She had begun her bus journey in Baltimore rather than Washington. She liked the fact that the bus took a circuitous route, straight over to Pittsburgh and then southward into West Virginia. On the way, she spent two nights in small, cheap motels that weren't part of a national chain, figuring that authorities trying to find her would check better-known places. She had no sense that anyone was following her.

This was the first really long bus ride she had taken. She had grown accustomed to quick, efficient airplane trips, with a rental car at the end, but she knew in the present circumstances, these were too easy for law enforcement officials to check.

Her clothes were wrinkled, her makeup needed freshening, and she had a stale, metallic taste in her mouth. Her muscles ached. "Oh for a spa treatment. Oh, for my Lexus," she thought. "What I wouldn't give for my Lexus at this moment." She also was trying to ration her cash, knowing that she would need every penny if her search were to take a long time.

She had looked up Hopefully on the internet, but the town's website was skimpy with information. "Situated near the Kentucky River, Hopefully is a town full of hope," it began. "It is located in the Knobs mountain range, just an hour from The Daniel Boone Explorers and Recreation Center. Its major sources of jobs are tobacco, soybeans, corn, and wheat farming, and the Paul Gregory's Chicken Farm, which yearly hosts Kentuckians for miles around at the P. G. Fourth of July Barbecue.

The knobs, she had learned, were series of small hills, held together by a core of limestone—nothing like the long ridges that were passing before her now.

She felt the town might at least provide some clues to the whereabouts of her husband, though she was going there on the flimsiest of evidence—a note with "Copperhead Club" written on it.

Where to stay was her first challenge. Hopefully's website showed only one hotel, a locally owned place with the ungrammatical, but forgivable name of the Hopefully Inn. She feared it might be dark and dingy and full of cockroaches, with the walls covered with ugly faded wallpaper and the bedspreads reeking of urine or mildew. She would try at least one night, and move to the nearest town, Purcells, in the next county to the west, if that didn't work out. At least Purcells had three motels.

Before leaving Virginia she had assembled informative reading materials. She settled down to read some sobering background on money laundering. She had an idea of what it was, but she never really thought much about it. She knew the general story. Money laundering was nothing new. It had mushroomed in America since the turn of the century. Dirty money could come from illegal gambling, extortion, insider-trading, and drug-trafficking. The practice of converting dirty money to clean money had become a sophisticated art, thanks partly to modern communications, technology, and offshore banks, which provided secrecy for their depositors.

Criminals kept inventing ingenious new ways to exploit this world of virtual money despite the government's efforts. They were often one step ahead. To do so required the talents of good lawyers who knew their way around the financial system. The government's case against Bob indicated that he had become an adviser for many undercover banks that did a huge business in laundering around the world.

Even more, the charges against her husband suggested that he was teaching attorneys how to launder money to support other criminal activity, including arms-purchases. She learned that many large banks in America and overseas engage in money laundering all the time, but without fear of a major crackdown by federal officials, who were always concerned that such a move would have a bad impact on the banking system.

From Stella's reading of the charges against Bob, many of the details about how he got caught were left out. "I wish I knew more," Stella thought. "I expected the government report to be a little more specific."

Stella read one study showing that lawyers played major roles in money laundering cases. It said that lawyers, working on behalf of clients, could use their own names to set up bank accounts, credit cards, loan agreements, shell corporations, and trusts.

They also could use their confidentiality privileges with clients when an investigation started. Sure, accountants, bankers, stockbrokers, and insurance companies also could play a role, but lawyers seemed to have the greatest ability to make money laundering succeed. And that made Stella more apprehensive.

She had made these notes to herself from her research efforts:

Once the money has been washed, that is, no longer associated with illegal activity, it can be used for almost any purpose, and mainly to enrich the people who get the dirty money in the first place. But because it can involve huge sums, money launderers try to spread it around or start new legitimate businesses without running up against the IRS reporting requirements.

Money launderers do everything they can to evade the law, which increasingly is not up to the task. For example, under IRS rules, a company that transfers $10,000 or more in cash is supposed to disclose it to the IRS. Often, the launderers will spread their money around to many banks, making sure that each cash transfer is less than $10,000. This practice is known as smurfing. It means that many companies have found these practices as a tempting way to get help on the side.

Stella wished she knew what Bob had done. How could he have been so willing to become a crook? Deep down, she felt Bob had a good heart. Would she ever know? She hoped to find out—and soon.

She could tell the bus was nearing Charleston as they passed motels and malls. The dome of the West Virginia capitol shone brightly. Even at this time of night, she could tell that vast petrochemical plants nearby were sending smoke into the atmosphere.

After stretching her legs, Stella found a soft chair inside the bus depot waiting room. The agent agreed to wake her when the bus to Kentucky arrived. She slept for three hours, dreaming of being lost in a forest of pine trees. When the bus rolled in, the agent woke her.

"Your bus is here," he said. She looked up at the clock—it was almost 5 a.m. She gathered herself together and washed her face in the bathroom. Then she climbed aboard.

She could see the hills around her as the sun lit up the horizon. She saw more petrochemical plants along the river and truck after truck filled with coal as she tried to imagine what mysteries might await her.

She sipped a cup of coffee, and it warmed her inside.

CHAPTER 12

Hopefully, Kentucky

B.J. perched near the top of Butcher's Knob at the east end of the county, surveying the hollows below. He wasn't looking for anything in particular, but he found this spot especially awe-inspiring. Here he could see the towering ridges to the east, no longer covered with haze from the day before. The crisp air had driven away all traces of man-made pollution. Green peaks of evergreen trees and shadowy valleys stretched to the horizon. A nuthatch scrambled down the side of a small maple to its left. A chickadee chattered behind him. B.J. took a deep breath of the fresh air and exhaled, emitting a long sigh.

He trained his zoom lens at scenes all around him, and found that isolation, even here in the hills, was relative. The zoom lens could see better than a telescope, B.J. thought. He spotted satellite dishes in front yards and rusted-out hulks of old cars sitting in backyards and in creeks. He felt like a voyeur, which he was in a way. But he'd been a voyeur for a long time and had gotten over any guilt.

Over to the south, he could hear Mr. Austrich's voice booming as he yelled at his kids in their frame house with a porch leaning to the left like a sailboat. Austrich worked in the coal mines in the next county, on the night shift, and so it was unusual to see him out during the day.

In one hollow, he caught sight of a boy and girl behind a barn. Bushes hid them for the most part, except B.J. could see them from above. They were making love with abandon. Someone, presumably the girl's mother, sat in the swing on the front porch of the house just beyond the front of the barn, oblivious to the youthful passion. It was, by all definition, a quickie, for they were doing the deed while standing, apparently so they could make a quick recovery after completion or in case someone approached while they were in the act. Her skirt was above her waist and her legs were wrapped tightly around him. With his large hands, he firmly gripped her bottom as they awkwardly maneuvered their bodies toward a satisfying conclusion.

B.J. took a couple of photos, including evidence that the young man had used a condom. He felt like a pornographer, but couldn't help himself. It might have been an erotic scene if it hadn't been so ridiculously bucolic and they so youthfully clumsy. The only other creature watching, a cow in the pasture next to the barn, mooed as the action became more frenetic. The young couple turned and laughed at the animal's complaint. Then a voice rang out. It was the mother calling her daughter. The girl put on her panties, pulled her skirt down, fixed up her hair, kissed him, and quickly ran around the barn toward the porch. The boy jumped over a back fence without being detected. B.J. clicked the shutter. The lad was smiling. The girl ran up to her unsuspecting mom and kissed her. The older woman put her arm around her daughter and smiled.

B.J. picked up his gear and moved to a vantage-point on the other side of the knob. There was a well-trodden path across the top of the hill, and a clearing in the middle filled with beer bottles and burnt wood. There were a few used condoms on the ground. Over in the bushes, a pair of black panties hanging on a limb fluttered in the breeze. He imagined the girl desperately trying to find them with nothing but a dying fire as light. She should wear white panties for hilltop assignations, he thought impishly.

It took more effort to reach the other side of the hill. B.J. made his way through thick weeds and rock. But when he finally reached the ridge, he told himself it was worth it. The panorama on that side was even more breathtaking. And in the hollows in the foreground, he could see very clearly. The dirt road that he'd taken to get there was visible just below him. He had parked his four-wheel-drive truck near the top, as far as he could take it. At the edge of the hill was a huge rock with a convenient crevice that would serve as a natural tripod for his camera.

He walked carefully to the edge and peered below. A small hill rose in the hollow on the other side. Near the bottom of it, a little shorter than a football field away, was an old wooden house with a porch all the way around it. A metallic blue car and a black SUV were parked in the driveway. In the middle of a mowed field below the house, a man was sitting in an old Adirondack chair, reading a book. Beside him on a little table was what appeared to be a beer bottle.

B.J. crouched behind the rock and reached inside his camera bag for his longest lens. With hardly a look, he retrieved it and snapped it into place. Like a cat stalking its prey, he moved ever so slowly into position so as not to be noticed by the man below. Resting his camera in the rock crevice, he steadied it and brought his subject into focus.

As he zoomed in on a tight shot, he couldn't recognize the man. He had a long red ponytail, a beard, and a mustache. He was wearing a Carhartt plaid shirt, jeans, boots and a Morehead State University baseball cap. B.J. clicked the shutter. The man put down the book, got up from his chair, and stretched his arms and legs. He sat down again and looked to his left as he picked up his book, preparing to resume his reading.

B.J. saw that another man—this one clearly well-dressed—was standing on the porch, and decided to take a shot of him as well. "I hope they don't hear this," B.J. said to himself as he squeezed the button to snap the picture. The normally quiet shutter sounded louder in the virtual silence of the moment. B.J. cursed himself for shooting just then. Silence magnifies the slightest noise. He should have waited for some ambience, like a bird singing or wind rustling through trees.

The man in the chair looked up immediately, straight at him. B.J.

thought he was well enough hidden to avoid being seen. The man stared straight ahead for a minute, then began looking left and right, obviously trying to find the source of the clearly foreign sound. After a minute or so, he looked down and resumed reading. B.J. relaxed. He had gotten his pictures without being noticed, so he aimed the camera again. The man picked up a cell phone next to him, said a few words and hung up. Casually, without looking up, he went back to his book.

Very cool, B.J. thought—too damn cool, so cool as to be conspicuous. Did he see a glint of the camera or just figure the sound was too familiar and there had to be somebody behind it? Did he wait to call to throw me off? He decided quickly it was time to get off the mountain and back home. He slid stealthily behind some trees and, once he was sure that he was out of sight he ran as fast as he could to his truck.

B.J. whipped his truck around the hairpin turns of the mountainside with a recklessness he did not know he possessed. Why he was so scared, he didn't know, but it was something about the man and the scene. It was just out of place. No one reads a book out in the middle of a field like that in these parts, and in February with small snow patches around. Why wasn't he on the porch? If he'd suspected that someone had been taking his picture, he could have shouted out something like, "Who's there?" But he hardly even moved.

B.J. rounded a turn with his wheels spinning and with dirt and rocks flying, only to confront a black SUV barreling toward him at high speed. There was not enough room for two vehicles, or enough time to avoid a collision. He swerved to the side of the road, but it was too late. He could see four men in the SUV, and they were just as surprised as he was. In the face of death, everything seemed to slow down. The passenger in the front seat had a huge rifle, nothing like he had ever seen. The driver of the SUV swerved to try to avoid him, but the vehicle hit the back of B.J.'s truck, which shoved its back tires off the road, and nearly into a ditch alongside the mountain. Then the SUV careered off the road on the other side and went down the hill, rolling over several times before crashing into a rock. B.J. saw the crash out of his side-view mirror.

B.J. gunned the engine and pulled out of the ditch, throwing dirt and stone behind him, and kept going. He knew he was breaking the law, but he didn't care. The men might be hurt, might be dead, but he knew they had come to get him, perhaps to kill him. If they were alive, they probably could find him by conducting a search of records, or some other way connected with his truck, which was easily distinguishable with its black and white lines on the side. He wasn't 100% sure, but he doubted that anyone connected with the SUV would file charges. If anything, they would come after him *outside* the court system.

Did they see his license plate number? Would they remember his face? Hell, B.J. thought, this is a small town. Everyone knows me. They know I drive this old wreck. They know where I live. It wouldn't take too much detective work.

He drove past the Copperhead Club as the sun was low in the sky, and headed down the road for home. His mom was waiting on the porch. She was in a bitchy mood. "B.J., I need my damn painkiller," she said. "Where the hell you been? And what did you do to the truck? Looks like you smashed into a goddamn concrete wall."

B.J. meekly explained that he'd spun on an oily spot up on Highway 6057-A and had slid into a tree. "Don't worry—I'll see if I can get it fixed," he said. "It still runs okay. I'll take it in tomorrow."

His mom patted him on the head. "Well, at least, the master isn't hurt," she said, smiling. "Now get the hell in the kitchen. I'm hungrier than a horse would be after a day plowing the field. We got hamburger meat and some canned green beans that the Weavers sent over. And let's open up a bottle of that Gallo."

B.J. couldn't cook, and he knew it, but pan-frying a burger and heating up beans wasn't so tough. B.J. couldn't always be around in the kitchen these days, so he tried to make sure there was enough food in the refrigerator for his mother to heat up when he had to go out. And

The Baron was a big help. He brought her food from the Hopefully Diner at least three times a week. The Baron seemed like a father to him, albeit a strange one.

At 10 p.m., B.J. turned on the television set to watch the news. There was no local news station in Hopefully, but they could pick up the Lexington stations on cable. Toward the end of the show, the news anchor reported a serious accident near Hopefully in which three men in a rented SUV were killed when it ran off a mountainside dirt road and hit a rock. There was no immediate identification of the men or why they were on that particular road. State officials had said the police were working around the clock to identify the mystery men. They were heavily armed with assault weapons. A man who lived at the bottom of the hill had discovered the wreck. He heard the crash and alerted authorities. B.J. was sure that this was not the man he had witnessed reading a book. He was sure it was probably Austrich, who yelled at his kids.

"A fourth victim in the crash is in the hospital, in critical condition," the news anchor said. "Authorities hope that he survives and is able to clear up the mystery surrounding the crash. But, when we checked with the hospital just minutes ago, he was still in a coma."

The news left B.J. in anguish. All he was trying to do was take some candid photos, not cause a crash. Now fear gripped him and turned his stomach upside down. He'd always been successful in avoiding challenges, but not one like this. He wanted to hide, but he realized there was no hiding from this one.

CHAPTER 13

Eastern Kentucky

S tella fell asleep amid the relentless monotony of the bus, only to be wakened when the driver announced that the town of Purcells was only five minutes away. Once again, the driver smiled and winked at her through the rearview mirror, enhancing her fears that he might have recognized her and might try to tell the authorities.

She had to get off at Purcells in order to find transportation to her ultimate destination, Hopefully, which was locked inside the foggy hills to the southeast.

The bus passed a Wal-Mart, three fast-food restaurants, two gas stations, and a used-car dealership on the road into Purcells. The driver helped Stella down the steps. He smiled and winked at her again. "Long ride, Miss," he said. "I hope you get some rest. Thanks for riding with us." He meant well, Stella thought, and at least he didn't wreck the bus going through the mountains; he had been ogling her through the rear-view mirror for the past 150 miles. With a quick look left and right, she surveyed the town and concluded there wasn't much of interest there, and a good cup of coffee might be difficult to find. No Starbucks here, no decaf latte or Gold Coast Blend, for sure. She settled for a Coke from the machine in front of the bus station and gulped it down, wondering how she was going to get to Hopefully.

Stella put aside her paranoia about the bus driver and asked how she could get a ride to the next town. The bus driver put down a bag he was toting for an elderly woman passenger and looked into her eyes and then at her breasts. "Name's Bill—Bill Smith," he said.

"Well, there isn't a bus as such over to Hopefully from here," he said. "There's a taxi, but that's kinda expensive. Look, I'll be glad to give you a ride tomorrow. I'm off then. I'll even provide the bed tonight. No cost. I promise not to touch you, though you could be mighty tempting."

"Thanks, but no thanks," Stella said, suddenly turning icy cold. "I'll just get a cab."

"Are you sure?" the driver said. "You can have my room all to yourself. I won't interfere." He held his hand over his heart. "I promise," he said.

She didn't want to tell him anything about herself, and she didn't want to make her problem of being alone without a place to stay a big issue. "No thanks," she said. "Really can't do it." She shook her head to emphasize the "no."

The driver looked disappointed, and turned a little sour. "I predict you'll ask me later when you find the only public transportation from here to there is by foot. Just trying to help. Here's my card, if you change your mind."

Stella didn't want to get into a fight. She thanked him and said she wanted to get into Hopefully sooner. A young woman with a heavy backpack sidled up to her. She spoke softly so no one else could hear. "This guy is a jerk. You need to get in touch with Maybelle Grimes. She sometimes drives Southeast Junior College students to Hopefully pretty cheaply, maybe for five bucks. She drives a van mostly for the elderly who need to get to the hospital here in Purcells from Hopefully. I'll call her if you'd like, to see if she can take you."

A few minutes later, Maybelle, a stout 30-something woman with a strong voice and bleached blonde hair in a long pigtail down her back, got out of a white van and walked over. She looked Stella up and down. "So this is the lady who wants to go to Hopefully," she said, a cigarette hanging out of her mouth. "Is there something wrong with your head? There's nothing there. Yeah, I'll take you, but you will have to lug your own luggage and stuff. That'll be $10 up front, please, so that there's no misunderstanding when we get there. I'm doing this as a favor to my friend who called about you. I gotta go over to Hopefully anyway to pick up some sick people. Just throw your things in the back and you can get in the seat behind me." Stella nodded, and with a groan lifted her heavy duffel into the van.

"What's your name?" Maybelle asked.

"Eloise. Call me Ellie."

"Well, Ellie, you are sitting in the quiet zone, so let's keep it that way. Do you like Bluegrass music? Alan Jackson?"

"Not really. Who is he?"

"Well, it's not my job to save the infidels," she said, turning up the volume of Alan Jackson's "Blue Ridge Mountain Song." Maybelle patted the steering wheel to the beat of the music and lip-synched words as the van rolled through town. "I cry every time he sings it," Maybelle said as she grabbed a Kleenex and wiped her eyes. Down the road to Hopefully, the van weaved through the mountains to the accompaniment of banjo and guitar music, foreign to Stella's ear as she contrasted it to the National Symphony or opera playing at the Kennedy Center.

After weaving through the Knobs, from one hairpin curve to another, the van rolled into Hopefully at lunchtime. Stella was thankful she had made the trip without getting sick. In fact, she'd worked up a strong appetite after having nothing but Coke and coffee for breakfast, and she found herself longing for the taste of L'Auberge Chez Francois's lobster bisque and grilled salmon with dill sauce. The fabulous restaurant in the Northern Virginia countryside was one of Bob's and her favorite places to dine. Hopefully was going to be a culinary desert, she was sure. Maybelle opened the door of the van.

"Thank you, Maybelle," said Stella, handing her a $10 tip.

Eying this, Maybelle smiled. "You look like you could use a hand with those bags, girl," she said. Stella smiled. A good tip works every time.

Maybelle picked up the bags and asked, "Why in the world are you coming here to Hopefully? Visiting a long-lost relative?"

"No, I'm just a painter looking for new scenery to paint," Stella said, hoping that Maybelle would accept her answer. "The knobs interest me."

"Really? Painting in Hopefully?" Maybelle said, shrugging. "You've gotta be kidding."

"Not at all, It's beautiful here," Stella said. Maybelle rolled her eyes as they walked to the inn.

"Where you from?" Maybelle asked.

"East Coast," Stella replied. "I've been traveling and painting nature's beauty in several states. I guess you could say I'm a vagabond painter right now," Stella said, hoping that would end the conversation.

"Okay, but where you really from?" Maybelle pressed.

"Connecticut," Stella said quickly, as she realized Maybelle was nosy, and she thought of her happy days in New Haven at Yale.

"I've heard it's pretty there. Never been myself. Good luck finding something to paint." Maybelle said as she dropped Stella's luggage at the front desk.

"Thank you again, Maybelle. Alan Jackson has a nice voice." Stella said.

Inside, the inn was better than she expected, with a brightly colored lobby and a big sofa in front of a TV set. The proprietors, Marshall and Sue Friendly, a retired railroad man and his wife, greeted her warmly and helped her to her room, which, surprisingly, was not dark and grim, but had white walls and sunshine streaming through two windows overlooking the courtyard.

Stella didn't take time to unpack her bags; she was hungry and ready to visit the Hopefully Diner just down the street.

A woman whose name tag read JENNIE greeted her and announced in a husky voice that she had a booth in the back.

Jennie returned with a glass of water and utensils. "Whatcha have, honey?"

Stella noticed Jennie's streaked hair, powerful arms and a strong smirk. "Do you have wheat bread?" she asked.

"We ain't *that* backward, honey. Whatcha want on it—turkey and cheese or Spam? We got a special on Spam."

Stella knew instantly she had committed the *faux pas* of being an uppity stranger, and Jennie had quickly cut her to size. She could think of only one way to make amends.

"Okay, baloney and cheese on wheat, but do you have low-fat mayo?" Stella smiled and said it in a way that Jennie could tell it was an apology.

Jennie laughed. "Tell you what: You have a turkey-wheat-bread-lettuce-and-tomato-without-the-mayo kind of figure to me, and that's what I'd suggest. Frankly, I'm out of baloney right now. We had a big crowd early. Diet Coke?"

Jennie came back with the turkey sandwich and a mountain of potato chips and plopped it on the table with the Diet Coke. Stella could already tell that probably anything she told Jennie would be quickly disseminated throughout the town and the county. "Here you are, honey—enjoy. I was just wonderin' when I was back in the kitchen: How did you ever wind up in our little town? We don't often get young pretty strangers like yourself in here."

"If you must know, I'm an artist and I like to paint landscapes," Stella said, figuring that a lie based on the truth would be easier to maintain. "I've heard about the beauty of the hills and decided to come to God's Country to see for myself, and maybe do a little painting."

"God's Country," Jennie repeated, with a hoot. "You left out the word 'forsaken'! Most of us who've lived here for a while don't see the beauty of it, I reckon, but I suppose it might be kinda nice to see for the first time. Me, I was born here, so I don't get that chance."

"Can you recommend any good places to go paint? I just got here and don't know my way around."

"Well, there's lotsa places. Everybody here likes to take pictures of Copperhead Knob. Ain't really a big mountain, just a knob that looks like one of those Egyptian pyramids. Go out 7884 'bout two miles past the Copperhead Club and just pull over by the right side of the road. There it is—pretty as can be."

At the mention of Copperhead Club, Stella felt a quickening in her chest. "Oh, I may have heard of the Copperhead Club," she said, perhaps too hastily.

"Really?" Jennie looked surprised. "You've heard of the Club? What did you say your name is?" Jennie asked.

"Didn't. Eloise. Eloise. . . uh. . . Heinz," Stella said, looking at the ketchup bottle on the table. "Ellie for short," she added.

"Okay, Ellie Heinz," Maybelle said. "This diner is a respectable business. The Copperhead Club is a honky-tonk, full of drunks and druggies and crazy people from all 'round who like loud Bluegrass music. I wouldn't be caught dead in the place. Owned and managed by a strange woman who came to town a few years ago. Ortiz—Lucinda Ortiz. She's from Mexico or someplace like that. Speaks good English, though. Gettin' a hillbilly accent, too. People like her, I reckon."

"Well, I kind of like Bluegrass," said Stella. "I might want to just go out there and listen to some. What do you mean that Mrs. Ortiz is strange?"

"Oh, she just keeps to herself. Doesn't come to town often and doesn't talk to many people. Drops her deposits off at the bank and heads back to the club. She must live there. Never see her in church. Think she's only been in here once. Tell you what—if you want to hear Bluegrass, you'll want to hear Jimmy Billingsley. He's the star of the show, and he's right over there at the counter."

Stella's eyes focused on a handsome young man with a ponytail and a goatee. He was working on a hamburger and french fries. He turned and caught her looking at him. He got up and came over.

"Jimmy Billingsley," he said, holding out his hand. "I couldn't help but hear you two talking. Ain't no privacy here. If you like Bluegrass, come on out. We'll be rockin'. Don't believe all that stuff Jennie says about the Club. We're good country folks just having a good time."

"I wouldn't if I were you," said Jennie, smiling at Jimmy but staring at Stella.

"Don't let the queen of the café sway you," Jimmy retorted. "I promise you'll be safe. Even pick you up myself."

"I think I can get there on my own," Stella said. She looked at Jimmy. He was at least 10 years younger than she, but he was certainly flirting with her. She couldn't allow herself to be drawn into something like this, she thought. She was taking enough risks already. She didn't want the danger multiplied. But perhaps Jimmy would be useful, a way for her to get to her husband, if indeed Bob were hiding somewhere near this town.

"Tell you what, Jimmy Billingsley, I'll try to make it just to hear you. You better be good." Stella said, cocking her head sweetly.

"I promise, I promise," Jimmy said with a half-smile.

CHAPTER 14

Washington, D.C.

Scott Herbert, President Everett's chief of staff, welcomed Dave Simon into his White House office. It was just down the hall from the Oval Office, meaning that it doesn't get much closer than that to the President.

Simon looked around at the photos on the wall showing Herbert and the President in places like Istanbul, Paris, and Beijing.

Herbert was abrupt, not a man to waste time. "Okay, Simon, stop playing games with me—where in the hell is she hiding?" he began.

"That's a good way to break the ice," Simon said dryly. "Well, as I told you over the phone, I don't have the slightest idea. She somehow just slipped away. Didn't leave a phone number or address, as she is supposed to do in the middle of an investigation."

"Don't bullshit me, Simon. You've never lost a client since I've known you. If you know where she is and you're trying to hide it from me, trust me, I'll have you prosecuted."

"Well," Simon said, "she hasn't been charged with anything yet, as far as I know. And no one has asked her to report in for more questioning. She hasn't been gone that long, so that to say she is missing is not exactly fair. I think she will show up in a couple of days. I think she is looking for a little peace from all this craziness."

"Nonetheless," said Herbert, "she *is* missing. You know we check up on these things if the President is involved in some way. She did issue

117

a statement supporting us at the hearing, and that was nice. But if she has disappeared, it brings up thousands of questions about us and our handling of this case."

"You mean you are now spying on us and you had her under constant surveillance, didn't you, yet she got away?" Simon shot back. "To tell you the truth, though, I don't think she has much to say."

"Maybe, maybe not—let me be the judge of that," Herbert snapped. "Let's stop talking about this bullshit that you're giving me. We know she's missing and you said you don't have the slightest idea of where she is. What the hell is she trying to do—find *him?*"

"She hasn't been in contact with me, so I don't know," Simon said. Why don't you check with the FBI? They should know a lot better than I do."

Herbert said the FBI hadn't volunteered any information, particularly since Bob was relatively close to the President. And, naturally, he added, the FBI could not and would not share any leads that it got.

"Do you mean the President is under investigation?"

"Could be, but he is as blameless as a lamb, trust me," said Herbert. "We're eager to find Jasper so that he can affirm the President's innocence to everyone concerned. Then things will be easier on the campaign trail."

"I think you have a greater chance of finding him than I do—or, for that matter, than Stella does," Simon observed.

"If you go to the media about this conversation, you'll be finished as a friend and a prominent figure in this town," Herbert warned. "You'll be a pariah in Washington. And if you don't try to find her, I'll hold you accountable as well."

Simon knew that this 40-something White House official could do him a lot of harm in a city that is a much smaller town than people realized. He tried a different tack: "You'll be the first one I call when and if she gets in touch with me," Simon said. "I'm not happy that she's disappeared on me, either. Look, she hurts me more if she runs away.

It means I have a client out of control, and I'm not happy with that. She obviously doesn't trust her lawyer, and doesn't respect my wishes on how to defend her. It's not in my self-interest to have her go underground. She knows all that."

"Do you think she's trying to find Bob and in some idiotic way confront him and kill him for his transgressions?"

"No, she isn't that bold." Simon said. "Look, she's entrenched with the society here. She's never done anything brave or different in her entire life. She's not a risk-taker, and she's very shy at heart. Why would she attempt such a thing? I just think she wants some privacy. It's really been tough on her."

"I wouldn't be that sure about her," said Herbert, "because she's lost everything she has ever cherished. The world suddenly has turned into a nightmare, and she's full of anger and resentment—and hate. If she calls you, don't give her a gun," Herbert said emphatically.

"In this country," Simon interjected, "anyone can get a gun if they want it badly enough. Why did you mention that? Do you know something I don't know? A gun? Stella? Ridiculous. She may be angry, but I don't think she's that angry or crazy."

"Okay. My boss has a personal interest in this case because he likes Stella and doesn't want to see her get hurt in any way. If she contacts you and decides to come back, he would love to meet with her and try to comfort her."

Simon let the words sink in, and nodded his head, but thought: Bullshit.

"Where do you think she might be?" Herbert asked. "The Caribbean? Canada? Maine? L.A.? Did she ever give you any hint about where she might be going?"

Simon again professed ignorance of where she might have gone.

"If you find out and tell us where she is, you know we'll have something for you," said Herbert.

"Like what?" Simon said with a smirk.

"Maybe a high-profile job at the Justice Department. Or if you don't want to work too hard, the Commerce Department could use some kick-ass leadership. You name it."

"Ambassador to France."

They both laughed.

"You're not serious," Herbert said. "You, the hard-boiled attorney with a cynical view of human nature—a diplomat—and to France?"

"Ah," said Simon, "Right up my alley. They don't get any more cynical than the French."

"I suppose if you deliver as proposed, anything would be possible for you," Herbert said. "And so we'll await that result."

The presidential aide, blessed with good looks, blond hair, and expensive suits, said his boss had a tough re-election campaign and easily could lose. Then he mentioned Ramos, saying that the President's re-election depended mightily on whether Ramos ended up supporting him. "The Latino electorate is in his hands," Herbert said, raising his voice. "If Ramos should choose Reyes Gonzales, Everett is toast." He said he was hopeful that Ramos would break his silence in the President's favor and hoped that Simon would use any influence he had to persuade Ramos.

"I don't have any inside channels to Ramos," Simon said. "I met him once and had a chat with him about politics. But he isn't a buddy. Just the same, you can be sure that if I do run into him, I'll try to persuade him to support the President." Simon said.

"I appreciate that," said Herbert. "If we lose, there's no telling what mischief the next President could do." Herbert thanked him for coming in, and they shook hands. A secretary came and took Simon out the southwest gate of the White House, where exiting presidential visitors aren't as visible.

Simon left with a smile on his face, but it soon turned to a frown as he hailed a cab along 17th Street, just outside the restricted zone in front of the White House and the Old Executive Office Building. He had decided he was going to sell some stock.

He admitted to himself that any President who would seriously consider him as an ambassador, even to France, should be suspect. What Herbert had said—offering a job to someone in exchange for information—probably was illegal, Simon thought. Be that as it may, such offers may be discussed more frequently than people think. Herbert was an intense man, accustomed to getting his way in his former political and business jobs. However, he could always say he'd only been kidding. Simon couldn't have proven otherwise.

Simon concluded that Everett, facing a tough re-election campaign, was extremely worried about this case. Obviously, he thought, the President didn't want to be connected with a money launderer in any way. He had witnessed what seemed to be an almost-desperate mood among the President's advisers.

And the line about wanting to comfort poor Stella had all but turned his stomach. "I think they'd be happy if she were in the grave right now," Simon thought. The very notion began to worry him more than it had before he'd gone into the White House.

Good God, he thought, suppose she did make her way to wherever Bob is and is trying to kill him or expose him and get him arrested? "Could she be losing her mind?" he asked himself. "That's like throwing yourself to the wolves."

Simon had acquired a reputation—valid or not—that he would do anything in his power to advance himself politically and economically, even if it meant abandoning old friends or partners.

But with this case, something had happened to Simon. Stella was a pariah and most likely was broke as well. He was helpless to assist her. But he would if he could.

CHAPTER 15

Hopefully, Kentucky

As the newly christened Ellie Heinz tried to sleep in the Hopefully Inn, she heard rumbles all night long—from trucks, cars and even an occasional train. A roach or two made itself at home in her room, and she unhesitatingly deployed a fly swatter that was conveniently hanging next to the door. She chuckled at the thought that she actually used to spend time at night downloading wind-chime variations from the white-noise app on her cellphone. What a waste of life's precious time, she thought. But she had to admit: This time, it wasn't the noise keeping her awake—it was the situation.

With $500 to her name, she was almost out of money. She was probably breaking the law. She had no real evidence that her husband was even here in this terribly isolated place, and she was angry in a way that ran deep into her soul. More than once, she asked herself: "Am I out of my mind?" Maybe she was, she thought, but she couldn't help doing this anyway.

She realized she was an amateur at this game, and tried to calculate her next steps in a way that wouldn't give away her identity or cause her to overstep her bounds. Yet she had never felt so betrayed. If she should see Bob, she didn't know whether she could actually kill him (if she'd been able to get a gun) or would merely wound him in a way that would cripple him for life. She bounced back and forth between thinking about outright murder and settling for just telling him off once and for all. No, that last one would be letting him off the hook.

Whatever the outcome, Stella wanted some satisfaction, something to ease her pain. She saw herself a woman wronged, turned into a fool by a cheating, secretive, self-aggrandizing asshole who may also have run away with her best friend. How could Alicia have done this to her, she wondered? "We were *friends*, for God's sake."

She had gotten past the crying stage. Now she was thriving on anger. But anger alone wouldn't get her what she wanted, Stella told herself. She had to think coldly and move as cautiously as she could.

Her immediate challenge was to get to the Copperhead Club, where she hoped to discover some intelligence that might lead her to Bob—and possibly to Alicia, too. The town was so small that it didn't have a taxi service, but she was sure that there were people who'd be willing to drive her somewhere for a few dollars and a good tip.

She thought about how she might get a gun. She had heard that acquiring a gun was easy in Hopefully, despite the state and federal gun registration laws. Supposedly, you could arrange for an under-the-table purchase with a little cash. But she didn't know how to do it without attracting attention. And it was still a dangerous move. What if they asked for her I.D. card? It would say Stella Jasper, not Ellie Heinz, and the jig would be up. Even if she could get a firearm, the consequences of her murdering Bob would be staggering. She certainly would spend years in prison and possibly be put to death herself. The thoughts kept her stomach in knots. She felt pain in her chest. Was she going to have a heart attack?

The traffic outside seemed to slacken about 2 a.m. and Stella finally dozed off, only to be wakened at 7 a.m. by a loud noise outside. She peeled back the curtain in her room, and saw two bears clawing at the garbage can, trying to get food. She called the front desk, and blurted loudly into the telephone. "Look, there are two bears outside my window, and this is very scary. What are you going to do about it?"

"Oh, yes, someone else has called," said the middle-aged man at the lobby desk. "We've called the police, but there's nothing they can do about it right now. It's a mother and her cub. Don't get scared. It's unusual, but we've seen them before at this time of year."

"Seen them before!" Stella shouted. "You mean you did nothing about it?"

"Don't get excited," the man at the desk continued. They'll leave soon, and they won't bother anyone if no one bothers them. The sheriff's office has sent a special unit who can take care of them if they get aggressive. If it takes too long I can get out the broom and bells."

"The what?" Stella asked, gasping audibly.

"The broom and bells—you know, a broom with some bells attached. Works most of the time, as long as you don't get too close. You just shake it above your head and walk slowly with your arms real big like you're King Kong.

"Isn't it dangerous to do that?" Stella asked.

"Well one time our former manager, old Fred, had to get stiches after he tripped on a garden hose running from a bear that charged, but he got too close and was trying to take a picture, too. Usually it works wonders."

"That's okay—I'll stay inside," Stella said, shaking her head in disbelief.

She opened the curtain again and stood nose-to-nose with the mother bear, with only a window and a screen separating them. Stella screamed and ran into the hall, wearing only her panties along with a light, silken top that hardly hid anything.

A man opened the door of another room and gave her an astonished look. "What the hell is going on?" he demanded.

"Bear!" she said. "Bear! Outside."

The man had a quizzical look. "Bear? Here?"

He reached inside his room, and threw her a bathrobe. She put it on and raced to the lobby. He wasn't far behind.

"Don't panic," the man at the desk assured them. "They're out and away from their den early. We usually see them in March or April. But we've had a mild winter, so they're coming out earlier than expected. They've just left our premises. "They're just looking for food. Now that it's daylight, they'll go back into the woods and hide. We hadn't seen bears in more than 30 years until recently," he continued. "But in the past couple of years, they've been coming back in greater numbers. They're a lot more brazen. We'll be watching. Try to get some sleep. We're as safe as anyone else in town."

Stella calmed down a little, but the whole town suddenly seemed more menacing to her than it had been before she'd seen the bears.

"I need to go home," Stella thought. "I've made a mistake coming here. Bob probably isn't here; he's not the mountain type. But where is he? Where's Alicia? She'd be scared to death of bears, just like me. If only this could be a nightmare and I could wake up with Bob holding me, Bob loving me. If only. . ."

The phone rang at 10 a.m. and, Stella, still sleepy, groped at the receiver from force of habit. It was Maybelle Grimes, the woman who'd given her a ride to Hopefully.

"Hello Eloise," Maybelle said softly. "Look, I'm calling to apologize. I was cleaning the van out last night and I noticed that the seat you traveled in was wet. When I looked more closely, I realized that it was piss."

"I didn't do that." Stella was aghast.

"No, no, I don't mean that you did it; it was poor Mr. Lambert, who is incontinent, among other things. He peed on the seat, and you sat in it. You may not have noticed it. I'm so sorry," Maybelle said in a soft voice.

Stella didn't know what to say or think, except "Oh, that's okay. Things happen."

Maybelle continued, "I'm calling also to apologize for being so rude on the bus ride. I wasn't being the nicest person, but I didn't mean any harm. I was just in a bad mood and I took it out on you. I want to somehow make it up to you. How about a late breakfast or lunch at the diner? I am local, so I know some things that might be useful for a painter in our town. I can tell you about some of the people here you may run into. And I'd like to hear about your painting."

Stella accepted her apology and, after a moment's hesitation, agreed to meet her. At first, she'd thought that getting closer to Maybelle could be dangerous. But then she concluded that she needed all the help she could get. And Maybelle certainly got around. Stella knew she'd have to be careful, but Maybelle could help because she knew Hopefully and the surrounding area well.

"Sure," she told Maybelle. "Can we meet at the diner at 11, in an hour or so, for brunch? I need to unpack."

Maybelle pointed out that people in Kentucky didn't do brunch very often, but said the diner was still open for breakfast at 11.

"Okay, see you for a late breakfast," Stella said.

"You got it," Maybelle replied, and hung up.

In her head, Stella made notes on what she planned to ask Maybelle when they met—about food, transportation, lodging, what the town was like, and who were the movers and shakers. More than anything else, she wanted to avoid any perception that she was on a quest. She hoped that talking to Maybelle would give her some credibility and reduce any suspicion about ulterior motives.

When she met Maybelle this time, the van radio had been turned down a bit, and she was dressed in what was a rather elegant outfit for Hopefully—a royal blue tunic top and matching jacket over sleek black pants and a nice pair of high heels.

"I want to apologize again," Maybelle said, "I feel terrible that I forgot to put the protective pad under Mr. Lambert. As soon as I can afford it, I'm going to install leather seats in the van; upholstered seats are terrible for the kind of older folks I drive around."

"I'm sure they appreciate all you do. How would they manage otherwise?" Stella said.

"I'd like to be a friend, at least as long as you're in this place," Maybelle went on. "It isn't often we get painters down here. You seem smart and 'with it.' I'm happy to help you get around, and even offer some advice. It must be tough to be alone in a strange new place. Y'know, we Kentuckians are known for our hospitality, but some of us have a different version of that: Be nice, but watch your back."

"I'm am happy to accept your apology, once again, and you don't really need to do that. I thought you were very funny on the bus ride."

Knowing better, Maybelle laughed. Some of that was acting, she admitted to Stella. "You should have heard what that man said when you came running down the hall that night, with hardly anything on, trying to escape a bear."

"How do you know about that?" Stella asked.

"The desk clerk told me when I called," Maybelle said.

"And what did he say?" Stella asked.

"He said the man from the room near yours told him: 'She has a nice ass.'"

"Creep," said Stella. "Well, he was no great representative of the human race—in body or mind."

"You know, you got me intrigued since you got in my van," Maybelle said. "Overall, you seem like you have a lot of self-confidence, but you give the impression that you're worried about something or looking for something or both. So, I thought if you want, maybe I could give you a few tips about this place."

"I've always been skittish about new places," Stella said. "But," she lied, "I have always liked little towns and their great hospitality."

Maybelle gave her a long stare, as if to say, "Have you gone mad?"

"You might want to rethink that a bit," she said. "Yeah, we're outwardly hospitable, but don't trust every one you meet here. Everyone knows everyone else, for the most part. We tolerate each other, but we don't really trust each other. Outsiders who come here shouldn't try to sound superior. We may not be the best-educated people in the world, but we sure as hell know bullshit when we see it or hear it."

"All I want to do is some painting for a week or so, and then I'm going home," Stella said. "I don't plan to socialize very much."

"Well, be careful," Maybelle cautioned. "We do have a few artists around here. They're mostly guys—one woman, I think. One of them got wounded a few months ago when he and a drunken railroad guy got into a fight. He was a young painter from Kansas, with high ideals, but he called our local guy a drunken oaf and called his girlfriend an ignorant nitwit. It happened in the parking lot of the Copperhead Club. The young painter got in his car and started to drive back to the inn downtown. They were waiting for him at Deadman's Curve. They shot his fingers off. He'll never paint again."

"Are you telling me I need a gun to protect myself just because I'm painting a scene?" Stella asked. "Is this Copperhead Club really dangerous? I mean, you know—the people and the atmosphere?"

"No, not extremely—but it's a bar, a nightclub, a place to get a drink and get drunk. Many do late in the evening. Early on, it's better. I'd say it's a step above a honky-tonk. The music is generally good, and you know how I love good country music. Are you interested in going there? Doesn't seem your cup of tea."

"Oh, yes, I definitely want to go, just to see what it's like. Also, a musician named Jimmy Billingsley has invited me to come and hear him play after I finish for the day. They say he's a good performer."

Maybelle stared at her incredulously. "You don't mean you've actually made a date with that guy?" she asked, aghast.

Stella saw the dismay in Maybelle's face. "What's the matter?" she questioned.

"He's the mayor's son, and they all love him at the club," Maybelle said, "but he's a man who likes good looking women, so be careful. You qualify as a good looking woman."

"I think I can handle him," Stella said, remembering the baby-boy face she'd seen at the café the day before. "And I'm also interested in meeting the woman who runs the place, Ms. Ortiz."

"Why?" Maybelle asked, clearly surprised.

"Because it's unusual to see a Hispanic person owning and running something in this part of the world," Stella said. "I like success stories and strong women. As I start painting again and perfecting my craft, I will be stronger myself. I hope to sell more of my work to the public."

Maybelle still wore her frown. "So you fancy yourself as a tough woman, huh, and you need to come to this little town for inspiration to launch a career you've dropped? Don't answer. Tell you what, I'll drive you tonight and pick you up, if you want. It'll make me feel better."

"Are you sure? I don't want to be a burden to anyone," Stella said.

"Look, I owe you one," responded Maybelle. "You had to listen to my music on the drive here, and believe me, I realize I didn't treat you right. So let me drive you back to the motel tonight."

"That's a deal," said Stella, smiling. She remembered she mustn't slip up and give herself away.

"I can help you get your painting done without much hassle," Maybelle said. "I know the lay of the land here, where the bodies are buried and how the back roads run. I know the mayor, the police chief, the councilmen, and the sheriff. They could be hard on you, a stranger in town, if they wanted. And that reminds me—I've got a patient to pick up now. I need to go, but I can wait for you to get your clothes that I soiled yesterday; I'll get them cleaned today."

"No, that's okay—I'll take care of them, but thanks anyway." Stella said.

"Well, how about if I drop you off at a painting site that's on my way?" Maybelle asked.

"Sure, I'll get my kit." Stella replied.

Stella returned to the inn and grabbed her art kit. It was strange, but she liked the idea of being called a painter again, even though she had stopped doing it years ago. And it was the only way she had to meet people here.

CHAPTER 16

Hopefully, Kentucky

B.J. hated nightmares. He'd tried to talk himself out of another one, but he knew it would be hard after such a tragic day and the deaths of the men on the mountain. Dozing off well past midnight, he dreamed he was alone in a forest on a wintry evening, depending on his fire to keep the wolves at bay. The fire soon went out, and the wolves closed in. He could see their shining teeth coming at him. He ran and fell over a tree limb across the path. As the wolves gathered around him one final time, he woke up in a sweat, with his heart beating fast. It was two o'clock in the morning as he quietly got out of bed, put on a pair of slippers and a robe, picked up his camera, and tiptoed outside.

The moon seemed especially bright, and he could see the trails on Copperhead Knob behind the house. At his desk in the barn, he quickly turned on the computer, took the memory card from the camera and slipped it into a computer port. With a quick scroll and a click of his mouse, small versions of each of his photos appeared on the monitor. Another click and there was the red-haired man with a beard and mustache, reading a book in the middle of a clearing, seemingly oblivious to the world around him.

B.J. zoomed in closer to the face, but it was hard to discern his finer features because the man's beard and baseball cap hid them. He might be relatively young, probably in his mid-to-late 30s.

"Why, red-haired man, are you sitting in the middle of a field 30 feet away from the house?" B.J. mused. "I know it was a chilly day when I took these pictures and you were letting the sun warm your back, but I think I could find a better place to relax and read than out there in the field in February. And who is this well dressed man with the navy blazer and blue shirt with khaki pants, with a bluetooth earpiece? Those guys in the accident knew you both, didn't they? You ordered them to come after me, didn't you? Why? Just for taking a photo? Why would you two need so many people to protect you? Or was it just the man in the chair you were protecting? Are you trying to hide from something terrible? Are you operating a meth lab?"

Since they were out in the open air, it didn't seem that the men were hiding anything, although admittedly they were in a very remote place. Maybe they thought that there was no one within miles, B.J. surmised. Maybe these men were hiding from the law. He knew they weren't moonshiners, who really did hide in the hills. Maybe they had something to do with drugs, but there was no evidence to back up that theory, either.

With the tragic accident apparently involving these two, B.J. knew that everything had changed, including the safety of his family. As he saw it, the man in a coma could awaken and remember that he'd seen a red truck with a distinguishing black-and-white stripe and a man driving it. Since this area was sparsely populated, it would be relatively easy to ascertain that B.J. had been the driver.

He knew that he had to rethink security at his house and even consider upgrading the weapons he kept there—a step that he'd eschewed because of his own antipathy to firearms and the possibility that his mother might object to them.

B.J. had little faith in the local cops, whether it was the police chief or the sheriff, even though his mother had once worked as a law enforcement officer. If he and his mom were to rely on the police for protection, he reasoned, their odds of surviving an attack would be low. First, the cops had neither the firearms nor the training to confront these adversaries, who had powerful weapons themselves. And then, of course, if he told the police what had happened, he might be arrested for failing to report the accident, even though his having done so in self-defense might be a credible excuse.

But deeper down, B.J. strongly suspected that the local authorities, including county and city officials, might be taking bribes from the drug rings that had grown up in eastern Kentucky in the past few years. He remembered the case of Gerald Brancombe, who had tried to sell drugs to half the county a few years ago. Parents went to the authorities a number of times to call for his arrest, but the police said they couldn't obtain the evidence against him, even though B.J. knew that Brancombe was the ringleader and could have easily been caught with a little effort. The suspect himself died of a drug overdose three years ago.

Law enforcement efforts also targeted widespread marketing and use of drugs, from prescription pharmaceuticals to marijuana and methamphetamine. And Hopefully hadn't seen the crackdown that a few other counties had launched against this menace. The same "pill mills" that brought illegally gained prescription drugs to the community had a free rein here and in other counties where local authorities looked the other way. Some of his former high school classmates had told him that, too, and adding that anyone who tried to buck this problem literally risked their lives.

So B.J. decided against going to the police and instead began setting up his own safety plan. He considered the old Matson hiding place on the knob to be their personal security safe house. His mom had been the inspiration for it, since she'd been the police officer who'd taken on the majority of local murder cases and other major crimes for so many years. In those days, there were incidents in which she'd experienced fear because of death threats to her and her family. Now, he concluded, he'd have to turn to the safe house again.

The safe house was perched near the top of the knob, at the end of a steep, winding lane that took an off-road vehicle to negotiate. As Molly grew more and more frail, it had become increasingly harder for her to go to the safe-house, even though B.J. had taken steps to make it less cumbersome. He'd built a zigzag path up to its entrance and a wheelchair ramp to take her the rest of the way. The truth was, she hadn't been up there in years. But when the time came for hiding, he'd take her on The Beast, an off-road vehicle that he kept in his garage. The Baron had purchased it, and B.J. had named it after taking his first wild ride up the knob. It was bouncy on the makeshift road, but it would work.

Yes, he told himself, they could use this fortress, which had been built long ago, but he realized that his plan had a second potential glitch: The criminals could just wait them out, until B.J. and his mother had to replenish food and medicine and other necessary stuff. He'd have to figure a solution to that one later.

B.J.'s first order of business was to protect himself and his mother, but The Baron was at risk, too, since he was associated with the family and his name would be mentioned if anyone came after B.J. or his mother. It was well known in the town that The Baron visited often.

Getting The Baron into hiding would be extremely difficult, if not impossible. The Baron had avoided military service because of various ailments, not to mention the anxiety he felt when threatened with injury whenever he confronted a foe. He also had suffered the taunting and beatings of more than one bully in his youth. He usually could talk himself out of a bad situation—a definite strength—but he never pretended that he was a hero. Moreover, the man was a public figure, the biggest and most recognized banker in the area, and someone who wouldn't want to go under cover for very long.

But there was one factor that could change the equation: The Baron was an utter and complete coward. Thin and wiry, he was afraid of his own shadow, and B.J. was sure he had never fired a gun. Yet he might be persuaded to let B.J. serve as a kind of bodyguard for him.

B.J. himself wasn't exactly a gun lover. He'd used guns to hunt, so he knew something about them. But he hated violence and he hated what having too many guns around could do to a community. And he knew that even hinting to his relatives about the heightened security risks might prompt them to call in authorities for protection—an approach that would be asking for trouble if the police and sheriff's office were on the take from the people who were threatening B.J.

Sooner or later he'd have to tell his mom and The Baron about this new threat in their lives—a threat that he thought could quickly materialize unless the critically ill man in the hospital remained in a coma or died before regaining consciousness.

B.J. looked at the photo again, this time zooming in closer to get details that hadn't been that apparent before. He focused on the beer bottle, wondering what kind of drink this man liked. After several attempts, he made out a brand name: Tutankhamen—a label he didn't recognize. He Googled the beer's name and found the information on the first try. It was brewed by a Cambridge company, using a secret recipe, supposedly from the family of King Tut of Ancient Egypt. And it was one of the world's most expensive beers, about $100 a bottle. "That's a nice way to spend an afternoon reading," B.J. thought to himself. Finding a beer like this in the hills would be difficult, if not impossible, although a bar obviously could order it to have some on hand. Another question for the Copperhead Club, he said to himself. The man also could have ordered the stuff himself. B.J. made a mental note of that. He would check with some of his friends at the post office and FedEx to see if they could help identify him.

But the more immediate question was how to protect his property and the lives of his mother and The Baron. B.J. mapped out in his mind where he would get the guns. He'd need at least two assault rifles and a couple of revolvers, plus plenty of ammunition. Neighboring McHune County hosted a gun show practically every week, and he was sure he could get something there. He knew the proprietor very well. He also had a hunting rifle of his own that he had put in his truck after the initial attempt on his life.

In B.J.'s mind, The Baron also would have to learn to shoot, and would have to do some target practice somewhere far out in the woods. The banker lived a lifetime of nonviolence, and turning himself into a gunslinger would be antithesis of the kind of man he is. He'd have to be convinced. Being afraid of one's shadow is one thing; saving one's life in self-defense is another. B.J. planned a strategy. He'd tell The Baron that the situation would give him an opportunity to protect his lifelong friendship with his mother, and a chance to show some bravery on her behalf. But what if The Baron feared it would drag him into controversy unnecessarily? "It's too late," B.J. planned to tell him. "You're in the middle of it, no matter what."

He thought of sending his mother to live with one of his siblings, but they'd repeatedly made it clear that they didn't want to take her, even for a few weeks. But beyond that, he knew that his mother would veto it if he tried to get her to move. She'd been a fearless policewoman in her day, and she still didn't scare easily. If he made up some story to get her to move temporarily, she'd be certain to insist on roughing it—or else refuse to take it seriously.

B.J. regretted that he couldn't go after the man with the expensive beer. Since the close scrape with his bodyguards, chances are that the man had left the area and gone to hide in another spot far away, unless there was some compelling reason for him to stay in the area, B.J. reasoned.

He slumped over in his chair after a while, falling asleep and encountering the wolf-dreams once again. This time the wolves had broken into his barn and into the locked, air-conditioned back room that housed his valuable things. They had bloody flesh hanging from their teeth following a recent kill and were pulling at his trousers as he climbed the knob and kept slipping backwards. He awakened sweating and short of breath. He got up and checked everything in the refurbished barn and unlocked the door to the back room to make sure his valuables were safe. They were safe, and he intended to keep them safe, even if he had to use a gun.

As the morning sun spread magenta streaks above the hilltops, B.J. went back to the farmhouse to fix breakfast and help his mom. It was Saturday and the bank would close at noon. The Baron was likely to arrive at the house around 1 p.m. and stay with Molly for the rest of the day. That would give B.J. the time to buy the weapons that he hoped would protect them.

Having slept in the barn to avoid letting his mother know how worried he was, B.J. hurried back to the house, hoping to get there before she awoke. But he found her up and about and upset with him for spending the night outside.

"I could have fallen and broken my neck, and you wouldn't be here to help me," she said peevishly. "Haven't you seen those 'I've fallen and I can't get up' ads?" Then she backed off. "I know you had a trying day, son, so please try to be in your own bed the next time." She understood that he was sacrificing himself to stay with her in a lonely town that didn't value his skills. "Thanks for the pancakes."

But B.J. knew the hard side of her personality would soon return. She would show that she was no pushover, that she'd deserved the job she had—as a cop. Molly-the-cop was still formidable, and most of the time she knew best.

So B.J. didn't bring up the issue with her. Nor did he mention it when The Baron showed up, at 1:15 p.m., carrying another one of Jennie's pies from the diner. B.J. decided he was going to do what was best—buy the guns, learn to use them, and bring them home. On the way to the gun seller's and back, he'd map out in his mind where to set up the best defense. He still had some time. The man in the hospital was still in a coma.

B.J. told Molly and The Baron that he needed to go to the auto dealer's downtown to check on an alternator that wasn't operating right and on an ignition problem that he couldn't fix. He also wanted to see how much it would cost to fix the big dent on the truck caused by the collision with his would-be murderers. "It might take a while," he said, "but I'll be back for dinner, and we can talk."

Having shot the photo of the strange, dangerous man, B.J. felt paranoid when he got back into the truck. Someone might be watching him now, he told himself, and he knew very well why. But he had to take a chance and improve his family's chance of survival in a world without much protection.

He'd grown up singing "My Old Kentucky Home," and listening to the Renfro Valley radio show that played all old country music standards. But something had happened to him as he entered his teenage years. Although he loved the state's natural beauty and reputation for hospitality, he began to view it with more of a sinister look as people began to mistreat him and dismiss him as Doofus. He recalled when football player Jesse Smits sneaked up behind him in the high school lunchroom and grabbed away his diagram of the lineage of the Tudor royal family in Medieval England. Glancing down at an open book with a picture of the rotund Henry VIII and Anne Boleyn, Smits laughed and said "Dream on, Doofus. I don't think you're going to get one wife, much less six." Smits wasn't the only one who poked fun. Other classmates hated many of the things that B.J. was beginning to love, such as Bach's fugues and John James Audubon's paintings.

B.J. had big ambitions back then. He knew he was smarter than many of the country boys, who had a limited vision of everything important in the public eye—the environment, the economy, the corruption in local governments across the state. For a time, he had imagined himself running for the state legislature someday. Now, he only wished that he and his family would be safe—and left alone.

CHAPTER 17

Hopefully, Kentucky

Maybelle spun the van through several switchback curves as she moved from one hill to the next and came closer to Copperhead Knob. Stella held on tight, her stomach feeling some of the sharp turns. Maybelle noted her discomfort with a smile.

"You gotta have an iron stomach to ride in some of these hills, baby," she said. "You certainly ain't no country girl. Hang on. One more switchback, and the road will straighten. They've always called this last curve The Circular, and you'll see why. Here we go!"

Maybelle turned the wheels sharply and they plunged downhill. It felt like a 360-degree curve, and it seemed as if the van would never stop turning. A car coming the other way had veered into their lane, and barely missed them as Maybelle jerked the van out of the way without losing control. Stella put her head down to fight off nausea. When they were out of The Circular, straight ahead loomed Copperhead Knob, shaped beautifully against the sky like an ancient pyramid, more symmetrical than all the other knobs in view.

The road wove back and forth through a valley of green to a straightaway—rare in these hills. Almost instantly the nausea subsided. On the left side of the road she could see a two-story wooden building with a covered front porch coming into view. Maybelle slowed down. "The Copperhead Club," she announced. "Here we are at honky-tonk hell," she said, laughing.

Stella could feel her heart beating faster, wondering if Bob or Alicia might pop out the front door holding hands at any moment and there would be a shouting match or worse right there in the parking lot.

She got out of the van, walked toward the club door, and stood frozen as she looked at the sign. The words "Copperhead Club" sent a small chill up her spine. The name was written on a big pane of glass, just above a beautifully painted rendition of a coiled copperhead snake with its fangs showing. The image was so realistic that Stella almost felt hypnotized by its eyes. There was a slogan below: "Come in and enjoy a bite." Stella almost smiled at the macabre wit.

The club, with its weathered brown shingles and green trim around the windows and doors, looked like an old bed-and-breakfast place that had been refurbished. There was a gravel parking lot, halfway filled, and a couple of large swings on the porch, with a bench on each side of the door.

Maybelle took Stella inside to meet the morning and early afternoon supervisor, Annalou McCinsky, and the people who would be serving that night. A few diners were finishing lunch. Inside, the dining room was clean and neat, surprising Stella. The walls were dark wood, and there were booths and tables that showed their nicks. Over a well-equipped bar was a deer's head; the animal probably was shot in this very county. From the ceiling hung six dimly lit chandeliers with fringed shades on the lamps. The more-or-less Victorian motif seemed to clash with this hard-drinking establishment that could likely get a little wild at times. In a side room were pool tables with neon Budweiser signs. Another room, without windows, had been added in back of the old house. Overhead were three wagon-wheel chandeliers. A few wooden benches were lined along the sidewalls. A mahogany bar and barstools ran along the back wall. The room and stage were small, so on a busy night the place would be crammed. She would see for herself tonight. She guessed that there were bedrooms upstairs, but there was no indication that they were being used, unless the manager lived up there.

There was no sign of Lucinda Ortiz. Annalou said she might be there in the evening, but she wasn't sure. "She's got some business downtown," she said. "Can I get you a drink? We've got Blue Wildcat on tap today."

"I'll have a ginger ale," Stella said, "and maybe something stronger later. Can't drink and sketch at the same time."

After Stella's ginger ale arrived, Maybelle said she had to go and pick up a patient and deliver her to the hospital in Purcells. But she said she'd be finished by 7 p.m. or so. She'd come back to the club to have dinner with Stella and then give her a ride home.

They left the club and walked across the road, down the path, and up the rise, which allowed Stella to have a good panoramic view of Copperhead Knob.

"You gonna be sketching next to the roadside?" Maybelle asked, breaking the brief silence. "This road can get busy when supper comes. There ain't any good eating places around Hopefully, and a lot of townspeople drive over here for dinner in the evening. Lunch tends to be a little slower, though."

"Well, I want to be pretty close to the club, so that if I get too chilled out here, I'll have a place to get warm, get a snack, or go to the bathroom," Stella said.

"Okay," Maybelle replied, "I'd suggest that you go down the road about 25 yards or so to paint. There's a path there that leads to a rise where you can see the mountain without the trees being in the way. A lot of artists like that spot."

Stella noticed there was a gravel road not far away that headed up a hill. "There might be several nice spots there, too," she said pointing, "and with more evergreens and a better angle. I could just go down that road to the top of that little rise. It would be spectacular. Would anyone care if I did that?"

"It's private property, and it's better to get their approval," Maybelle said. "Their house sits way back on the property. He's run off artists from time to time. There's a gate and a "No Trespassing" sign right at the turn, then the road turns to dirt the closer you get to the house."

"What's the name of the people living there?" Stella asked.

"Matson—Molly Jo and B.J. Matson," Maybelle said. "She's a retired policewoman from Hopefully, and he's her son, and he takes care of her. Her husband is dead, and her other kids live elsewhere and don't come around much. People call her son 'Doofus' 'cause he dresses like a country hick most of the time. I don't know too much about them. She's famous for killing a bank robber a long time ago. She shot him right in the head without blinking. She was the toughest cop the town has ever had. B.J.'s fiancé was killed in a car crash a long time ago. He's a loner who takes a lot of pictures, for some reason. I don't think I'd mess with either one of them."

Just then she heard a gun go off. And then another shot rang out. She flinched and looked for cover, but Maybelle told her to relax. About a mile down the road there's a shooting range, she said, and there's a window between 2 p.m. and 4 p.m. in which they can shoot at targets for a fee. Once in a while, they hold a contest. "You can't see it from here, but it's about a half-mile down 7884 and then a side road into the range," Maybelle said. "The place is well locked up and very professional," she added.

Hearing the weapons going off frightened Stella, but she was determined to show her toughness even if she was faking it most of the time.

"Just guns," she said, "—so what?"

They hurried back to the van, where Stella zipped up her jacket, put on her cap and sunglasses, and tucked some bottled water into an outside pocket on her backpack, which she put over her shoulder and headed down the road. "Thanks again, Maybelle. I'll see you later," Stella called as she waved goodbye. Then she began thinking: Are you around here somewhere, Bob?

Stella got to the path and climbed up the rise, which gave her a good panoramic view of Copperhead Knob. She could see why everyone liked it, and it supposedly had been painted dozens of times, but she didn't remember seeing a copy of any of the renderings. It was almost too much of a cliché, thought Stella, to paint a scene that poses so well *au naturel.* She really thought that the Copperhead Club itself would be far more interesting as the subject of her work—a place with pretensions of being one of the best restaurants in the area at a time when it had one of the biggest, if not the biggest, clientele of young drinkers to be found in these parts. Violent, too, she thought, if Maybelle's story about the artist who got his fingers shot off was true.

She knew that even though it was February and spring colors hadn't arrived yet, she had the talent to produce a solid, colorful representation of this hill and the sky around it and even get praise for it. But deep in her heart, it seemed more like copying the obvious without inducing the kind of emotional—and yes, say it—*spiritual* effect she wanted to achieve. It wasn't a religious plane she was trying to reach, but the style of painting with the courage and emotional maturity to enable her to paint with the delicacy of her soul—whatever that was. She had an idea how all the old masters had done it with their various styles, and somehow she couldn't jettison these influences with a snap of the finger. In the past, when she'd tried to be bolder she found herself copying others who had broken with the artistic traditions of the times.

At first she sketched the knob—good and solid—as close to a photo as a sketch can get. Then she made note of the colors. In February, the knob was still devoid of full deciduous trees, especially dogwood and crab apple trees in bloom. Their empty branches could still be beautiful, but they were tiresome and unimaginative to her. Maybe they'd be okay for postcards, but not for her.

She turned around and looked back at the Copperhead Club. "I'll give it a try," she said. To her it was a sinister place, where devilish plans were being hatched and where people would betray one another. She felt she didn't need to walk back to copy it. She knew what it looked like and she let her emotions take control. This was the first time in her life she had faced such hardship and such rejection. This was the first time she didn't know what to do or how her life would turn out. Everything was at stake, but nothing was at stake—because she had nothing. What happened to my life, she asked herself? Tears streamed down her eyes as she sketched furiously. She let go of her old control. She sketched without hesitation, letting hate, destruction, betrayal, fury, and loneliness direct her strokes. She sketched another version and another.

Then she grabbed her red pen and began an abstract sketch as she had never done before. She couldn't resist the urge to use broader-nibbed red and black pens. They were shining like fire in hell, while an added light-blue pen depicted the end of innocence. In the center was a woman—presumably herself—surrounded by this conflagration.

She finished the last stroke and stood back. She was pleased with the imagery of it all. "There," she said. "I might buy this one." I probably would be the only one, she thought. Like all artists, she needed encouragement. But there would be none of that today.

Stella was confident that her identity hadn't been compromised yet, and thought she ought to go to dinner and see a show that evening. She hoped to pick up something that might lead her to Bob, or at least give her a hint. It was her only choice, too. She suspected that Ms. Ortiz might have an inside track or even be part of a scheme to enrich her husband and other compatriots. She told herself she needed to go into the lion's den to see how they reacted.

Before she left for the club, Stella started sketching another picture of the knob. In this one, the bare bark of the trees, combined with a few evergreens in the foreground, took on a new life, preparing the stage for the knob in the distance.

Stella heard a rumbling and turned to see a red pickup truck with a black-and-white stripe pulling up to the spot where she was standing. It stopped right behind her.

CHAPTER 18

Hopefully, Kentucky

B.J. had begun his trip back from McHune County right after lunch, with a tarpaulin covering the truck bed that carried his new equipment—four rifles and four handguns and what seemed like enough ammunition to equip an army platoon. He hated guns, but he wanted to be able to employ every option available to deal with potential assassins. He even contemplated making poison darts for the old bow-and-arrow that he'd used as a child.

After he'd bought the weapons and ammunition, the gun dealer, Mark Julius, had spent an hour showing him some basics about how to use them. Julius, 45, sported a military crew cut, a gold tooth, and a black tank-top with a drawing of a laughing rattlesnake bearing the legend, "Just *Try* to Tread on Me!" B.J. had respected him for years as an expert on guns.

"Let's rock and roll!" Julius exclaimed, by way of getting started. After 10 tries of aiming at tin cans sitting on posts, B. J knew how to load, aim and shoot with some success, but he realized that he'd need a lot more practice to be able to hit a target consistently.

"Mark, don't tell anyone about these purchases," B.J. said. "You know, Mom and I live in an isolated spot, and I'm worried that some druggie might try to break into our house and steal guns and Mom's meds. There's a new shooting range near the Copperhead Club," he added. "I'm going to go there and practice until I'm more confident and feel better about all this."

"Well, I don't think you'll shoot yourself in the foot," Mark had replied. "Just remember to keep the safety on until you absolutely need it. I hope you won't need to."

B.J.'s animus toward firearms had been strong, but now he could see why people were attracted to guns: Power. "You can either be scared of your own shadow, or you can swagger with the knowledge that you have a .45-caliber pistol tucked in a holster around your waist," Mark Julius had told him. "You know the saying, 'Knowledge is power?' Well, give me a guy with knowledge and one with a shotgun, and you tell me who's gonna win out," he'd said with a smile.

When B.J. got into his truck, he tried to memorize Mark's pointers about how all the weapons worked and what their strengths and weaknesses were. His heart raced and his head pounded as he remembered that he'd only hit the cans three times.

Passing the Copperhead Club on his way home, he noticed a strange sight. A pretty woman was sketching a picture in the dead of winter, and he stopped, admiring her rendition of the knob. "That's very nice," he said aloud, surprising himself that he was trying to have a conversation with her. She looked somewhat familiar.

"Thank you," she said. "Are you the guy who owns the land there past the gate?"

"Yes."

"Would it be okay for me to move inside your gate? I have a feeling the view is much better," she said.

"It is," B.J. said, "but how do I know you won't roam all over our property?"

"You can either watch me or trust me," she said.

"I'll think about it," B.J. responded. "But I can't do it now."

"I'm not going to be here long," she said. "Only a day or two more. I'll even do a painting for you, for free."

"There's something you should know," he said. "This can be a dangerous place, and if I were you, I would go back home."

"Well, I don't have a home right now. And why? What's going on? I am going to the Copperhead Club tonight, and I certainly want to be safe. Besides, I'm going to get a ride from my new friends, Maybelle or Jimmy," she said.

"That's all I can say," said B.J., and he rolled up the truck window, drove over the ridge, opened the gate to his land, and drove up the hill, leaving behind marks of his truck's tire treads. Stella looked at her watch. It was 4 p.m.

At that moment in Purcells, Maybelle was looking at her watch, too, as she waited to see whether the patient she'd driven there was returning to Hopefully.

The hospital said the patient would need another test on the next day, and that it would be better if she stayed with a relative in Purcells for a night before returning home.

Nodding, Maybelle went to her van to head back to the Copperhead Club, only to find that the engine wouldn't start. The battery seemed okay, but the crankshaft just wouldn't turn over. It was almost closing time for local service stations, so she had to find help quickly. The one car repair shop she knew was pretty reliable, but it was located on the other side of town.

Maybelle first tried hitching a ride, but most people drove on past her. Finally, a familiar face—an old friend—stopped to give her a ride. The station was open for gasoline and soft drinks, but the mechanics had all gone home hours ago, and the young man in charge didn't know the first thing about fixing cars. At Maybelle's prodding, he called his boss and discovered that he'd gone to a local eatery with his family. The station's owner would come down to look at the problem, but it might be a couple of hours. And there was no guarantee that he could fix it, since he might have to order parts. In the meantime, the van would have to be towed from wherever Maybelle had left it.

Maybelle looked at her watch. It was 5 p.m.—time for her to meet

Ellie at the Copperhead Club.

When Stella, still getting used to being called Ellie, walked into the club, she asked if someone could keep her art kit and backpack until she went home. She was supposed to have dinner with someone, and was waiting for her to drive from Purcells, she explained. She waited 15 minutes when the woman at the desk said there was someone on the phone for her. The call was from Maybelle, who explained that her van had died and that she probably wouldn't be able to keep their dinner date if she didn't get some help soon. "I don't want you leaving there with Billingsley—I'm very uncomfortable with that man," Maybelle added.

"Come on, Maybelle," Stella said. "I'm a big girl, and I know how to handle myself. I've told you that already."

"But you don't know this guy," Maybelle said. "I just don't trust him. Can't tell you exactly why, but I wish you wouldn't go out with him."

"Well, Maybelle, I trusted you to pick me up, and now you can't. So how do you suggest I get back to my room?"

Maybelle said she'd try to find someone to give Ellie a lift and would let her know, even though it might be difficult to find her in the mass of bodies stomping to live music at the club. Stella said fine, and she would expect a call. Now, after all that trouble and Maybelle's behavior, Stella was confused. "What is driving this woman?" she asked herself. "She's become overly solicitous—why?"

Just then, Jimmy Billingsley, in leather jeans, boots, and an open shirt showing a tuft of chest hair, walked in the door and came over to say hello. He was polite and charming, and asked about her sketches. "Did Copperhead Knob show you its real personality?" he asked. "I'll bet you demanded it and got it. You would be hard to resist."

Smiling, Stella said any of her discussions with any hills that flatter her were off the record, but "they've never gone all the way, and they never will." Jimmy understood the putdown, and backed away from his attempt at being charming. He told her to enjoy the evening with her first big encounter with country music. "And, if you need a ride back to the hotel, I'm available," he said. Noting that he was scheduled for the first set at 9:15, he took his guitar and walked through the dining area to a door at the back of the restaurant. Behind it, music played, people drank, and the ambience was far different from the club's sedate country dining room, which seemed to appeal to older people.

Stella felt a little apprehensive, but she would go in as soon as she had a sandwich and a drink. She wasn't sure whether this was just a crazy waste of time or a possible link to Bob. Maybe Jimmy could help her, maybe not. Her gut instinct told her never to trust a stranger, but she might have to if there was a chance that he or she might know where Bob was.

There was only one door from the restaurant side to get to the honky-tonk part of the Copperhead Club, but Stella later learned that people could also enter it from the back of the building without being seen in the restaurant. The music was loud, the talking was even louder, and there was constant movement by the largely young crowd. Waiting for a drink, Stella stood behind a woman who appeared to be about 20. She wore a pair of skin tight jeans and a sequined tank-top—a little chilly for a February night, Stella thought. When the woman looked around, Stella introduced herself. "Excuse me, hi. Do you know where the bathroom is?"

The woman responded, snapping her chewing gum. "It's over there by the bar. I'm going that way. You can follow me."

Stella followed the tight jeans to the dingy bathroom, which was barely the size of a broom closet and had graffiti all over the walls. She thought about walking out of the club entirely, but decided she'd have just one more drink. Luckily, when she came out, there was one stool at the end of the bar next to where Geraldine had perched herself. She, too, appeared to be waiting for someone, but Stella didn't pry.

"Hey, again. I'm Geraldine," she said with a smile, sipping on a cranberry vodka. "Where're you from?"

Stella ignored her question. "I'm Ellie. I'm a painter, and I sketched the Knob this afternoon," she said. "Lovely place. I'm also thinking of doing some portraits."

"It's not very pretty right now, but just wait until the dogwoods and redbuds come out—it's real pretty then," Geraldine said. "That's cool about the portraits. I wonder if you could paint my boyfriend, Roger, and me?"

Stella said she could, but she would not be in town long. "Oh," Geraldine said, "Roger works right here at the club as a maintenance man."

Stella jumped at the chance. "Is he here tonight?" she asked. Geraldine pointed to a young man with a beard, who was standing next to the bar. He wasn't quite so casual as others, wearing a pair of slacks and a blue dress shirt, without a tie.

"Wait here," said Geraldine, walking over to Roger to tell him. He nodded, and flashed Stella a wave to let her know he'd be over in a little while.

At this point, Jimmy and his band, *The Avengers*, took over. Jimmy told the audience there were many important people there tonight, including Ellie, an artist, who came here to "paint these old hills" and "show the world what a pretty place this is."

"Raise your hand, Ellie!" Jimmy said. Stella waved, feeling warmth in her face.

"Does he always call out people's names like that?" Stella asked Geraldine.

"Oh yeah. It's part of his thing. Last week, he mentioned me, and a guy visiting from Louisville who was a horse trainer."

Stella, the connoisseur of fine opera, ballet and symphony music, had not yet acquired an appreciation for contemporary pop, rock, country, or bluegrass music. She wondered if she'd be able to stand the noise that was about to come. She'd expected twangy country music, the kind she used to hear on the radio as a young girl at her aunt's house. She hadn't realized that in recent decades country music had evolved into a more mainstream sound, with a heavy influence from rock. The old-fashioned country songs, slow and sentimental and often tragic, were still a part of any country musician's repertoire, but new singers and new musicians had broadened the genre for a wider audience. Jimmy did a little bit of both, combining older songs with the new. His voice ranged from mellow baritone to deep rich bass sounds, and his fingering of the guitar strings showed a talent she couldn't believe. Although Jimmy had three musicians backing him up, he was clearly the star, and the audience appreciated every note.

She couldn't believe she liked it so much—and she applauded loudly. Jimmy accepted all the congratulations from the clientele, and then came over to her. "One more set, and I'll be glad to take you home," he said.

"I'm still waiting for my ride, and I think she'll be here soon, but thanks anyway," Stella said. She looked at the clock. It was close to 11 p.m.

Stella went back into the dining room to check whether she'd gotten a telephone call. Maybelle had left a message. She still hadn't been able to get the car fixed, and it might be tomorrow before she could. But Maybelle again urged her not to ride with Jimmy. Stella was beginning to feel uneasy about it, but the choices were narrowing. There was no cab company in Hopefully. The hotel didn't have a bus, or any workers who'd be able to get her. Maybe she could find someone else whom she could trust to drive her back. She went back to the clubroom.

Geraldine and Roger came over to say they were grateful that she could paint them together, since they were planning to get married. Stella said she'd be happy to do it, and told them not to worry about the price. And then she couldn't help herself. Impulsively, she reached into her purse and pulled out a photo of Bob. "I was wondering if you've seen this man around here," she said. "He's an old high school buddy I've been trying to find, and supposedly lives around here somewhere. I can't find his name in the phone book. He goes by Bob."

They both looked at the photo and glanced at one another, and

Roger said, "No, sorry, but if you leave your number, we can call you if we do." They seemed to be telling the truth. She thanked them and asked if they could do a sitting for her the day after tomorrow—in front of the Copperhead Knob. She was about to ask them for a ride to the motel, but Geraldine got a call from her mother telling her to come home quickly because she was feeling sick. "Roger will have to take me," she said. Stella looked around the room and decided that Jimmy was her best choice.

After his last set, Jimmy came over to her and offered a ride. "You've got to promise to be a good boy and get me home safely, with no other stops," she said. He nodded, and she smiled. "Let's go," she said.

When Jimmy pulled the SUV out of the parking lot, he turned left instead of right. Stella immediately wanted to know why.

"I have something I want to show you in this moonlight, he said. "It's close and too good to miss. It'll only take a minute."

"No!" she said emphatically. "You promised not to make any stops. I need to get back to Hopefully now."

"Relax," Jimmy said, "I'm not going to hurt you. Here—I'm turning to go to the river, just over that little ridge. Here you can see Copperhead Canyon in all its glory. It's why they use the word copperhead around here so much. It's a local landmark that you've got to see."

Jimmy locked the doors, and Stella frantically tried to find the switch on her side that would unlock it. He pulled to a stop, and said, "If you look to your left, you can see the vision of a copperhead in the water." He put his arm around her and she grabbed it and pushed it back to him.

When she did this, Jimmy kissed her on the mouth, and grabbed her breast. "Stop it!" she screamed.

"Come on, it's what you want," Jimmy said, putting his hand on her other breast and pulling her toward him. "You know I'm not going to hurt you. You're too beautiful for me to do that."

She fought back with a punch to his nose, which sent him reeling backward while she unlocked the door. "Damn, you little witch he yelled.

She managed to wrest open the door and push herself halfway through it, but he pulled her back inside. She bit his arm with a ferocity she never thought she had and broke loose from him, jumping on the sandy ground outside. He went after her as she ran, grabbed her and smacked her in the face. She went down.

Just then bright lights went on, and she was blinded momentarily. They were truck lights, and in front of them stood a man. She realized she'd seen him earlier. He had a rifle in his hand. "Don't move, Billingsley—stop it now, or I'll blow off your head!" B.J. barked. He'd parked his truck at a spot where Jimmy couldn't have seen it. It had occurred to him that she was talking about Billingsley in the late afternoon when she'd mentioned 'a new friend Jimmy' might drive her home. He feared that the mayor's son would eye this new woman in town as his latest prey. He would go to "The Rock" just in case his suspicion was correct. If it was, he would be there to save her.

Jimmy stopped in his tracks and expressed surprise to see who was threatening him. "Is this the Doofus I see before me, trying to interfere with a little lovemaking?"

With this, B.J. fired twice, and ripped a hole in a tree right above Jimmy's head. A small limb fell on him, knocking him down.

"Okay, okay, Doofus," he said. "I'm sorry. It was just a misunderstanding."

B.J. asked Stella if she'd left anything inside the SUV. Yes, she said, her back pack on the front side.

"Go over and get the bag," B.J. told her. She did it quickly, without comment.

Then B.J. ordered Jimmy to throw his cell phone in the sand. He did, without saying a word.

"Go now, or I'll kill you and bury you at the bottom of the river with a rock tied to your body," B.J. said, surprising even himself. "No one will find you. And if I were you, I'd skip town now so you can't be arrested tomorrow after this young lady tells her story."

"Okay, okay, I'm going, but if she presses charges, I got a bunch of witnesses saying how she came on to me—sorry, but it's true," Jimmy said as he jumped in his SUV and took off. B.J. watched until the night sky covered the SUV's taillights and there were no more engine sounds—only silence.

Stella was still reeling from the blows, almost as if she'd had a concussion. B.J. gently lifted her in the truck. "We're going to the hospital in Purcells," he said.

"No, no, no, I can't," Stella insisted. "I'll be all right. No one can know that I'm here. It's a matter of life or death. Please trust me. I know I'll be okay."

"I can't risk it—it could be a fatal concussion, for all I know." B.J. countered.

She implored him again. "Please, I just want to get in bed and get some rest. I will be all right. I'm not very woozy right now."

"No, you have got to go to the hospital," he said.

"Please," she said. "I'll be fine after I get out of this place. You can't take me to the hospital now. Please believe me."

"Okay, is there someone I should call and let them know you've been hurt, or someone who can pick you up? Do you live anywhere near here?"

"No!" Stella yelled. "I know this doesn't make sense right now, but I'm from out of town, and I can't let anyone know I'm here. Just don't ask me about it—okay?"

B.J. was taken aback by the mysteriousness of this woman, but considering he was stocking guns to fight off possible assassins, he really was not in a position to question it. He looked at her closely this time, as if to understand something he had not understood before. "Okay, let's go," he said. He helped her to his truck.

"Where are we going?" Stella asked.

"Home. You now have permission to visit my property. But I'll be watching you. My mom's there. You need to tell me how you feel, so that if your condition changes, I can get you to the emergency room. Don't worry. I'm harmless. But I need to hide you from Billingsley so he can't come after you."

B.J. was afraid that Jimmy would be waiting in ambush if he went down the same road. He turned right at the road ahead and proceeded to take a roundabout way back home. But first he checked with Stella to see if she felt better. She said the pain was easing, and she didn't feel as dizzy. "Then I'm driving into downtown Hopefully. You'll go to the hotel and pick up your luggage and other stuff. Pay your bill by putting cash on the bed—that is, if you have cash."

"I do," Stella said. She wondered whether she should insist that he just drop her off, but something in her gut told her she could trust him.

B.J. sped through the hilly terrain, and Stella closed her eyes to avoid sickness. She went into the motel to get her things, put the money on the bed, along with a big thank you and a tip. She explained that she had to leave early because of an illness in the family.

It was then that she saw her bloody face and her black eye in the mirror. Her shirt was torn and her body was covered with bruises. She had intense pain in her neck.

"Oh, my God, look at me," she said, with a gasp. Tears started to come. In the bathroom, she splashed cold water on her face, and, grabbing a fistful of Kleenex she slowly, carefully, wiped away some of the dried blood. Then, with a solemn, intense look she stared at herself. "You are the new Stella," she told the image in the mirror. "And there's one thing I promise you from now on: No one else will treat you this way anymore, even if I have to die in the process. I will not back down. I never, *ever* will let this happen to you again."

She came out to B.J.'s truck and said, "Okay, let's go. I hope no one knows where I am."

They rode in silence, and soon they passed the club and headed up the hill to B.J.'s house. He put her in his old room and told her he'd be in a room just down the hall. He brought her an ice pack to put on her eye.

And he asked if she wanted water. He was so gentle and kind.

Someone else came to the door. "He's a friend," B.J. assured her. "We call him The Baron. He's the town banker. He won't hurt you. Get some rest."

She could hear them talking for the longest time before she finally fell asleep.

CHAPTER 19

Hopefully, Kentucky

The Baron sat in his office, looking at bar charts and bank deposit trends next to a line of perfectly aligned Cincinnati Reds bobbleheads. He'd decided not to go to Molly's. He hoped she would understand. When The Baron had something on his mind, whether it was a biscuit or bank receipt, he was on it like a bloodhound for hours— or even days—until he had satisfied his quest. It was a well-worn joke among bank employees to call the back office the 'hi-Baron-nation' den on some days. He needed to look further at the statistics. He wanted to get a better idea of why the deposit totals had increased so much in the past couple of years. He wondered why some of the mom-and-pop businesses in the area were depositing thousands of dollars more each week than they had been at the same time a year ago, or maybe longer than that. He suspected that some of the small businesses outside of Hopefully were being used to launder drug receipts, passing them off as profits to the outside world and to federal tax authorities. "What else could it be?" he wondered. "It sure as heck isn't just food and really good cocktails. Is it a prostitution ring? Is someone making a fortune off illegal cockfights?"

The Baron knew that money laundering posed a conflict-of-interest for bankers. They got more deposits, of course, but many of these would be illegal. Companies engaging in money laundering in this way mingled dirty money with regular receipts, making it hard to tell which

165

was which. And this was usually the first step in a more complex money laundering system that involved a number of corporations.

In recent years, he had turned his attention to the Copperhead Club for its mixture of food and entertainment. One thing that caught his eye was that the club had chalked up a 25% increase in receipts over the past year—a highly suspect figure. Three years before that, it had barely been breaking even. Could it be that all or most of these extra gains had come from drug receipts?

It was true that the club had been far more successful recently with the addition of a popular musician, Jimmy Billingsley. Also, the new owner and manager, Lucinda Ortiz, had done a good job in separating the restaurant from the more raucous room in the back, which was the honky-tonk part of the operation. But that large an increase in so short a time was an anomaly. In the past, a really hot business might see an increase of 8% in that kind of time period; a jump of 25% was a whole different story. This was Hopefully, not New York City.

If The Baron's suspicions were true, it would be very difficult for him to disentangle profits from dirty money, so he made a mental note to contact the IRS to express his concerns. One side of him was reluctant to do this, since it would reduce the size of deposits from the club. He knew the manager, Lucinda Ortiz, very well and found her very credible and seemingly very honest. But there was no question about the statistics. They didn't lie.

He pulled a bottle of bourbon from his drawer and poured himself a drink, straight up. He'd seen so much over the years in the growth of his bank, and now there was talk of consolidation. He wanted to do his own due diligence on the bank and its customers before the sale took place, if indeed it ever would take place.

Something else was bothering him. He couldn't get his arms around it, but it had to do with a sense of danger in the area. The number of drug addicts had grown markedly in recent years, and it seemed that not much was being done about it. At the local McDonald's there were kids with holey jeans, flip-flops, and unkempt hair who liked to hang out at the edge of the parking lot for hours, huddling around cars and sitting on the curb. Whenever a car passed on the way to the drive-through, they'd morph from loud, obnoxious wildebeests to quiet lambs, with glaring, paranoid eyes. Even the federal government seemed lax in investigating the various reports of drug use in the area. And, surprisingly, the community seemed willing to tolerate the practice.

The Baron also feared that drug dealers or moonshiners might be paying off city and county officials. He had little proof of that, but there clearly were grounds for suspicion.

That could be the reason for poor enforcement. If public officials were accepting bribes, The Baron reasoned, they were hiding it well. He had known these officials for years, and never thought for a second that his old friends would be involved in such schemes. After all, they had sworn to uphold the public trust and set a good example for the rest of the citizenry. Mayor Billingsley a crook? No, he couldn't even imagine that. He and his family had served the town for years. But he remembered that Molly had not been one of the Billingsleys' best friends.

When Molly left, she felt that the authorities had become more lenient in prosecuting some employees of the police department. As she saw it, some of them should have been in jail for their misdeeds, such as stealing parking violation receipts, most of them near the courthouse when people were on jury duty or when they were eating at the café. This was how the police department made money, Molly said, and it was tainted money to her.

He smiled when he thought of Molly and her toughness and her clear sense of right and wrong, which demanded that even the tiniest misdemeanor should be prosecuted to the fullest. No looking the other way for her. She never hesitated to punish a crime, no matter how small. That may not be the way the world works, but it's the way it ought to work, The Baron said to himself. "Justice has no favorites, except for those who apply the law fairly and without prejudice." He stayed up later than he'd intended that night, checking his desk clock to discover that it was nearing 2 a.m. He shut off his computer, popped a cinnamon jawbreaker in his mouth, lined up his bobbleheads again, packed up his stuff, and headed for the door when the telephone rang. It was B.J. "I need your help right away."

"Why, what's wrong? Molly...?" The Baron asked.

"Wait until you get here," B.J. said. "It's very important. I'll be in my office in the barn. It's not about Mom. She's okay."

The Baron was on his way.

CHAPTER 20

Hopefully, Kentucky

In the spare bedroom on the first floor of the Matson farmhouse, Stella awoke to see a wrinkled old woman with salt-and-pepper hair pointing a gun right between her eyes. The woman's hands were quivering and the gun touched Stella's nose. "Who the hell are you, bitch, and what are you doing in my house?" the old woman shouted. "Don't make a move or you're dead!"

Stella screamed. The old woman's hand was shaking, and so was the gun. Stunned and horrified, Stella was afraid the woman would pull the trigger any second if she made another sound or moved an inch. Suddenly someone ran in shouting, "No, no, Mom! It's okay, it's okay."

Responding to her son's shouts, Molly lowered the gun and looked at Stella with some doubt. "Who the hell is she?" she asked B.J. suspiciously.

"She survived a rape attempt last night," B.J. said. "And I brought her here. You were asleep when she got here. She needs our help. Now, let me have the gun."

"Well, since you say so, but you could have told me," Molly said, slowly moving the barrel of the gun away from Stella's nose.

B.J. said it was so late when they got home that he'd decided to let Molly sleep through the conversation. He gently took the gun, which was still touching part of Stella's cheek.

"It's not loaded, Ellie, not to worry," he said.

"The hell you say," Molly said. "You can't hide ammunition from me.

I'm a cop, remember."

Confirming this by checking the gun, B.J. said loudly and with authority, "I want the rest of the ammunition, Mom, and I want it right now. You know you aren't supposed to have loaded weapons at your age." Molly sheepishly handed over a box of bullets that she'd stuck in her apron. "You better not be hiding any other bullets," he told her.

Molly said she had no other ammunition hidden anywhere. B.J. took his mom at her word, realizing he could never trust her and her uncanny ability to find where he had hidden it.

Stella was struggling to get her heart rate down, staring straight at the ceiling and mumbling, "oh God, oh God, oh God." Molly apologized. She'd thought Stella was an intruder, she explained—someone who'd come there to find the jewelry box or B.J.'s coin collection under the bed.

The Baron then came running into the room frantically, wiping sweat from his face with a monogrammed white handkerchief. He breathed a sigh of relief that there was no one dead or bleeding anywhere. "I'm sorry, Molly, I didn't see you last night. I had to work late. It was past midnight and I was going to go home when B.J. told me to come here quickly." The Baron said hello to Stella, who was still frozen in place with a deer-in-the-headlights gaze.

B.J. told Molly that Stella needed to shower and dress and then get her sore neck looked at. "How much pain do you have this morning?" he asked Stella.

"It's not as intense," Stella said. "There's a little soreness in the neck, but no lasting head pain. I feel like the time when I had a bike wreck 10 years ago. In a few days, it was much better, but I had a headache for a week."

"I've got some pills," said Molly, suddenly warming up to Stella. "I believe they'll help. You need a real doctor to look at that neck and the rest of you. Who in the hell did this to you? I will go out and personally kill the bastard."

"I'll tell you in a minute, Mom, but he's a real lowlife, and that's another story. We need to take care of this woman first," B.J. said. "She says her name is Ellie Heinz and she says she doesn't want anyone to know about the rape attempt or any charges filed. Why? Because she says she came here to spy on her husband, who may have come here to meet up with her girlfriend from back home."

Stella nodded her head.

"But it's a lie," B.J. said, "and she's not very credible. After we got home, I pulled up Google News and saw her face. I realized where I'd seen her before, and I know who she really is. This is Stella Eads Jasper. Her husband disappeared after she and the world discovered he was part of a major league money laundering operation. She's done an outstanding job of disguising herself—outstanding. She fooled me, too, until I looked up some of that testimony on YouTube, and there isn't much doubt. Her husband escaped with millions of dollars. No one knows where he is. But isn't it strange that she's here now? Does she know something the rest of the world doesn't know—the location of her husband, who left her virtually penniless?"

"Good lord," Molly said, waving to The Baron. "I need a glass of Scotch."

Stella began crying as she shook her head and nodded, confirming what B.J. was saying. She feared the shotgun was going to end up between her eyes again at any moment.

"I thought she looked familiar," Molly said, "but she certainly fooled me."

B.J. went on addressing his family. "What I don't know is whether she's in cahoots with her husband to meet somewhere here in Kentucky and escape with the loot, or if she has somehow, someway, found out where he is, and he doesn't know that she knows the truth. She either wants the money or she wants to do him severe harm, possibly wipe him off the planet. What I can't figure out is why the hell she would want to hook up with Billingsley."

"That good for nothing, low-down scoundrel. I could have guessed it was him," Molly said.

"Mom, I told you that that's another story," B.J. said. "We'll talk about him later. We have to deal with this situation first."

Stella sat up and spoke firmly. "Billingsley—yes, he's an asshole, but my husband Bob Jasper is much worse. Yes, I have told myself I'd like to kill him because he's taken away my life," she said. "But I don't think I really can. Right now, I just want him found, and prosecuted. I want to know why he did what he did, to ask him why he ran away—as I think he did—with my closest friend, Alicia. I swear to God."

"What made you think he was here?" The Baron asked.

"I came here because he had written 'Copperhead Club' on a notepad at home. I could make it out by looking at the indentations and then using a light pencil to shade over it. I think there was a phone number, but I couldn't make it out."

"Copperhead Club could mean a lot of things—maybe the name of golf clubs, maybe some other places with the same name," said The Baron. "Maybe you're just guessing."

Stella said that she had checked the name on Google and it does refer to a golf club as well as other private clubs, but this one in Kentucky is so secluded that it is a good place to hide. "He told me not long ago about airline transfers recently through Louisville, a place that he rarely mentioned before. Although it was a bit of a guess then— maybe woman's intuition—I really believe that I may find Bob hiding somewhere nearby."

"And why hasn't someone in Washington noticed or said that you are missing?" The Baron asked.

"I don't know," Stella said. "Maybe they're waiting to see if I get spotted, or maybe they're too embarrassed right now to admit that I gave them the slip. But it's only been a few days since I left and made my way here without getting detected. My goal is to find him and look him in the eye and ask him how he could have done this thing to the person he supposedly loved. I'm not here for loot or money—I just want closure," Stella said, weeping.

Molly told Stella about her work as a policewoman in the past and said everything works the best if people go through the proper channels.

"Mom, I am afraid the local police, and the sheriff, too, have been tempted by the dollars that they can make by failing to prosecute people the way you did in the old days," B.J. said. "I suspect they may be on the payroll of some of the big moonshine dealers or maybe even drug dealers. If so, they won't prosecute or arrest her if she tells her story, and then her life will be in big danger. Don't you remember the case of the shooting down on Main Street where drug paraphernalia was found and no one ever did anything?"

Molly thought for a second. She had been Madame Enforcement in the old days. "But if the enforcement process is corrupted, we have to replace what we've got," she said. "These people are the worst sort of vermin. If Chief Larson is corrupt, I want to be there for his arrest." And for the first time in her life, she felt that perhaps too hasty a prosecution could spoil the broth of a developing criminal case—especially a case that could lead to her son's being charged with a crime.

But B.J. knew that the old Molly was still there, hard as ever. To her, he knew, these steps could be mere excuses on the path of blurring justice. She'd been successful in the past in following a clear path of prosecuting the commission of a crime, no matter how many shades of gray could dampen the lines of enforcement. Now, these strange and complex facts—plus her son's involvement with this woman—had created a curtain of gray that softened her black-and-white world.

Then B.J. spoke again. "Mom, I have something else to tell you. It happened as I was taking photos and enjoying the scenery on Butchers Knob, a truly isolated place. I took photos of a man dressed like a local, but I've never seen him before. There was another man, too, but I can't make out his face on my camera. He was dressed in city clothes. I believe the man in the chair heard me when I moved just enough for him to tell someone was there. He just casually took out his cell phone and called some bodyguards in an SUV who'd been parked near the top of the hill. I ran like crazy, got in my truck at the end of the road near the top of the hill, and roared down the road, only to see the SUV coming straight at me. We sideswiped each other, but I was able to hold on and avoid falling down the cliff while the SUV rolled over and fell to the bottom. One person survived, but he's in a coma. I didn't report this to police or anyone else because I didn't want them to come after me if this one person survived. And he might. That means we may all be in danger."

"Benjamin James—that's illegal, and you know it!" she shouted at B.J. in the same tone she used to scold him when he was a three-year-old and had snatched Oreos when he wasn't supposed to. "You did something I never thought you would do, and you've disappointed me to the core."

"It's self-defense, Mom, but it's also defense for our family. If this one person survives and identifies me, or even my car, vaguely, people will tell them who I am, and they'll be coming after me," he said. "I couldn't do that to you. I know these policemen, including the sheriff and maybe the mayor, too, are corrupt. When's the last time they prosecuted someone in a drug crime? Back when you were still on the job, I'd guess. And we all know that drugs are everywhere in this county and they're ruining an entire generation."

"It's true that all the enforcement took place before the current Mr. Billingsley took over," Molly conceded. "His dad was a very good man when he was mayor and he supported an active anti-drug policy. But I do have my doubts about his son, Stewart."

"Look, Molly," The Baron interjected, "you need to listen to B.J. Half the town agrees with what he's saying, and I've also seen it from another side. I suspect that some local companies, including the Copperhead Club, are laundering dirty money, and no one's doing anything about it. I hate to think that Lucinda Ortiz is involved in such a thing, but I'm going to inform the federal authorities in Louisville of my suspicion, and I hope there's some follow-up."

"There's nothing on this planet I hate worse than a corrupt public official," Molly blurted out, her forehead veins popping from the inner conflict she felt between tough enforcement and situations that blur the lines between right and wrong.

Stella couldn't restrain herself any longer. "You said you took photos of a man you didn't recognize. Where's Butcher's Knob? When did you take the picture? Do you think the man could be Bob? Please, please, let me see the photos."

"Maybe it *is* Bob," B.J. said. "I can show you the pictures this afternoon, but first we're going to a shooting range over in the next county so that you can learn how to use a weapon. I need to know if you're with me and are trustworthy. I have to protect my family, but you're free to go if you want. I'm not getting into the kidnapping game. If you go, you have to promise me you won't jump on your husband's side, if indeed he *is* here. If you leave us, you can't see the photos I took. And know if you do leave and try to hurt us, there may not be someone pulling the gun away from your forehead next time."

"I can't wait," Stella said. "Please believe me; I want to find Bob and I want to send him to prison." Stella said. "I have to see those photos *now*. You've got to let me see them. It'll only take a minute for me to recognize him. If it isn't Bob, then I'm probably on a wild goose chase, and I'll leave."

B.J. looked at his watch. "Only a minute? Suppose it's him? What are you going to do? Report him and go back home?"

"I honestly don't know," Stella said. "I just want to know *why*, that's it—why would he treat me that way, giving me no warning, treating me like trash? I'll be honest. I *have* thought of killing the bastard. I've come this far down on the scale of what it means to be a human being. He took everything from me—everything. Don't you understand?"

"I understand, but you can't kill him," B.J. said. "I don't think you're that kind of person. I can't let you get close to a gun unless you promise that you won't try to kill him."

Stella thought for a minute. Her hesitation made B.J. a little nervous.

"Okay," she said, "I promise. If it is him, I'll alert the FBI and they can arrest him." B.J. wasn't so sure she wasn't just trying to please him at that moment rather than to make a firm promise. He knew it would be a gamble on his part if indeed she should come face-to-face with Bob Jasper. "Let's go to the computer out in the barn," he said.

He took her to his studio in the barn. She was expecting a mess inside, with lots of papers and books and photos everywhere, but not in this case. Although the furniture was old, B.J. was almost obsessively neat. There were some very nice paintings on the wall, but she didn't look at them closely because she was obsessed with the idea of seeing her husband.

B.J. led her to the computer, and inserted his photo memory card in the slot. With a few quick strokes, there was the photo of the man reading a book, with a beer beside him.

"Oh my God," said Stella. "He's camouflaged his face with that red beard and mustache. He has thick brown hair, you know, and he always gets it trimmed every week. He's usually very well-groomed. Let me look closer. Just look at that long red hair. If that's him, it's a very good disguise. Do you see the way he cocks his head at an angle when he is reading? That's the way Bob reads. And he likes to read outside like this when he can. I can't tell from this, but he looks to be roughly the same size. I'm trying to picture Bob behind all that facial hair and the cap, and him being out of his business suit. I'd have to say, yes, this man could easily be him."

"You aren't 100% sure?" B.J. asked.

"Well, 75%, anyway."

Stella noticed the beer bottle beside him. "Zoom in closer on that," she said. "Look, it's Tutankhamen! Oh, my God—the same beer down here, too! Where in the hell did he get that while he was in hiding? He *loves* the stuff, I'm telling you, and that does it for me. That's really him. I'm 100% sure."

She looked at the computer screen and put her nose right up against it. "I'm coming after you, you bastard!" she cried. "That King Tut beer did you in. Oh, did I tell you, B.J.—it costs at least $100 a bottle, one of the most expensive in the world? I tasted it, but it didn't turn me on like it did him."

Stella wanted to know where the lair was. "About 10 miles or so, in a very secluded hollow," B.J. replied. "I suspect he's found another place somewhere, but I don't have the slightest idea where. It was a rental house. I checked that out. This is a small point, but I'm going to see a friend of mine I've known since high school. If there's Tutankhamen beer sold around here, he might know since he does a lot of business delivering to stores in Hopefully. They might sell it at the Copperhead Club. Bob could have ordered it and had it dropped off there, or he could have used a fictitious name and had it delivered to one of his helpers."

"Bob's not a man to take chances, especially stupid chances," Stella said. "I suspect he bought it somewhere on his way here. I can't believe he had it delivered."

B.J. had some second thoughts about not turning himself in immediately when he was nearly killed by the man's hired guns. If he could prove that he had found Bob Jasper was hiding in the county, it obviously would help his case. But one fact stood over them all: He had refused to report his role in the crash that had taken the lives of three men, and perhaps another.

B.J. worried that he himself would be the next target if the lone survivor were able to give a general description of the car and possibly even his face. The man's bodyguards would be coming at him very quickly, with guns locked and loaded. The leaders of the town and the county knew B.J. as an odd loner who traveled the hills, constantly taking photos. He really didn't fit in. Some would love to put him in jail immediately because they were uncomfortable around him. Others called him a laughing stock and a momma's-boy. B.J. had developed a strong bent toward paranoia. In Hopefully, that was one way for an offbeat personality like him to survive.

B.J. showed her the second man whom he had photographed. His face was blurred because he apparently had moved just as the shutter clicked. He had an authoritative look about him, but B.J. couldn't place him as anyone he'd seen in Hopefully or the surrounding areas.

"The navy blue jacket and khaki pants are like a uniform among some government workers, particularly staff people, but I can't make him out in this photo—it's too blurred," Stella said. "Seems clear that he's not from around here, though."

B.J. nodded his head in agreement.

Stella was mystified. "Even though this man's face is blurred, I feel like I know him," she said. "It's in the way he looks and dresses. Maybe if we kept on looking, we could find him."

"How so?" B.J. asked.

"If he *has* been here, somebody probably has seen his face," Stella reasoned. "My money says that this person works in D.C. and came down to see Bob for whatever reason. I have no ideas otherwise. It appears to be someone he trusts." Tears came to her eyes. The hurt was still there. Where was the trust with her?

"Look, Bob Jasper has destroyed my life," she went on. "Look at me, for Christ's sake. I want to stare at him—to see if I can understand it, to see why I was so blind all those years. I was married to a fucking criminal who told me he loved me."

B.J. said he couldn't figure out why such a man wound up here in Kentucky. Sure, the hollows were isolated in some places, and sure, no one expects a prominent person to come here and stay. But there were plenty of other unlikely places where life would be more comfortable. Maybe Jasper did the best he could under the fast unfolding circumstances, and he knew that he would take a giant risk every time he moved in public, especially if he tried to leave the country. B.J. said Jasper might have left Kentucky and headed for some other spot. But the danger might increase exponentially if he tried to move, because the criminals for whom he had worked might try to kill him as someone who knew too much. Obviously, the government was trying to find him and the well-dressed man, too.

"Stella, there were a load of people in the car when it went over the cliff, and I suspect he has more protectors than that," B.J. said. "We can try to find him in this area, if he hasn't already slipped away. I'll try to help you, but if we do find him, we must stop and go public. Confronting him is too dangerous, and downright foolhardy."

Stella listened to him and nodded her head affirmatively as she wiped her tears away. But B.J. wasn't sure that she'd keep her promise.

CHAPTER 21

Hopefully, Kentucky

After getting her medical van fixed the next morning, Maybelle Grimes left Purcells and headed for Hopefully, where she wanted to meet Ellie as soon as possible. On this trip, she didn't play her country music—a sign of how stressed she was over last night's events.

She went to the Copperhead Club, driving past the small area where Ellie had been sketching the day before. Using her cell phone, she called the hotel, where she learned that Ellie had checked out well before dawn, leaving a cash payment in her room.

Maybelle was stricken with terror and guilt, fearing that something terrible had happened to Ellie—that she could even be dead.

Stella had left no forwarding address or even an explanation for the abrupt departure. Maybelle checked with Hazel Fines, a friend who'd worked late at the club the night before, and asked if she'd seen Ellie, the woman painter. Hazel was a petite lady, with big eyes and other features that made her the spitting image of Popeye's Olive Oyl. "Yes," Hazel answered, "she seemed to be enjoying herself all evening. Apparently she was looking for someone—a man in a photograph. She'd asked Roger and Geraldine if they'd seen him. Jimmy Billingsley gave her a ride back to the hotel around midnight or so." But she added that Billingsley turned left when they left the club, which would have taken them down by the river, an alternate but longer way to downtown Hopefully.

Maybelle immediately put two and two together, but she wasn't certain that they added up to four. Every scenario she thought of didn't make sense. Would it be possible that she and Billingsley had found some time to have sex, and then he gave her a ride to downtown Hopefully? But why did she check out so quickly without even going to the front desk? Billingsley was a scary character and had acquired a reputation for using his star quality when it came to women. She remembered that one girl told her that Billingsley liked rough sex, and that she vowed never again to get into a vehicle with him.

She suspected that something had gone wrong in Billingsley's SUV, but no one had seen anything as far as she knew. She could file a missing person's report with the police, but she had no evidence of any wrongdoing. For that matter, this woman could just as easily be headed back home. This wouldn't have happened if Ellie had refused to accept a ride with Jimmy, she thought, even if it meant she'd have had to spend the night in the club.

Maybelle asked Hazel to keep an eye out for Ellie and to let her know as soon as she heard anything about her. Hazel was pretty sharp. Instead of a waitress, she should have been a nosy news reporter, Maybelle thought.

"Oh, by the way," Hazel remembered, "I saw her talking to B.J. Matson very briefly yesterday as I was walking on my way here. B.J. was going home. He had a loaded truck, and the entire load was under a thick green tarpaulin, kind of old and faded. I thought that was kind of odd since there wasn't a cloud in the sky. B.J. stopped and looked like he was saying something nice to her, maybe about her art, and she pointed to the hill where B.J. lives and appeared to be asking him a question about it. B.J. shook his head no, and then drove off up the driveway toward his home."

"It sounds like a first meeting of the two of them—an introduction," Maybelle said.

"Yeah, that's it," Hazel said. "B.J. usually isn't that outgoing." She promised to watch out for further signs of B.J. and Ellie. Then she blurted out: "Your makeup is all wrong on the left side, Maybelle. Blush is too low. Go fix it before you leave."

"Call me if you get anything," Maybelle said, heading to the ladies' lounge.

Hazel stood and pondered a minute about B.J. getting together with this sophisticated visitor from the East. Doofus and Snob Ellie? She laughed at the prospect. "Nah!" she said to herself.

Hazel started doing 10-minute lookout shifts once an hour—partly because Maybelle had been a good friend, and partly because her curiosity was getting the best of her.

About 1:30 in the afternoon, Hazel stuck her nose to the window and saw a red pickup coming from the Matson's home. B.J. stopped, got out and opened the gate, moved ahead, and got out and closed the gate. He turned onto the main road. As B.J. drove past, he seemed to be talking to himself—or to someone hiding in the truck? There was no one in the passenger seat. The green tarpaulin was still covering something, but Hazel couldn't tell what it was.

She called Maybelle and reported: "B.J. just came out of the house with a covered load in his truck. I didn't see a passenger, but he appeared to be talking to someone as he passed me. Someone could have been under that tarp. I went outside and watched him turn on the McHune County road. I have no clue why."

Maybelle said she'd try to catch up with B.J.'s truck, but not in the medical van. She'd use her old white Chevrolet, still a reliable car, and see if she could be lucky enough to find B.J. and find out if he knew anything about Ellie.

Maybelle took a short cut across the southern part of Knob County that led into McHune County. Just as she prepared to turn right onto a road that led into McHune, B.J.'s truck passed her. She tried to follow from a good distance behind, and finally saw him turn onto a road out in the country. She went on past. A sign said, "McHune Shooting Range."

That was odd. In Hopefully, Doofus had always told people that he hated guns. And although he was a big guy, he was never a bully. Something was pushing him in the opposite direction, and Maybelle thought she knew what it was. The truck no longer was in sight; it apparently had gone over a ridge that led to the shooting range. She could hear guns going off, though not all in one spot.

As she moved slowly to the top of a ridge, Maybelle reached for her binoculars and focused on a woman. It was Ellie. B.J. was standing next to her, along with some guy who seemed to be an instructor. Maybelle told herself she knew all she needed to know. Ellie was staying with B.J., and she was learning how to shoot a gun.

Maybelle backed up, turned around, and parked in a place where Stella and B.J. couldn't see her car when they drove out. She scurried back to the ridge, watching every move that Stella and B.J. made. After two hours of waiting for them to finish, she saw B.J. put the guns in the back of the truck and she watched Stella climb in next to the guns and lie down as B.J. carefully pulled the tarp over her. "What on earth!" she said to herself. "Has B.J. drugged her? Is he some kind of sociopathic serial killer, abducting women and hiding them under tarps? Or are he and Stella up to something?"

For Maybelle, the answer hinged on whether Ellie might actually like B.J., regardless of whatever kind of weird shenanigans they were up to. She hadn't looked upset or threatened the whole time, and had even giggled loudly on a couple of occasions. "Impossible," she thought. She didn't know whether Ellie was promiscuous or prudish or just a woman lost in a strange territory and in need of help. All that was clear was that Ellie was bent on learning how to shoot a gun.

"Jeez," she said, "Annie Oakley and Doofus. And I thought this town was *boring*."

CHAPTER 22

Hopefully, Kentucky

When the truck came to a stop in front of the house, Stella couldn't wait to get her feet on the ground again. She'd been bounced around for 30 miles, unable to see where the truck was going, and getting sicker the longer she laid on the old mattress that B.J. had provided. When B.J. hit a pothole, as he did six or seven times, she felt as though the bottom was dropping from her stomach. Every part of her body ached. Her black eye was still swollen, and her neck still hurt from Billingsley's punch.

B.J. came around and gently lifted her off the back of the truck. He had an urge to touch her and rub her back, but he drew back and started unloading the guns.

She walked around to restore her sense of control and to stretch her legs to keep them from cramping. Oh, how she wished she were in the McLean Spa, enjoying a seaweed wrap and mani-pedi from Isabella Ravyn. "Damn you, Bob" was her latest mumble to herself, complete with gritted teeth. Her face turned red as she thought of her miserable husband and her friend Alicia. She looked carefully at B.J. and at the weapons. "Do you really think I can handle any of these?"

"Of course you can," B.J. said. "You have a better feel for all of them than I do. And to top off that, you have a very good eye. You hit the target more than I did. You're learning fast. We'll go back again."

"I surprised myself—I kinda like it," she said. "I hate to admit that in a way, I wish I had one of these babies here when that asshole tried to rape me," she said, pointing at the guns. "Well, let him try again." She laughed. "I didn't know I had this much of a criminal mind and foul language within me. Damn, let me at the bastards."

B.J. didn't quite know what to make of the newly energized woman who had suddenly walked into his life. She had seemed vulnerable, sweet, and gentle at first, but now that she was going through some sort of free-wheeling metamorphosis, he genuinely feared she'd become reckless.

"You have to promise me again," he said, "—you won't kill your husband unless it happens to be genuine self-defense. I'm not going to give you a gun unless you make that solemn promise to me right now, one more time. And you'd better mean it this time. I have enough troubles to worry about getting charged with aiding and abetting a homicidal scorned woman." He'd repeatedly questioned whether he should have taken her to the gun range at all. It was inviting trouble. But not doing so might have put her in direct danger.

She looked into his blue eyes, wondering if this was a serious plea. This chubby man is decent and kind, she thought, and he's going through a bad time in his life, facing down a group of assassins trying to find one lousy photograph.

"I promise," she said quietly.

"One more time—and louder," B.J. said.

"I promise, I promise—for God's sake," Stella, beginning to become annoyed. B.J. stared at her firmly. "I promise that I won't try to kill the son-of-a-bitch," she repeated one last time, "—unless he tries to kill me first."

"You did well out there on the range, too, B.J.," Stella said. "Is it true that you've never used a gun before?"

"My mom tried to teach me when I was younger," B.J. said, "but I was terrible at it back then and I hated the idea that guns could be so forceful in our society. My mom kept trying to teach me, but the more she did, the more I resisted. Finally, she gave up and left me to my own devices. Isn't it ironic? Now I'm going to try and learn to shoot to protect her."

He told her about his mother's background, including the famous incident in which she'd killed a bank robber in Hopefully and made a reputation for herself. Some of the people she'd arrested were murderers and although she was threatened a few times, she was never afraid. She could always take care of herself. "She still has those steel-like nerves, in case you didn't notice," B.J. said. "It's hard to follow a mom like that," he said. "Now I feel that I have to do it."

"I'll have your back," Stella said, standing like an Army sergeant displaying a new confidence that she hadn't previously seen in herself. "You can count on me and my Betsy here," patting the new pistol she'd put in a holster.

"You know, Stella, I'm guessing that Bob still isn't too far away. Maybe in some lonely hollow somewhere where few people venture. But I don't know why, really. If his cover's been blown in this general area, it might seem smarter if he moved somewhere else. But then he'd have to go on the move and that might increase his chances of getting caught. But he's got a new look with the red hair and beard."

"He's waiting for something or someone," B.J. continued. "When I took his picture, I knew right away that he wasn't a Hopefully guy. He had an expensive beer, and he was reading a book about the game of chess. I know because I zoomed in on the title."

"He loves chess," Stella said. "He's a fanatic about it. I'm pretty good at the game, but I wouldn't play him at all. In our early years of marriage, he played in chess tournaments." Stella told B.J. she'd had dreams all last night in which she was chasing Bob through a gigantic chessboard. She kept losing him behind one of the knights, but after tripping on a pawn, she'd grab his ankle and pointed a gun in the middle of his back, saying, "Checkmate, you bastard."

B.J. smiled at this latest manifestation of the new Stella spirit. This green-eyed woman was beginning to grow on him. He didn't want her to leave.

Stella told B.J. about the young couple she'd met at the Copperhead Club. They had asked if she could paint them for their wedding. "I might have made a mistake," she said, "but I showed them a picture of Bob to see if they had seen him around. I called him a friend."

"Had they seen him?"

"No, they said they hadn't seen him, but now I'm beginning to wonder," Stella said. "The guy works as a maintenance man at the club. He may have mentioned to other workers there that I was asking about a man in a picture. Maybe one of them might have seen Bob."

B.J. said he didn't know the couple and couldn't help with that. "But you know that if Bob has any contacts with the people at the Copperhead Club, he'll find out that you're in town. We'll try to keep you under cover as much as possible."

They finished carrying the guns inside the barn, and once again Stella was impressed with B.J.'s organizational abilities and his choice in art. "That one hanging over there is beautiful," she said. It was a painting of a Kentucky cardinal feeding his mate. The bird's feathers looked almost three-dimensional. "Who did that?"

"I don't know," B.J. said. "I got it at a thrift shop."

"Really nice," Stella said. She moved up close to him, touching his arm lightly. "B.J., I truly appreciate all you've done to help me. You are a brave soul to have taken on Billingsley when he was trying to rape me. You didn't have to do it, but you did."

B.J. couldn't think of anything smart or elegant to say. "I didn't want him to commit another crime and get away with it," he said. He felt a strong urge to kiss her, but it was a single moment of passion and it quickly passed.

"You know I live with my mom. I lost my fiancé," B.J. said. "She died in a car crash on the road home from work. Her grave is outside the window, right over there," he said, pointing to a headstone. "I still love her dearly."

"What was her name?" Stella asked.

"Melody. Melody Meredith," he whispered.

"Beautiful name," Stella said, nodding her head in respect. She stared at the grave. "I'm sorry," she said. "Tell me about her."

"She was popular, smart, funny, and beautiful. Most of the guys she dated or was interested in after high school just left," he said. "She felt alone and distraught. Then she and I got together. We discovered that we liked to joke around and to talk about music and politics. We moved in together. She got a job at a call-center over on the other side of the mountain, and I'm sure if she had lived, she would have become manager of the whole shebang. Then, one night, when she was driving home, a truck filled with coal moved around a switchback curve too quickly and hit her car. She didn't have a chance."

"Oh, no!" Stella said, as she put a hand over her mouth in anguish. "I'm so sorry—so very sorry." She moved close to him again, and hugged him. He reached around her waist, and touched her bottom softly. She didn't protest. Tears came to his eyes, and he dropped his arms to the side.

After another moment of silence, she smiled and looked him in the eyes, which brightened suddenly.

"Would you like a drink?" he said. "I have a domestic brand, $4 a bottle usually, but $2.99 on sale. Premium stuff."

"Sure." She smiled broadly. "Can I have this pistol?" she asked, picking up the .45-caliber Beretta. "This is the one that will nail him if he gives us a rough time."

"And who might that be?" he said.

"Those people who want to kill you. Or my husband, or Alicia, or Jimmy Billingsley—whomever."

They both laughed at her use of proper grammar here in a barn in Eastern Kentucky. "Whomever," he said, chuckling at the irony. "We're now seeking out the dastardly Whomever."

"Whomever could be quick and accurate on the draw," Stella teased.

"I'd like to get more practice, even if I have to ride in the back of the truck, hidden by a tarp."

Again, she moved closer, looking into his eyes. She embraced him and kissed him on the cheek, but before he could advance any further, she pulled back.

"I need to see Bob face-to-face," she said.

MARCH

CHAPTER 23

Lexington, Kentucky

At the University of Kentucky Medical School in Lexington, Carlos Mendez blinked his eyes and then opened them.

He was in a hospital bed. It was night. There was no one around. The last thing he remembered, he was in an SUV at the top of a hill, racing to stop an intruder. Then everything went blank.

Now he could hardly move. Desperate to see a human being, he tried to yell out for help, but he could hardly speak. He tried again. He noticed a little device next to him, designed to enable a patient to switch channels on the TV set. Besides the TV controls, it also had a microphone and a button. He pushed the button.

"Hello—may I help you?" came the quick response.

"Where am I?" Carlos asked, bewildered.

"Wow!" the nurse said. "I'm coming to your room right now."

Soon his room was swarming with people. "Hello, young man," one of them said. "It's so good to see you back with us."

"How long have I been here?" Carlos said. They told him he'd been in a coma for a week. They couldn't believe he was awake and talking. They hadn't expected him to survive. But the oddest thing: no one had come forward to claim him. They knew he'd been in a terrible accident with three other people, but they had died, and apparently he had no one else. He didn't have a driver's license or any other kind of identification. He seemed to be an immigrant, but he didn't have a green card. That meant he'd been in the U.S. illegally. And, for now, he was an unknown.

"What's your name?" the head nurse asked.

"I think it's Carlos," he said. "I can't remember my last name right now." He was lying, but they accepted it at face value. He asked what had happened to the other people in the car.

"They're all dead. You're the lucky one."

He was sad for all the others who'd died. Suddenly, he felt the tears. The men had been his constant companions for nine weeks as they worked to keep a man hidden from the authorities. But he couldn't talk about them.

"Do you have a family—someone else we can call?"

"Not that I know of now—I just can't remember, and I think I need to get some more rest."

They left him alone, but under close watch. The office staff had already called the authorities, and the police would soon be on their way.

A young doctor on call came to see him. He told Carlos it was a miracle that he had come out of the coma and was talking. "I think your memory will come back after a while," he said. "But right now, this is very good news for you."

Carlos waited for the moment when he'd be alone. It finally came in early morning after he'd been awake for a few hours. He knew what he was about to do was risky.

He picked up the telephone and dialed nine, and then a number. When he was asked to give a message, he spoke in Spanish. "Carlos here—old, red GM truck, black-and-white stripe, dents all over, a guy maybe in his mid-30s, probably local, Kentucky license plates. That's all."

Later the police met with the hospital staff. They instructed them not to tell the general public about the patient's miraculous recovery—"it would help us with the investigation." If the other person involved in the accident were to hear about Carlos's improved condition, they reasoned, he or she might be tempted to do harm to Carlos or even skip town.

The police didn't know that Carlos had already spread the message to other bodyguards. And they didn't know that Carlos would lie every time he was asked to describe the other vehicle.

Retribution, such as it was, was going to be a private matter.

CHAPTER 24

Hopefully, Kentucky

At sunrise on a cool March morning, B.J. took Stella on the trail to the top of Copperhead Knob. Springtime wild flowers were starting to show their heads and glisten in the dew. Birds in a cacophony of sounds kept silence away.

It was good to get out and for Stella to feel well again, well enough to master The Knob. B.J. and Molly had insisted that Stella rest up after her ordeal with Billingsley. Staying with Molly and B.J. had a calming effect. She felt these people were genuine—they really cared about her. With the little money she had left, she offered to buy groceries. They refused. She felt obligated to "earn her keep," so she learned how to cook some simple meals and clean up the kitchen. After two weeks, her black eye was almost gone and her head was clearer. "You're getting your wits back," Molly said. "Now, you'll be able to get the S.O.B. and put him away." Stella wasn't sure if Molly had meant dead or alive.

Stella had adopted B.J.'s green, fleece-lined hoodie. It was big and toasty-warm and matched her green eyes. B.J. jokingly called her "Turtle" when she wore it.

"I want to show you the safe house," he announced. "This is where we'll come if we hear that the survivor of that crash comes out of the coma. I've been working on this for years. I think you'll find it pretty efficient.

"I can't even imagine such a thing," Stella said. "I can't wait to see it."

"I could take you in The Beast—our ATV—but it's a nice day to take a hike up the mountain if you think you're up for it."

"Sure, but I would like to take a ride on the ATV some day," Stella replied.

"Okay, we'll do that, too," B.J. said, with a grin.

Stella loved the way the old hill was shaped. From a distance, it was like a pyramid. But up close, the limestone rocks and the trees looked like any other side of a hill. B.J. took Stella's hand as they negotiated ruts in the path and, in some places, tree limbs. He'd tried to keep the trail as clear as possible, but he didn't always have the time or inclination. "Be careful," he said matter-of-factly. "It's a little early for copperheads to come out, but I've seen them when temperatures get warmer. I've seen them really dirty, just like they've just emerged from their winter sleep."

"Uh-huh," Stella said with a gulp.

They didn't take the rugged road that switched back and forth, choosing instead to follow the trail that goes straight up. That cut the distance, but it was harder to negotiate. Homemade "No Trespassing" signs were scattered here and there, and took away from some of the beauty. Stella guessed they didn't always keep strangers out, but if B.J. ever caught anybody on his hill, he'd ask why the person was there and warn him or her to leave.

When they'd climbed high enough, they watched the panorama unfold—a deep, dark-green valley, with other knobs far off on the horizon. Soon, they were near the end of the road, where one could not see much of the ugliness below, such as old rusted cars and houses needing paint. Stella remarked: "This place dresses well, even if the clothing isn't clean."

She spotted the Copperhead Club building, which looked elegant so far away, showing itself off surprisingly well, as if it were shaking off a drunken haze from the night before. She could see that there was one car out front, perhaps belonging to the man who came to clean up early each morning. She wanted to meet Ms. Ortiz and see if she could provide some help in finding her husband. As she thought about this, she squeezed the Beretta she now carried—with B.J.'s okay—in a holster attached to her belt. He thought she could handle herself now, after her shooting lessons, and it had become her pet. Stella mused: "I wonder how this gun and holster would have looked attached to one of my Gucci belts?"

"There's the river," Stella said, pointing to the left as they ascended. The Kentucky River snaked through the valley below, and took a sharp turn near the base of the Copperhead Knob, just as the poisonous snake itself might do, when it prepared to strike. The sight evoked happiness and sadness—and it reminded Stella of Jimmy Billingsley's attack. There it was—the little sandy beach down to the left, and the winding pathway that rose on that side to the top of the hill. From this vantage point, B.J. had witnessed Billingsley's attempt to rape another woman, a few days before the one involving Stella.

They sat on a makeshift bench—made of two felled trees—for a brief rest. The panorama of miles and miles of green, with a river cutting through the terrain, was even more stunning on this crystal clear day, and they took a while to take it all in. "I wish I'd thought to bring my sketchbook," Stella said. "This has possibilities." On this morning, a rosy color added a softness that was rarely seen. B.J. pushed forward.

"That's where we're going," B.J. said. "Wait'll you see this." Ahead was an outcrop of limestone about 15 to 20 feet high that would be hard to negotiate if you tried to climb over it. To get to the top of the hill, one had to take a well-traveled path to the left in order to bypass this block of stone. They went the other way on a path that B.J. had cleaned out for wheelchair entry.

Stella looked straight ahead. Chiseled into the rock was a metal door. "This is neat," B.J. said, by way of introduction. He opened the door with a key, revealing a dark chasm inside. He turned on a generator just inside the door, and soon afterward he flipped a light switch. Suddenly, the size of the hole in the hill became apparent. Behind the stone exterior, the family had built a large living space with electric power and fresh water. There was enough room for several people to live for a long time in isolation—a genuine "safe house."

Stella looked at this in awe. "Incredible," she said. "How in the world did you get this done? And why?"

"I guess because my mom and dad didn't believe in a world that was inherently good," he said. "She was a cop, and a damned good one. She had seen too much evil, and my dad and siblings were truly afraid that someone with a need for retribution would do her harm. So they decided to build it. After 9/11, they thought the safe house would also protect them from a nuclear attack or some other terrorist attack. We dug out a lot of dirt, but the natural opening on this side of the limestone outcrop made the job easier than you'd think."

"How long did it take to get it like this?" Stella asked.

"At least three years. Putting in the electric generator, running the water line from the natural spring, and getting the television antenna up were the most difficult projects." Leaning against the stone B.J., continued, "This stuff is known as dolomitic limestone, and it was used long ago for building homes and public buildings in Kentucky. So, as long as 100 years ago, the state decided to come here and cut some of the stone to build a new government building in the capital at Frankfort. Our family owned the land, so we sold them the stone. They didn't need all of it, and the state covered it up as best they could. They carved into the wall and left stone everywhere. When we started on the project, we didn't need new materials. Just a plan. The Baron has been here; he thinks it's as much a trap as it is a fortress that would protect us."

"Well, has it ever been used for that kind of purpose?" Stella asked.

"Not until now," B.J. said. "But maybe we're going to make it worthwhile this time around. I never intended it to be a place where we could defend ourselves with guns, although that was the vision when Mom and Dad had it built. So it was built in a spirit of paranoia, I guess. Mom came across a lot of strange people in her police work, and she knew that some of them would like to come and get her. In particular, she helped put away a mean S.O.B. who chopped up his landlady. Mom figured out who it was by finding hidden tire treads near the scene. He always threatened to do the same to Mom if he got out of prison. He still sends threatening letters sometimes. When someone broke out of the prison where he is, that was enough for her to speed up construction of this place. Then there're the ones who are already out—like Jackson Jones. Mom calls him 'the arsonist.' He's already tried to set fire to our trash cans."

B.J. turned a switch on, and a closed-circuit monitor screen dropped down inside the safe house. It showed three different views of the trail out front. "There are actually six cameras out watching all this. And we have a siren if people get too close without our permission. Right now, the alarm system is off."

"If we have three guns going against invaders, they'll back off," B.J. said. "And we probably can kill them all."

"There's only one door," Stella said. "It also could be a deadly trap."

B.J. hit another button. There were two doors to the left, which sprang open at the command. "And there are piles of stone outside to hide behind so we can continue firing at our opponents."

All this reminded Stella of the kids at home playing cops and robbers at the local playground fort. It all felt sort of like she was in the middle of a big video game.

"I was about to close this place down and forget the upkeep until this man who may be your husband came up here in the hills." B.J. said. "I've always hated guns, but my family wanted to protect ourselves from revenge-seeking assholes. But nothing ever happened—at least not until now—Bob Jasper, and now you." They both laughed. And, in an odd way, she felt completely at home in this hole in a rock, smelling like wet leaves, with a crazy hillbilly who had a crazy cop for a mother who had a crazy boyfriend who just happens to be the town banker.

The safe house was well stocked with canned goods and cereals and such—nothing perishable of course, unless someone caught some fresh fish from the river. "We could live here for a month if we had to," B.J. said. "So you're right, if they wanted to wait us out, I suppose they could. But if our cellphones and communication worked, we could also call the police."

"Who you say are corrupt," Stella said, referring to the police.

"Right, Stella, they are—but they'll protect us if some drunk climbs up here with a gun in his hand, threatening us. We'd never be in danger, but we don't want to shoot some crazy drunk in the middle of the night."

"You've retreated up here for some strange reason, B.J.," she said. "You mentioned it as kind of a hidden fortress before, and I can't believe you spend so much time up here."

"I guess I have my reasons?"

Stella was insistent: "Is there some hidden aspect of this I can't see? Are you afraid the sky is falling? This is sort of excessive, don't you think?"

"I work up here a lot." B.J. said.

"Doing what?" Stella asked.

"Just stuff related to the hills. I take a lot of photos and stuff, you know."

"Well, I saw the photo of what appears to be my husband, but what else do you take photos of?"

"Just these mountains," he said. "Just pictures of life."

"I'd like to see them. I know you have some pictures hanging in the barn. I don't see any here. Where are they?"

"Maybe another time," B.J. said. "Now I have to get back down the hill and check on Mom."

Before she left, Stella stopped at the door of the safe house. She knew B.J. was a little bizarre, especially for a man who grew up in these hills. Now even this gentle man who had saved her and who had vowed to protect her also scared her because of his peculiar ways.

A little over two months ago, she had lived in the midst of

Yuppieville, with all the amenities and comforts of life—where art and theater thrived and where government and politics were a source of constant conversation.

The sun had stolen the morning's cool. She took off the hoodie and tied it around her waist. On the way down, Stella and B. J decided to take a more difficult route down the knob, a route that any mountain climber might want to train on. To get down, you needed to go from one boulder to another. At one spot two boulders stood about two feet apart. Stella leaned forward and put her palms on one rock with her feet still on the other, and giggled about her shirt riding up. As her body sprawled across the gap in a gigantic V, B.J. shouted "Don't move!" About two feet underneath her belly button was a den of coiled copperheads. "Oh, my God, oh, my God, what do I do?" Stella shrieked. She could see their shades of brown scales, which blended perfectly in the nest of fallen leaves. The slits of their eyes were closed. She feared that if she moved, they would wake up, lunge, and sink their fangs into her—and she would die right on top of the rock.

B.J. slowly climbed the rock where her palms were. "Stella, trust me," he said. "We're just going to inch ever so slightly—bit by bit." He grabbed her hand. She began to move her palms, little by little, until the forward part of her body was almost fully on the first rock. Over the next four minutes, she turned her body from a V into a flat line, with her lower legs dangling in the air. "Come on, we've got this—we've got this," B .J. said. He pulled her with one last tug until they both tumbled down the rock into a patch of leaves. The snakes still hadn't moved.

Stella burst out in tears, shaking like she had never had in her life. But B.J.'s mind was somewhere else. He'd seen enough close calls with poisonous snakes in the hills not to be phased by it much. It was part of the knob existence.

He thought of copperheads of different kinds, lurking with their poison and daring you to take one false step into their territory.

Here, when you walk you have to make sure where and who the

enemy is. B.J. knew all about the snakes and their behavior, but not so much about the people out to end his time on this planet with one quick strike.

CHAPTER 25

Hopefully, Kentucky

Lucinda Ortiz, owner of the Copperhead Club, had just come out of the bank in downtown Hopefully when she saw Mayor Billingsley heading into city hall. His puffed-up eyes and drawn face spoke of anguish, strange for an ample man who usually greeted people with a slap on the back, a broad smile, and a big hello.

"Come into my office, Lucinda," he yelled over the sound of a coal truck rolling down Main Street. "I need to talk to you. I have bad news which affects you, too."

"You look like somebody hit you with a sledgehammer," Lucinda said, as she settled into a chair in his office and accepted the cup of coffee that he offered.

"That's a good way to say it," the mayor said. "Jimmy has skipped town. Gone. Just like that. He wrote us a note saying he's going to Chicago to start a new career. No communication at all with us. No cellphone that will work. Said he needed to get away from here and build a new life."

"Oh, my God," Lucinda said. "This is so sudden. I'm so terribly sorry to hear this. I see why you're so upset. Did you alert the police in Chicago? I used to live there. Maybe I can help."

"Thanks for the offer, and maybe I'll take you up on that. But I haven't heard anything yet. I'll call the cops there, but I doubt if that'll lead to anything. Jimmy says he'll write and stay in touch, but I have my doubts. I wonder if this is the last we will see or hear of him. He's been growing distant and acting more moody these days. We did everything we could for the boy. I'm both hurt and angry at the same time."

"I don't blame you. I understand," Lucinda said, looking at the mayor with that serious, focused look that made her a formidable companion. Tall, well-dressed, poised and in her 40s, she charmed people, particularly hard-nosed men, with a constant smile and an ability to pay careful attention to everything a person said. Her speech indicated an excellent proficiency in English, along with her native Spanish.

"You know, we sent him to a good college, which he screwed up, and he had the gall to come back home and blame us. We bought him a car, told him he could go to any school, anywhere in the nation, but he didn't want to do any of that. Oh no, he wanted to do drugs, and thank God, we think he's cured of that, though not cured of drinking. He's a gifted musician—but at what cost? He'll never follow in the Billingsley tradition of being a mayor or a town leader, and he's got a bad reputation among some women in town, all of them sluts probably," the mayor said.

"You must be devastated."

"No, not totally devastated," the mayor said. "Sad, but hopeful. You know, they don't call this place Hopefully for nothing. You have to have a lot of hope to live here, as you know." By the look on his face and his obvious anguish, Lucinda thought his "hope" statement lacked sincerity; it seemed to be a political cliché he was mouthing. Mayors are prone to that, she thought.

"I know your personal loss is great and I feel it, too, even more so because I'm losing something, too," she said. "I'm going to need help to find a replacement half as good as he was up there on the stage. He was a major reason why our receipts are up, and why we're thinking of expanding. I need another Jimmy—and soon. There aren't that many around these parts. It may take a little sweetener to get someone who comes close to his talent," Lucinda said.

Tears gushed again. "Sorry," the mayor said, "but I can hear him singing now. "I loved his rendition of 'God Bless the USA,' " he said. "Look, I'll start asking around for someone to replace him. I'll check with a couple of other mayors I know."

"Thank you," Lucinda said, gratefully.

"Tell me something, Lucinda. I don't go to the club very often, as you know, because I have to be loyal to my downtown businesses. But in his note, Jimmy says my wife and I would hear some stories about his being a 'Lothario.' I've heard him talk about women now and then, but do you have any knowledge of that?"

Lucinda paused. This was a sensitive topic. "Yes, he's had that kind of reputation, but I've never actually witnessed anything."

"What do you mean, Lucinda? Don't be so damned wishy-washy. If you know something, please tell me. We haven't been friends for nothing. You can tell me. I need to know."

"The only thing I have heard is that, if you're a woman, you don't want to go out with him if he's had too much to drink. I know nothing first-hand—just casual statements from some girls about being afraid of him."

The mayor's heart sank. He'd avoided drinking for 30 years because of that family problem. He wrung his hands, rubbed them in his hair, looked at the floor, and fought off a tear once again. He'd barely avoided a rape accusation himself through the intervention of his own father. Like father, like son, the mayor thought—only the son could be even worse.

"The last thing I know about Jimmy is that he gave that woman painter, Ellie Heinz, a lift to the hotel the other night. Hazel Fines at the club told me."

"What? I didn't know that," the mayor said. "Do you think that this woman could have gone off with Jimmy?"

"All I know is that this woman appeared to take a little shine to him when he was performing," Lucinda said. "Based on what Hazel said, he even welcomed her to the club when he got up to entertain. I guess it's a possibility they took off together. And I don't know anything about her. Do you?"

"No, I don't. Tell me more. Where'd she come from?"

Lucinda said this "Ellie person" had come to town in a medical van driven by Maybelle Grimes, who dropped her off at the Copperhead Club so she could paint the mountain and go to see and hear Jimmy's music.

"That's a bit strange, don't you think?" the mayor said. "Why would she want to paint The Knob in cold weather, before spring has sprung around here?"

She told the mayor how Stella had shown one of her staff members a photo of a friend she'd been trying to find for a long time, and wondered if he'd seen him. "My guy, who helps with maintenance, didn't recognize him. You're right—the whole thing is a little strange."

"As you know, around here, we're highly suspicious of anyone who asks odd questions," Lucinda said. "I'm glad she's left town, if that indeed is the case, but I'd still like to know something about her visit here. I'm going to ask some friends of mine to find out everything they can about her. I'll let you know if I find out anything."

"Thanks," said the mayor. "Maybe she's with Jimmy. It'll be important for us to know what's going on. Probably nothing, but worth checking out." He didn't say why this was so important, because both of them already knew why.

"How many years have you been here, Lucinda?"

"Six and counting," she said. The mayor knew her story, how hard she'd worked at odd jobs in the States after emigrating from Mexico. She'd obtained her green card and received a scholarship to study business at the University of Arizona. Her talent showed as she went on to get a master's degree in business even as she worked for several companies, including financial houses in Chicago.

When the job offer came to go to the hills of Kentucky and manage the Copperhead Club, she hesitated, but finally decided it was a good opportunity to test her skills and build a place from nothing. Besides she was sick of the noise and grime of a big city. She had no idea that she'd be the first Hispanic resident of Hopefully. When the owner passed away suddenly, the owner's family sold it quickly to Lucinda. The club went from deep losses to break-even status in a relatively short time, thanks to the better music and better food. She lured a young chef straight out of culinary school in Chicago to improve the restaurant, and he also improved her sex life. Some people disapproved of what they called her loose morals here in this small town, but they didn't boycott the place— far from it.

"I have to go, Mayor," Lucinda said. "Maybe Jimmy'll change his mind and come back. I know you're deeply worried about him. I sure hope we can find a replacement at the club if he doesn't return. I'll see if I can find out more about this strange 'Ellie person.' Some other staff member may have heard her say something. It could be a clue."

After Lucinda left the mayor's office, she looked back at his window. He had his head down as he pounded the table with his fist, as if to say, why, why, why? Lucinda felt sorry for him, but she knew of many others who'd suffered more. He knows nothing about real loss and deprivation, Lucinda thought. The average person in Mexico can tell you in a minute about that, because poverty is so prevalent. It's a virtue to escape it, even if the rules are bent to make escape possible.

Lucinda walked outside. On the street corner were a couple of guys in their 30s. They wore torn T-shirts and baseball caps with the bills turned backwards. They were smoking and laughing. She recognized them. Jimmy had called them by their first names, Joe and Jack, and they often came to hear him play. Their parents frequently had dinner at the club. Joe and Jack drove old beat-up cars that appeared to be ready for the scrap heap, and she knew that their parents lived right on the edge of bankruptcy.

Down here, Lucinda mused, too many people were already living on the scrap heap of drugs and deprivation, and if it weren't for federal programs of one type or another, some might be bankrupt or starving. That was just a reality.

But all in all, she loved Kentuckians more than people from all other states where she had lived. For the most part, she thought, they were smart, honest, caring, solicitous, hospitable, blunt, industrious, and creative in many ways, especially with their vocabularies. Downtown Hopefully, which had only a handful of stores, offered little to improve these qualities. Many people had to go elsewhere to work, but they loved their little town and the people they'd known all their lives.

Her thoughts turned to Jimmy Billingsley. The boy had spirit, she thought, and he had pride. And he had the courage to gamble energy on an enterprise, even if it were misguided and wrong, like the Transylvania University incident. He was also good at finding drugs and making a profit from them. He knew his music and, against the wishes of his uptight mom and dad, he'd started a country music group unlike any she had seen anywhere. He's lucky he's not in jail, she thought, and if he'd stayed in Hopefully a little longer, even his parents couldn't excuse him from his brazen attacks on women. That could never be condoned by society, she knew that—and he would have to suffer the consequences.

The best thing that Jimmy's parents could do would be to find their son and encourage him to turn himself in and ask for mercy—because with his record so far, he was bound to get into deeper trouble later on. She'd get her chef to ask his friends in Chicago to keep an eye out for him. Perhaps he'd be performing at some small sports club, hoping to break out into the big show.

But the tragedy saddened her deeply, and, as she began the search for a new musician for the club, she thought of her own survival.

CHAPTER 26

Hopefully, Kentucky

A skim of fog covered the hills and hollows at daybreak. B.J. sat on the front porch swing, meditating over the possible danger ahead. A mild wind, barely strong enough to move the forest leaves, touched his tortured face. "I'm not ready to die," he said to no one in particular. "Please don't let it happen yet. There are things I still want to do."

He mouthed the words so softly that no one else in the house could hear them. B.J. was neither a churchgoing man nor a religious one. But he had a spiritual side to him that most of his friends had never witnessed, because he practiced his religion, if one could call it that, in quiet, introspective moments alone. His mother didn't have much room for meditation and churchy behavior, though in a weak moment she'd once admitted to being spiritual, whatever that means to a woman who'd killed a few errant men and women in her day. But Molly, too, was feeling the uncertainty of the moment, though she didn't dwell on it in talking with B.J. or with The Baron.

Stella had been more or less adopted by the Matsons. She loved getting shooting lessons from a new coach—Molly, the retired cop. There was no ammunition permitted in the house, however. The bullets and shells would be dispensed to Stella at the shooting range. After that frightening morning when Molly held a gun to Stella's face, Molly rediscovered her maternal instincts and treated Stella like a young girl who needed to be taught some things about living in Kentucky, as she saw it from a police officer's point of view.

Holding Stella's gun, Molly said, "Your Beretta is your friend, and you must treat it with respect, but with authority. You only shoot as a last resort, when there's no other possibility of resolving the situation. Treat this gun like your best friend, but be aware of the fact that it is a deadly friend." She tried to show Stella the trick of the locally famous Matson move, where Molly would shoot perfectly at the range target with her left hand while holding a cup of coffee in the other. It was all about the knee-bend, which Stella could not seem to perfect.

Stella learned how to be more precise as she practiced holding, pointing and aiming at an old dartboard that Molly had attached to the dining room wall. Sometimes, she'd glance at her reflection in a mirror on the left and think, "Is this really you—Stella Jasper with a gun, not a paint brush?"

One day, about two hours after breakfast, B.J. said it seemed like a good day to take a ride. Would Stella like to go to the firing range?

"Sure. Let's go," Stella said, grabbing her backpack. For Stella, the shooting range was not just a place to unleash her emotions, but to breathe the air and to escape the gnawing feeling that she was being held in captivity.

There were a couple of reasons that B.J. wanted to leave. Just like Stella, he sought to become more proficient with guns—which he intended to use in self-defense, he told himself. Since there had been no update on the man in a coma in Lexington, he reasoned that Jasper or his men would not know who caused the deadly accident; they would not be coming after him with heavy weapons immediately.

Stella was sure, too, and she wanted to go get Bob right then and there. From the moment Stella saw the Tutankhamen beer bottle, she was sure she was looking at Bob in disguise. "Funny," she thought, "he's changed his looks and I have, too. We probably wouldn't recognize each other at a distance. "You goddamn Tutankhamen beer jerk. You have no idea I know you're here. You thought you were smarter than me." It would be simple: She would call the authorities, they would arrest him, she would be vindicated, and she would get her life back.

But she couldn't. B.J. had saved her life and now she had to save his. She would have to be patient and hope that Bob stayed in hiding until the man in the hospital died. If the man lived, however, he'd identify B.J. and Bob's thugs would be after them.

What should they do? Was there a chance that Bob knew that she was in town because she'd made some clumsy choices when she showed up in the Copperhead Club? Was it possible that some of Bob's allies might have been undercover in the club and recognized her, even in her partial disguise? B.J. wasn't sure, but he thought a metallic blue car in the club lot that night looked similar to the one that had been parked next to the black SUV that nearly ran him off the mountain. Was there someone in there trying to find out who caused the accident on the knob?

B.J. was scared stiff about taking on gangsters who had automatic weapons, such as the men he'd encountered on the knob. Even though Stella was becoming more skillful with a weapon, B.J. felt he himself was not. He wasn't sure he'd ever be ready to shoot at a person. Then he remembered someone who might help. He'd take Stella out to shoot and then go meet Wally Ponz.

Wally, whose real name was Walton I. Ponz III, owned Ponz Delivery Service. He might have seen strangers on the trips that he took every day in the hills or in the valleys. B.J. tried to reach Wally earlier, but the man proved hard to reach, as he traveled all over four counties surrounding Hopefully. Wally left B.J. a voicemail while he and Stella were on top of the mountain, saying he'd meet up at 1 p.m. over in Big Bull, a small settlement in Showalter County that sponsored a bull festival every spring. There were no bullfights, but they did stage a much-scaled-down version of the famous running of the bulls in Pamplona, Spain.

Once again, Stella hid from view as they drove to the firing range.

Once again, they swore the range owner to silence about their target practice. Unfailingly, they arrived an hour before the place opened, and began firing almost immediately. It was fairly apparent both of them were improving rapidly—particularly Stella, who surprised herself with her ability to hit so many bull's-eyes. Although Molly's lessons were conducted with unloaded weapons, they were beginning to pay off.

All that considered, they hadn't noticed that Maybelle was continuing to watch their every move—from a distance. She'd found a perfect spot where she could camouflage herself by arraying a few leaves on her head and then monitor B.J. and Stella from behind a tree. This time, Maybelle had a video camera with a high-quality zoom lens—and she captured everything. When Stella pulled out her Beretta from a holster with lightning speed and hit the target in the center, Maybelle burst out, "Wow, this is incredible!" Luckily for her, she was beyond earshot.

After practice, the two marksmanship students headed back to Hopefully and to the safe house, with Stella once again riding under the tarp. "Time for you to go inside," B.J. said to Stella when they arrived. "I gotta go meet up with Wally Ponz."

"Why can't I go?" she protested. "I'm in this, too, and besides I could help him identify my husband."

"No," B.J. said. "Wally is a strange bird—different from anyone you've met. He does better one-on-one, but doesn't get to the point quickly. I can't really tell him why I've come to see him. We went to high school together, so we've known each other a long time. I'll use that to see if we can find out if he's seen your husband, the same guy I saw in the hollow."

"But you might need me as a backup," Stella said.

"We don't have to shoot Wally," B.J. said, putting out his hands, palms out, as if to say stop.

"All I need are a couple of six-packs and a McDonald's on the way," B.J. said. "Oh, yes—and a couple of moonpies for dessert. I hope Wally knows something. I may be gone the rest of the afternoon. You stay inside the house while I'm away."

He knew Wally Ponz all too well. It might take hours to get any significant information from him. He'd be unresponsive to direct questions such as: "Seen any strange men recently who might have moved in somewhere near?" He remembered a conversation during his last visit with Wally.

"Hey Wally, do you remember who moved into the Kohl house in Last Man's Holler?"

"Old Man Kohl was a mean sumbitch, wasn't he?" Wally said. "Always pulling out his chest hairs. He used to throw his opened pocketknife around, too. I don't think he ever hit anybody. I'll never forget his toothless grin. Last Man's Holler needed some nice people."

"You know, Wally, you have the best memory of anyone I ever saw. You could be making millions if you used it more. Now tell me, does someone nice live where he used to live?"

Such an approach usually produced a back-and-forth stream of consciousness about everyone in the area, and where they lived, and how he, Wally, felt about them. You had to know how to milk the truth out of Wally Ponz, and B.J. was good at it.

After insisting one last time that Stella stay in the house, B.J. headed for Big Bull. He was paranoid enough to think that he might be followed—especially by a metallic blue car—or that he might put Wally in danger. So he drove down the hill to Route 7884 and turned as if to go down by the river—except that he pulled off the road right after a sharp bend and quickly turned onto a dirt road, where he parked behind some bushes and a tree. Soon a woman driving an old, white Chevrolet passed by. As soon as he was confident that no one had seen him, he roared out of the side road and went the opposite way. He didn't have to go downtown. He turned a mile short of that, and went south on Route 2455. He pulled off after driving about a mile, and waited to see if anyone was following him. There were only a couple of cars, one driven by an old woman poking down the road, the other by a young man in a

Jeep Liberty, coming home from the coalfields. No white Chevrolet. No metallic blue car. He resumed his driving.

Wally had a unique business. He delivered all kinds of goods, including groceries and packages, all over the area. If anyone had an old sofa to transport and couldn't get a truck, Wally was the man for the job. People who were unable to shop for groceries could count on Wally. He did well for himself by becoming a close friend to his customers, who loved to see a family-owned business survive.

His trucks bore an awkward motto: "We Deliver What They Won't." But it was true. He'd been asked to deliver everything from doughnuts to drywall, from candy to liquor. He was adept at loading his truck with an odd mix of things in a single trip, like when he managed to haul live chickens in a plastic kiddie pool. He always stayed within the law in delivering whiskey or beer in dry counties. He told clients that he would be happy to deliver one step away from the county line, and it was up to them to do what else they had planned. He'd gone to authorities to qualify for every kind of delivery possible.

Wally was enterprising, and he believed in investing in his own future. He bought three trucks, including a refrigerated model, to haul goods. For personal use, he drove a vintage Ford truck that would soon be 15 years old, and he fixed it himself. When things got tight and deliveries were down because of a bad economy, he "fired" himself first and did some car repair work on the side. He'd have done car repair full-time, he supposed, but he loved the beauty of this part of Kentucky and he enjoyed talking to people in all the counties around.

Wally, at 34, was paper thin, about 6-foot-3, with brown hair, brown eyes, and a short handlebar mustache. Always dressed casually, he liked to show off his Western boots and the belt with the big silver buckle that he'd bought on a trip out to Arizona.

Before Wally became a business owner, he'd had only one or two changes of clothing—usually a pair of jeans with holes in them, a faded T-shirt with a peace symbol on it, a denim jacket, and a nearly worn-out pair of running shoes. Occasionally, he'd peruse an album to see the old photos. "Pretty handsome dude, there," he'd say to himself.

When B.J. drove into Big Bull, he didn't believe how small it was. There were only four or five streets in the town, and Wally's home was nearly in the center. The annual "Bull Run" didn't actually take place in town, but in a nearby pasture. It didn't quite match up to the Pamplona race; not many people got hurt in the Kentucky versions because there was more room to run. "We're gonna have to fix that," Wally said once. "Gotta get some excitement going, even if we have to kill one or two." B.J. hoped he'd been referring to the bulls, not the runners.

Wally came outside to meet B.J., and they embraced immediately, patting each other heavily on their backs.

"Been a long time since we were in high school," Wally said. "I remember that stupid looking uniform your mom dressed you in. "Your mom gave you a T-shirt with CRIME DOES NOT PAY on the front and SUPPORT YOUR LOCAL POLICE on the back. Not cool. It didn't go over very well with those of us who looked to break the law with a little bit of drinking and pot smoking. Would you like a drink?"

"I got some beers and burgers with me, and I thought we could talk over old times," B.J. said. "You seem to be going well." Indeed, Wally had prospered for a guy who never went to college and had dreamed up his own company.

They opened cans of beer and went inside Wally's office—a single room with a bathroom and a lot of old pictures on the wall and a couple of soft chairs.

"Look what I have for you and your friends if you want," Wally said. "These shirts were left from our last festival. The red shirts were emblazoned with RUN WITH—NOT FROM—THE POLICE, and SUPPORT BIG BULL POLICE in smaller letters. They both laughed, remembering the ones that B.J. had had to wear. B.J. thanked Wally for the stack of shirts.

"Where do you *really* live?" B.J. asked.

"At the crossing of highways 1156 and 1375. It's only three bedrooms and a bath. It was plenty big for us."

"Us?" B.J. asked, his curiosity suddenly piqued.

"Yeah, you know—Deborah Stein, good Jewish girl up here in the hills. Mighty hard for her, trying to be friends with people here. She did try, for a couple or years or so. But they just wore her down. We split so she could stay with her momma over in Lexington. Divorced. Never had kids."

"You were going to marry Tripsy Bluebaker. Didn't it work out?"

"Yeah, I know. But she wouldn't smoke or drink. What kind of fun is that?"

"I don't smoke or drink," said B.J.

"Yeah, but I don't have to marry you."

B.J. changed the subject. "Do you remember JoBeth and John Walker?"

"Yeah, they lived in that odd hollow over near Preparatory Place. Two kids. Nice. Lived next to the Rangers, Mary and Josephine, I think, and way up there on top of the knob is a home owned by Bill Beathle. Big family."

"Any new people in that hollow?" Wally answered in the negative, but then he said, "in the next hollow up that line, there's a new couple, with a dog, and a man with a fine looking Lexus right next door."

Wally was on a roll, reciting where everyone lived, which he loved to talk about with someone who cared, someone who'd gone to school with him. "Here, have a beer," said B.J., prodding Wally gently about who lived when and where, about the history of the place where they lived, and about who might have been a good or bad hombre.

Wally downed the burger and french fries, washing them down with beer. The moonpies lasted only a second or two. And then the two old schoolmates laughed.

"I got a surprise today," Wally said abruptly. "Someone said they'd seen you with a woman."

"Who told you that?"

"Uh, I think it was someone at the Copperhead. They saw you talking to a pretty lady out on the road."

"Yeah Wally, I just met her a couple weeks ago. She was out sketching a beautiful picture of the hills. I don't expect her to be around much longer."

"Too bad, B.J. You need to settle down with a woman. Know what I mean? Been a long time since your girlfriend died, you know, on that awful curve. It was so sad, and I think about it all the time. But you gotta let go sometime. I heard this one was good looking, but that's all I know about her. Just think about a night in bed with her."

B.J. changed the subject, figuring his personal life wasn't Wally's business. "Tell me about your business and where you go in a week's time. Must be six or seven counties. Think of all the old times. We used to visit them all in one way or another, by foot or by car. You know, like Devil's Hollow. What's going on there?"

Wally covered all the people he knew of in that small settlement, and then began to talk about others. They drank and talked most of the afternoon. The beer was soon gone and Wally uncorked a bottle of red wine. B.J. asked if he'd seen any place that was unusual or where it was hard to get to know the tenant.

"No, no, but wait. A new guy just moved in at the Cottingly's old house in Viable—you know, in Shepherd County, deep in the heart of the knobs. Really isolated. It was sold when the widow passed last year. Not sure who owns it now. Seems odd that he's the only one there, except now and then I've seen some people around."

"Do you know the hollow we used to call Ringworm?" B.J. asked. "It was curved in a near-U at one point."

"Yeah, I got a picture of that somewhere," Wally said. "I'll check it out, just to see how things are changing."

"Did you meet this strange guy? What's he like?" "Didn't meet him at all," Wally answered. "He never saw fit to order anything from me."

"Not even a beer?" B.J. asked.

"Not even a beer or anything else to drink. He must be a strange recluse, or something. You see people like that at times."

B.J. felt he had reached the limit in pressing Wally. But Wally kept up the conversation. "You ought to write a book, B.J. You've been around these counties as long as many of the old people around here."

"Thanks a lot for the compliment," B.J. said sarcastically. "I'm afraid I'd have to destroy too many reputations and people would come after me." He patted Wally on the shoulder. "Not you, my friend," he added. "You are the salt of the earth."

"Why don't you come to work with me?" Wally suggested. "I pay pretty well for this part of the world. We'd make a great team."

"You mean I could visit all these sites up here and get paid for it, too?"

"Yes," Wally said.

"Well, it might be fun for a day or two—if I could bring my friend along with me. You know who," B.J. said with a wink. "And you wouldn't even have to pay me. It'd give her a chance to see how real Kentuckians live before she leaves."

"Sure, you can bring your assistant," Wally chuckled. "But you'll have to accept pay. It actually would be a big help to me. It'd give me a chance to do some work on my car and paint the shed out back. I'm *serious!* Take your friend along and enjoy the natural beauty of our Kentucky's mountains. She'll want to paint every one of them. She might even decide to stay."

"Could I pick the counties to visit?" B.J. asked.

"Well, you'll need to make deliveries, but I bet they'll be all the places you'll want to visit."

"Well, I don't have a trucker's license or a license to sell," B.J. said.

"No worries, as long as *my* license is in the truck. You're just an employee."

B.J. thanked his friend, and said he'd think it over and call him back in a day or two. He would see if Mrs. Edinbrock was available to stay with Molly while he would be gone. Molly was always content to have her "visit" because she liked to play Scrabble and munch on Mrs. Edinbrock's version of Chex Mix. Mrs. Edinbrock was also content, because The Baron paid her well for her service to Molly.

On his way back, B.J., still feeling the effects of the liquor, looked for a white Chevrolet. He was nearly home, and there was one parked in the lot at the Copperhead Café, identical to the one he saw on his way to Wally's. Could be a coincidence, he thought.

B.J. got home at 8 p.m. "Where in the hell have you been, you big shithead?" his mom asked. Stella just stared at him.

"Don't you remember Wally Ponz, Mom?"

"Absolutely," Molly said. "Before I retired, I arrested him three or four times for drinking and taking drugs. What kind of company are you keeping, B.J.?"

B.J. said Wally's story was a successful one; he was an enterprising young man, shaking off drugs and alcohol. And he had a new—and very profitable—business.

"He's a really good guy, Mom," B.J. said. "Wally had a girl—a Jewish lady—but they've gotten a divorce. He's looking for another woman. I can tell. Wally is one of the finer citizens of this area."

"Really," Molly said skeptically. "I'll believe that when I see it. Never trusted a drunk or a druggie. You know how I am."

"Yes," said B.J., "but you're wrong about Wally."

"Just give him time, honey—just give him time," Molly said. B.J. thought to himself that that was the first time in 10 years that Molly had called him honey. Maybe there was hope. Or maybe she'd been around The Baron for too long.

"What'd you find out?" Stella asked. "Does he know where Bob might be?"

"There's one possible place, but it's not for sure," B.J. said. "We need to figure out a way to check it out without being seen."

B.J. ordinarily was cautious. But perhaps the drink had made him a little more decisive. "How would you like to drive a delivery truck with me for a day or two?" he asked Stella. "Wally will let you and me work for him traveling up and about country roads in and out of hollows. I think he may suspect that I'm up to something unusual and might need a cover."

"How do you know that?" Stella asked. "Has he told you he'd let you have a truck so you could snoop around this area? Does he have a possibility?"

"Not quite," B.J. said. "He didn't say that, but that's what he meant. I can read Wally's code."

"What? A code? That's ridiculous," Stella countered.

"I saved his ass once—and kept him out of prison," B.J. said. " He wants to repay me, I suppose.

CHAPTER 27

Hopefully, Kentucky

Maybelle was growing more and more frustrated with her attempts to tail B.J. He'd managed to slip away from her a couple of times. It seemed pretty obvious that he had an inkling that he was being followed, or at least that he was worried about it. He would do U-turns in odd places and even drive backwards down side roads when no one was looking. One time she saw him at a distance, sticking his head out his truck window repeatedly, staring at a parking lot as though he was a prairie dog popping out of a hole. Every time he managed to slip away, Maybelle became that more determined to find out what he was up to.

It was almost like a game. He'd given her the slip for an entire day, and there's no telling where he went. She couldn't guess, but she was dying to know. To make sure this wouldn't happen again, Maybelle decided to get more help and use a different tactic.

She decided to call Hazel Fines, her friend at the Copperhead Club, again. Hazel, who had a knack for detail and a good bit of intuition besides, was probably the nosiest person in town. Hazel would extend her hours, get there early in the morning, and tip Maybelle off if B.J. and "Ellie" happened to leave their compound, as Hazel called it. She stashed binoculars under one of the restaurant tables. Hazel had the finest ears in the whole town, and she always heard the sound of B.J.'s truck—or any other vehicle, for that matter—when it crunched the gravel driveway just outside the Copperhead Club. Maybelle had called on Hazel more than once because of her talent as a busybody.

Hazel found three other Copperhead Club companions to watch for B.J. and maybe Ellie. Maybelle had figured that, together with a couple of other spotters, as she called them, she'd almost certainly be alerted anytime B.J. went out. She could keep the white Chevrolet parked at an intersection close by, where she wouldn't be seen. If Hazel or one of her friends called in a tip, Maybelle could use a rental car to follow B.J. She'd already signed one out for the week—a dark gray Toyota Camry, which might be less noticeable to B.J. She was all set.

Maybelle knew that B.J. had odd sleeping and waking hours, and, in fact, he slept little. She had stayed up late a few times to witness that erratic cycle. She camped on top of a ridge behind the Copperhead Club, and from there she could see when lights were on in the house or barn. Often, the barn lights were on most of the night. A few times she thought she saw a light on the knob that lay behind the house, but she dismissed the idea. "No way—not at this time of night on a mountain," she thought.

The surveillance began. When B.J. turned the lights out, Maybelle stayed at a friend's house until 7 a.m. and then went back on "the watch," as she called it. She had to rush to get ready. Hidden off the main road at an intersection, she sipped her coffee and munched a sausage biscuit from the diner, waiting for a call. "No wonder cops eat a lot of doughnuts," she mused, smirking. "This is terribly boring."

At 10:20 a.m., Hazel called. "Maybelle, one of those Wally Ponz delivery trucks just went up to the house. It looks as if it's Wally himself. I'll keep you posted."

Her heart rate rose suddenly. Wally Ponz? What can he be delivering over there? Groceries, maybe? Drinks?

Ten minutes later, Hazel called to alert Maybelle that the truck was coming back down the highway. "I can only see Wally in it," Hazel said. "But this one is one of those panel trucks where you can't see much. There could be people stored in the back. He's coming your way. He should be there in five minutes."

It was a quandary for Maybelle. If she thought B.J., Ellie, or both, were hidden in that truck, she would follow. If they weren't, she'd have left her post open—and possibly lose track of them altogether for the entire day. It was playing the odds. She needed another person to help in this. Clearly, given the circumstances, B.J. had become cunning about avoiding unwanted spies.

After much thought, she decided to gamble, follow the truck, and see what happened. She could retrace some of the route if Hazel suddenly called to make another report. B.J. and Ellie might not be in Wally's truck; they might come out later in B.J.'s truck.

She would stay far back so as not to make anyone suspicious. The truck wasn't going very fast as it approached Maybelle's hiding spot, hidden by the trees on an intersecting road. She could tell that Wally wasn't talking to anyone when he passed her. He crossed the intersection and kept going. Within a minute, she pulled out and followed him.

Wally began noticing a gray car that seemed to be following him at a distance. He whistled "She'll be Coming Around the Mountain" and "My Old Kentucky Home" as he drove deeper and deeper into the county. Finally, he came to a sharp curve that took him 90 degrees to the right. Then the road turned straight for a mile. He stopped at the end of the curve, so that the driver behind him couldn't see that his truck was sitting on the shoulder of the road.

Maybelle took the curve at a moderate speed, but was surprised to see Wally's truck on the shoulder of the road and Wally waving a white handkerchief. She stopped the car.

"Hello, ma'am. Saw you back there behind me, and we're kind of far from the main road. Might you be lost and need some direction? I get down these roads every day, and I see lost people all the time. Wouldn't want that to happen to a nice lady like you. Kinda dangerous out here by yourself." Wally said.

Maybelle, though surprised, never let on that she was following him.

"Oh, I hope I'm on the right road," she said. "I'm going to Providence County to see some friends in Salamander."

"Oh, yes, you're doing fine," Wally said. "After this straight stretch, the road to Salamander is off to the left. I have to turn right and make a delivery to Cow Bell, a little community of people who always need stuff they can't get at the grocery there. What did you say your name is?"

"Maybelle," she said, trying not to feel deflated. "I live up near Purcells, and I drive a medical van that goes all over the place. Take people to the hospital and doctors, stuff like that, you know."

"Ah, I've heard about you. I will say this: No matter what others may say about you, I think you are a fine Christian woman. You work so hard to help all those poor people who need a ride to the hospital and to the doctor's office."

"What's that supposed to mean?"

"Hey, don't get so sensitive," Wally said. "This is God's Country we are living in here, and we should all be good friends and able to take a little joke. As I say, Maybelline,..."

"Maybelle!" she corrected.

"Maybelle. Nice name, too. Maybelle, there are good people living in this area and there are terrible people. One way to separate them is to know that good people don't cave in to the many temptations that destroy us. The terrible people are those who cave in, and the bad thing is that they are running these counties. You are one of the good people."

Maybelle asked him where he was going.

"Oh, after my delivery to Cow Bell, I'll just go back to Big Bull where I have my office. It's just off to the right a few miles. It's about 25 minutes from Hopefully. Come and see us sometime."

Maybelle said thanks and drove off, taking the turn to the left, a move that she hoped would buttress her story. She still didn't know whether B.J., Ellie, or both were hiding in the back of the truck. She also sensed that Wally was on to her story—call it an intuition.

She got beyond the turn and stopped after a couple of miles, then turned onto a dirt road and made a U-turn so she was facing the main road. She called Hazel Fines, who reported that she hadn't seen B.J. and Ellie leave the compound. Maybelle thanked her for her help. Then she made another call that lasted only briefly.

Maybelle wasn't lost and she wasn't disoriented. She was confident that she'd made the right decision—and that Ellie and B.J. might be in the Wally Ponz truck. Perhaps she should have insisted on seeing whether the couple was riding with Wally, although that would have been overstepping her bounds and probably would have been counterproductive.

After waiting 10 minutes, she decided to go back to her parking spot near the Copperhead Club, where she might be able to catch up with the elusive couple again. The day was still young. But just as she started to move out, Wally Ponz's truck came down the highway again and turned onto the same dirt road right next to her. He got out and asked, "Do you need any help?"

"No," she said, "sometimes I get a bad headache when I am driving, and I just had to pull over and rest."

"I understand," said Wally, clearly skeptical about her story. "Well, if you want to go to the doctor, you can park this vehicle here and I'll drive you to a pretty good doc about 10 miles or so down the road. Or I can take you back to my office in Big Bull. It's up to you. I've got some drinks in the back here. What can I get you?"

"Let me look," she said, and got out of the car and peered into the back of the panel truck and saw no sign of any passengers. "I'll take one of those root beers," she said, "and thanks."

"You're welcome. I've got some ice for that drink," and he gave her a paper cup with the drink, and a straw too.

"Do you want me to wait here a while to make sure that you feel better?" said Wally.

She said she was feeling better already, thanks to him. "I gotta go," she said, after sipping a little of the soft drink.

"See you back in town one of these days," said Wally. "I gotta make some more deliveries to make sure I stay afloat."

Maybelle was more interested in what might have happened to what she suspected might have been Wally's cargo—B.J. and Ellie. "Where did you let them off?" she muttered to herself. And after his truck was out of sight, she made another phone call.

CHAPTER 28

Washington, D.C.

Ramos showed up at the White House on a cloudy day in Washington. He didn't think any outsiders recognized him or even paid attention. His chauffeur drove through the Southwest gate, where tall shrubbery blocked the view of tourists and others on the street. There would be no news story about his visit, he reckoned, unless the President publicized it. And that he doubted.

After he passed through the security desk, a young woman greeted him and told him she would escort him through the building. Even though he'd been in the White House many times, he'd always felt a sense of its importance, the fact that so many crucial decisions had been made in there.

In a moment, it seemed, he was at the doorway of the Oval Office. The President greeted him, and Ramos noted his square jaw and still-winning smile. "Welcome, Placido—I trust your family is well," President Everett said. "Have a seat by the fireplace."

"They are well, thank you, Mr. President."

"You probably aren't surprised that I'm seeking your support for a second term, Placido. It's a tough time for anyone to run, and I know my ratings are way down. But you could help get them up just by saying you'll support me. I want to tell you that the presidency is on the line for our conservative party, and we need prominent citizens like you to help."

"This means I would have to campaign for you all the time?" Ramos asked.

"That would be very nice, but I'm not expecting you to do that," the President said. "What I need is, you know, an endorsement now, and for you to speak out for me every chance you get. And to spread the good will out to Hispanics, who might be the tipping point in the election. Reyes Gonzales is getting favorable numbers in the Hispanic community in all the polls."

Ramos listened, letting Everett fill the pauses that invited him to respond. "You know how important this election is to our country," the President said. "With you on my side, we can pull off a miracle. And that is very important, very important, because if the liberals get back in power over these tough years, we'll regret for the rest of our lives that we didn't work harder to keep control. With all due respect, I hope you'll soon become part of the action in this campaign, and that is to support our philosophy, which I know means much to you, and thus prevent the demise of our country."

"You know, this is nothing personal, Mr. President," Ramos finally responded. "I can't see what's in this for me. Credibility is very important. It is so closely tied with reputation. Frankly, I'd like to be President myself, and I think I'm qualified for the job, but there's no vacancy now. However, you can make a vacancy—the Vice Presidency. I'll be frank with you, Mr. President. The only way I can be on your team is if you choose me as your running mate. I'll bring votes you don't have. Even beyond the Hispanic community, there are also a lot of conservative moderates who need assurance that they have a voice. With me as Vice President, you can even swing a little to the right in the election."

The President was stunned to hear Ramos's proposal. "The only problem, Placido, is I already have a Vice President, and he's a good leader and a good man."

"He's a liability, and he's sick," Ramos said. "He might not last the rest of the year. I saw him only a week ago. I love him as you do, but he's past his prime, and I'd be a better candidate hands down. People know me and respect me. I have business experience and political experience.

"I hear you," Everett said. "Why don't you come out and say why you *really* want to be number two? That's not like you. Why in hell do you want to be the Vice President? Nobody really wants to be Vice President."

"Well, I'm certain that you're going to live a long life, but I know everything there is to know about politics and how to win, besides. Who knows?—I could run for President, too, one day. I'm certain I'd do a good job for you as Vice President, because I'm a good, articulate spokesman for the administration, and I'm a team player. And, yes, I'm still ambitious about politics and rising to a higher level. The party loves me. I know foreign heads of state by their first names. And I'm an excellent spokesman on administration policy on any topic you can think about."

"What's more," Ramos added, "I've always loved my country. I want it to be bigger and better. And I believe that, together, we can have a terrific administration that will solve some of these terrible problems."

There was a pause before the President spoke again.

"I must be honest and ask you," Everett said, "is this about you making more money than you have now? You're a multibillionaire, so I'm asking whether you're driven by money that would come your way after your term is over?"

"I will not accept a salary—all of it will go to charity," Ramos said. "I've been a successful person and I want to pay back the country because it's been good to me. I've learned much about the economy and how to create jobs."

"Placido, you know how difficult it would be for me to pull this off. As much as I like you, I have to be honest. You've never run for a federal office, but here you are suddenly asking to be on my ticket. For all your political wherewithal, believe me, running for an office at the highest level is no easy job. Furthermore, you know as well as I do that the press would have a field day with this. I can see the headlines now: 'Vice President Wilbur Hill abandons race. What does he know that we don't?' "

"However, there's already been speculation that the Vice President might decline a second term because of his health. There's a political window that's not often there during a re-election run. I wouldn't rule it out entirely. We have some unusual circumstances. And you might be the answer we need to get past our political troubles. I need to consult the Vice President, who's a very good man."

"Let me warn you: I can be a very dull man," Ramos said. "I love my wife, and I've never cheated on her. I like to gamble once in a while, but I don't do it much. I love horse races and play blackjack in Vegas."

As for the Vice President, Ramos said even more plainly than he had before, as sad as it was, he thought Wilbur Hill was dying. "If you stay with him, you'll lose the election. It's a high price to pay for a friendship and for letting him stay on the ticket."

"But do you have something else up your sleeve?" the President asked. "Just what is it? I need to know. You're human, like all the rest of us. What are you really after?"

"Even though I have many conservative views, I feel strongly about immigration reform and the poor people I know in Mexico and other South American countries, who feel there should be a more lenient policy on immigration. I also think you should increase the number of immigrants coming into the U.S."

"Okay, I'm willing to take up immigration reform," the President said, "but will you support me if I don't pick you? That's all I want to know."

"I doubt it seriously, Mr. President," Ramos answered. "Once in a lifetime a chance comes along, and I've always taken them when they've come to me. This is another one of those times. The choice is yours, not mine, but you could get a lot from picking me. If you don't, I'll stay at home and not even participate in the election. I can help you get re-elected or I could help you lose. It's your choice."

The President thought Ramos was one of the most arrogant people he'd ever encountered in politics—and that was a mouthful. Still, because of Ramos's importance to the campaign, which might well falter without him, Everett couldn't just reject him.

"Thank you, Placido, for your candor, and I'll get back to you soon."

"I'll be waiting," Ramos said. He shook the President's hand, said goodbye, and followed a staffer out the door, through the same secluded White House gate.

The President sat in the Oval Office and pondered what just happened. Ramos was super-slick, and was looking out for his own best interests first. On the other hand, there weren't many politicians he knew who *didn't* look out for their self-interest ahead of everybody else's.

Ramos had provided a logical scenario for a victory, and he had no doubt that Ramos would work for him diligently if he were on the ticket.

Just how would he be as a campaigner and a nominee? He'd never been truly tested in this arena, Everett thought, but with his intelligence, knowledge, and smooth speaking style, he could be one of the best vice presidents ever elected.

The President thought how lucky Ramos might be in the political arena. And that luck might continue if he joined the Everett ticket. Four years from now, Ramos might get the chance to run for President himself.

What about Ramos's running for President after his term is over? That's essentially not my problem, Everett mused. The people decide whom they want for President, not me. If Ramos is nominated, he'll have to win the presidency on his own.

Everett walked to the windows behind his desk and swayed slightly, as he was prone to do when he felt stressed. He clinched his fist around a monogrammed stress-ball that one of his daughters had given him.

Just then, Chief of Staff Scott Herbert came bursting into the room with a pile of papers and folders. "The Senate Majority Leader is pushing for the executive order today, Mr. President. Do you think we should go ahead?"

"No," Everett said quietly. "We're not making big decisions today."

CHAPTER 29

Hopefully, Kentucky

B.J. and Stella drove the Wally Ponz truck through a labyrinth of country roads in the knobs section of Kentucky to the place called Viable. It failed to live up to its name. The town, if that's what it was, was no more than a crossing of two country roads, surrounded by hills. The only "viable" part of Viable appeared to be several homes at the bottom of the hill, off the road to the left. There also was a country store of some kind.

"This is our stop, and we're way back in the sticks," B.J. said. "That's the Shepherd Market that Wally told me about. We're going to deliver some goods to the owner, Josephine Oeuvre—Natty, for short."

Stella said she loved the name—not Natty, but Oeuvre. "It has class," she declared. "It means *a work of art*. It's French."

They turned left and drove down the hill, past a lane of trees and a large open field, to find the semblance of a town—about 16 houses on a lane, eight on each side, and Shepherd's Market, which had a gasoline pump outside and an air hose for tires. All the houses looked empty except for one, and they couldn't tell for sure about that one.

The door jingled when Stella walked into the store. She heard a stirring in the back, which was about as packed with goods as a place could get. The shelves were high and close together, as if they'd been designed for only thin people to move through. There were candies and fuses, aspirin, and bug spray, cans of vegetables and meat, sewing kits, and bread. There was baby formula and diapers, and reading glasses with cleaner for them. Rakes, hand tools, and a snow shovel hung on a back wall, next to the anti-freeze, engine oil, and a package of rock salt to thaw the ice in winter or make ice cream in summer. It was a miniature Walmart, without the low prices.

"You must be Josephine," Stella said to a thin, gray curly haired lady wearing a work apron with lots of pockets.

"That's right, but you can call me Natty."

"We're here today subbing for Wally Ponz," Stella said. "We're going to help him a bit for a couple of weeks. My name is Ellie. Ellie Heinz."

"Is Wally okay?"

"Absolutely. Here's something Wally thought you'd like. They're the first ones ready out of his greenhouse," Stella said, as she handed over a small plastic bag of lettuce and onions.

Natty pulled out an onion and smelled it. "These will be so tasty in my potato soup or on a salad. What else is Wally growing? Besides his greenhouse, he always has a big garden, too. I bet he's already plowed it. I don't know how he has time to tend it, but he brought me good stuff last year. I hope he can find good strawberries again, so I can make my world-famous strawberry malt, with fresh berries. It was a real hit last year. You don't get that at the Dairy Queen. Tell Wally I'll pay him for all the stuff you're bringing in today when he comes by."

"Sure, we'll tell him. You know, the scenery is so beautiful here," Stella said. "You'd think some people tired of living in a busy city might want to settle down in a restful place like around here. Wally wondered if any new settlers were around. He's always looking for some new customers. Are there any houses he should visit to check out possible shipments?"

"None I can think of," Natty said. "Every once in a while I hear of people moving out and people moving in. Wally may know better than I do."

"Wally mentioned the old Cottingly House up on Route 844," Stella said. "Have you heard anything about that one?"

"Hmm, I don't remember," Natty said. "The house up there has been sitting empty for some time. I know that. It could be there's a person in there, but I don't know for sure. You'd have to check. I doubt it, though. It's in one of the most isolated areas around here."

"Most of the houses around here look empty. Where do all your customers come from?" Stella asked.

"Well, there are two boarded-up houses not worth fixing. The others may look empty, but they aren't. People are out working, you know. There are people all around here in little settlements in the hills and hollows. You just can't see them from here. Also, there's a bunch of people about 20 miles away who come to their second homes in the Dogwood Project. It has a golf course, a lodge, vacation homes, and a nice restaurant. A lot of my customers come from over there. They like the country feel of this place a little better. We like to be touristy here, but the real reason is for my strawberry malts."

Natty was looking at Stella's waist. "You're pretty thin, you know, but unless my eyes deceive me, you're wearing a gun." Stella had forgotten to take it off—a decided mistake.

"Oh that—don't worry, I'm harmless," she said. "I don't know the area well—only been here but a few days—and I just feel more comfortable out here with it on. I'm sorry I disturbed you."

"No, no, no. I just meant to ask, what do you want for it?" Natty asked. "I got guns at the house and one under the checkout desk here, but I sure like the looks of that one."

Stella smiled. "Maybe I can get you one," she said. "They're for sale at a shooting range I go to. But you know, maybe I can't. You have to sign ownership papers," she said. "You know—government rules."

"Nobody seems to care around here, Ellie," Natty said. "If you got money, you can buy purt'-near anything you want."

B.J., who had dressed in a nice, laundered shirt with a tie and dress pants in line with Wally's dress codes, unloaded the rest of the groceries that Natty had ordered. "We have to go, but I hope you can make a strawberry shake for me sometime," he said.

"Glad to—right now," Natty said. "I have a few frozen bags of strawberries left. Just take a minute. Ellie, do you want one, too?"

"I know it's wonderful, but I'll pass this trip. Maybe next time," Stella said.

Natty scooped up the ice cream, added milk and strawberries, malt, and her "special" ingredient (homemade strawberry jam with a touch of bourbon), and the blender hummed.

"Delicious," B.J. said after the first sip.

"It's the best in these parts," said Natty, an Oeuvre who had shown off her oeuvre with an oeuvre.

B.J. praised it again and gave her a five-dollar bill. "I gotta get down to Mrs. Beasley's house," he said. "I've got her prescription medicines and she needs them today. I'm not sure how far she lives from here."

"Poor lady," Natty said. "She's got high blood pressure, and I know she can't get out. Just go down to the bottom of the next hill, turn left, about 10 miles. She's on the left-hand side of the road. There's a sign out front with the house number and also a sign that says Beasley. She's got a dog, Max, who likes to bark a lot. Take these dog biscuits and Max will love you."

B.J. said thanks, and then Natty interrupted him: "Hide your damned gun before Mrs. Beasley gets hers out," she warned Stella. Mrs. Beasley knows how to use it. Killed her first husband with it. He abused her, you know. Her second husband is a keeper though."

When they drove away, Stella looked over at B.J. and asked: "Did she really kill her husband?"

"Dunno," B.J. mumbled.

It was a relief to them when a man who identified himself as Mrs. Beasley's husband answered the door, and he welcomed the two delivery people into the house. The dog came running in, barking, but Stella quickly gave him a couple of biscuits, and all was well. "Glad you got here," the man told them. "I meant to get her pills yesterday, but I had to change the tire on the car and by the time I got there the pharmacy had closed. Come on back here. Bertha, your medicine is here."

Bertha, who was resting in her bedroom, took the prescription gratefully, and said she was going to rest some more. "I see you've met my husband," she said. "He's a dear."

Mrs. Beasley paid them, and they got away quickly after that. In the truck, Stella looked at B.J. And they both laughed.

They made several more stops for Wally, then turned to the major item of interest: with increased excitement, they'd been talking about the old Cottingly house all day, but they didn't have a real picture of it from the Internet. Stella thought they should check it out. The possibility of finding Bob, and maybe Alicia, there was causing her to shake her knees uncontrollably.

The house was along Route 844, but was actually off the road by about half a mile. The side road—if you could call it that—was all dirt, and was rutted and uneven. B.J. drove at a snail's pace because he didn't know what kind of pothole would be coming next.

B.J. stopped suddenly. "We can't do this," he said. "If Bob is down there, he's going to see us long before we see him. If that happens, he can slip away without any trouble or his buddies can open fire, and that'll be the end of us. I think we should circle around and try to find another side road that would have a good view of the house."

Stella didn't want to show her disappointment because she believed Bob might be there and wanted to confront him immediately, but she realized the wisdom of what B.J. was saying, and agreed.

They went down several dirt roads and lanes, none of which got them anywhere close, until they came to a road that went up a steep hill. Pine trees stood on either side, and it was a one-lane road most of the way, except for occasional two-lane stretches where drivers going the opposite way could pull over to pass.

The hill ended in a curve, with a large area on the right side of the road serving as a scenic overlook. They looked down, and there was the house—white clapboard and in pretty good shape. It was getting dark, but there were no lights in the house and no vehicles that they could see. It looked deserted. There was only one road going to the house, and this one wasn't it.

Soon a black truck came from the opposite direction and pulled up next to them. An elderly unshaven man had a shotgun. He spoke with authority.

"Do you guys ever look at 'No Trespassing' signs? They're all over the place. Now if I were you, I'd get off my property and go back where you came from."

"Oh, I'm very sorry, sir," said B.J., with a soft Kentucky accent. "You know, my girl and I were just looking for a quiet place to, well, you know what. We don't mean any harm. " Stella leaned over and put her head on B.J.'s shoulder, rubbed his chest, and winked at the man.

"Go somewhere else for your nookie," the man with the shotgun said, laughing. "I reckon plenty of guys been getting their poontang right here where you folks are parked. I might as well put up a sign announcing Doin' the Nasty Lane and charge admission."

Stella frowned at his crude remarks and said: "Gee, do you think people need to have permits to enjoy good places for assignations?" She stopped, took one look at his puzzlement over the meaning of the word, and added, "No, not a chance."

He swung his head to the left to spit the tobacco he had been chewing. "Well, on your way now," he said sternly, waving his shotgun.

"We're going, but can you tell me anything about that house sitting down there, with nobody living in it?" B.J. said. "I might be interested in buying a place like that."

"Yep, there *are* people there, but I don't know them," the man said. "Strangest thing. One night there's someone there, the next night, not. It's like for occasional use, you know? He's probably like you two. He's got a girlfriend somewhere and he goes back and forth. Either that, or he's an ax murderer."

Neither Stella nor B.J. found this very funny as they backed up, turned around, and headed down the hill. B.J. was glad that Stella was still sitting close; he missed her hand on his chest.

They saw the headlights of a car in the distance. It was heading away from them—toward town. They didn't know which house it had come from.

Stella rubbed B.J.'s neck and said, "Come on, B.J., let's drive up to the house. It may be empty but you never know. I'm not afraid of the bastard. I've got a gun if necessary, and I know he won't kill me."

"No way," said B.J. "It's too dangerous."

"But there's no one there. And how are we going to cross it off our list for sure if we don't check it out?"

"No way," B.J. repeated firmly.

But Stella could be persistent, a character trait that had become stronger in recent weeks. B.J. came to a near stop when a squirrel ran across the road, and Stella took the chance to go for it on her own. She pushed the door open and started running.

"Dammit," B.J. grunted. He knew he was fighting a losing battle that was going to end either with them going to the house or him tying her down in the truck. He knew Stella would find a way to go the house, even if she had to go beg Natty or a stranger for a ride. He pulled to the side abruptly, put the truck in park and chased after her at full speed.

"Stella! Stop!" he shouted. "We can go, but we have to make it quick. It's getting dark. Stella!"

She slowed to a walk.

"I'm going, B.J.—don't try to stop me!" she said, pointing her finger at him as she struggled to catch her breath.

He grabbed her arm and they walked back to the truck to find a better parking spot. It took them a good 20 minutes to get to a place where he could hide the truck and also not be seen from the house. Buckling on their guns again, they got out and started walking. He was thankful that the moon was out to light their way so they wouldn't step in water or trip over something. In fact, he thought warily, he'd never seen a moon this bright.

B.J.'s heart began pounding, as caution and fear showed themselves. "Stay under cover," he whispered to Stella. They walked across the wide lawn (which he noticed hadn't been mowed recently) and looked through a window. The place seemed deserted. He turned on the flashlight fearful of what he might see—such as the barrel of a gun.

Stella slipped away from him, jumped on the porch, and started yelling at the top of her voice. "Open the door, you son-of-a-bitch. Here I am, your wife, coming here to shoot you between the eyes if you show yourself. But you're not good enough for that—oh no, you fucking coward. Don't worry—I won't kill you. I'd prefer to put you in jail for a lifetime, and expose you for the crook that you are. I'll never forgive you. You misled me, cheated on me, and left me all but penniless without so much as a warning. Come on out, God damn you! Come on out!"

B.J. put his hands over her mouth, for fear the man with the shotgun at the next house about half a mile away might see or hear her—and blow them to kingdom come. But there was no visible move in that direction. The man seemed to have disappeared and gone back to his own home for the night.

B.J. shined the light into all the rooms, and decided that the house was empty. Through the front window, he could see an empty bottle of something on a dining room table. Stella had the better eyesight. "He's been here," she said breathlessly. "That looks like a beer bottle. Maybe it's a King Tut. Probably drank it last night or today."

"You don't know that," B.J. said. "For all you know, it could be a Budweiser, left by a drifter passing through."

They walked around the house and found nothing else that indicated that the house might be occupied.

"Let's open the door if we can," Stella said. "It's the only way we're going to know." But B.J. objected, saying he didn't want to be accused of breaking and entering, and the chances were dim that they'd find anything else. More surveillance would be required, they said to each other. "Let's get out of here," he said. "This place gives me the creeps."

Angry, he told her flat out that she couldn't let go with another outburst like that if she wanted to live through this ordeal. He made her promise she'd never do that again. She promised.

When they got back on the main road, Stella had a theory. "I think Bob's got several places he stays in and he mixes it up every night," she said. "He could afford to pay the rent on several homes out here on land next to the Daniel Boone National Forest."

"That makes sense," B.J. said. "He could spend a lot of time on these roads in the knobs, going from place to place, like a man without a country. Even though money laundering is a serious crime, and can put you behind bars, it isn't murder. Is your husband a killer? I don't know. But I do know that he can't hide forever."

On the wildest conjecture, B.J., trusting no one these days, stopped the truck abruptly. Stella followed him with a flashlight to the back of the truck, and watched him climb in and open a crate that was left after all the deliveries. "Nope. None here."

"What's not here?" Stella asked.

"Bottles of Tut. I know it was a crazy idea, but I just had to look," B.J. said.

They hadn't seen Bob, but Stella sensed that he was close by, possibly even observing them as they attempted to find him. It was a weird feeling.

"You know," Stella said, "Bob was good at paying people for the little things that they do. If he's been around here as much as I suspect he has, he's probably getting some help from people who struggle to make their jobs and their businesses do well. Natty and Wally are solid citizens, but he might be buying their silence with some good tips. Just a guess. Afterall this time of trusting people, I'm beginning to suspect everyone."

"You're thinking just like my mom," B.J. said.

There was silence.

"Did I make a good enough date for you back there on top of the hill?" she said touching his arm. "Been a long time since anybody ever accused me of that—well never."

B.J. smiled. "Plenty good," he said.

"By the way, you look pretty handsome in your shirt and tie," said Stella.

The bright moon lit up the back roads as their truck hummed along. They pulled into Wally's place at 10 p.m. Wally welcomed them and wanted to know if their trip had been productive. "A little," said B.J. "Natty made me a great milkshake."

"Sounds great," said Wally. "Come on, I'm driving you back to your house with my sedan over there." B.J. got the bag with his guns in it, and they both headed back to Hopefully. They laughed at Wally's stories about Maybelle trying to follow them—and how B.J. and Stella were in the back of the truck at their first encounter with Maybelle, but not the second time when he'd let Maybelle see the cargo.

Then they were quiet. They didn't know why Maybelle had followed them. "We've got to be careful no matter where we go," B.J. said.

Meantime, back at the Cottingly house, the man who'd been hiding in a closet when Stella and B.J. were outside sat on a couch with his companion, who'd been hunkering down in the bathroom. Each of them had another King Tut.

CHAPTER 30

Washington, D.C.

Dave Simon sipped a glass of red wine as he watched the evening news. The lead story chronicled the President's low poll ratings, with voters complaining about the impact of a terrible economy, the high unemployment rate, turmoil at home and overseas, and the decline of personal savings everywhere. With a challenger's advantage, Reyes Gonzales had an answer for each of these complaints, and his poll numbers were rising rapidly. Scandal also was a factor in the President's sagging approval ratings, with Bob Jasper's disappearance amidst charges of money laundering near the top of the list. People thought the Everett Administration was slimy at best and hideously corrupt at worst.

"He's toast," Simon said to himself, as he took one last swallow. He agreed that finding Jasper and putting him behind bars would help, but that wouldn't be the end of the President's troubles. He tried to think ahead about how the race would shape up. "It'll be nasty," he thought, "— nastier than any race I've ever seen." It wouldn't be the first time that a politician had to turn to negative campaigning—tearing down the other candidate—to win an election. It might work; it might not. Certainly it's the only chance the President has at the moment, Simon thought.

And then over the TV came a bulletin from veteran correspondent Matthew Andrus. "The White House said tonight that Vice President Hill has been diagnosed with liver cancer and is undergoing treatment in Washington. His doctors say he has a good chance of recovery over the next few months, according to the White House. President Everett said he was hoping and praying for the Vice President's swift recovery and return to work. There are no plans to invoke the 25th Amendment to the Constitution and replace him, according to a top White House source." Most likely that source was Herbert, Simon speculated.

"Wow," thought Simon, "that *is* a surprise. "Hill has a serious illness and may not be able to continue working. The President didn't say anything about the election. That's a very draining job—to run for re-election. The campaign might kill him if the cancer doesn't."

And so, Simon thought, maybe Everett would have a shot if he finds a strong and popular running mate who can help articulate a positive message for the country while also attacking the other party. He'd also need someone who'd be able to boost Everett's appeal in the most important swing states—Florida and Ohio.

There were several younger politicians in Everett's party who could fit the bill. People who could appeal to moderate, middle-class Americans who'd grown tired of ideologues who had simplistic approaches to government. Some prominent business people could and should be on the list, too, Simon thought. Ramos would be a possibility if he were interested, but he'd rejected such opportunities in previous elections, and liked to ride above the political fray.

Simon had a stake in the election, too. Usually money and prestige drove him like a runaway locomotive. Scott Herbert had put it on the table: He could have a top job in the administration almost immediately if he could discover where Stella was. He wouldn't have to meet her and bring her in—just give the White House the location. That would be enough to tip off the press and FBI. The White House was guessing that if they found Stella, they'd find Bob Jasper and put him in the slammer and declare a victory.

But Simon wasn't so sure about that scenario. He guessed that Stella had gone underground to try to find Jasper. If someone this angry had a gun, she might kill, he thought. He didn't want Stella to make such a mistake. He didn't blame her for wanting to hurt Bob, and he felt some responsibility to try to find her and talk her out of such an outlandish scheme. He hoped that Bob would just turn himself in.

He also wasn't sure about the relationship between Stella, her husband, and Alicia, and just how Alicia would fit into the picture, even though she had been Bob's lover. Could her disappearance be a sign that she was going to join Bob and then flee the country, using his riches to live a nice life? Could be, Simon reasoned. Anything sounded plausible in this case, but he certainly hoped that his client had had nothing to do with Alicia's disappearance.

Simon concluded that Stella was more resourceful and gutsier than he ever figured—enough to make him respect her abilities for the first time. In the old days, he'd written her off as a lightweight. But no more.

But how to find her? He made a trip to her former apartment in Arlington—the one where mostly Hispanic people lived—to see if he could turn up any information. The women who'd seen her last said they had no idea where she went. Simon figured they might be lying, but he wasn't sure, and he had no reason to question them. They told him they loved Stella and hoped that he could find her and put her in a safe place.

Shortly after 10 p.m., the phone rang. Simon hadn't expected any calls. He hesitated at first to pick it up. The caller I.D. said ANONYMOUS, an intentional attempt to remain unidentified. He picked up the receiver. "Dave Simon," he said.

"Are you Stella Jasper's attorney?" a woman asked.

"Yes," Simon answered.

"Mr. Simon, I know where your client is—the one with the Claddagh ring on her pinkie finger. I think she needs your help before she gets killed. Listen: Up the road from the Copperhead Club. That's all I can tell you. I'll say it again. Up the road from the Copperhead Club. Goodbye."

"Wait!" Simon shouted. "Where the hell is that?" There was a click and a dial tone. Simon had no way to trace the number. He'd received weird tips about Stella before, but something about this one made him think it might be legit. While Stella wore her Claddagh ring everywhere, it wasn't detectable in most photos or TV shots. Only people who'd been near her might notice it. He jumped up and went to the computer, and fired up his search engine. He found Copperhead Clubs in several states. He was baffled which one to take, and then he remembered: The woman had a soft Southern accent, not as pronounced as some, but still Southern. He saw one Copperhead Club that looked like it was a restaurant and bar with live country music. It was in Kentucky.

He used the search engine to see what was around this club, which sat almost all by itself across the street from a hill. Google maps didn't show a road going up the hill, but when he put the actual satellite pictures on his computer, he could see the road and the house at the end of it. "Bingo," he said. Now he felt 99% certain.

Using his computer, he booked an 8 a.m. flight to Lexington, Kentucky, and reserved a rental car.

He didn't call Scott Herbert, despite the offer of a lucrative position in the government. He wasn't sure whether he was making a good decision or a bad one, but it felt better this way. He realized he didn't have much time.

He also worried that someone might be watching his house— something that probably had been the case since Stella disappeared. And so he decided he'd have to sneak out without being seen. He packed a few things and turned off all the lights in the house, the last one in his bedroom. Slowly, in the pitch dark he began walking, holding his hand to the wall to get to the basement stairs. He succeeded without knocking anything down. He walked across the room, up a few stairs and into the alley outside. His car was still out front. He was in the back. Wearing dark pants and shirt to blend in with the night, he began walking, hoping that no one was taking notice.

He went from alley to alley, and then saw Union Station three blocks ahead, and he realized he'd have to walk in the open. He waited and then joined a group of sightseers who were strolling from the U.S. Capitol to the station to pick up the subway. He joined them without a word and left them at the cabstand out front. He waited in line to get a taxi, but when he did, he felt a relief. "Reagan Airport," he said.

Simon belonged to an airline club where he could eat and rest in the frequent flyers' lounge, and he took advantage of that. It also reduced the chance that anyone would see him.

During the long night in the airport, he second-guessed his decision, thinking of the privileges and income that might have awaited him had he just given the information to Herbert. But then he had an unusual thought: He wasn't going to succumb to the usual Washington slime and throw his client under the bus. He owed her the benefit of his legal expertise and political acumen. Stella was going through a rough time, discovering all in one day that her husband had abandoned her and had stolen all her money. It was unforgivable that her husband would do such a thing. It would be even more so if he, her lawyer, were to bail on her as well.

CHAPTER 31

Hopefully, Kentucky

The next morning, Natty Oeuvre called B.J.'s house and asked to speak with him or "that nice delivery girl" who had helped him deliver her orders. B.J. took the call.

"I'd like to ask you and your friend to supper tonight," Natty said. "I'll invite my friend Bud Jackson and we'll have some good country cooking—fried chicken maybe, and one of my prize-winning chocolate pies. I don't get around very much these days, and I'd love some good, intelligent company."

The invitation seemed strange to B.J., who asked Natty to wait until he summoned Stella, who had suddenly discovered the rich taste of grits with scrambled eggs and sausage, Kentucky-style.

"This may sound crazy, but Natty Oeuvre wants to invite us to supper," B.J. said, turning his palms upward to show that he hadn't the foggiest idea why. Stella took the phone, and Natty repeated her invitation. Stella accepted, adding, "Between Molly and you, I won't have much of a figure left." Natty laughed and said she'd see them at 7 p.m.

When the call was over, Stella looked at B.J. quizzingly. "What on earth?" she asked. "Why would she suddenly invite us to dinner?"

"She must know something or she wants to get some information from us," B.J. said.

"—Or both," Stella added. They debated whether they should go or stay. Stella feared she'd blow her cover by saying something wrong at the meal, or that B.J. would call her Stella instead of Ellie.

B.J. checked with his mom and The Baron to see if they would stay in the safe house until they got home. Molly objected, insisting that she could take care of herself, but then relented. "We'll try to be home by 11," B.J. said, trying to reassure them.

Stella asked Molly and The Baron if they knew much about Natty. Molly said Natty's husband had died of a heart attack 10 years ago and had left the store to her. Early in their marriage the two of them had worked over in Purcells, with a firm that set up computers for small businesses. "She was a lot better at the job than he was," Molly added. "They got robbed once or twice, I think, but she never had much cash for the robbers, who happened to be local people on drugs. After that, I heard she wanted to volunteer for the police department, but I don't think she ever did. She's kind and she's funny, and she's a very good cook. I bet she doesn't go to church, though, because she hasn't yet forgiven the Almighty for taking her husband."

"I can relate to that," Stella said sharply.

"You know, it's tough to be a widow in these parts," Molly said. "I'm blessed with a son who takes care of me. Natty didn't have a son, so she's more or less adopted Wally Ponz, whom she helped get through some of his wild years. She taught him a little about business, too."

In the evening, before sunset, B.J. drove the off-the-road vehicle to the safe house, with Molly and The Baron on board. They had a portable radio, a bag of "birdseed"—Molly's munchies of rice crackers and nuts—a case of beer, and a deck of cards to help them pass the time.

"Look, there's some wildflowers starting to show their heads," Molly exclaimed. "I'd forgotten how beautiful it is out here."

"Yes, it's God's Country," The Baron agreed.

B.J. helped Molly get in the wheelchair, rolled her up the ramp, turned on the lights, and got all of them inside with no trouble.

To avoid being followed, B.J. decided to take The Baron's car, which was parked on the other side of the knob, where he had picked up The Baron in the afternoon. He and Stella walked along a path around the knob near its base, and then to the car parked nearby. The path couldn't be seen from the road.

They were off. B.J. told Stella that he never dreamed he'd be in an undeclared war with no ending and with very little intelligence about the other participants.

"I know," Stella said. "Weird how life is. Do you remember the Forrest Gump movie? Forrest said, 'Life is like a box of chocolates; you never know what you're gonna get.' You're right, B.J., and maybe I should start thinking right now about leaving," she mused, "just to make it safer for you." He reminded her of the car crash on the hill that killed two of the men who were, presumably, Bob's bodyguards, and the fear that he, and his family, could still be attacked if they found out that he was responsible. So if she left, it wouldn't entirely remove their trouble. No matter where they went, they felt they had to tote their guns with them as if they were back in the Wild West.

Natty Oeuvre's house was on the hill, just down from the store they'd visited earlier. She greeted them with a warm hug and introduced them to Bud Jackson, a muscular guy who could have played football in college.

Inside, the house was a treasure trove of antiques she had gathered over the years—marbletop tables, a pie-safe that held an extensive collection of Tea Leaf china and Bybee pottery, old-fashioned desks, a player piano, and ancient weight-driven clocks.

"This is wonderful!" Stella said, admiring the personal museum. Fried chicken, mashed potatoes, green beans cooked in bacon grease, deviled eggs, an iceberg lettuce salad, cornbread, and sweet tea provided a hearty, traditional Kentucky supper. "Nothing fancy," Natty had promised, and she was right. However, she announced that she did have champagne to top off the meal—the same champagne that Wally had sold her a year ago. They ate heartily and merrily, including the chocolate pie, although Stella sensed that Natty was nursing some kind of hidden gloom.

Stella managed to remember that her name was really Ellie Heinz, and she prompted B.J. to call her by that name all night. They talked about traditions in Kentucky and inquired about her painting career, which, she admitted, amounted to nothing. Bud Jackson was an outdoor man who loved to fish and hunt and talk about the reemergence of bald eagles in some areas of the state. Natty couldn't stop talking about her customers and her antiques, but she confided later in the evening that she watched cable television news all day long, even when customers were in the store. "Anderson Cooper is always on," she said. "I swear there's two of him—how can he be in New York in the morning and in Ohio or some other place, diving with sharks, later in the day?" Stella wished she had the time to keep up with everything, but said she couldn't.

After supper, Natty said, "Ellie, come with me. "I want to show you some more of my collections and a special powder room of antiques where there's a pitcher and washbowl in a dry sink that I love. Pardon us boys, a little girl talk."

They went upstairs talking about old photographs placed neatly on the staircase wall. Antiques surrounded them like old memories, old realities, and old assumptions. In the hallway, Natty put on a country CD and turned up the volume.

Suddenly Natty became very serious. "I have a quick message for you," she said to Stella, grabbing her hand and leading her to a nearby bedroom. "He said to tell you he knows you're here in Kentucky, but he can't meet with you or be seen with you. He said it's too dangerous. He said he knows you're deeply angry with him for what he's done, but that he couldn't help himself. He said he's a human being, and far, far from perfect, that he's broken laws and the vows of your marriage. He asks for forgiveness. But he cannot—simply cannot—meet directly with you."

Stunned for a moment, Stella was silent, the color draining from her face.

"Do you mean to tell me you talked to my husband Bob? You've been deceiving me all along? How could you?" Stella shouted as she kicked over a wastebasket, spilling all its contents.

"Shhhh, they'll hear you," Natty said in a stage whisper. She squeezed Stella's arm and pleaded with her to control her anger. Yes, she admitted, she had talked with Bob face-to-face. "But he insists that you cannot see him. I befriended him only recently when he came looking for a place to stay. He wanted to hide. It meant a little money for me, and I swore I'd help him and keep everything confidential. He's wondering how the hell you found him, and if you've told anyone."

"You've been toying with me all along, haven't you?" shouted Stella "You know who I really am because he told you. I'm so pissed now that I could turn you in for aiding and abetting a criminal. How could you do this?" The screech in her voice grew louder. "And no, I haven't told anyone! Why do you think I'm going by the name Ellie fucking Heinz?"

She picked up an early American vase sitting on a shelf and cocked her arm as she prepared to throw it. Natty grabbed her arm again. "Shhhh! You don't want to do this, Stella, if I can call you that now. Believe me, this is the best I can do. I'll tell you what: I'll contact him as soon as possible to see if I can arrange a meeting. We'll keep the cops out of it. You can have your talk privately, give him a piece of your mind, and report him. And I agree: He's the king of all assholes."

"Let's go. Let's do it now," Stella said, grabbing Natty's arm. "I'm tired of waiting around."

"No—I need to find him again," Natty said. "He's moving from place to place. I suspect that within several days, he'll either come back or he'll send someone to pick up another case of King Tut beer, which I store for him. He doesn't carry a cellphone or anything that can be traced. He's very paranoid about everything and everybody. I help with food and supplies—stuff like that. But here's the problem: He trusts no one, and that probably includes you. You have to promise you won't try anything funny. You also have to realize that no matter how many pleas you make, Bob is likely to turn you down. He said to tell you this: 'Go home, forget about me.' "

"No way!" Stella rasped. "Not only is he a complete fucking jerk, he's crazy! I won't rest until Bob is behind bars. He says his life is in danger? How so? He could be arrested and put in jail without getting hurt."

"I don't know," Natty said, "there are devils who'd like him dead. If you persist in trying to find him, *your* life could be in danger, too. He says that hiding in various places all the time is very hard, and he's thinking of moving out of this area, although he doesn't know where to go. I'll keep my promise to ask him, but I don't think he's worth it. I'd advise you to forget him."

"Not a chance!" Stella shot back. Her red face, wet with tears, couldn't hide her anger—and sadness. She pounded her fist against the wall, rattling the antique figurines on the shelf, crying over what she'd just heard. Natty tried to console her.

"There've been days when he hid in my house," Natty said. "Now I don't have a clue where he is. You've got to remember—I provide food and his beer when he needs it. He doesn't tell me where he is."

Natty said Stella would have to take a vow of secrecy before she'd try to set up a meeting. "You have to swear to me that you won't tell anyone about this, because purely and simply, my life could be in danger, too. Look. I'm probably violating the law just by speaking to him because he's a fugitive at large."

"I've got to tell B.J.," Stella said. " This affects him too. He won't betray you—I pledge to you, on my word of honor. And you know B.J., too. He's a solid person, who believes in carrying out his promises."

Natty nodded her agreement, and clasped Stella's hand. "I hope you'll take my advice," she said. "You can have a long and beautiful life ahead of you if you leave this area as soon as you can. Take B.J. with you."

"I wonder if Wally Ponz has ever seen Bob?" Stella asked, seemingly ignoring Natty's advice.

"I don't know," Natty said, "but I wouldn't be surprised. He's all over this area with trucks and knows practically everybody. It'd be hard for anyone to hide from Wally. And he watches everything. He's our spy, really. He might have seen Bob, but he wouldn't know who he was talking to."

Stella remembered the bottle of King Tut left in what had seemed to be a deserted home. If Wally *had* taken it to Bob, he'd lied to them about it. But, perhaps a lie in such a situation might not be so bad, she reasoned, and was in fact understandable. He might be trying to protect clients and himself, even if it meant doing business with a money laundering crook. And I'm not really one to talk, she told herself; I'm living a lie too, with a new name and new look, to find a husband who's taken away my entire way of life.

Natty handed Stella some Kleenex and told her to clean up her smeared mascara. She also warned Stella that she'd have to go out and do a good acting job in front of Bud and B.J.—to pretend that she had been admiring hand made quilts, and other antique collections. "Smile, and tell them what fantastic furniture I have," she told Stella. "And I'll be careful to call you Ellie," she said.

And so it went as they talked about Kentucky folklore through the end of the evening.

On their way home, B.J. seemed puzzled. "That sure was a strange evening," he told Stella. "Here we thought Natty might have some other reason for inviting us than just for dinner, but not so. Bud is a nice, funny guy. I had never heard that story about paying monthly rental fees for a tuxedo on a corpse," B.J. said laughing. Stella said nothing. "It was nice to get away from our worries for a little while," B.J. continued. "I hope The Baron and Mom are having a nice evening playing cards in the safe house." Again, Stella said nothing.

"What's wrong?—You aren't talking," B.J. said.

She told B.J. that what she was about to tell him was unbelievable but true, and a deep secret, and that he'd have to promise to keep it a secret. When he agreed, Stella told him the story. B.J. slammed on the brakes and the car came to a halt. "*FUCK!*—This changes everything," he said. Abruptly, he stepped on the accelerator and turned the car around.

"Where are you going?" Stella asked.

"Back to Viable to pick up Natty," he said. "I don't think we were followed, but it's possible. From what you've told me, her life could be in danger. Someone trying to get Jasper might have followed us, and they might try to hurt her because they know who you are and they think you know where Bob is and you may have told Natty. We just don't know."

They returned quickly as they could and roared into Natty's driveway. The house was dark, with no lights. Her car was still in the driveway.

"Oh no, where is she?—We were just here 20 minutes ago," Stella said. They went to the front door. It was locked. They called out, but there was no answer. "Oh no, B.J. Her car is still here. I think you were right to be afraid for Natty. Something terrible has happened, but I don't know what. Let's check all the doors. She may be bound, gagged, dead, or..."

"No, let's get out of here," B.J. said as he grabbed her arm and started running back to the truck. "Someone might be waiting for us inside. Let's go. We need to calm down and think clearly what we should do."

With his heart racing, B.J. gunned the Lincoln's engine as they sped toward home. He turned on the radio to his favorite public broadcasting station in nearby Purcells and got the report that he never wanted to hear. Citing confidential sources, the broadcaster said the sole survivor of a mysterious mountaintop crash in which three others died had miraculously awakened from his coma. The man had been speaking to authorities, the broadcaster reported. There was hope that the person driving the other vehicle could be identified and arrested.

"Yikes!" Stella said. She reached over and squeezed B.J.'s thigh.

"The men protecting Bob could've found out where I live by now," he said. "They could be at the house as we speak. I can't take you there now."

"Well, if you're going to the house, I'm going with you," Stella said. "You might save my life, and I might save yours. I know how to handle a gun. So do you. Besides, the reason this is happening at all ultimately is because of my husband," she said, feeling guilt. "I owe it to you."

"But I'm not only thinking about you. I'm also thinking about my mom and The Baron," B.J. said. "Worrying about you could well be what puts this whole thing in the wringer. Please don't insist on going in there with me."

"You need backup," Stella declared.

CHAPTER 32

Hopefully, Kentucky

B.J. pushed the accelerator harder as headlights of something behind them showed up in the rearview mirror around every curve. "Are we being followed?" he asked, raising his voice a bit louder each time.

"I don't know," Stella said, looking over her shoulder to check the road behind. "Oh no!" she exclaimed. "I can see lights, sort of laying back, not getting too close. At this point, I'm afraid we *are* being followed, dammit."

B.J. hit the steering wheel as he rocked back and forth. "We never should have gone to dinner tonight," he said. "We never should have gone—never, never."

Stella thought he was probably right.

"We just weren't careful enough," B.J. shrieked. "I'm really worried that Bob Jasper's hired guns are going to be waiting at home. Natty and Bud could have been tortured, killed and carried off, never to be found," he said.

"I'm worried about Molly and The Baron," Stella interjected. "Let's hope that no one has tried to get in the safe house. They're old and they don't have any way to defend themselves."

B.J. agreed. "I know, I know, I know!"

"Damn, damn, damn—those sons-of-bitches better not bother your mom and The Baron, or you for that matter. I'm so glad you got these guns for me." Three months ago, she never wanted to leave her Northern

Virginia bubble. Now the shallowness of it all made her sick. She knew evil lurked. "We're going to be okay, aren't we?" she asked nervously.

From the glow of the instruments on the dashboard she looked at B.J.'s face. He was sweating profusely. She found a tissue and handed it to him.

She had no illusions about her husband's being at the Matson house. No way, she asserted. It would be a bad place to hide. If anyone trying to kill B.J. were at the house, he also did not know that she, Bob's wife, was going to be there with him. Bob had cheated on her, robbed her, and abandoned her, and there was obviously no love for her whatsoever. In fact, if they killed her, it was to dispose of another of his problems—her obsession with searching him out and trying to shame him.

"The car lights are still behind us," B.J. said. "If they get to the house, they can't be seen well in the dark. They could alert any other intruders about us, too. They would simply meet us at the gate." He told Stella there was a side road they could take that passed by the mountain, but on the other side from their house. And the turnoff would be coming up soon.

"I'm calling Noah," B.J. said.

"Whoever he is, do it fast," she said, with tension in her face. "He's an old friend," said B.J. He pulled out his cellphone, highlighted a name, and hit the call button. It rang a couple of times, and Noah Williams picked it up at the other end. "B.J. here. Noah, I'm calling because I need some help—badly, and quickly. Could you please help me? I know it's late."

"I'm up—I've been reading," Noah said. "What's up, brother?"

"Noah, look I need for you to help me right *now*," B.J. said, emphasizing the *now*. "Something's come up that'll take me too long to explain. But I'm in danger. It may be a bit a risky," B.J. said with a nervous sound in his voice. "I'm on Route 910, heading home, and I'm worried that some bad guys are following me. I want to lose them so I can get back to my family and make sure everything is okay at home."

"Hey man, slow down," Noah said. "Take a deep breath. Why would a bad somebody want to follow you?" B.J. said he'd explain later.

"Okay," Noah said. "What can I do?" B.J. saved Noah's butt a couple times when he was in debt and being stalked by an ex. B.J. also invested some money in Noah's hauling business, and Noah paid him back with interest. B.J. promptly reinvested it. Noah didn't hesitate to help B.J. now.

"Do you have one of your semis at the house?" B.J. asked. When Noah said yes, he said, "I want you to block the road for me after I pass your place. Up at the bridge, you know, where it's only one lane. Just for a little while. Like maybe a half hour or so. I'll owe you big time. I'm in The Baron's white Lincoln."

"No problem. Anything for you, man," Noah said. "I'm on my way. Are you sure you don't want me to call the police?"

"No, no, no," B.J. said. "Those guys'll only make it worse."

B.J. took a right, then a left onto a road that paralleled the main road, but wasn't well traveled. The smaller road spun around sharp curves as it climbed along the side of a hill.

Up ahead, he saw Noah's house on the right, with a big semi truck idling out front.

"That's Noah," he said. B.J. flashed his bright lights on and off, and Noah pulled the truck behind him as soon as he passed. Up ahead was the bridge, a one lane structure that went over Clary Gorge, which fell 100 feet below. B.J. roared across the bridge on the way home. Noah stopped when his truck got on the bridge. No one else could pass. No less than a minute later, an SUV drove up with two men in it. The driver stuck his head out the window. "Hey, you," he said testily. "What's going on? We need to get to town."

"Sorry, I have a bundle-branch block in the heart of my engine," Noah told him. "I just called someone to tow me out."

"How long will that take?" The man asked.

"About an hour, sir. I'm very sorry."

The men in the car turned around and headed down the hill to see if they could retrace their course and catch up. But at the next turn, they came upon another semi, traveling slowly down the hill. It took another 10 minutes before they could get around this truck, also one of Noah's trucks with Ethan, his neighbor, driving.

When he could no longer see the SUV's headlights as they drove farther, Noah called B.J. and told him about the "bundle-branch" excuse he had used. He'd first heard the term applied to a heart malady from which his mother had suffered. They laughed.

"Anything else I can do for you, friend?" Noah asked.

"I don't think so at the moment," B.J. said. "I don't want to involve you any further. You have a family. Be sure to tell Ethan thanks for his help."

"I'll tell him. I can still call the police," Noah offered.

"No, no, don't do that. They're part of the problem. You've done your thing. Just wish me well. We don't know whether mom and The Baron are okay. They're in the safe house. I'm going to go around the mountain rather than go up the driveway, just in case someone's waiting. I know this all seems crazy, but I'll explain later."

"Good luck, man," Noah said. "Let me know if there's anything else I can do."

After they'd hung up, Noah realized he was deeply troubled about what his friend was facing. "What the hell has he gotten himself into?" Noah wondered. "Being chased? That's not the B.J. I know." What had he done to get in such a mess?

In The Baron's comfortable car, Stella didn't feel the sense of panic that she might have felt in the past under such circumstances. She was thinking ahead, not knowing what the circumstances were. "I want Noah's cellphone number," she said. "And I'd like to borrow yours."

They knew by now that the car following them had gone away and guessed they probably were headed for the front entrance to the Matson home. "There might be others," B.J. said.

On the small road, B.J. looped around the knob and turned left at a dirt road. The road went to the bottom of the mountain, where there was a padlocked gate, with a sign saying, "No Trespassing." It was the same spot they'd left hours ago. They'd parked under a tree in a grassy area about 40 yards to the left. It would be hard for anyone to see the car from the road. As best they could tell, there was no one around. They toted their guns over their backs in bags they had purchased at the shooting range. The pistols were holstered. The moon was bright overhead.

Moving slowly and quietly, they made their way around the knob until they spotted the house, some sheds, and the barn that also served as B.J.'s office. The lights in the house were off, as were those in the barn. There was one room in the barn that had no windows, and that was where B.J. kept most of the stuff he valued. But the intruders wouldn't want any of that. They'd want B.J.

"Stay here," he said to Stella, as they stood behind a large shrub deep in the shadows. He moved closer and tried to stay in the shadows or behind a shed—although someone in the windows might spot him there. It was quiet—too quiet. He clutched his rifle, ready to shoot.

"Don't move, son," a masculine voice behind him boomed out. "We have you covered four ways. Put down your weapon if you want to live a second longer."

They'd hidden in the shadows just as he had feared. There were six of them, and maybe more inside. He didn't know. He dropped his weapon as directed.

"So you must be B.J.," the leader said.

"Who wants to know?" B.J. asked him.

"I'm Butch Jellico," the man said. "We work for the Kentucky State Police as an undercover unit." He flashed a badge and put it back in his pocket. B.J. didn't have time to read it, but it looked authentic.

"You need to know that we just arrested five people who were on their way to your house. We caught them at the gate down there, and we've taken them away. We're investigating the circumstances of the accident on the hill here a while back in which everyone was killed except for one person, who has just come out of a coma. He indicated the person in the truck that hit them was you, B.J. We believe that they were a bunch of hired guns protecting a criminal, that's all I can say. Can you tell us what is going on? What's this all about, anyway?"

Feeling some relief, B.J. spilled out the whole story—his photos, the collision on the hill, the constant worry that he and his family were going to be hurt, the extraordinary effort to protect his family because of fear that the authorities downtown would do nothing. "It was an accident on the hill, but I was too scared to report it. I was afraid they would kill the whole family."

"We're here to help," Butch said. "Now, can you get me a copy of the photo, so that I can know who led this gang of people? Do you know where the leader is?"

"No, I don't know where he is," B.J. said.

"Well, who is this person? Do you have a real name for him?"

"I don't know anything for sure," B.J. said. He didn't want to give up the fact that Stella—still hiding outside in a bush somewhere—was 90% sure it was Bob Jasper, the lawyer accused of laundering millions of dollars. "But it must have been someone very important, at least to somebody. I don't really have an answer."

"Well, it would help if we could see the photo or photos," Butch said. "Then we might be able to recognize him and get to the bottom of this mess."

B.J. said he would show the photos if he would agree not to put them in the public domain. He did not want them to be on the Internet or in the news in any way.

The officer thought this a reasonable proposition, and added that B.J. could be reasonably sure that police would not charge him with leaving the scene of an accident. B.J. was relieved that he would no longer have to worry about possible retaliation for the deadly accident.

At his computer, B.J. showed the officers the photos he'd taken. The first one showed Jasper sitting in a chair, sipping a beer. He enlarged it for Butch. "Send me a copy of that," Butch said, and B.J. did.

He showed the other photo—a man with a blurred face. Butch looked at it carefully. B.J. watched Butch's face, and for an instant there was a sign that he had recognized the man.

"I can't tell who this is," Butch said, "but send me that one, too, if it's not too much trouble..."

B.J. complied.

Butch thanked him for the photos and said that the Kentucky State Police would undoubtedly be in touch once the investigation is over. With a rounding up of weapons and fast goodbyes, the officers were on their way.

Stella had climbed the hill and hadn't stopped until she'd gotten to the safe house. At night, the climb was treacherous, but the moon was out and she knew the way. When she got to the door, she used the key that B.J. had given to her and went inside. There was a small nightlight. Both Molly and The Baron were asleep in the same bed, a touching sight. The Baron opened his eyes and mumbled. "Just checking on you," Stella said softly. The Baron said okay and turned his head the other way. Stella quietly locked the door and started back down the knob.

She saw a couple of cars moving down the road as she neared the bottom of the hill. She heard men's voices in the distance and was terrified that she might never see B.J. again, and that her own hours on earth were numbered. When she saw the outline of a man move up the hill and decided that it clearly had B. J's stride and shape, she literally fell to the ground in relief.

B.J., who'd been happy at first that the appearance of these men meant that his house would unlikely be attacked, now took a more sober view.

"I worry that they weren't as thorough as I had expected," he said. "You know, they said they'd arrested people and had taken them away, but it wasn't clear what these people were doing. They certainly seemed legit—they all had badges and sirens and the rest. But now that they're gone, I admit that I'm wondering about them. It seemed that all they wanted were the photos."

Just then they saw lights from a vehicle coming up the road. B.J. and Stella reached for their guns. As the lights drew closer, it became clear that they belonged to a very large truck, just like the one owned by B.J.'s old friend.

The truck stopped in front of them and Noah, brandishing a rifle, stuck his head out the window.

"Everyone okay?" he asked cheerfully.

CHAPTER 33

Washington, D.C.

In the Oval Office, President Everett told his Chief of Staff, Scott Herbert, that he doubted that the Vice President would be on the ticket in the upcoming election.

"He's really much worse off than I thought," the President said. "It appears the cancer is metastasizing. Unless a miracle happens, he won't last the year."

"Very sad," Herbert said, knowing that the President admired the man as a straight shooter who believed in making tough decisions when necessary, even if it hurt politically in the short run.

"He has a vision, and I love that," the President said. "It's too bad the problems are so vast and so controversial now."

"Out of respect for the Vice President, I won't announce any decision yet as to who will replace him," the President continued. "But I would like to give the American people a clue about the type of person I'm looking for, just to settle the uncertainty. They need to know as soon as possible. Of course, Ramos is at the top of the list. He's loved by the conservative movement, and he's pragmatic and brilliant."

The President looked Herbert in the eye. "You see right through me, don't you, Scott?" he said. "This is purely political—to bolster my presidency. If Ramos says anything in my behalf, it'll help my standings in the polls and it'll make more people listen to me."

"What are you going to do?" Herbert asked.

"Basically, I'm going to ask Ramos to accompany me on my campaign trips around the country," Everett said. "He can reassure people that we're on top of the world's problems. He's like a god out there with the voters. And I want you to go with us as the campaign chief of staff to observe him and help him with speeches. I don't want him freelancing. I've already spoken with Ramos about this, and I think he's willing to do it. Let's face it—he knows he has a good shot at being V.P."

"Excellent idea. When do we start?" Herbert said.

"Next week when I go to your home state, Kentucky, then West Virginia and Tennessee. Inform Ramos and go ahead with the planning as soon as possible and check back with me," the President said.

A little later, after sketching out some preliminary plans, Herbert called Ramos and said to get ready for the ride. Ramos agreed to go.

"If the response to your trip is as positive as we fully expect, Mr. President, Pennsylvania and Ohio should come next." Herbert said.

"I'll leave as soon as possible as an advance man." He had advanced trips all the time as a campaign aide when Everett was a member of Congress and later when he ran for President. Normally, a man in Herbert's position wouldn't act as an advance man, since he'd be needed to give the President advice on broader political questions and substantive issues. But Herbert loved to do advance work—to talk to the locals, spread the official message, and even pick the best places for the President to eat. Benjamin Johnson, Herbert's deputy, would step in and substitute for him while he was away. He was confident that the White House staff would operate smoothly.

Herbert called Ramos. "We're going to introduce you to the American people as a politician rather than a businessman," Herbert said. "You'll be great." Herbert told him that by going to border states, he'd enjoy a heartier welcome and that he'd be able to sound more like a populist than he would be anywhere else. Even though many people in these states are on welfare, food stamps, and Medicaid, they're still very conservative," he pointed out. "They'll love you there," Herbert said.

Everett had never given Ramos a hint about what his chances for getting on the ticket would be if he accepted this assignment. He said only that he was going to ask several prominent people to help with the campaign. Ramos, who had never lacked self-esteem, was confident that he would outshine the others. To him, it meant that he had the vice presidential nomination in the bag.

Everett had to be careful about how he pitched this trip to the American people. He didn't want it to backfire, and give the dozens of "talking heads"—the commentators and outside contributors who populated talk radio stations and cable TV networks—an opportunity to accuse him of exploiting the Vice President's illness for his own political gain.

So the President called a few of his media contacts to tell them about what he was doing and try to persuade them that there was no politics involved. He knew that some of them would question his motives anyway, but they would still feel obliged to quote the President as saying that he was just trying to rally the country at a troublesome time. It would help unify the party, he would tell them.

One of those "talking heads" asked the President why were they launching the series of campaign speeches in those states. "Well, we have to start somewhere," he said, "Why not Kentucky, Tennessee, and West Virginia? They're all good solid states with hard-working people and strong historical ties." Referring to his strong standing in the polls in the Bluegrass region, Everett added: "Most Kentuckians I've encountered have been very good to me."

CHAPTER 34

Hopefully, Kentucky

Looking a little rumpled after a quick flight from Washington to Kentucky, Dave Simon parked his rental car in the Copperhead Club lot, then went straight to the Matson house driveway, opened the gate, and walked up the dusty road. Huffing and puffing, he climbed the porch steps and knocked on the door. His watch said 3:30 p.m.

An elderly woman answered, brandishing a gun that she'd pointed at him.

"Who in the hell are you?" she barked. Suddenly, a chubby man ran to the door and grabbed the gun away. "Mom, I told you to stay away from guns," he said. Molly walked away, visibly fuming over this order.

"Can I help you, sir?" B.J. said. "And pardon my mom. She's a former cop."

"I'm Stella Jasper's attorney," Simon said. "Could I see her?"

"What makes you think that anyone with that name would be at this house?" B.J. asked.

"Some woman who didn't give a name called me yesterday at my home in Washington, D.C., and told me where Stella was. I'm worried about her. So is she here or not?" B.J. recognized the man from the TV hearings, and knew he was no imposter. But would Stella want to talk to him now?

Just then, Stella walked to the door and stood behind B.J. Her eyes popped open when she saw him. "Dave Simon, I don't believe this is

293

you!" she said in astonishment. "How'd you find me? But before you answer, I'd suggest it'd be smarter if you turned around and went home. You need to leave now—for your own good."

"Is it really you, Stella?" asked Simon. "Behind all this short, black, funky hair, and crazy glasses to boot? What a disguise that is! You could have fooled me."

"Dave, you need to save yourself," she said.

"I'm not going anywhere right now," Simon said. "When I got a call about where you were, I felt I had to come. Everyone's trying to get me to tell where you are. The White House even offered me a job as a diplomat in Paris, for God's sake. When I heard where you were, I thought I ought to try to see you and find out whether I could help. I didn't tell those bastards in Washington where I was going. So here I am. Hey—what's with the tattoo of a phoenix on your neck?"

"It's just part of my disguise. It's only a temporary one. Dave, you've put my friends here and me at great risk. How do you know the FBI didn't follow you? If the government is seeking you out, they can do it without your knowledge."

Simon assured them he had taken extraordinary steps to avoid detection, such as walking out of his house in total darkness and almost tiptoeing through alleys in the back of his house. "I don't think I was followed," he said.

"Why should we trust you?" B.J. demanded. He turned to Stella. "Should we trust him?" he asked.

Stella looked at Simon for a few seconds, pausing, and then at B.J. "Dave is a complete asshole, a pain in the neck, a person who is highly ambitious, but yeah, I trust him. He told me the truth more than once— even when it hurt. We can trust him."

So over the next few hours, Stella and B.J. told their stories. They told him about Natty and Bud—that the two of them may have been murdered. As Simon listened, he looked at Stella with more respect. This woman was truly amazing, he thought. Who would've thought that clueless Stella would remake herself into a Rambo Girl—a woman who before this would have shied away from just touching a gun, let alone firing one.

Simon regarded B.J. as a diamond in the rough. Here was a mountain man in overalls and flannel shirt using an extensive vocabulary to discuss government, politics, justice, and who knows what else. He was at ease jumping from discussions of appellate law to how Stella's watercolors sometimes resembled Monet's "Water Lilies." If he were wearing the Washington, D.C., uniform—with a dark-blue suit, shirt, and tie—he probably could lead a boardroom discussion anywhere in the country. His Kentucky accent, with the telltale long *i*, was noticeable and would identify him as being from Appalachia. Despite his knowledge and command of the language, he seemed shy. He was clearly worried about Stella and his mother—and frightened about the predicament they were in.

Simon could understand why Bob wouldn't want to meet with Stella, especially if she knew anything about his criminal behavior. If he still loved her, he wouldn't want to make her a target, as he himself almost certainly was. "He's hiding, but he hasn't gone completely underground," Simon said. "Can't figure it out. It's pretty dangerous."

"Now, as for these photos you took, B.J., I'm sorry you gave them to someone you don't know," Simon continued. "You think you can trust this Butch Jellico, but you can't be sure. The person could use the photos to identify and kill Bob, especially if Bob stays around here."

The landline phone rang. B.J. answered. "Oh my God! Thank goodness! We didn't know what happened," he said. Then: "Okay, I'll get her. Stella—pick up the phone. Stella, it's Natty."

"Oh, Natty, I'm so happy to hear your voice and to know that you're okay. We were scared for you and Bud last night. We were being followed and we thought someone had linked you to me and that that same someone might have harmed you. So we came back to your house and all the lights were off. Where were you all?

"Oh, I'm sorry you did that," Natty said. "We're fine. Bud left right after you, and I went to bed shortly after that. All's well."

"But we yelled for you and you didn't answer," Stella said.

"I didn't hear you," Natty replied. "I had earphones on, listening to WHG's late news on the radio. I'm sorry you were scared. I've been thinking maybe I should get a dog that would alert me if I had any visitors. Anyway, Bud and I are fine."

"This is really important," Natty said. "I've talked to Bob again and he's agreed to see you, but this next part will be painful for you to hear. He says it'll have to be the absolute last time you will see him. As traumatic as this is for you, you'll have to accept his terms or you'll never see him again."

"Why? What did he say? Natty, what did he tell you?"

Then: "Did he mention Alicia?"

"I'm just relaying his message," Natty said. "He'll have to explain when he meets you."

"Okay, I accept his terms," Stella said. "I can't wait to see the damned S.O.B. When and where do we meet?"

"Tuesday—9 a.m.," Natty said. "Go to the Cottingly house on Route 844—way out in the sticks."

"So Bob has been there. B.J. and I went to the Cottingly house the day we delivered Wally's stuff. We didn't find anyone there."

"I talked him into this," Natty continued. "I told him that you've come all this way to find him, and no matter how big a shit he is, he should do it. He is your husband, for God's sake."

"But Natty, you told me last night that he said couldn't meet with me because it was too dangerous for me to know too much, for fear I would be pulled into the story and become a target," Stella said.

"I'm sure he won't give you any details about his wrongdoing and connections, so you won't have to worry about being a target," Natty said. "The Cottingly house is safe as long as you aren't followed."

"Well, I'm not so sure," Stella said. "He has bodyguards and I don't. I know it's a big risk, but I want to do it."

"Put the phone down a minute," Simon told her from the other side of the room. "Let's talk. Let's not jump into something crazy." He agreed that Stella would be taking a great risk by meeting Jasper at this moment. He wondered why they couldn't meet almost immediately, and why it couldn't be on Stella's terms. Maybe she should forgo the whole thing until she was more certain of what reception she'd get. Could she get there without being followed? He also worried that by meeting with Bob, Stella could be vulnerable to charges of aiding and abetting a criminal suspect. It all would depend on what happened, he said, and he encouraged her to tell police about it immediately after the meeting and let them know where Bob was.

B.J. didn't like it. "I'm afraid it could be a trap," he said. "We just had a group of guys who broke into our house, claiming to be undercover state police. I'm starting to wonder if these people are really who they said they were."

"Natty, do you know any undercover State Police?" Stella asked.

Natty said she knew nothing about any State Police. "Look," she said, "Bob said to take it or leave it. He'll be ready Tuesday morning in the house. You know how to get there. Go in the side entrance on the left of the house."

B.J. said he was wary, but Stella agreed. "I'll be there," Stella said, and hung up. Turning to B.J. and to Simon, she said, "I have to do this. I won't rest until I see him."

"You're more courageous than I gave you credit for," said Simon. "I can't really object. This is why you came here—to find him. I can only advise you to be prepared by considering every possible outcome. It doesn't seem to be in his self-interest to hurt you."

Not trusting either Bob Jasper or Natty, his confidante, B.J. said he wouldn't go to the house without weapons. He didn't understand why Bob had chosen the Cottingly house, except that it was remote. He thought back: It had a big yard. He tried to remember how many trees or other possible shelters it contained.

"I'm going with you," B.J. said. "And I have an idea—maybe we can rent an armored car."

"Come on, B.J.—you've got to be kidding," Simon said with a snort. "An armored car out here?"

"Yes, believe it or not, my friend Wally Ponz, who may be a little weird, bought an older model armored car that he used in his delivery fleet. I think I saw it the other day on the lot next to his house. I'm texting him now." B.J. asked if he could borrow the special vehicle.

In less than two minutes, B.J.'s cell rang. "Of course you can have Bertha," Wally said. "What's going on? Have you got some crazies running around your place? Are you playing war games in the woods? Do you need for me to go with you wherever you're going and protect your back?" he added jokingly.

"I know you'd do anything in the world for me, but I can't let you ride with us," B.J. said." I'm a *friend*, too, you know."

Wally sounded disappointed. "Where, exactly, are you going?" he asked. "I'd like to know something about where old Bertha is going to be." Against his better judgment, B.J. told him that Ellie's ex-husband was in the area and that she was afraid of him, but she needed to talk to him. He provided no more details. "What we are thinking of doing could be dangerous," B.J. replied. "We don't want to involve you, Wally. Using your car will solve our problem. We'll tell you about it next week. Right now, I don't have time to explain it. Natty can tell you."

"Okay—it's not a problem—but I'm worried why you can't tell me. You're my buddy, so come and get her—now, if you can—while I'm here. I've got deliveries this afternoon."

"Okay, we'll be there soon."

Bertha was sitting at the end of Wally's driveway when B.J. and Stella arrived to pick up the armored car. "Wally, I can't thank you enough, I owe you a big one," B.J. said. He got in, took the wheel, and waved to Wally, who watched, speechless, as Stella followed in B.J.'s truck down the road.

Back at the Matson house, Molly offered Simon a bed for the night as well as dinner.

Simon smiled and nodded, saying he'd be grateful for both if it wouldn't be a burden. "There's a small bedroom upstairs that isn't being used, Molly said.

The Baron brought food from the diner downtown. To Simon, it was a feast—fried country steak, biscuits, cabbage, macaroni cheese casserole, Jell-O salad, plus a homemade apple pie for dessert (with ice cream, of course). To help wash it down, Molly supplied a white wine made somewhere in Kentucky. After the pie, she offered Simon a little bourbon whiskey. Both were surprisingly good.

As they sat in front of the television set, their mouths nearly flew open when they heard a local TV bulletin: The President was coming to Kentucky. First, he'd stop in Louisville and Lexington. Then he'd head to the knobs, and he was scheduled to speak in Hopefully on Monday.

"Hmm, I have to think about this. There's going to be a huge crowd coming to see and hear him. I may need to close the bank for a few hours," The Baron said.

When the newscast reported that the Vice President had been diagnosed with a serious health condition, Molly, suddenly a political analyst in her own right, linked the two announcements instantly. "He's trying to get people to like him again, to put aside all this shit about Jasper, but it's not going to work. They can see right through his tactics." Even so, she conceded, "it's really something for Hopefully to have the President coming here. Imagine that! My, my!" The Baron nodded.

Simon agreed that it was astounding news, but he took issue with her assessment. He wouldn't be surprised if the President's strategy worked. He understood visits to the big cities Louisville and Lexington, but he just couldn't understand why the President had chosen Hopefully, Kentucky. It would be so ironic if it turned out that Jasper was hiding somewhere in the nearby hills at the same time the President's men were looking for him.

After parking Bertha and the truck, Stella and B.J. helped themselves to dinner. Simon asked if he could see the photos of Bob. Stella had B.J. show them to him while she cleaned up the kitchen. The Baron usually did the kitchen work, but he'd left early that night to get back to town. Stella filled the dishwasher with Molly's "brown-drip" china, put the leftovers in plastic containers, and wiped off the brown laminate countertops, musing that they were far easier to clean than her red Pyrolane enameled lava tops at home." She carefully lined up the kitchen cooking tools next to the stove, and she hung the dishtowel, just so, on the hook near the sink. She knew that The Baron would expect to find everything in order when he returned the next day.

As Simon entered the barn, with its rustic exterior, he was fascinated with B.J.'s office setup. No cows or goats on bare ground with bales of hay, but a shiny wooden floor, a desktop Apple computer on a long white desk with small shelves of discs, tiny busts of Beethoven, Bach, and Mozart, and interesting scientific models of various molecules. The walls were plastered and adorned with framed photos of natural subjects. In a corner was a case of shelves holding cameras and photo paper. "Hey, these framed photos are beautiful," Simon said. "This is an amazing workroom. You sure could have fooled me. What's in there? A darkroom? Do you develop your own pictures?"

"Maybe," B.J. said.

B.J. pulled up the pictures of the man seated outside with a King Tut beer bottle near. When Simon looked at B.J.'s photo, he was amazed how much a change in facial hair and a few small cosmetic changes could completely alter a person's looks. "Is this really Bob?" Simon asked incredulously. "It's hard to tell."

"Stella thinks it is him," said B.J., "but she's not 100% sure."

"Who's the other person in the photos?" Simon asked. He referred to the one in which the face had been blurred because of camera motion. "He definitely looks familiar, despite the blurred details," Simon said.

"It's possible that I've met this person or seen him on TV. He's dressed in professional clothes. Look, his neck is mostly clear, and that could tell us something. That jaw looks pretty straight and pointed. And the blond hair. Let me think about it some more."

"I had to move fast because I sensed that people were coming, and I blurred the picture," B.J. said.

"It's too bad," Simon said. "He could be far more important than Bob Jasper, I suspect."

"Stella told me that identifying Bob in the photo wasn't as certain as she would have liked because of the long red hair, cap, beard, and mustache," B.J. said. "It's a great disguise. She said she thought he almost looked like a ghost, someone she dreamed about. There are similarities and there are some differences. Sometimes she is haunted about it. The thing that clinched it for her was the King Tut beer. That is apparently his favorite," B.J. said.

When they came back to the house, Simon said he wanted to accompany B.J. and Stella to the Cottingly house hideaway on Tuesday morning, but they both nixed it. Bob hadn't approved her lawyer's coming. Only Stella could come, B.J. said.

"This is what lawyers do, anyway," Stella added. "They sit back and wait for the witnesses to tell them what happened. And besides, there's always a chance you could get hurt—and then you could sue us for millions of dollars."

Simon couldn't help it. He was laughing for the first time in a long time.

CHAPTER 35

Hopefully, Kentucky

On Monday afternoon, Route 7884 into Hopefully was jammed. A gaggle of white trucks bearing television crews led the motorcade, followed by a line of black sedans carrying President Everett, Scott Herbert, Placido Ramos de la Torre, and Gladys Ratkin, the Secretary of Agriculture. Dozens of police officers guided spectators through screening machines and ushered them into cordoned areas on both sides of Main Street. The Christa Lynn Hair and More beauty shop and Kevin's Hardware offered spectators small American flags to wave. The Hopefully High School band and the girls' drill team, dressed in their shiny blue-and-gold uniforms, marched down Main Street and took their places next to the stage. Mayor Billingsley, sporting a new suit, shirt, and tie, shook hands with people in the crowd and climbed onto the small stage put up by the two Krikien brothers, Dan and Bill, who generally were acknowledged to be the best carpenters around.

It was set up in front of the diner, which offered an electrical outlet, with a long extension cord, to power the microphone. Ray, another Krikien brother, had gotten the public address system working just before the President arrived. Mildred, a Krikien sister, had come early to attach red, white, and blue crepe ribbons to the edge of the stage and on the nearby telephone poles.

The crowd spilled into every nook and cranny on the sidewalk as people from neighboring towns flooded in. The sightseers brought entire families and even some of their pets.

Simon and Stella weren't there. They didn't want anyone from Washington to recognize them. They urged B.J. not to talk about Stella (a.k.a. Ellie), if anyone like Maybelle or her gossipy friends should encounter him.

As they watched TV from a few miles away, both Simon and Stella looked at the faces to see if they recognized anyone in the presidential entourage. Simon thought he might spot some, since he knew many Washington figures by sight. Scott Herbert stayed near Secretary Ratkin and Ramos and occasionally whispered in their ears. Herbert appeared to be looking closely at faces in the crowd. Once the camera showed Herbert on his cell phone.

"Look," Stella said, "I think that guy standing next to Herbert is the state police undercover agent who was here the other night. I didn't see him very well when he was at the house because it was dark and I was hiding behind a tree, but he might be the same man. He told B.J. his name was Butch Jellico. It seems odd that he's standing right there next to the White House chief of staff."

Simon nodded his head in agreement. "He acts like a Secret Service agent, but I'm not sure. He said he was a state policeman? But that doesn't make it so. The Secret Service is always all over the place, but not next to the chief of staff. I'm going to check on that Jellico guy if I can get a friend back in D.C. to call me."

"I don't recognize many faces, except for Herbert and maybe this Butch guy," Stella said. "I just feel like they're looking for me. Herbert has been looking for me for a long time, as you confirmed when he called you into his office to grill you about my whereabouts."

"Here comes Ramos. He's a big man—so much taller than the President."

Whenever politicians came to Kentucky, B.J. and Molly always watched their speeches. Kentuckians were proud to be living in the state where Abraham Lincoln was born. President Everett had visited the state two times in the past year, one to honor war heroes from the state and one for the opening of a new "Made in America" car factory nearby.

Ramos was an excellent choice as an introductory speaker for the President. He didn't talk down to the Kentuckians. In a low-pitched and powerful voice, he said, "President Everett understands your problems and knows how you can improve the economy here in Kentucky." In Louisville, he had added: "I was poor once like many people in this state, and most of them are smarter than I am."

"The President loves this state," Ramos had said at a rally in Lexington, which was held in a street near a block called Cheapside, where slaves had been bought and sold before the emancipation. "The President loves and respects you as well as anyone in the country. My grandparents were from Bolivia, and they had to work hard in this world in order to make ends meet before they brought my parents here. They and I are proud of our accomplishments and proud to be Americans."

"You know, Stella, Americans would appreciate Ramos de la Torre's approach," B.J. offered. Indeed, #runramos was a trending hashtag. The tweets were mostly positive. NBC and Fox News included excerpts of his speeches along with those of the President. CBS featured an interview while Ramos was in West Virginia, using a similar theme.

After Mayor Billingsley's welcoming remarks, Ramos introduced Everett with a short speech similar to the one he'd given in Lexington and Louisville, but inserting a line on how much the President loved Eastern Kentucky people.

Everett took up a similar theme. "You're the heart and soul of America," he said. "You are hard workers and good family people, and you know when Washington is giving you a bad deal. I have worked hard to create jobs and save our public retirement and medical care programs for your children and your children's children. Now, I need your support.

"I came to Hopefully because it's representative of so many hard-working communities in this country," he said. "We can't snap our fingers in Washington and make something happen. It's you who make it happen—especially when it comes to jobs. If I'm re-elected, I will be your advocate in Washington for a new and vibrant economy that will come into being because of unity and hard work."

The President could spout off platitudes like this all day and seemingly never tire of them. But because he was such a good orator, he could make anything seem wise and wonderful, no matter that he was speaking in grand generalities. Like Jon Stewart or Bill Clinton, the President also had the kind of beer-at-a-barbecue persona that was so valuable for politicians. He was the kind of guy you'd want to talk to if you were standing around a fire-pit, because he could combine economic statistics and cow jokes with ease. He had a knack for sounding as though he'd made up everything he was saying spontaneously, without letting on that it had been the product of three speechwriters. He eschewed teleprompters. And he smiled broadly as the crowd cheered loudly, "Ev-er-rett, Ev-er-rett, Ev-er-rett."

Stella saw a scores of faces she hadn't seen before—probably people from neighboring towns coming to witness this historical moment: President Everett Comes to Hopefully. She saw Herbert shaking hands with Stew Billingsley, the mayor and father of a rapist.

All the while, she prepared herself for the face-to-face with Bob. When Natty called to schedule the meeting, Stella felt as though she'd been declared the victor in a quiz show or some sort of contest. She had won, and this was her prize.

One thing nagged at her: She still couldn't figure out why Bob hadn't yet moved to another area. After all, several people, including Natty and maybe Wally Ponz, had seen him with a disguise.

She was anxious about seeing Bob again and hearing him talk about what he's done and, above all, why. She would find out on Tuesday. And her journey, she hoped, would quickly come to an end.

CHAPTER 36

Hopefully, Kentucky

B.J. checked Wally Ponz's old armored car on Monday afternoon after returning from the Ramos speech. Wally was fascinated with old cars, especially the rarities. He had bought "Bertha" at an auction a few years ago and fixed its myriad problems. B.J. gassed it up and checked the tires and all the important gauges. A test drive showed that the engine was in fine shape.

Early the next morning, with a cool breeze blowing, B.J. and Stella began loading up. They took guns and ammunition, a camera, some water, a pair of binoculars, and lunch. B.J. also made prints of the photos he'd taken just before the collision on the hill. He wasn't quite sure why he did it, but it seemed right. They figured it would take them more than an hour to get there, and that would give them some time to survey the surroundings, this time in daylight.

As they lumbered down the road in the armored vehicle, Stella said once again that B.J. didn't have to drive her to see Bob—a move that might well put his own life into jeopardy.

He looked at her with a smile. "I know I expressed my disagreement for going to this meeting with your husband," he responded. "But you know, we've become partners in this crazy adventure. Too many times in my life I've been a chicken, afraid to stand up for myself. I don't know why, but I don't feel that way anymore."

"I don't want anything to happen to you," Stella said. "It wouldn't bother me if you were a coward, but I know you're not. You proved it to me out on the riverbank that night. With me, you have nothing more to prove."

At Viable, B.J. turned on Route 844 in search of the old Cottingly house. He pulled to a stop when they arrived at the long driveway leading to the dwelling. It was 8 a.m., and they still had an hour to kill.

"I have an idea," B.J. said. "Let's go down that narrow road up ahead— the same road you and I took when we got busted by that guy on his property. That was a good view of the house from there, and maybe we'll see some movement. If the old man catches us again, we'll start making out," he added, smiling.

Stella agreed as she rubbed B.J.'s shoulder. It took less than 15 minutes to get there. They could see the house clearly. It was bigger than they remembered, with a large porch in the front. Two cars sat parked next to the house on the left side, with room left for one more car near the side entrance.

A garage in back of the driveway appeared to be closed. There was no movement, and that was good, they thought. "Looks okay, doesn't it?" Stella asked. "I expected two cars—one for Natty, and the other for Bob and maybe some of his cohorts."

The house was a long way from the main road, with a big yard encircled by lots of shrubs and trees where people could hide. B.J. took out his binoculars and scanned the area around the house. Briefly, he thought he caught a glint of something near a bush, but whatever it was went away. He scanned the area for several more minutes, and concluded that the glint he saw must have come from the dewdrops reflecting the sunrise.

They waited silently and patiently to see if anyone else came by. No one did. Finally, at 8:50 a.m., B.J. declared, "I think it looks clear. Let's go."

Slowly, B.J. turned around and headed back to the main road and on to their destination. The entranceway took them down a tree-lined, gravel drive that twisted and turned several times before the house came into view. The yard was huge, and Stella estimated the house was 150 feet away from the forested area.

They took the open parking space next to the house. When the old vehicle edged to a stop, the kitchen door opened and Natty stuck her head out. "Hurry up, you two!" she called with a sense of urgency in her voice. "You need to get in here as soon as you can. We have a lot of work to do and we don't want to waste time. I worked hard to set this meeting up, so let's get a move on."

B.J. and Stella grabbed their guns and ammunition and ran into the house. Natty held her hands up. "No guns at this meeting," she said. Stella responded with ice in her voice. "Look Natty, I wish I could trust you, but I need to protect myself and B.J. here in the event we're threatened in any way. I'm not going to shoot anybody except in self-defense. You have my word on that. To me, this is like a wild western. You've got *your* guns; I've got mine. It's a balance of power."

Natty produced a walkie-talkie and spoke into it. "She insists on having her guns. Promises not to use them if we do the same." A male's voice responded. "Okay, we have a truce."

"Who the hell is that!" shouted Stella. "Is that Bob? This bullshit walkie-talkie is not going to do the job. I need to see him *now*! Either get him, or I'll call my lawyer and tell him where you are and what you are doing and suggest he send some forces up here. And you, Natty! You'd be guilty of aiding and abetting a criminal by protecting Bob. Look, I want some goddamn answers from the horse's mouth, and in a hurry. I've come too far and waited too long for this moment. Where is the S.O.B.?"

Natty told her to stop being hysterical and that she would get her wish in good time. But Stella wouldn't stop. "Look, he's my husband," Stella screeched. "He ran away from me. He promised to meet me right here. So let's do it!"

Just then a man wearing black pants and a black shirt ran up the stairs and right past her, heading for the door. His red hair was pulled back, showing a wired device in her ear. He had a pistol and what looked to be an AK-47. It was Bob, she computed. He never looked at her. He was disguised as he'd been in the photos, with lots of facial hair. Stella yelled, "Come back, you asshole!" She tried to follow him out the door, but Natty stood in front of her to restrain her. "Trust me, Stella, he needs to do this first." Bob was outside no more than a minute. He walked around the cars briskly and looked up, as if he were showing off his face to the world. And then he came back in, and ran past her to the downstairs, without speaking.

"Okay, you want your meeting, you've got it," Natty said. Sit down! We don't have long." This was not the kind and gentle Natty of a few days ago.

Suddenly, Maybelle Grimes came upstairs, glanced at Stella and B.J. and announced. "It's working."

Both Stella and B.J. were speechless. "What the hell do *you* have to do with this?" Stella demanded. "Aren't you a two-faced bitch, too, working for my crook of a husband! You should be ashamed of yourself, Maybelle. I trusted you, too, but you lied to me and now you're taking advantage."

"We'll explain," Maybelle said evenly. "Hurry up. There's a reason for speed this morning. I'm not who you think, so please shut your mouth for just a moment."

Natty invited them to sit on a large couch in one corner of the room. It faced an empty chair. "Have a seat on the sofa. He'll be right out," Natty said. "He's in the next room. You have to understand—Bob does not *want* to talk to you; it'll be difficult for him."

Bob walked in shortly and sat in the chair, facing his tormentors. His bill cap was pulled down over his eyes. Stella jumped up but Maybelle grabbed her arm and told her to sit down and stay down. Stella said, "I don't know what the hell is going on, but you'd better tell the truth. Bob—why? Why didn't you tell me what you were into? I thought you loved me. I want you to tell me, right now if you're still sleeping with Alicia?" Bob shook his head no and turned to face the window. Natty said Bob had had a short fling that lasted only a couple of weeks. He'd cut it off, but he didn't know where Alicia was now.

"You made my life miserable," Stella resumed. "You ran off leaving me broke and confused, and you ripped apart the life we had." Bob shook his head yes. What she'd said was true. Stella jumped up and Maybelle pulled her back down, this time using an arm-lock to keep her down. Natty explained again, "He says that a friend got him involved with 'Robinhood' because it was for a good cause—a way to help fight worldwide terrorism. Funneling money to the Middle East with Security Now as a front was easy, and it was addictive because he always got a healthy portion of the take. It destroyed his sense of judgment. "At first, he didn't know the money was mainly coming through the cartel." Natty said.

"Whoa—wait a minute—whoa!" Stella said, wrestling to break free of Maybelle's grip. "What's Robinhood? What cartel? I know about Security Now; Bob and I have contributed to their charities. But what's this crazy kabuki dance you guys are pulling here? Stop talking for him. Let him answer, Natty. Let him answer, and let's hear if it comes from the heart. Do you have laryngitis, Bob? Talk!" Maybelle held her tightly. Natty looked exasperated.

Bob replied in a high-pitched voice. "We're running out of time—they're coming," he said. "This completes the interview." Then he fell silent.

This wasn't Bob's beautiful baritone. She freed her arm from Maybelle's grasp, jumped up, and grabbed his shirt.

There was a moment of silence. She let go of his shirt. "You...Are...Not...Bob. Who are you?" she screamed. "What the hell is going on here? This is some kind of trick you're playing. Where's Bob?"

"Yes, it's a trick, but not directed against you," the man said. "Maybelle, Natty and I are all members of an FBI team here to flush out the drug dealers and money launderers whom Bob may have dealt with in the American cartel known as Robinhood. If he has worked with them, they'll want to dispose of him in order to maintain their secrecy.

"We began this operation setting up a sting," he continued. "We want to catch enough of the operatives alive hoping they'll lead us to the capo of the operation. If our plan works, they'll be coming after me thinking I'm Bob. After Bob was arrested, the timeline for the operation was for only a few weeks. But you showed up unexpectedly and we had to adjust that. Originally, we were hoping that you and your friend here"—he nodded toward B.J.—"would leave the area. Then we found out that he's a local and wouldn't be leaving and that you weren't going to go back until you found Bob. So, Natty, Hazel Fines at the Copperhead Club, and Maybelle have been on the surveillance-and-protection team hoping to keep you safe. When you showed the picture of Bob in the club, Lucinda's people knew you weren't Ellie Heinz but rather Stella Jasper, and that you were looking for Bob here in Kentucky. The cartel suspects that Bob may have told you about some of his illegal business. You're a liability to them. We believe they may have followed you. If so, we're ready."

B.J., who'd been stone-silent and shocked by the fake Bob's revelations said, "Oh, that's just great! Stella and I are guinea pigs." His voice was quivering. "Why do we have to be here? Come on Stella, let's get out of here."

"No, B.J.," Stella said. "Where is Bob?" she asked.

"I'm sorry, but he's not here," Maybelle said, as she hurriedly handed Stella and B.J. bulletproof vests. "Hurry—put these on."

"Why?" B.J. asked.

"There's more to the story," the Bob-imposter explained. "As I said, I work for the FBI. When we came here we were not sure if sweetlick… …""Sweetlick? What's that?" B.J. and Stella said simultaneously.

"It's—

A shot rang outside.

"The hood!" a male voice yelled from downstairs. "Come on!" Maybelle cried, as she led Stella and B.J. into the basement.

Halfway down the stairs, beeping sounds could be heard. At least five men in bulletproof vests were looking at a live video feed on a huge communications console. Cameras were sweeping the entire perimeter of the property. An armed man with a semiautomatic rifle was approaching the farmhouse yard from the left. Another man was on the center hill. It looked like war.

"It worked!" the man who had pretended to be Bob exclaimed. "I told you they'd be here soon after Stella arrived. Gotta go." Someone helped him with his bulletproof vest, then into a shirt and jacket. Soon he was outside, protecting himself by hiding behind Wally's car. Judging from the cameras, it was an extensive attack led by at least 20 enemy gunmen.

As Stella watched the operation, the government men who'd been lying in wait made their appearance. Agents, completely dressed in camouflage combat gear with green-and-black greasepaint smeared on their faces, had hidden behind the cottage in a shed, in the garage, under the porch, and some behind a large rock to the right side of the field. And that wasn't all.

A helicopter was overhead, and then another—a sound that was rarely heard in the knobs of Kentucky.

Natty advised everyone to get down, find a corner, just in case one of the intruders got through the protection outside, however unlikely. Stella and B.J., looking horrified, were still processing what was happening. "Who are all these people? What is really going on?" Stella asked Natty. "This time tell me the truth," she screamed.

Natty shouted: "This time you have to promise you can stand the truth, because I am getting damned tired of listening to your screaming complaints."

Stella nodded her agreement as she shakily got out her pistol and her assault weapon. And began to load them. "Don't point those things at me," Natty said, "or I won't tell you a thing." Stella said Natty wasn't the target and not to worry.

"I'll tell her," Maybelle said. "Here's the truth: We were really surprised when you showed up in Hopefully." But before Maybelle could finish, there was a loud explosion from out front—maybe a grenade.

Stella ducked and looked at B.J. Something seemed to snap inside her. As she would recall later, in the chaos and with all the trouble she had gone through it was as though she could hear herself being called to join in the battle.

Somewhere deep inside her, she could hear Wagner's "Ride of the Valkyries" summoning her to go to war. She'd seen the opera at the Kennedy Center last year. Now it had real, practical meaning for her. This was *her* moment, it said to her. She'd been so frustrated. It was time to fight back. Innocence lost, maybe, but she felt a responsibility to act. She couldn't resist the power of the music and the power of sweet revenge—despite the high risk. She put on her armor and shield. She was Artemisia, surprising and defeating the Rhodians. She was Joan of Arc. And Wonder Woman.

"Cover me," Stella told B.J. She got up and started running for the door. "I've got to do this."

"Are you crazy?" B.J. yelled. "Don't go out there. You're not ready for this."

And out the side door she went, ducking behind the armored car. B.J. ran after her. Bullets whizzed around them.

As she was taught at the gun range, Stella kept her cool and didn't fire indiscriminately. She looked to her right and saw the man who'd been impersonating her husband. He was looking straight ahead and didn't see that one of the enemy shooters had crawled to the side porch and was taking aim at his head. With a quick turn, Stella swung her pistol around and shot the intruder before he could pull the trigger. The fake Bob turned and saw her, and nodded with gratitude.

In the meantime, B.J. looked to the right of the house and saw the old road where he and Stella had parked just before they came—the very road where they had stopped that night when the owner found them "getting it on."

There was a car parked in the same spot now, a small lookout that offered a good view of the house. He could see a very tall man running through the weeds and rocks trying to get to the car. He started up an incline. "Halt, or I'll shoot," B.J. yelled at the man, immediately jumping behind a tree. The intruder stopped, crouched down, and fired back at B.J. The shot tore into the tree trunk where B.J. was hiding, sending out a splinter that sliced his forehead. He began to bleed.

B.J. aimed for the man's legs and fired. The man let out a sharp yell and dropped his weapon, which tumbled back down the hill out of reach. Even with a surface wound on his forehead, B.J. caught up with the man before he could get away. He took one look at him. It was Butch Jellico, the same one who had broken into his house.

"You coward—hiding behind a State Police badge," B.J. shouted. "You were trying to kill Jasper. We know that now."

"You fat bastard," Jellico muttered, as he winced in pain.

Five of the government's men surrounded Jellico and handcuffed him.

It had seemed like a lifetime, but the shootout was over in 10 minutes.

The two helicopters that had been circling the area during the fracas left. A large black bus made its way to the clearing in front of the house. The government contingent had the invaders in handcuffs, linked together with an interlocking chain. They boarded the bus. Agents kept looking for any snipers who might have escaped, but everything seemed quiet. They'd prevailed because of superior numbers and the element of surprise. "This was well-planned," Stella said. Later, they would learn, the government forces had killed four and wounded 15 among 20 attackers. Escape routes were blocked as soon as the shooting started, but one attacker had gotten away.

Limping from a gunshot wound that grazed his left leg, Bob's imposter followed Stella back into the house. He'd been wounded, but not seriously. Quickly a medic rushed over to treat the bullet wound. The man looked at Stella. "Thank you for saving my life," he said simply. "That was good shooting out there."

"I can't believe I did that," Stella said, smiling. Then she turned serious again. "Please tell me about what just happened," she said. "Why were the helicopters here? What's going on?"

"My name isn't Bob," the man responded. "It's James Timber. I used to work undercover in Washington for the Drug Enforcement Administration. While I was there, I found out that a new deadly synthetic drug called sweetlick had caught on in America and that a group of Americans had formed a U.S.-based cartel called Robinhood to market sweetlick along with other drugs. It caught on first in big city hubs like New York and Chicago and it's now making its way into small towns and rural areas where it is being made. We haven't found the drug here yet, but we know from Bob that Hopefully is a hub for cartel operations and that plans for making the drug around here are in the works.

"Now I'm FBI, and we believe that some high-level officials in the administration are somehow how linked to this cartel and are using the money for a clandestine political purpose such as getting money and weapons to the Middle East to defeat ISIS. Because of this, they may have a more benign view of drugs, and feel they're morally justified getting tied to the cartel to get the funding for their supposedly higher purpose. Bob worked with wealthy and high-level officials at Security Now, a philanthropic group in Washington. What we've seen so far suggests that Robinhood is somehow linked to this group and may be the main source of funds going to the Middle East. Of course, Bob and the capo, along with other top cartel operatives may feel they are doing good like the storied Robin Hood did in Sherwood Forest. However, that Robin Hood didn't keep a good portion of the money for himself like Bob and the others."

"Where's Bob? Do you think he knows who these people are?" Stella asked.

"He probably does, and maybe even knows the kingpin, but he isn't here," Timber replied. "Natty can tell you more about Bob. Stella, I'm truly concerned about your safety. You need to be protected, too. One of the cartel hitmen got away today, and we don't know what we'll learn from the people we captured. Your life is in danger until we get them all and the capo. I'm confident that Bud's men will find them, but I don't know how soon."

"Who's Bud?" B.J. asked.

"Oh, didn't you see Bud today? He was in charge of the entire operation. He's Deputy Director of the FBI. You met him at Natty's house."

B.J. looked at Stella in disbelief. " Oh my God! Buxton R. Jackson, the Deputy Director, here in Kentucky. Whoa! This is *big!*"

"So was that you or Bob I saw from the hilltop?" B.J. asked. "Who were the men who died on the winding road on the knob? Who was in the hospital in Lexington?"

"They were some of our best agents," Timber said. "We were hoping to entice the local drug dealers to come out there near your place. We were practicing for the operation. We had only been there two days. I was watching and learning all of Bob's mannerisms, but I never could imitate his voice. I tried but just couldn't get it right. Our tech men were setting up shop at that house like we set up here. That day Bob thought he heard a noise and told the guys to check it out. You know the rest."

"I didn't know my camera was that noisy," B.J. said sadly. "I really feel terrible that I caused those men to die."

"Then, James Timber, I can't believe that you know nothing about Bob," Stella said, exasperatedly.

"I promise you, I don't know where Bob is now," Timber said. "The FBI picked me to play Bob because I resembled his looks. When we put on the same disguise, with the hair all over our faces, it was definitely hard to tell us apart. That reminds me: I wouldn't mind having a King

Tut beer right now."

Several agents stopped to thank B.J. and Stella for helping. They praised Timber, telling him they thought the operation was perfect. One was Bud Jackson. "I hope some of these buzzards will talk and we'll finally bury Robinhood," Bud said.

"Mr. Jackson, you sure fooled me at Natty's house." B.J. said. "I admire you and all of the FBI personnel who keep us safe."

"Thank you. Agent Timber here, and all of the locals who joined us in the operation have been real pros. I'm proud of them."

"Mr. Jackson, I came here to find my husband. You must know where he is. Please tell me." Stella implored.

"Mrs. Jasper, for his protection and yours, it's best that you not know. Perhaps I'll see you again sometime in better circumstances," Jackson said as he shut the door of the SUV waiting for him.

"I think I understand the enormity of the operation now," B.J. said to Timber. "At first, I felt that you used me, you used us, you put us out here like guinea pigs. You didn't care about our lives; you cared only about your mission. We could be dead now. It's terrorism with a capital T."

"Why did you and Mrs. Jasper go outside and risk your lives?" Timber asked. "You didn't have to go outside at all."

"I was trying to save *her*, not you," B.J. told Timber. "By allowing her to go outside, you forced me to follow her lead. She's been through too much hell in the last few weeks."

"We took every precaution," Natty said.

"The FBI thought it would be worth it, if we could find out more about sweetlick—who was calling the shots, who the liaison is between the cartel and Security Now," Timber explained.

He said he couldn't help the fact that Stella's husband was a crook and also a turncoat. "No matter what, it would be best to forget him, especially after what he's done to you," Timber added. "And from now on, no matter what happens, you'll be in danger if you should try to get in touch with him. If you and I stay around here, the kingpin will think Bob is still here. You'd have to love him very much to risk your life like this all the time."

"I don't love him anymore, but I still want to see him and let him know how I feel, and I still don't know what happened to Alicia, either. When you were in training with Bob under custody did he mention her?" Stella asked.

"I don't think so," Timber said.

A member of the FBI team yelled to those inside the house. "You have to see this," he said. They all walked outside. Down the driveway toward the house came a man pushing a handcuffed captive who had been the one shooter who had escaped. His captor held a gun at the man's head. B.J. instantly recognized Wally Ponz and ran to meet him.

"I caught this fellow trying to get away in his car," Wally said. "I blocked the driveway and got behind a bush. I shot out his tires and then all his windows and threatened to kill him if he moved another inch. He gave up. I've had these handcuffs for as long as I can remember. I figured this might be the time to use them. '

"You could have been killed," B.J. said, as others took care of the prisoner. "You're a crazy fool, but I still love you."

"Guns scare the hell out of me," Wally said. "But I'd do anything for you and Stella. I just couldn't let you go by yourselves." Wally blushed when Stella hugged him and then kissed him on the cheek.

"I think we're even now, Wally," B.J. said. Wally nodded. They both smiled. "Let's get a drink," Wally proposed.

An hour after the attack, a white Camry pulled into the driveway, and was immediately stopped. They looked at the driver's credentials and checked his car. One of the officers called Timber. "This man says he's Dave Simon, attorney for both Stella Jasper and B.J. Matson. Shall I let him through?" Timber told the officer to wave Dave through.

Simon got out and rushed to his clients. "You guys have done a terrific job," he told them. "From what I heard briefly, on CNN, two locals joined in the fight. I knew it was you two. It scared the hell out of me. I'm amazed." Then, he added, "Are you okay?

B.J. and Stella nodded.

"This was quite an operation—*huge*," Simon continued. "Apparently several FBI divisions were involved. I've been told that the agents subdued all the attackers. But it was a danger that shouldn't have gone this far.

"In your photos, B.J., the other man with the blurry face is none other than Gerald Jennings, a deputy U.S. attorney general. I finally recognized him by a scar on his neck. So this was a wide-ranging government operation from the get-go."

Simon said he'd been on the telephone with a friend who worked with a high-level agency, and his contact had been very pleased with the result of the operation. He certainly believed that there would be more arrests.

"Did you ask your friend about Bob?" Stella asked. "Where is he?"

"They won't tell you," Simon said, "but they hinted to me that he's part of the government's witness protection program. Although the government said he'd been charged with the crime and couldn't be found, he actually was in custody at all times—but we don't know where. The FBI director hatched this operation. I'm betting that Bob didn't have enough information about the cartel's operations when he was caught, and so this whole plan was cooked up to see if it could catch a number of top money launderers in action."

He looked at Stella. "I'm sorry, I think he's gone forever. No doubt they've changed his identity and moved him to some faraway place where he would never dream of living. I'd guess he doesn't have any real money of his own anymore, but now the government is paying the tab. I suspect some prison time may be involved in this. Hard to say."

Simon also said that the FBI would be monitoring lots of telephone calls as it investigated the attack. "They wanted to see if any money launderers or cartel operatives might have panicked and made telephone calls, texts, e-mails, or tweets they otherwise would avoid," he said. "It might be a few days before they know anything on that."

Stella listened quietly to Mr.- Know-It-All Simon as he proudly told all the details of the operation in which she had just participated. "Wait 'til I tell him about Robinhood and sweetlick," she mused.

"Speaking of calling, Mr. Simon, I was the one who called you and gave you the clue to Stella's location," Natty interjected. "I didn't want to say too much in case my phone was tapped. We were hoping you'd come and persuade her to return home."

"You did the right thing calling me," Simon said. "Okay guys, I've got to head out of here and get back to Lexington to catch my plane. I'll call you, Stella." Simon said.

"Thank you, Dave," Stella responded, waving goodbye.

"After the last truck was loaded with all the FBI equipment and the last agent climbed in the SUV waiting, Natty sighed. "Well, I guess we're finished here at the old Cottingly house. I've got to go through the house, shut off the plumbing and electricity. My, my, look at all those bullet holes," she added, pointing to the punctures on the wall of the front porch. "They were a little too close for comfort."

"Natty, how did you get involved in the operation?" Stella asked.

"That's my country store near Viable," Natty said. "The FBI thought it would be a perfect cover for their operations. They didn't want any of the locals to know what was going on. Plus, I'm a cousin to one of the agents. That day when you stopped by with Wally's deliveries, three agents were in the room in back of my store working."

Stella remembered the dinner that Natty had given for her and B.J., along with Bud Jackson. "You took me outside and told me that you had talked to my husband, and he wanted us to leave town," Stella said. "That doesn't make any sense now. Back then you were urging us to get away. But today, you sent us into the middle of a trap with a fake Bob as the bait."

"What I told you was accurate," Natty said.

"Then my husband really was, and maybe still is, somewhere in this area?" Stella asked. "You told the truth once, and then you lied?"

"What I told you was accurate," Natty repeated.

"Is he still here?"

"No, no longer. I wanted him to be here. But a bunch of agents grabbed him and flew him out of here before you came. They didn't want to risk having him on the ground during the shooting. They want him in a courtroom one day, testifying against people we caught today. That's okay, but I think he owed you a face-to-face meeting, so if nothing else, you could scream at him."

"Right," said Stella. "That's all I wanted to do. It's silly, I know, but all I wanted was an explanation and some of the details about why he'd done what he did."

Natty pulled something out of her shoulder-bag. It was Bob's wedding ring in a small envelope. "He wants you to know it's over. It *is*, Stella, except for one other thing. She pulled out another envelope. He made a video. It's on this disk. I made him do it before he left to go into hiding," she said. "I hope it helps. After you watch it, you must destroy it. Otherwise, I can't let you see it. It's too risky for Bob, you, and me."

"Okay, okay, I promise." Stella twirled Bob's ring around her finger. It reminded her of good times filled with fun and love. For a moment she felt she couldn't breathe or swallow. "Thank you, Natty," she said with a gulp.

"Don't tell a soul," Natty whispered. Then she turned around and left the house.

APRIL

CHAPTER 37

Washington, D.C.

President Everett smiled broadly when Scott Herbert walked into the Oval Office on a warm Tuesday morning. Herbert looked very serious and concerned as he walked in, but he relaxed—and grinned with relief—when the President shook his hand vigorously.

"I think my trip to Tennessee, West Virginia, and Kentucky was a sign that the tide is beginning to rise," the President said. "The latest *Wall Street Journal* poll has me up by five points since then. You're to be congratulated, Scott, for staging the trip—great events. You know those good Kentucky folks well. What's your hometown there? I forgot."

"It's Purcells, Mr. President."

"It's close to Hopefully. Isn't it?"

"Yes, Mr. President. It's just over the mountain. Yes, I think you're back on the way up, Mr. President," Herbert said. "Secretary Ratkin said she'd be happy to go on more trips, and I think Ramos enjoyed himself. Now all we have to do is make sure that Ramos doesn't have any presidential ambitions of his own this year and suddenly decide to run against you. It's okay if he runs in the next election, and I suspect he will. But not this year—though I'm sure he's tempted."

The President grimaced as he thought about that. "That's fairly simple to solve," he said. "Just make sure he understands that I won't appoint him Vice President if he's thinking of running for President right away."

"I will," Herbert said, smiling. He relished his position as a sort of presidential deputy, who was responsible for a lot of details at the White House, including important matters of politics.

"I'm serious about putting him on the ticket," the President said. "The other candidates are good, but none is as popular and, frankly, as talented as Ramos. But let's see how the others perform. We have a little time, but not much." Herbert nodded in agreement, but the President noticed that his chief of staff appeared preoccupied.

Everett started to ask Herbert if something was wrong, but at that moment he noticed that his secretary's light was on.

"Yes, Miss Swope."

"Mr. President, your appointment—Brenton Charles, the FBI director—is here," Miss Swope said.

"Brenton Charles said he has something urgent to tell me, Scott," the President told Herbert. "You can stay if you'd like."

"Thank you, Sir, but I have some appointments to prepare for," Herbert said, heading for the side door. "Please call me if you need me." Everett said he would. The President had never seen his chief of staff so anxious, and he intended to question him further about it once he got through with the meeting with Charles. But first, he told his secretary to put through calls to Ramos and Secretary Ratkin. Then he asked her to send Charles in.

Brenton Charles was a tall, straight-laced man with what seemed to be a permanent scowl on his face. He also was an assiduous worker who loved a good drink at the end of the day. He'd taken a tough job at a time when the threat of domestic terrorism had skyrocketed.

This day Charles looked especially grim. He shook the President's hand and went straight to the core of the matter. "Mr. President, this will be difficult for you to hear, but we have some serious problems with some high-ranking officials in this administration. One of them is Scott Herbert."

"You're not serious!" Everett said, genuinely taken aback. "Scott is one of the best public servants I've ever met. What's going on?"

"Sir, we believe he ordered a gang of killers to eliminate Bob Jasper and his wife, Stella, about 40 miles from where you were speaking in Kentucky. We came across it in one of our sting operations. We used an imposter to play the role of Jasper. The real Jasper is helping us and is in witness protection because of what he knows about Robinhood—an American cartel that's involved with money laundering activities—and its political connections in the U.S. We don't know for sure, but there's danger it seems all around, and a genuine fear that others in your administration might be involved."

"Others? Like who?" the President asked.

"Sir, we're not sure," Charles said. "Jasper has given us leads. We'll know more when Scott Herbert talks."

Everett looked shocked. "You must be kidding," he said. "Scott is the last person on earth I'd suspect of such a thing. He went with me on my last trip. Yes, I heard about the incident yesterday, but the details were very murky. Why didn't you fill me in then?"

"I'll be frank, Mr. President," Charles said. "Obviously, Scott hadn't told you about Robinhood, and it took some time to nail down his role in the case. When we did, we were reluctant to notify you about it immediately for fear that he'd find out that we were on to him, alert the cartel, and run away."

"I don't understand—I can't believe that Scott would want to kill anyone," the President said, holding his head in his hands.

"Sir, we believe that he's involved with funneling illegal money from the cartel through the Security Now philanthropic group downtown. Jasper was laundering money for Robinhood, and the cartel was one of the principal donors of funds for aiding Middle East fighters. We know of their interest in some of the causes that you personally are passionate about, such as sending weapons to the Middle East to fight ISIS. That's what we discovered in the investigation."

"How do you know for sure that Scott is involved with the cartel?"

Everett asked.

"Jasper told us, and then on an intercepted call, we have Herbert saying to 'go ahead and do it.' We're 100% positive it's his voice. It turns out that the man who received that call was Butch Jellico, one of our former undercover agents who got a job a couple of years ago as an agent for the Kentucky State Police. We now know that Jellico has ties to the cartel, too, and he's one of those who were involved in the attempt to kill the Jaspers. Now he's in custody. We knew that something was going to happen. We had some good local agents, hired just for this case, as well as our own people. They put together a strong force against the attackers, and we overwhelmed them."

Charles said the most worrisome thing was that the cartel had managed to make such big inroads with senior U.S. government officials without anyone's knowing until now. He speculated that the cartel had been trying to frustrate U.S. enforcement of money laundering and anti-drug laws by corrupting officials who were close to power within the government. There were few higher than the top adviser to the President, he said, and the bureau was "lucky that we caught him in the act."

Everett recalled that it was Herbert who'd suggested that he, the President, should go to Kentucky and include Hopefully in his itinerary. "Just a few minutes ago, he told me his hometown of Purcells is near Hopefully. "So he was near the site where this happened? This makes me sick. I never would have thought that Scott could be mixed up in anything like this," the President added, sadly. "Who's running the show for the cartel? I can't believe the kingpin is anywhere near Hopefully. But why did the FBI choose that place for Bob Jasper to hide?"

"Bob Jasper told us that a club—the Copperhead Club, located not far from Hopefully—was a hub for the cartel," Charles replied. "There's no evidence that the new drug sweetlick was sold on site, but Bob told us that the club was a training site for money launderers and that there had been discussions of starting up a sweetlick lab nearby. The owner of the place, a woman named Lucinda Ortiz, was using the top floor of the club to conduct classes—you know, ways to get around the system—that kind of stuff. It was very unobtrusive, and only Ortiz and her people knew about this. The Hopefully area provided us with two excellent informants who discovered who Ortiz's operatives were. Those people are all under arrest, except that Ortiz is nowhere to be found. This is very unfortunate because she could give us precious cartel information. We're looking for her. She disappeared a few days after Stella Jasper arrived in Hopefully. As far as we know, none of the other cartels has anything going on like this. Jasper was trained by Ortiz long before we discovered his involvement and learned how to move money from bank account to bank account—usually in foreign countries—to launder it.

"The other interesting part of this is that Stella Jasper, his wife, went all the way from Washington to Kentucky to confront her husband. The media thought she might have been involved, and frankly so did we, at first. But now we believe she's innocent. She just wanted to find him, confront him and turn him in. Once she was discovered in Hopefully, those who wanted to kill her husband watched her movements very closely, because they thought that she eventually would lead them to Bob Jasper. I'll have to say that she was excellent bait.

"In fact, she was inside the house that came under attack. We tried to protect her from the shootout, but we had no idea that she, being a refined woman from Virginia, would do something very foolish and yet very brave. She joined the gun battle. In fact, she helped save the life of our top agent, the one masquerading as Bob Jasper. I might add that B.J. Matson, a local who accompanied Mrs. Jasper, also helped capture Butch Jellico, wounding him before he could escape. Jellico was a real defector who went over to the other side about a year ago. There might be other turncoats connected with this crime. We're still investigating. In this sting operation, we hacked computers and used wiretaps and other means to try to get cartel members in this country to take steps that would expose them. This has to be a big blow to the cartel."

"I'm astonished," the President said. "It's my own administration, and I didn't know all this was going on. I can't tell you how upsetting that is."

"Unfortunately, because of the situation, the FBI couldn't tell the White House about the op," Charles said. "With Herbert working here, we knew he'd just alert the killers. Bud Jackson was also in Kentucky, Mr. President."

"The Deputy Director? Why?" Everett asked. "Why wasn't I informed?"

"Same reason, Mr. President. Herbert may be involved with arms shipments to the Middle East. Other members of your administration are under investigation."

The President leaned over and pushed the intercom button.

"Miss Swope, please get Bud Jackson on the phone immediately."

"Yes, Mr. President."

"Can you tell the public that I knew nothing about this?" Everett said. "First the Jasper thing, then Herbert and my staff. Such corruption will hurt my standing with the citizens of the country. You've got to set the record straight as far as I am concerned—*now!*"

Charles looked him straight in the eye. "I have no evidence that you knew anything about it," he said. "But you're right. A lot of people remember Richard Nixon and Watergate, and they're going to be suspicious. I'd suggest you put everything about this case that involves your administration on the record. The FBI has been on the trail of arms going to the Middle East to fight the terrorists for weeks. Only recently, since Bob Jasper disappeared, has there been a connection with the cartel and funds being transferred through Security Now. There are many wealthy donors and well-meaning honest people who'll be shocked to find out that the organization is involved in such activities. It's going to be hard to pin down the names of the leaders of these operations in the United States.

"I still can't believe Scott; I trusted him," the President said grimly. "He stepped out of this office just before you came in. The White House was his life. I thought I knew him. I thought he was one of the best. I can't tell you how hard it is for me to say this: Let's arrest him now."

"That's underway, sir, as we speak," Charles said. They shook hands. "We'll keep you informed," he added.

"Mr. President, Bud Jackson, FBI, is on the line..."

"Thank you, Miss Swope, put him on," Everett said as he looked at the desktop photo of his wife, Joy Olivia, holding the Bible for his inauguration.

When Herbert left the Oval Office before Charles came in, he decided not to stop because he knew what was happening. He knew about the debacle in Kentucky, but had no idea that anyone would know about his role in the whole thing. Yet Charles's appearance in the Oval Office convinced him that he'd been found out. His instincts were always very good on things like this. In any case, just to be safe he had to hide. And finding a safe place in a hurry could be extremely challenging.

When he was recruited by the capo, Herbert was reminded that it was a dangerous position and that if he ever got into trouble he should call "Barry," who was close by. They gave him a cellphone number to call and request immediate help. He'd always kept a low profile and rarely called someone else to do business on behalf of the cartel. But when the Jasper incident came along, he and other top cartel leaders knew that Jasper could expose them and would have to be eliminated as soon as possible. Herbert realized he should never have been the one to make that phone call to Butch Jellico ordering him to assassinate Bob Jasper. He should have passed the buck to someone else.

He also remembered that Jellico had e-mailed him B.J.'s photo of a man he had thought was Jasper. The FBI must know about that, too, Herbert thought. "I walked into a trap," he said to himself.

He strode quickly from the southwest gate and hailed a cab as soon as he had left the White House complex. He picked up his cellphone and called Barry, and told him that he feared he was going to be arrested for the Kentucky "problem." Barry told him to look for a blue Honda Civic at the side entrance to the State Department. "It'll be waiting for you in about five minutes," Barry said. "Don't worry—you're going to be fine. *We're* going to be fine."

Herbert got out of the cab at the side entrance to the State Department and saw the Civic—his escape car to another state, another identity and another life. He had done good work for The Man. Lives in the Middle East had been saved. Laundering money for a good cause wasn't such a heinous act. The Man would find another job for him. As Herbert approached the Civic, a black SUV that had been moving down the street in front of him slowed. There was a quick flash, and Herbert fell to the pavement, killed by a silencer-equipped pistol. The SUV, whose license plates were covered, moved on.

"Call 911!" yelled a woman who'd been walking near the spot where Herbert fell. "I think a man has had a heart attack."

Scott Herbert didn't have the chance before he died to tell Barry that he suspected his cellphone had been tapped—a fact that would eventually lead to more arrests for Americans involved with Robinhood and cripple its actions in the United States. Funds for arms in the Middle East would have to come from other sources.

CHAPTER 38

Hopefully, Kentucky

Even though Stella was dying to see Bob's video, all she and B.J. could talk about when they were driving back was the spontaneous shootout. It all seemed like a horrible nightmare, but it wasn't; it was very real. They had shot people themselves and had walked past bloodied bodies. A video of Bob talking would be nothing compared to that.

"Okay, you scoundrel, where are you now?" Stella said aloud, as she prepared to play the DVD they'd given her. "You think you've shit all over poor little Stella? Well, you have another thing coming, you miserable S.O.B." Her face was red and her hand shook as she inserted the DVD into the player. She invited B.J. to watch it with her. She needed someone to help alleviate the pain. She took a deep breath and hit the PLAY button.

When she saw Bob standing there, with a beard down to his Adam's apple, her demeanor changed abruptly. "Oh Bob, you look so ratty, not anything like my handsome lawyer with the big blue eyes I once knew," she cried.

Bob began in a slow, halting voice.

Hello, Stella. At Natty's suggestion, I'm doing this little clip just for you. You must destroy it after you watch. It's exceedingly dangerous for me to do this. Your life and your friends' lives also are in danger because of your connection to me. I'm breaking the rules of my protection doing this. Stella, I don't have much to say about us that you don't already know by now. I cheated on you. I broke the law. I left you with such little money that you're broke now. I was a terrible husband. I know that. I've known that all along.

When I finished my first money laundering job for the cartel, I knew that our marriage was going to be threatened, but the whole thing was intoxicating. I was making easy money like I'd never made before. Would you believe, I stuck with them and laundered for five years? Then when a high-level official offered me the chance to work for him, I was too weak to resist. Because a lot of the money was being funneled to the Middle East to buy arms for fighting ISIS, I said, 'Well, it's for a good cause; I need to help out.'"

During the time I was laundering funds in the import-export business, I handled their money conservatively when I invested it, but not so conservatively when I took my cut. You were absolutely clueless, and it made me think less of you at the time.

Later on, I began to respect the innocence you had toward our marriage. You tended to look the other way when you suspected that I had cheated or was thinking of cheating. As time went on, I cheated a lot, but not so much with Alicia. That lasted maybe a week or two. I knew George would kill us both if he found out.

When I got caught, someone came up with the idea that we should make it appear that I knew a lot and that the cartel would be better off if someone killed me before I spilled the beans. The idea was to put them into positions where they would have to come forward and take some action against me because in their minds I knew too much. The FBI and the Drug Enforcement Administration came into my office about six months ago and told me that they knew I was laundering money and would arrest me on the spot if I refused to cooperate with their plans. They were suspicious that somebody very high in the government was on the cartel's payroll. They wanted to see if they could discover the identity of that person through me. I was a man with some inside knowledge of the White House and I might pull the cartel out in the open. I knew it would be risky and my life would be in danger, but I figured I didn't have a choice. I'd have to testify. I agreed to their plan. I'd disappear and go into "hiding" from the government.

Even though I wanted to tell you, they told me I couldn't and that I needed to vanish from the Washington area immediately. Unfortunately, I had to leave you just like that with a lot of pain and debt. In the long run you won't have to pay it, I think. Someday, some way, I hope to return some of the money, which you deserve.

On the set day, I took a train to Philadelphia, and there I wound up in a van that drove me to a secluded place in Kentucky, a place I told them about. There the feds hoped to lure people desperate to kill me. I had been there before. In fact, I was sent there in the beginning to visit the Copperhead Club, where I attended training sessions with a person who taught me all about laundering money. It was done in a soundproof room upstairs. Lucinda Ortiz, or "Oz," as she was known to the cartel, was my teacher.

If anyone was curious about activity upstairs at the club, they were told that Lucinda was teaching a course to small business owners on how to manage their finances. That would be the cover story, a story that probably was never told. I don't think any of the locals were curious enough to question Oz. But upstairs, Oz was on her game; we learned all the tricks. The Copperhead Club is a major site in the U.S. for this training. If Copperhead is closed after this federal operation, I'm sure the cartel will open up another training spot—unless the kingpin is caught.

When the guy you know caused that accident in which some of my bodyguards were killed, we worried that the cartel had found us too quickly; all of our resources weren't in place yet. We were only doing a practice for my stand-in, who was training to be me. But we were relieved to know that it was your friend B.J., who apparently took photos of the assistant attorney general from D.C. and me instead of someone's taking pictures from the cartel. Stella, when you went to the Copperhead Club with my picture from your wallet, Oz apparently alerted Butch Jellico, the turncoat hired by the cartel to find me.

Butch and his group kept an eye on you and your friend B.J. to see if you might lead them to me—or so I've been told. If you did, they'd know that you probably weren't innocent, but a partner in my misdeeds. Butch had been fired by the feds some time ago, and wasn't in on the police sting operation. He bit hard on the information available. From your encounter with him at B.J.'s house, he knew what I looked like. By now, I hope to God that the operation was successful—that Butch and his hitmen got their comeuppance. By the time you see this, it'll be over—and I hope you and your friend survived. It'll be a big deal. The feds are hopeful that someone they catch will talk and will lead them to the big fish.

I can't tell you any more; I've said too much already. I'm in witness protection, and I'm not going to tell you where I'm serving my time while I await the trial. That would only endanger your life.

Now, I'm sorry for so many things. I think of the mom-and-pop businesses that continue to be hurt by the cartel. I think of all the messed up kids and adults hooked on sweetlick and are paying big bucks to get it. I wore blinders when I laundered. I'm a selfish, disgusting, miserable human being.

I'm sorry that I screwed up our marriage, and that it turned out this way. I'm not going to say I love you, either, because I don't believe in lies anymore. I'm a crook, but I'm trying to get back my heart. That being said, Stella, we had our good times, our happy times, but you know that that's over. I gave Natty my ring to prove it's over for both of us. I won't be coming back. All I can say is, I'm sorry—so sorry."

And there's one final thing: Remember the night you screamed at me at the old Cottingly House and you thought I wasn't there? Well I was. I was hiding in a dark closet. I heard every word of your diatribe. I'm not the man you married and you aren't the Stella I married. You've become one tough lady. And I'm proud of you. Stay safe, SCC.

Hearing their love code, SCC, Stella wept quietly for a few minutes. Then all of a sudden, she took off her muddy hiking boot, picked it up, and threw it at the television screen. It hit the screen hard, but luckily the fling didn't have enough force to smash it to smithereens.

"What do you think, B.J.? How could I have been so clueless?"

B.J. came over and held her tightly for the longest time.

"You didn't answer," she said, with a hint of hurt in her voice.

"I hope you start forgetting as best you can," B.J. said. "The past is the past."

"Speaking of Alicia," Stella said, "he only mentioned her once, saying that they had had a short-lived affair. Where is she? What happened to her?"

"I have no idea," B.J. said.

"Natty and Bob say for me to destroy the disk, but I don't want to. Where can we hide it safely?" Stella asked.

"I'll take care of this," B.J. said. "Remember, you promised Natty. You should never look at it again anyway," B.J. said emphatically.

"I don't want to," Stella said.

Then B.J. said, "You shared this DVD with me; now I have something I want to share with you."

" You do? What is it?"

"We have to go to the barn to see," he said.

CHAPTER 39

Hopefully, Kentucky

In the corner of B.J.'s workroom, next to the computer, there was a locked filing cabinet taller than he was. "You've been asking me what I do in here, and I'm finally going to show you," he told Stella as he fiddled with the lock before it opened. From the second drawer, he pulled a stack of photos. She flipped through them to discover they all were of the same subject, but taken at different angles.

"Mmm. Nice pictures, B.J. But why the 180-degree panorama? What're you planning to do with them?"

He opened the door next to the filing cabinet, took her hand and led her into a room filled with color. From the floor to the ceiling hung unique and overpowering works of art. He pointed to a painting at least six feet wide and four feet high. "Be honest," he said. "You're the critic. Don't hold back just because we're friends."

She looked at the painting, awestruck, and then again at the photos that she still was clutching. The oil painting was of the scene in the photos, yet so different from mere photography. Shades of green, red, blue, and yellow danced in a fantastical way, reminding her of some of Chagall's works. But it was different from anything Chagall ever did. It also reminded her of some of Van Gogh's works because of its swirling clouds, curving lines, and luminescent sun.

At first, the dancing colors hit Stella in the eye as if they were stirring to be part of the creation itself with no form or function, just a paradise of color. On closer look, Stella could see a three-dimensional scene of nature, featuring birds of all types, other animals, trees, mountains, a river, and bright flowers blooming in spring. Then, with a little shift of perspective, the colors seemed to merge into objects—a forest, a flower, and a woman picking apples, with sparkling colors dancing around them. And, as she moved to another vantage point, they merged into pulsating colors pleasant to the eye. The three-dimensional effect was incredible. It was almost holographic, practically three paintings in one.

"You did this?" Stella asked.

B.J. nodded.

"And they've been here all this time without anyone's knowing? They're incredible, beautiful," she said, obviously stirred. "I've never seen anything like them or like your technique. It's oil. What's its surface? It's not canvas, wood, or paper."

"It's Mylar," B.J. replied. "I started using it when The Baron gave me some leftover materials after they refurbished the bank. I found I could get a 3-D effect using the flexibility of the material. The 180-degree photos gave me the prospective views I needed. I love working with Mylar. I don't have to prime it, and it takes to texture beautifully."

"Now I understand why you took so many photos," Stella said. She studied another, smaller painting. It was what seemed to be a thousand varieties of green, mixed with other colors, all seemingly pulsating and dancing on the surface with translucent fury, as if one were standing in the forest and experiencing life's essence. Everything was suggestive but indistinct, except for one bright luminescent orange ray of light breaking through at the top and illuminating a small red cardinal to the left of center. It was a simple idea, but she'd never seen one quite like it. With delicate strokes and brilliant colors playing the game of life, he had turned the forest into something like a Garden of Eden all his own.

"Magnificent!" she exclaimed. Indeed, she was astonished. "Do you have more?'

"Yes."

"Do you know that you have a goldmine here?" Stella asked. Stella could appreciate the delicacy and accuracy and emotional power required for painting like this, and to top it off, he was using a brand new technique in the art world. "How long have you enjoyed art?" Stella asked.

"I got interested in high school, got an A in the class. Then Melody bought a set of oil paints and some canvas for me and told me to have fun with it. She passed away soon after that. I quit painting and started taking pictures for fun. Then one day I was painting the front door of our house. I put down some of the Mylar to protect the floor from drips. I was just about to throw out the Mylar when I noticed a lot of paint drops fell on it. That started my experimentation with oil on Mylar. One of the first ones I did is in the window of the Copperhead Club. Have you seen it?"

"I love it," Stella said. "I thought it was a copperhead painted on glass. I like the caption about going in there to get a bite."

B.J. had at least 50 paintings. Stella said they were very marketable, and that B.J. should consider letting her do just that. In fact, she knew of a show coming up in Washington where he could display some of his paintings.

"How about all the photos?" she asked.

"I have them all here," he said, as he pulled out one album after another. They displayed Kentucky's beauty—the bluegrass region and its horses, limestone ridges on the Kentucky River near Harrodsburg, and the wild and breathtaking Red River area. There were photos of captivating faces of little children and the very hospitable and kind people of Appalachia, but there also were albums of beautiful mountains whose tops were flattened by strip-mining and albums of the sad faces of people standing in unemployment lines. She saw the themes he was pursuing: A state wrestling with poverty, but one that was filled with beautiful landscapes and people.

"Do you think you can come to Washington?" said Stella.

"Somebody's got to watch Mom," B.J. responded.

"Maybe she can come," Stella said. "Maybe The Baron can help her."

She was certain that B.J.'s work would be a huge success once it was widely seen. "I'll start the process by calling up some of my old sources in Washington." She knew her old friend Marie, an artist, would welcome her back in McLean and Marie would help her get the ball rolling for the art show. "I'll get my life back." Stella said.

"Wait a minute," B.J. said. "We can't do it."

"Why?" Stella asked.

"Because the media will know you're out of hiding and so will the cartel. You'll no longer be able to hide from them. You need protection. I don't know if the government can get some kind of protection for you or not. In any case, let's forget the whole art show thing."

"B.J., I can't stay here or anywhere else hiding from the unknown forever," Stella said. "Someone who was at the Cottingly house is bound to leak to the press that I was here in disguise. The word'll be out. I'll just have to face the world of risks, dangers, criticisms, suspicions, and God-knows-what-else. I can't get up every morning worrying about what might happen to me."

"I guess I'll have to be the worrywart, then. I can't bear losing you," B.J. said sadly.

"You won't lose me," Stella said. "You have a talent that needs to come out. I do watercolors—with not much talent. But you—*wow*! I can't let you hide. Your work has to be shown, period! I'll be okay, you'll see. As time goes on, the cartel will realize that I know nothing. They'll forget me, especially after the kingpin is caught. It will happen. I have faith."

"Stella, I'm not as sure of that as you. You don't understand. I've never felt...."

She cupped her hands around his face, and kissed him on the forehead. "B.J., stop worrying. I'll be all right," she said, as he began to gently run his fingers through her hair. After unbuttoning her shirt, he picked her up and carried her to the couch.

JUNE

CHAPTER 40

Hopefully, Kentucky

B.J. and Stella, along with The Baron, Molly, Dave Simon, Wally Ponz, and Maybelle, decided to have dinner before Simon ended his most recent visit to Hopefully and headed back to Washington. They chose the Copperhead Club over the Hopefully Diner because they said they wanted to try the new menu, but in reality they wanted to experience the excitement of the now famous restaurant in a small Kentucky town—a place where national television crews visited and talked to the town folk about the Robinhood cartel headquarters that had operated upstairs, about Lucinda Ortiz and her disappearance, about the terrible drug sweetlick and the discovery of the laboratory that was on the verge of making it down a dirt road off of route 732.

The Copperhead Club was especially crowded and noisy this evening. The Baron suggested that many out-of-towners were bringing new dollars to the town. Bank deposits were up. Entrepreneurs from all around were out to make a buck where the whole drama had begun. The Club had T-shirts, caps, coffee mugs, and aprons emblazoned with B.J.'s art with the "Come in for a Bite" sign. Hazel Fines loved the attention and was always willing to be photographed next to the sign. The food was good as well, and people who came for music weren't disappointed either. A twenty-something man had replaced Jimmy Billingsley, and everyone thought he was just as good as Jimmy—if not better. "Never think you're irreplaceable," Molly exclaimed, in one of her profound moments.

Maybelle and Wally added to the occasion by announcing their engagement, with a wedding scheduled for the fall. As Maybelle sported her new ring, everyone drank to the couple's success. "He tried to fool me when B.J. and Stella were riding in his big van, but I knew they were there all the time," Maybelle said. "I just let him think I believed what he said."

Wally laughed and said he wasn't talking.

The Billingsley family had done its best to suppress the painful news of their son—from his arrest in Chicago to his sentencing. The mayor had refused to pay for his son's bail, so Jimmy would have to sit in a cell and sing to himself.

Missing was Lucinda Ortiz, who'd been tipped off about the government sting and escaped, perhaps to Mexico, the government thought. She left the club high and dry. None of the Hopefully locals knew what would happen to the club. Would it be auctioned and the proceeds go to the town to establish a badly needed public park? John Stuart, a businessman in Purcells, and his wife, Elizabeth, a songwriter and performer, already had made it known they were interested in buying the club and making it more "upscale."

Simon said government sources told him that Lucinda likely would go undercover for a while, and probably would change her name and her looks. One thing was sure: She'd never return. The cartel would take care of her one way or another.

Soon their conversation turned to the presidential race. "I can't believe what's happening," Simon said, with the big grin of a man who enjoyed politics, "and all because of what happened here in this little corner of Kentucky. We're likely to have a new candidate for president because there's no way that President Everett is going to be able to withstand this scandal. How can he possibly survive, with his chief of staff working for a drug cartel, then getting murdered a few blocks from the White House?"

"Really, you think the President is going to have to quit?" Stella asked.

"No doubt about it," said Simon. "The party's elders already know he's toast. His approval rating is under 30% and the party can't allow any sitting president go into the election that vulnerable. It would be a landslide on top of a landslide, and it would leave his party so weak that it may never recover from the political blow and possibly never get back into the White House. Give him another week, at most, before he sees the light of day. He's not a selfish man. It's too bad."

The Baron said that Everett seemed to be a nice guy who'd gotten caught up in a scandal not of his own doing. "I like Everett, and I don't believe for a minute that the President knew about any of the drug cartel stuff," The Baron said, "but I think there may be more to the story than we know."

"Well, yes," Simon conceded. "But this will be the final nail in his coffin. The press won't let us forget that he's been under investigation for rewarding campaign donors with his energy bill, and most people think he botched the military operation in Syria. We'll probably find out more dirt later. These stories are kept alive and will hurt both the President and his conservative base."

"He's played the game like all presidents." Simon continued. "He's looked out for his interest groups and he's gotten too cozy with lobbyists who were corrupt. For example, Bob Jasper lobbied for scores of business sources here and abroad, and working behind the scenes he's gotten a lot of things done. But Jasper was also a big contributor, and in this game money talks—loud."

"As best as anyone can tell," Simon said, "the President is not involved in any way with Herbert's drug cartel, but there's some evidence that he knew about political contributions that might have been illegal. He's probably just like any other president on that score. You know, the person who says, 'okay, but just *don't* tell me about it.'"

Simon said Herbert was so corrupt that he thought it was part of ordinary behavior. "He even offered me a decent position in the government if I could tell him the whereabouts of Miss Stella over here. They wanted to find out where she was, and silence her ASAP, even if it meant a permanent silencing. It was clear they were willing to go that far. So when I found out where Stella was, I came straight here, and I didn't tell a soul. I certainly didn't trust Herbert."

"What's going to happen?" Molly asked. "How does all this play out?"

Simon said he'd heard that Ramos had already made up his mind to run for the presidency, figuring that Everett would decide to bow out, sooner or later. "Actually party insiders figure that Ramos has a better chance of winning than Everett," Simon said. "The party is weak, but has a very strong figure in Ramos, and I predict he'll surprise everyone with his competence and, frankly, his electability."

Just then, the TV over the bar showed the President making an announcement. The Copperhead Club grew quiet. Everett told the American people that Vice President Wilbur Hill had just submitted his resignation because he was battling cancer and would be unable to serve, and, under the 25th Amendment to the Constitution, the President was appointing Placido Ramos de la Torre to replace him. "I trust the Congress will confirm him," Everett said. "I also am asking the party to nominate Mr. de la Torre as my running mate this year," the President continued. "He's highly qualified, with a wide spectrum of interests, and he'll serve our country well, now and into the future."

The President acknowledged that the Jasper incident had dealt a major blow to his administration politically, but swore that he had known nothing about the Herbert scandal and was innocent. "I thought that Scott Herbert was my friend, but really he was a felon and a spy, and I condemn him for his treachery. He was killed by a desperate cartel, and we will not rest until we find his killer, find the cartel's leader and the rest of its members. They will be brought to justice. The Robinhood cartel will be buried forever."

Simon dismissed the President's remarks as a futile holding-action. "He can't give up easily, so he wants to test the waters. But give it another day or two. He'll cave. He'll look at the numbers and then he'll cave, for the good of the party. He's under incessant pressure from the Majority Leader, and every conservative pundit on Fox News. The people I know are desperate for it to happen as soon as possible, so that the party can get on with nominating a new candidate."

Looks of amazement and sadness showed on the faces of the club's patrons. The sudden change in the national political scene had been so stunning to Simon and those around him that they shook their heads in disbelief. For a minute the club's noise level was at a whisper until Joe Mantle, a local mechanic who'd been watching the President's TV appearance from the bar, blurted out: "That sumbitch should resign right now!"—no one challenged his outburst.

"Can you imagine a Presidential election with two Hispanic men as candidates?" Stella said. "Ramos is second-generation and Gonzalez is fourth. Both have had extraordinary careers, but Ramos is clearly the richest, with all his business connections."

"If it comes down to those two, I think Ramos will pull off the upset because he's more talented," The Baron replied. "Remember his introductory speech here weeks ago?"

"Yes, I do," Maybelle said.

"Ramos is a hell of a candidate—smart, a good speaker, empathetic, good looking, successful, but a conservative with a heart," Wally said, chiming in. "I think he showed a lot of confidence and competence when he came here."

"You know, I met him—in fact, last year—when I talked to him briefly at a White House party," Stella said. "We chatted about some of his philanthropic work. He's very impressive, and his wife is beautiful. I remember Bob spent some time talking to him too. "

But The Baron and Molly had a different point of view, arguing that Gonzalez was chosen by the party's political structure, while Ramos had never been involved in party politics and hadn't gone through the rigors of a political campaign, and wasn't familiar to the party or the voters.

What's more, the Latino electorate tended to lean liberal overall, which was not going to make it easy for Ramos. Oh, he'd managed campaigns all right, but being a candidate and a campaign manager are two different things, The Baron said, with Molly nodding.

The political talk continued until dessert was served. Wally and Maybelle shared some of their wedding plans and then left, holding hands. Molly was getting tired, so The Baron asked B.J. for help in getting her back home. Simon said he'd have one last drink and then drive Stella back to the house.

"You did well, and you should be proud of yourself," Simon told Stella after they were alone. They talked about Washington and ambition, and how politics had changed in recent years as a new set of social conservatives had increasingly tried to dictate how human beings conducted their lives. Simon told her that she could expect to get some of the money that Bob had earned legitimately, and it could amount to a million dollars or so. He said he was working with the government in this regard. She thanked him, but said she didn't want any of the money. If she did receive any, she would give it to a charity that worked with poor people addicted to drugs. It made her sick to think that in recent years she had lived a high life in McLean from the millions made off their addictions.

"Are you going back to work in D.C.?" she asked. Simon said he knew nothing else and that he might indeed consider a job in the executive branch if it were offered and if Ramos were elected. But now, he wasn't sure if he'd be wanted after his decision to come to Kentucky without telling the White House about Stella's whereabouts. She assured him that he'd be fine when he got back to D.C. and said she'd look forward to seeing him there.

"And what are you doing, young lady?" Simon asked. "You and B.J.? You two make an interesting couple. He's smart and talented, and from what you tell me, he may explode on the world's art stage. You're helping him find his dream. You're also talented and smart, capable of big things. But this is just between you and me. You've just been through something very dangerous and, like it or not, there may be some very angry and desperate people who want to harm you. These cartels are vicious, as we both know, and they'll think of nothing to attack an individual just to make a statement."

Stella sighed. "I know," she said. "What do you think my chances are? I know it's possible they might come after me, but I hope it isn't probable."

"I couldn't say for sure, but it's something you are going to have to face if you intend to go back to Washington or wherever, whether you're divorced or not. You already have experienced how desperate and ruthless this cartel can be. Its leaders killed one of their own— Herbert. You'd be useful to them if you could help them locate Bob. The government may offer you protection, just as it did with Bob, you'll have to change your identity and your name. *Poof!*—and you'll be someone else. It would mean that you, Stella, would disappear just like Bob. Do you want to do that? It's safe. It's like insurance against being Mrs. Bob Jasper, the chief bait for the government trap in Kentucky. But it's a real catch-22. You'd be safer by asking for protection. But you no longer would be you—the smart and very pretty lady who promises so much to the world."

Stella listened quietly. "It's a tough call," she said, finally. "I haven't fully realized my dilemma, Dave. I can't go underground. It would violate all my goals, and overturn my lifestyle. I want to be recognized for what I want to do, which is to promote B.J. I'd hate to go underground—hate it. I might change my mind if my situation gets desperate enough, but you know, I can truthfully say that I knew nothing of the world that my husband created as a money launderer. All I did was look for him so I might be able to find out what had happened and to tell him off, face to face. I was never part of his world."

"Oh, they won't forget you," Simon said. "If they think they can hold you hostage or perhaps torture you in order to give them information about Bob, they'll do it. You have to continue to say that you know nothing. If that's your choice, then you have the Salman Rushdie option. You could still be public, but no one could know where you live, and you'd have to move frequently and take extra precautions everywhere you go."

"Every reporter in America would like to talk to you right now," Simon continued. TV networks are pleading for you to come forward for exclusive interviews. Of course, Stella, you can make a fortune off of a book deal if you want. God, what a story! Socialite wife of money launderer Bob Jasper seeks to find him in Kentucky, and then, without her knowledge, becomes a main figure in a sting operation conducted by the federal government—and it works! She decides to protect herself, and winds up killing one of the attackers in a shootout, saving a top agent's life. And through all this, she discovers an exciting new painter who helped her during her ordeal in Kentucky. Now, I could sell that story."

Stella smiled. After some thought, she told him that she was leaning against asking for witness protection. "You know when that creep Billingsley tried to rape me, and beat me up, I looked in the mirror and vowed that never again would I allow others to control me. So I'm not going to get pissed if the government decides to watch over me. But I'm *not* going to ask them. I know there's some risk, but I want to live."

"I respect your decision, but as your attorney, I'd hope you'd go for safety," Simon said. "You could still live as a Nellie or a Jacqueline from South Dakota, painting and enjoying life without threat."

She smiled. They got up. He embraced her and kissed her on the cheek. "Safety first," he said, a bizarre phrase for the courage he wished that he had himself.

"I'm tired of hiding," Stella said flatly.

SEPTEMBER

CHAPTER 41

Hopefully, Kentucky

B.J. got in his mother's face. "Okay, I want to know right now," he demanded. "Where's the gun and where are the bullets? You keep hiding them. Mom, I'm leaving. The van is right outside, with all my paintings and my clothes stuffed in it, ready to go to Washington and maybe New York. And what're you doing? You're being stubborn."

The furrows on Molly's forehead seemed deeper than ever. "Look, I told you, I'm old," she said. "I get things mixed up, and it's easy to forget the last hiding place for my guns and bullets. So I don't know."

"Did you say gun*s*?" B.J. asked. "How many guns do you *have*? Do you know how dangerous this is?"

Molly showed a wry little smile, and simply shook her head.

B.J. said he'd refuse to leave home until she told the truth and revealed the hiding place. "Why are you being so difficult?" he demanded. The Baron, who had come to see B.J. off, looked totally bewildered as to what to say or do as their voices kept getting louder and louder.

Just then, Maybelle came in, along with Mrs. Edinbrock, who was to be Molly's caretaker for the rest of the day. When B.J. told Maybelle about the standoff with his mother, she took Molly by the arm and led her into the next room for a chat. Fifteen minutes later, they returned.

"B.J., you're going to have to give a little here," Maybelle said. "These are the same guns Molly used in the police department, and they're important to her. They're souvenirs of her existence, and they give her a measure of safety when she's alone. So she's proposed that she'll turn over the key to where she hid the guns to the person who's here with her, taking care of her. But I think she's right about one thing: Despite her age, she knows about gun safety. She promises to be careful. She remembers her training, and how she helped Stella. She'd only act in self-defense. Don't worry. We'll take care of her, B.J. I'll be around a lot. You've got to trust us."

Finally, B.J. calmed down. "Okay, when I'm away, you can keep the guns as long as you stick to these rules," he told his mother, "but if you don't, I'm going to have someone take away the guns." For all of Molly's promises on this subject, her son still didn't trust her. But he was happy with the support she'd be getting while he was out of town. There would be someone to watch her during the day, and usually The Baron would take over at night. B.J. didn't know how long he'd be gone, but he planned to return to Hopefully as soon as he could. He'd been to Washington only once before, with his high school graduating class.

Noah drove up in a small truck to say goodbye. "I see you're using one of my smaller air-conditioned vans to carry your art work," he told B.J. "Don't worry. Your paintings will travel just fine. We'll take good care of them."

"Thanks, Noah," B.J. said. "I'll never forget that bundle-branch-block trick. I looked it up," he said with a chuckle. "A bundle-branch block is a condition in which there's a delay or obstruction along the pathway that electrical impulses travel to make your heartbeat. Doctors use pacemakers to fix it."

"Speaking of pacemakers, this campaign for the presidency has really sped up," said Noah. "I can't believe what happened. The country is still in a state of shock that President Everett quit because of the scandals and recommended that Ramos run instead. I don't know y'all, but I don't think that's ever happened in our country right before an election. It's proving to be a brilliant choice. Everett would have lost, no doubt about it, and I think Ramos might pull it off. This is one crazy election year all right." Noah said shaking his head.

B.J. agreed. "I liked what Everett said when he stepped down just before the convention. He said, 'I want the party to win, but I understand they can't win with me.' He clearly didn't have a choice when all this stuff broke open. But you know, I think Everett is innocent of any wrongdoing."

Noah said that Ramos had learned to fend off attacks that he had anything to do with the corruption which resulted in the death of the White House chief of staff. He said he wasn't part of that administration when all that happened, and he definitely did not condone such corruption. "Everett is Everett, I am Ramos," is the way he put it. That tactic seems to be working.

Then Noah surprised B.J. "Are you afraid?" he asked simply.

"What do you mean?" B.J. said.

"Well, you were in all the news stories as being active in that big shootout with the people from the cartel a few months ago," Noah said. "You know, those people are noted for practicing their own brutal brand of torture and murder. Whew! They're really bad dudes. I guess Lucinda Ortiz is gone, and they've squashed all attempts to manufacture sweetlick around here, but until they get the big guy, the capo, there's always a chance some thug may be around to get you. Maybe you should cool it for a while—hide somewhere else. I'm your friend, B.J., and I don't want to see you get hurt."

"Well, I really played a less visible part in all that," B.J. said. "Stella was right in the thick of it, and she isn't trying to hide, and she doesn't seem to be all that afraid. But you know, you have to take your chances in life, while being careful, of course."

"I understand why you want to be free, but why don't you take some time off and go underground for a while, rather than having a big art exhibit that might attract a lot of people?" Noah suggested. "You can sell those paintings without going out in public very much."

B.J. said he'd lived in the sticks for so long that he was desperate to see more of the world, to get a little attention if that was possible. "Why do we live on this planet if not to pursue our dreams?" he asked. "Yeah, I'll take my chances. As much as I hate guns, I'll keep one handy if I have to."

His cellphone rang. It was Stella. "See you soon," he said to Noah, and then pushed a button—she was on FaceTime.

"Hey girl, you look great!" B.J. said. "You know, I like the curly red-haired lady better than the black spiked-hair lady I first met," he said, grinning.

"Oh you do, huh? Hey, B.J., I have great news. You won't believe this, but I just spent the afternoon with my contact, and she's agreed to put on an exhibit, based on just the one painting of yours that I took with me. So we can start talking about that when you get here. Maybe we can do it sometime later in the fall, perhaps around election day. I don't want to wait much longer if we can swing it.

"The second bit of good news is that the real estate agent will have an open house this weekend. He already thinks he has a buyer. How great is that! If I sell the house quickly, I'll be free of more of the past. It'll be easier to move on with "Stella-Act II—whatever that is.

"Oh, and you'll never guess—the White House social secretary called me today to have lunch at a fancy restaurant downtown."

"Are you selling out to this fluff again?" B.J. asked.

"No, I essentially said that I would consider it, and I would do it if it were possible in the weeks ahead. I said I was very busy, but I would keep her posted."

"Sounds like the typical Washington brush-off. Except, this time, you're doing it to them."

"That's what I meant to do. I hope it worked. You know this isn't my future—our future—whatever. It's a self-imposed trap," Stella said. "There are plenty of friends out there in the world."

B.J. signed off, saying he was about to get on the road with his load of paintings, and he'd see her the next day. After they said goodbye, B.J.

gave his mom one last hug and shook The Baron's hand, thanking them both profusely for helping make this trip a reality.

"Your family is very proud of you," Molly said. "You know, I've gotten 10 times the number of phone calls from your siblings than I did before all this came up. They'll want to spend more time with you whenever you have it," she said.

"Whenever can be a long time," B.J. said. "Are they still calling me Doofus?"

"You know, that's funny—none of them did," Molly said.

NOVEMBER

CHAPTER 42

Federal Prison in North Carolina

❝Four-hundred twenty-three, four-hundred twenty-four, four-hundred twenty-five, four…" Melvin Wright counted the holes in the tiles above his bed, again. "There's gotta be something more in life than this. I hate this. I hate my name. I hate my looks. I hate being here. I hate myself." Melvin, the former Bob Jasper, sat on the side of his bed, held his bald head in his hands, and yelled, "Guard! Has the New Yorker magazine come yet?"

On this day the U.S. marshals called Mr. Fowler, their psychologist, to talk to Melvin, because he was becoming more and more talkative to himself as Bob Jasper. It was as if another person was in his cell at all times. Besides talking to Bob, he had started playing chess and poker with his imaginary self.

Melvin had been confined for 10 months, waiting and waiting for something to happen with his trial. Still nothing. Piles of newspapers and magazines were in the corner of his small room. He had read them all. The television was on, but he wasn't watching. For days Melvin was glued to the television during the presidential debates. Talking to Bob,' Melvin said, "I knew from the start that Ramos was going to win. He knew how to spread the manure neatly and have people believe in it."

"Bob, I feel responsible for the way the election turned out. I think if I hadn't been caught, Everett might have been re-elected, and everything would have been fine. I don't know how the FBI caught me. It's driving me crazy. They said they found out through a big deposit of money in a foreign bank that insists on secrecy. They say they found out all about it, and with little effort. I don't believe them. Someone had to rat on me. Maybe it was Oz. The last time I talked to her, she seemed upset for some reason. She said she wasn't being compensated enough. She was well paid, for God's sake. We even bought the Copperhead Club for her. We'll never know if she blew the whistle unless she's caught. The Man loved her, so I think they're together.

"I'm positive it wasn't that crazy chief of staff, Herbert, or the others who were in on Security Now. Some of them didn't really know what I was up to—at least I don't think they knew. They just went along for the ride, enjoying big bucks from Robinhood and fronting money for their cause in the Middle East. No, I just don't know. Still, I'm not sure who got me.

"Look, Bob, I can't tell you how much I miss the excitement of politics and government, I miss the behind-the-scenes efforts to help lobbyists and big business and getting money from the system for scores and scores of companies and various interest groups. These people who have the political power to wheel and deal with taxpayer money do it without shame. It's how they stay in power. I loved to go from agency to agency to secure funds, and even many interests around the world. I loved those trips to Paris and Rome. Oh, God, if only I could get witness protection in either of those two cities. That's wishful thinking, for sure.

"Sweetlick—I have nightmares about kids getting hooked on sweetlick. It's deadly. I didn't know about it when I first went to Hopefully to work with Oz. I knew it was pulling in lots of dough, and I knew they were going to start making it there, but I didn't know it could kill.

"I'm absolutely scared to death about the cartel's efforts to get me. I know they're cut-throat. Literally. They're vicious. You never know who you can trust. Lucinda was a sweetheart on the outside, but a devil on the inside. I think they're coming after me."

"Here Mr. Wright. Here's your mag. You're sweating. Are you feeling okay? It's not that hot in here. Here's the New Yorker you asked for. Whaddya think of the cover? Funny, huh?"

The only time Melvin's "Bob Jasper" would disappear from the room was when someone would call or a guard would interrupt their conversation. He seemed like a five-year-old child talking with an imaginary friend, and acted like one, gleefully becoming animated, when a piece of mail came with his name on it. Under witness protection, very few pieces came, but one day, Melvin got a surprise—a DVD from Stella. He thought she had made it sometime in late summer but it didn't get to him until right after the election. One of the federal agents at the big shootout turned over the DVD to the U.S. marshals, and it eventually got shipped to the prison. The DVD began with beautiful Kentucky scenery—green hills and valleys with purple ironweed and white Queen Anne's lace growing in abundance. "There you are with short black hair. I like your natural red hair better, but no matter what color—blue, brown, black, blonde, red, you're still gorgeous. Your voice is stronger, more assured than it used to be; you were always mild and meek," Melvin thought.

He played the DVD over and over and could almost recite it. Stella said:

This is Copperhead Knob here in Kentucky. Over there at ground level is the Kentucky River and at the bottom of this knob you can see the infamous Copperhead Club. Looks familiar, right? You've been here. Well, look, Bob, I wanted you to see something else.

This is one of my paintings that I am proud of. I may or may not sell it, but people tell me that they would like to buy it. No one has told me that for years. After all that has happened here and presented in mainstream news, I probably could sell dozens of paintings even if they weren't well done.

I am going to be honest with you. I didn't cheat on you all that time when you were cheating on me, but I am doing some dating these days since you have left me for good. Not too long ago, I was so angry with you I could have shot you between the eyes. Good thing you wouldn't meet with me down here in Hopefully. You probably saved your life, because I was pretty pissed then. And I had g-u-n-s, GUNS! Here's a warning. I hope you don't lie about my involvement, or even suggest I knew about your illegal activities. You'll regret it. And, oh that reminds me, I don't want to be part of this federal witness protection program you're in. Nope. I'll take my chances. I doubt if they will be coming after me. It's you they want.

I hate DVD goodbyes, Bob. This is the first and the last one that I will send to you. I wish you all the best for the rest of your life. I promise you this: if anyone asks me where you are, I won't lie. I will tell them I don't have the slightest idea, and I don't care. And it'll be the truth. So I won't try to contact you anymore and I hope you'll do the same.

Stella smiled as the video scanned the hills around her, and then went dark.

Melvin started talking to the black screen again. "You're not the woman I married. Not at all. I wish I had your courage, which is a bit foolhardy, mind you. I'm a coward, through and through, and I'm not afraid to admit it. I really fucked up. I can't explain it, but you seem more playful and alive, especially since you have rediscovered your watercolors, and God help you, you can shoot a gun. Ironically, I told you in my DVD that, in essence, I don't care for you. I meant that at the time. But now, it's tragic, but I love you. Not for what you were, but for the soul that has emerged. Perhaps you were always there, but camouflaged underneath a shallow Washington image. In a way, I guess I never really knew you. I guess D.C. is often like that—a bunch of turtles walking around sluggishly with some other completely different life form underneath their shells. You know what? I understand the word 'tragedy' like never before. My tragedy."

Melvin cackled as he read the New Yorker from cover to cover. There were still pages and cartoons involving the freakish election just past. "Hey Bob. Ramos is amazing. He knows how to fend off everything that can hurt him. Like Ronald Reagan, he's covered with Teflon. Can you imagine winning with 55% of the vote? Landslide on top of landslide, wasn't it? Poor Gonzalez. His party is devastated. Despite a Spanish surname like Gonzalez, he couldn't win the Hispanic vote, even though Ramos got into the race late."

"Hello Mr. Wright. I'm David Fowler. I work with the marshals. Could we talk?"

"Sure, Mr. Fowler. I was just talking to Bob here. We were thinking of playing a game of poker. Want to join us?"

DECEMBER

CHAPTER 43

West Virginia

A light snow fell as Stella drove her car toward Alderson, in West Virginia, a welcome area of gentle countryside, surrounded by Appalachian ridges.

The Christmas season announced itself on the lawns along this winding road with decorated trees, plastic Santa Clauses and reindeer, and Nativity scenes.

In the distance, she could hear church bells ringing. What was that tune? "Go Tell It on the Mountain?" How appropriate. She found the church on the right, pulled into its parking lot and sat for a moment. It was the carillon bells of Alderson's Mountain View United Church. The wind subsided and the snow fell gently on the ground. She listened and made a note to herself about the name of the church and its address so she could send a contribution when she got home.

Her cell phone rang. It was B.J. in Washington. He was excited. "I had no idea this was going to happen." He said that his paintings got a great write-up by a Washington Post reviewer who attended the exhibition. It was a show that one of Stella's long-time friends had made possible. He said he sold three paintings in a week and believed that, with the newspaper article, he would sell more and at higher prices.

"Let me read this to you," he said. "Quote: 'He is incredibly inventive; the three dimensional effect is unique in this kind of oil work. I hope we will see more of his paintings; we'll sell them all.' So you know what else they said? They called me a Kentucky phenomenon, a hillbilly who knows how to splash inviting colors on Mylar and achieve amazing depth and dimension effects that make for a fresh and inviting style.'"

"Don't sell any more until I get back," Stella told him. "We want to test the waters for demand. Their value will go up now."

She loved to hear B.J.'s excitement over his work of all those years. It made her smile and she couldn't wait to see him.

Yet, after she hung up, she felt a strange uneasiness getting back onto the road. Driving a car alone can do that to you. She reflected on the events of the year, and how she was taking a risk with every public appearance. She remembered how last January, almost a year ago, she was afraid of going to a strange new place where no one knew her. Now everyone knew her.

She felt a little vulnerable out in the West Virginia mountains, so far from home. This was the first time since leaving Hopefully that she was so isolated from city civilization and from an easy 911 call. Anyone could have followed her.

She thought of the Copperhead Club and how it might survive with its new owners. The club was doing okay so far, perhaps because of its newfound notoriety. She wondered if Lucinda Ortiz would ever be found or if the cartel's kingpin would be caught.

Then her thoughts turned to Ramos. Now that he had won the presidency, she wondered, would he be the same man she remembered at the White House party? Or would the power of the office overwhelm him? She recalled what Dave Simon had said about it: For the immediate future, he will be treated like a god. "Let's hope he doesn't act like one," Simon had said.

The snow seemed to fall off a bit. Signs on the highway were few and far between, so Stella checked her GPS to make sure she was on the right highway. She was. She knew she was in unfamiliar territory in more ways than one, but she had to do this.

The mountains had lost their leaves for the most part, making the patches of hardy evergreens even more noticeable. The snow wasn't expected to be heavy, according to the woman forecasting weather and the local radio station. "Thank goodness the radio is on to keep me company," she said to herself.

A sign announced the Federal Correctional Institution. She had read that some folks called this minimum-security prison "Camp Cupcake" even though the inmates did not feel it was so easy. Here Martha Stewart had spent a few months in jail and so did Lynette "Squeaky" Fromme, the woman who took a shot at President Ford when he was in office. It was a camp-like facility, with dormitories and cabins, but with no observation towers that would stamp it clearly as a prison.

She parked her car in the designated visitor's spot and went to the entrance. Officers verified her scheduled visit, examined her possessions for security purposes and then took her to the visitors' area where inmates visit relatives and friends. No lunch here, but she could get a cup of coffee and some snacks from a vending machine.

Stella waited five minutes, then a thin, tall, woman with cropped blonde hair walked straight to her and put out her hand.

"Hello Stella." Alicia said softly.

Stella smiled at her old friend. They stopped short of an embrace or even a handshake. Too much had happened between them to try to be cozy now.

Alicia put it on the table. "I'm glad you came. I have so much to apologize for, and appreciate your giving me the opportunity to do it. Have a seat."

It was the last Saturday in the week before Christmas. Despite all the troubles these women had been through, and despite the rift that now existed between them, they were keeping the tradition.

It was a year since Stella's lunch with Alicia at the Bastille in Northern Virginia. Now, here she was in prison and very much alive.

"I have much to tell you," Alicia said. "Here's the first thing, cutting right to the chase. Yes, it is true that I had an affair with Bob, but it was very short, only a week or so. You have every right to want to kill me for that, but hear me out."

She told Stella that she and her husband George Valiant had gotten involved in money laundering with Bob because it seemed so easy and so profitable. Alicia said her husband showed her how to transfer funds from one international bank account to another simply on the computer. It was addictive, she said, as she and George were getting richer and richer. Their import-export business was a good front and the laundering fed her penchant for gambling that she had thrived on during the day-trading 1990s but then lost.

"The FBI caught Bob. Why didn't they get George?" Stella asked.

"There's got to be a reason. I'm sure Bob has told them everything, now that he is in witness protection. Maybe George has left the country. I don't know. We haven't communicated at all since I left. Maybe he's hiding in France, Austria, or Germany where he's done a lot of business. He started taking more and more trips away from home. I was alone a lot and that's when I seduced Bob over a year ago. It was a terrible mistake, and I hope you can forgive me."

"All I can say is that I will try," said Stella. "But I can't tell you how disappointed I am with you. You were my friend, my closest friend. I still don't understand it. On top of all that, you disappeared. Why did you do that? People thought I had killed you."

"I had to get away," Alicia said. "Before I left, George was drinking more heavily. He was mean and verbally abusive. I didn't want to take it any more. I knew Bob and George were mixed up in something so big it scared me. I was afraid something terrible was going to happen to me or you. So I cut my finger a little to get some blood, put it on the carpet, smashed a vase, and then ran off. I hid in Ohio for a time, and then moved to Jackson, Mississippi—a world away from where I had lived. I put on a southern accent and worked as a waitress. I saw George on the news. I could tell that he was really distressed about my disappearance. He thought that I had joined up with Bob, and that somehow you knew it. Obviously, not true."

Stella said, "But you came back?"

"Yes," Alicia said. "Once I was away from George those first months, I realized I didn't love him and I couldn't stand who I was anymore. I knew I'd be caught sooner or later. So I turned myself last July. I have been here in Alderson since fall. You know, someday I will be testifying against my own husband, can you imagine that?"

Stella smiled. "You no doubt have been a model prisoner."

"I want to get out of here, Stella," Alicia said. "I'm like Martha Stewart. And when I do, I want to start a second life. Don't know how or when, but I will try."

"Bob is gone from my life," said Stella. I haven't seen him at all and probably never will. I have filed divorce papers. There's another man in my life. I am very devoted to him for saving my life."

"Really."

"He is a painter, a photographer, a straight shooter, and is very courageous. He's from Kentucky."

"Kentucky, land of fast horses and fast women, as they say," said Alicia, with an ironic kind of laugh. "I have read about your relationship with B.J. Matson and his developing fame with a new type of art work. Although I am confined here, we have TV. B.J.'s work has been all over the Internet and people have shown me copies. I love to hear him in interviews talking about how he uses his photos to develop a three-dimensional perspective. Is it true that you discovered him?"

Stella said that B.J. had discovered himself, and that the only way she had helped him was to make him understand he was really good. She told Alicia she wasn't sure where the relationship was going. "I definitely want to help him as he tries to make a name for himself in the art world, and prove that he is a great artist."

"Well, I think you are a great artist, too," said Alicia. "Have you used the paintbrush I gave you a year ago?"

"Yes, as a matter of fact. I have a painting for you, Alicia, as soon as you get out," Stella said. "It's one I painted of the Copperhead Club in the knobs of Kentucky one hot day last summer. Here is a photo of it. I like it a lot. Yes, you helped me get back into painting, so thank you." Tears welled up in Alicia's eyes. "I didn't mean to make you cry," Stella said.

"You've changed," said Alicia. "You're tougher, and that's good. You have every right to hate my guts for life, yet you don't. That takes some real strength."

"You know, it is really hard to forgive you. I can't really forgive you, Alicia, at least not now. What you did was despicable. I just want to call a truce. And I won't bring it up again."

Stella told Alicia that she looked as good as anyone could look in her khaki prison garb and that when she was out of prison, she could easily make that the style nationwide.

"You were always the fanciest dresser," Stella said. "I tried to keep up with you, but I realized that was futile."

"I don't have any desire to get involved with that social scene in Washington anymore," said Alicia. "It took me a long time to realize how unimportant it all was the grand scheme of things. I like to talk to real people and try to help those in need. I might be a broken person now, financially, but I can still be a volunteer in helping people start up businesses and also teach them to give more of themselves than they do now."

"That's a great goal," Stella said. "I'll hold you to that promise.

They both smiled. "It's time to go," the officer said. "Wrap it up."

"Good luck to you, Stella," said Alicia.

"Good luck to you, Alicia," said Stella.

They knew that they had been more truthful than on their previous luncheons. They did not know whether their old holiday tradition would die or continue.

Alicia walked to the door with her. "Perhaps we will meet again," said Alicia, and Stella nodded her head yes. With one final wave of a hand, Stella was on her way.

With the help of an escort, Stella reached her car, brushed off some of the snow, and hopped in. She thought she could see Alicia waving her arms from an upstairs window.

In a flash, Stella was around a corner and on her way back home. It was her turn to cry.

CHAPTER 44

Washington, D.C.

Ramos couldn't sleep. Leaving his wife in bed, he went to the kitchen. He found a beer in the refrigerator and sat in the living room couch to enjoy a drink in near-total darkness and to reflect. It was a good American brand, by no means a King Tut, the kind that Bob Jasper and federal investigators enjoyed and used to help lure their opponents into the trap. "King Tut," he laughed. He wouldn't fall for that one.

Here he was, up late, in the Vice President's home on Massachusetts Avenue in Washington. It would be a little more than a month before he would become the President and move into the White House. He wondered, with a smile, what his dad and mom might say, and his grandparents, long since gone. His dream was coming true. He could imagine their pride. He pictured his parents and grandparents and said, as if they were listening, "I did this for you."

Events of the last few months played magically in his brain: His sudden emergence as Vice President, and then the scandal of Herbert knocking Everett out of the race, leaving him, Ramos, as the main candidate for his party. He had trained so many candidates on how to campaign for top political jobs, and he knew the ingredients necessary for a contender: A quick and nimble intelligence, the ability to identify with voter concerns, a powerful and expressive voice, and plenty of money. He had them all and even more: An insatiable drive to be the top man in the country, an ambition greater than his opponents.

"Sweet," he said, as he remembered the debates in which he was the clear winner over his opponent. And sweet also was that mystic ebullience he felt when the voting returns clearly indicated that he was going to be next President of the United States. He also thought he was number one in many ways, but this was, as he might say in American terms, "off the charts."

As for appointing Dave Simon as a top official in the Justice Department, Ramos decided a low position in the Labor Department would be better—and calculated that the ambitious Simon likely would turn him down. He took another sip of beer.

In a month, he would be the President and he would have to be even more careful about confidential reports (some from outside the government) that would come his way. But he had always been a careful man, circumspect in every aspect of politics, business and life. He knew he was highly skilled in covering his behind. And he did not think of himself to be a bad person when compared with other political figures who had run the country.

His first job was to be the best President he could possibly be, of course, but he told himself he would never forget to help those who got him here. He would figure out how.

Then there was yesterday's news story that topped off his elation. He had thought about it off and on all evening. President Everett had called in the morning with exciting news and thanked Ramos again for working with Bud Jackson and the FBI in planning and carrying out the Kentucky operation. He remembered that day very well, watching from above in the helicopter. The cartel thought they had him in its back pocket. Lucinda even said so. He had played his part well.

News of the arrest spread quickly. An aide had left top stories of the day for his perusal. A first edition of the Miami Herald was on top. The headline read "George Valiant Captured." It said that George Valiant, a czar in the import-export business had been taken into custody. Valiant's private plane, "Victory," had made an emergency landing at the Miami

International Airport on Friday. Valiant, his pilot, and his passenger, Lucinda Ortiz, were en route to their home in Belize from Europe when their pilot, Bernie Vendor, radioed engine trouble. No one was injured.

"Valiant is the husband of Alicia Valiant, now in prison and associated with the Bob Jasper money laundering affair. Since Bob Jasper's arrest and the sensational events that took place last March in Hopefully, Kentucky, the FBI has had George Valiant and his businesses under surveillance.

"Two weeks ago, one of Valiant's export companies was shut down when it was discovered that 50 pounds of sweetlick, a synthetic drug, was found in a shipment of Kentucky bourbon to Poland. With this evidence of drug smuggling, the FBI has been watching and waiting for Valiant to set foot back on American soil.

"Lucinda Ortiz, the former owner and manager of the Copperhead Club had disappeared from Hopefully, Kentucky, before the FBI completed its sting operation, which resulted in a fierce shootout. A source said the Copperhead Club was the hub of the Robinhood Cartel network and that Ortiz was the director.

"During the time Valiant has been under the watchful eye of the FBI, he has been featured in news stories. Six months ago he gave a speech at a luncheon to the Economic Club in Los Angeles, where he declared war on the latest government regulation of exports. He was also mentioned last month as a possible Secretary of the Department of Commerce."

"Well, George," Ramos thought to himself, "the only secretary you'll ever be is in your prison cellblock. The cartel, which you created, is dead, and sweetlick has been swallowed for the last time. It will not return. Not on my watch. Your ex, Alicia, has saved countless lives—and U.S. dollars. Alicia Valiant ended up a hero. Her anonymous tip about Jasper and you put us on track, and that's where we are going to stay." He picked up his beer and smiled.

"Even if a snake is not poisonous, it should pretend to be venomous."

—CHANAKYA

CPSIA information can be obtained at www.ICGtesting.com
Printed in the USA
BVOW05*2324091115

426439BV00002B/2/P